TALL DARK & DAMAGED

Damaged Heroes: Book One

Sarah Andre

BEACH READS
3250 Bonita Beach Road, 205-204
Bonita Springs, FL 34134

Edited by Anya Kagan, Touchstone Editing
Cover Design by Christa Holland, Paper and Sage
Formatting by Anessa Books
Manufactured in the United States of America
Beach Reads First Edition June 2016
ISBN-13: 978-0997560701
ISBN-10: 0997560703

DEDICATION

To Scott, the love of my life, for creating a world where I can pretend to be the empress of everything.

In loving memory: John A. Dawson, Annie Joe Dawson, John H. Dawson, and Mary Dunbar. I miss you all so much.

And of course, the breathtaking house on Sheridan Road.

ACKNOWLEDGEMENTS

My eternal gratitude to:

Hank Phillippe Ryan for reading enough chapters in 2013 to tell me the story started twenty pages in.

The exceptionally talented Anya Kagan, of Touchstone Editing, for taking a hot mess of words and ideas and once again shaping them into a romance novel. I'm getting an amazing craft education one tiny margin balloon at a time.

Maura Kye-Casella, my fabulous agent, for your years-long patience. *One* day I'll be rich and famous!

Christa Holland of Paper and Sage for the hottest cover *ever*.

Faith Williams from The Atwater Group and Arran McNicol for copy editing and proofreading at the drop of a hat.

My BFFs, Lark Brennan and Susan Breeden, for the critiques, advice, support, and talking me off the ledge several times over this story. And the last one...

Gayle Evers, as always, for your remarkable insight and honest advice. Twice! You should not recognize this third version.

My Kiss and Thrill blog mates for the cheerleading, unconditional love and support, and the ongoing publishing and marketing advice. It's one big Workshop about Puppies given by Twins!

The Prosecco-drinking 2014 Dreamweavers for being the most fabulous GH group of support, love, lessons and advice. I'm so lucky to be among such formidable talent.

The 2010 restoration staff at Joel Oppenheimer Inc.

in Chicago for teaching me about restoring paintings with smoke damage, and answering amateur questions I had for future plots.

M.E. Stanton and R.S. Andre for relentlessly reading and correcting passages about business, hostile takeovers, and private equity firms. Good thing I'm a writer, not a businesswoman. Love you!

Ginny Engler for your guidance through the complicated maze of Medicare Part A, B and D, Home Health and long-term health insurance. You're a godsend to confused writers and senior citizens.

Sue Kinzie, Karen Stupalski, Ida Carlson, Colleen Stenholt and all the members of Bonita Springs Newcomers Club for welcoming me, inviting me to share my passion, and all the lovely compliments that end with: "When's the next book coming out?" Here it is!

This is a work of fiction. All mistakes are mine, but then again, I wouldn't call them *mistakes* since it's a story in my head that I simply wrote down. :)

CHAPTER 1

DEVON ASHBY CUT the engine. "I can't believe someone tried to torch the place."

On the other end of the Bluetooth earpiece, his cousin grunted. "Happy fucking birthday to your old man, right?"

Devon climbed out of the rental car, and inhaled the chilly night air. Yep, overlaying the scent of Lake Michigan and decaying fall foliage was the distinct whiff of acrid smoke. If it hadn't been for the foolish risk of his siblings' lives, he'd have shaken the perpetrator's hand. "Gotta go. I'm about to walk into the lion's den."

"Don't screw this up," Eric said. "Go in, make nice, get out."

"Relax. I'll lay that olive branch right on a Wickham silver platter. *After* signing for the trust."

"I'm popping the champagne now."

Devon clicked off and stuck the earpiece in his overnight case. Wind buffeted his coat, its high-pitched whistle and the swishing clack of tree limbs the only sounds in this sleepy suburb. Fine gravel crunched underfoot as he headed toward his childhood home, majestic and formidable in the strategic landscape lighting. Christ, how he used to despise this mammoth symbol of wealth and power and success. Now the thick stone veneer and white-trimmed windows tantalized his adult sensibilities. He'd own a mansion like this one day—only in White Plains or New Canaan. He'd come a long way since leaving Chicago, and after tonight, he'd have it all.

Crisp leaves skittered past his ankles as he passed the Poseidon fountain centering the stately circular driveway. The statue's trident was raised in triumph at the harvest moon. Talk about symbolism. Devon saluted the sea king, and bound up the marble steps guarded by life-sized stone lions. He vigorously pressed the doorbell. The deep, gonging chime—so familiar—raised goose bumps. *You shouldn't have come. Go home and have the documents express-mailed.* As if in agreement, a gust swirled in off the lake, slicing icy talons through his wool coat. Devon scowled at his thoughts and swiveled so his back took the force of the wind. Still, a thin shiver rolled through him.

The massive oak-and-wrought-iron door slowly opened. Golden light and warmth spilled out onto him, like the first rays of a spring sun. At the sight of the ageless butler, Devon broke into a wide grin. "Hey, Joseph."

"Good evening, sir. It's a great pleasure to see you again."

Devon stepped past him, fighting the childish urge to embrace the man who'd adopted his father's role too often to count. "It's been a long time," he said instead, as if the older man wasn't aware of his twelve-year absence. Inwardly he winced. *Talk about lame.*

The door closed with an echoing *thunk*. He should unbutton his overcoat and comment on the weather, but the words died on his lips. One glance around the vast hall evoked memories that crushed him like a steroid-laden linebacker.

The Christmas mornings he'd flown down the sweeping staircase into the formal living room where his presents lay. The black-and-white art-deco tiles, and that dumb game of all-white-tile hopscotch Frannie used to coax him into. Or how they'd race each other past these glowing wall sconces to a dinner as abundant and comforting as his mother's smile. The ache he thought he'd conquered so long ago almost doubled him over. Who'd expect to be ambushed by *good* memories?

Behind him, Joseph coughed discreetly. Devon consciously steadied his breathing and fumbled with the coat buttons. "How is Mrs. Farlow?"

"She's well, sir. Very busy with the festivities tonight. May I wish you a happy birthday?"

"Thanks." Devon grinned as he handed the coat over. *Happy birthday.* The phrase restored the confidence he'd had climbing out of the car. "I'll try to stop in the kitchen later and see her myself. I've missed her apple pie something fierce."

The butler bowed, a shadow of a smile touching his lips. "She'll enjoy seeing you again. I'll put your bag in your mother's old bedroom, if that's all right with you."

Devon nodded. "Any news about the fire?" The question clearly caught Joseph off guard; family members would never have asked the help, but Devon had long ago parted from the Wickham ways.

"No, sir. Very little damage to the theater itself, but your father's art gallery needs restoration."

"Do they know who did it?"

Joseph flushed and swallowed. "I don't believe so, sir. An arson investigator was here most of today."

Devon nodded. It wouldn't surprise him if the investigator found multiple people with a motive. In fact, if he'd been here Tuesday night, no doubt he'd be the number one suspect. "I'm glad no one was hurt." He gazed around the foyer again, seeing the opulence instead of the memories, and his shoulders relaxed. "Are they in the dining room?"

"The party moved to the formal library for dessert and coffee. Dinner was served at eight." Joseph's dry tone held volumes of warning.

Devon glanced down the long hallway at the arched doors gleaming in high polish. Even after all this time, he knew what lay in wait. Just like with Henry VIII, when one person displeased the old tyrant, they all got punished. And Devon was an unavoidable hour and a half delayed. He broke into a grin at the challenge ahead. The fearlessness he displayed in the boardroom was a direct result of growing up here. "I'll handle him."

"Yes, sir."

He headed swiftly toward the living room, elation growing. Tonight, on his thirtieth birthday, the provisions from his mother's trust came into effect. It had been a long, difficult twelve years, scraping and clawing his way from a broke and homeless eighteen-year-old to an up-and-coming force in Manhattan. This gift from his mother couldn't come at a more perfect time in his career. He'd already signed over the inheritance to secure a business loan. The high-risk venture had required the personal guarantee; banks were still too cautious. But the property was a steal, the value from developing mixed-use dwellings too substantial not to snap up. And he wasn't nicknamed Renegade because he invested cautiously. This deal would ensure his status among corporate giants.

At the arched doors, Devon straightened his tie and shot his cuffs. Soft strains of classical music wafted from within, one of Mozart's violin concertos. A woman laughed, throaty and melodic. He inhaled deeply, grasped the century-old crystal handles, and thrust both panels open. The laughter died mid-note. Time came to a freeze-frame halt, as if the guests posed for a portrait. His sister, Francine, hair shorter and darker than he remembered, held a china cup to her mouth. Beside her, his half-brother, Rick, had a chokehold on the slim neck of a Château Latour. Across the room, two men sat in wingbacks, their backs to the door, profiles turned to the platinum blonde—the source of the laughter—her mouth still open. And beside her, too close for any misinterpretation, sat his father: majestic, patrician, and grim. No one would ever confuse the etched wrinkles on his face for laugh lines. An expression flashed across his face, too quick for Devon to catch. *Regret, maybe?*

The old man broke the spell by glancing down his hawk nose at his Rolex. "Ah, the grand return of the prodigal son. My eldest, who goes by a different name…"

Nope, not regret. Devon managed a half-smile, but already his olive branch goal was faltering. "Happy birthday, Harrison." The irony that his father and he shared a birthdate when they had nothing else in this entire world in common…

Someone cleared his throat, and Devon's gaze swept over the men again, who'd turned in their seats to face him. He nodded to George Fallow, the family lawyer. He hadn't aged well by the looks of his sunken cheeks and hunched posture, but the fact he was still here even though Devon was so late was a great sign. Hopefully the trust business could be concluded tonight.

"Honey, Wesley," Harrison said, "this is my eldest son, Devon Wickham."

Really? "Ashby," Devon corrected.

"Grown men don't use their middle names—unless they're rednecks from the South." The condescending tone baited, and Devon's muscles tensed.

"Ashby is my mother's maiden name." He looked pointedly at his father. "Or had you forgotten?"

Those ice-blue eyes sparked with animosity, but when Harrison continued, his voice remained affable. "This is Honey Hartlett and Wesley O'Brien."

A second passed as Devon waited for how they related to the Wickham birthday dinner to be disclosed, but no explanation came. He nodded once to each of them. Honey responded with a thin-lipped smile, and the young blond guy studiously ignored him.

"Sit down, Dev," Frannie said sharply. She patted Rick's arm, and he rose with a grumble. Devon clapped him on the shoulder, murmuring a greeting as he passed by. The last time he'd seen his half-brother, Rick had been a chubby nine-year-old. Their communication over the years had been infrequent and stilted, a shattering example of the collateral damage from that horrific night exactly twelve years ago.

Devon sat beside his sister, and they exchanged a hug. They, at least, had kept in touch through email and holiday video calls. She was thinner than her screen presence, her skin the kind of bluish pale that came from exhaustion. The divorce must not be going well. He grasped her hand, ice-cold and twig-like in his, and squeezed.

An enormous silver tray on the cocktail table before them held coffee and Wickham china. "My dear," Harrison murmured, and Honey immediately leaned forward, pouring coffee with an elegant tilt of her wrist. She looked about the same age as Frannie. How long had she and Harrison been dating? Frannie hadn't mentioned her the last time they'd spoken.

When Honey handed Devon the coffee, her cornflower-blue eyes regarded him coolly. Clearly she knew about his black-sheep status. He thanked her, though he didn't intend to stay at the party long enough to finish it. "I'm actually here for—"

"Drink your coffee," Harrison interrupted. "If there's one thing I've learned in my vast years, it's to enjoy the company of loved ones over business."

Devon sipped the piping-hot liquid to stifle the

abrupt laughter rising up. Never had a man less deserving of the title "father" walked this Earth. He was pretty sure Harrison knew it, too, and couldn't give a shit. Not to mention the man had run through three wives… *Loved ones over business.* Yeah, right.

Still, Devon was in his father's house, and an olive branch could turn into lucrative business contacts or partnering on future ventures with Wickham Corp. Why not take the high road and try to build a bridge across the great divide? "Frannie told me about the fire last night," he commented. He didn't tack on Joseph's update about the arson investigator.

"Yes, last night was quite dramatic," his father answered, his tone lacking any drama.

Interesting. The fire had been in the old-fashioned theater, but it shared a wall with Harrison's climate-controlled art gallery, filled with masterpieces. "Is your art damaged?"

"There's too much oily soot covering the paintings to be sure." Another clipped response. His father wasn't the kind of guy who kept his displeasure under control like this. And back in the day, a three-degree temperature malfunction in either of his two galleries was considered catastrophic. This was a freaking *fire.* What had changed? Maybe it was the fact that the perp might be in this very room. Devon glanced at the faces surrounding him, all filled with the usual tension associated with just being in his father's presence.

Francine crossed her legs. Her foot nudged Devon's twice. "I saw workers in the gallery this afternoon," she said to Harrison, then threw Devon a pointed look.

So? He gave her an imperceptible shrug. His disinterest in art was in direct proportion to his father's obsession for it.

"Some woman with red corkscrew curls," she added sharply. A buzzing began in Devon's ears.

"I hired Moore and Morrow Art Restoration." Harrison poured himself more coffee.

Corkscrew... Moore and Morrow...? *Hannah Moore? His* Hannah? Something must have registered on his face, because his sister widened her eyes like: *Yes, idiot, that's what I've been trying to tell you!*

The buzzing grew louder, and goose bumps covered Devon's arms. Hannah had been *here* today? Regret at missing her flashed through him a second before his heart squeezed so hard he squinted. Yet another "twelve years ago tonight" memory, the wreckage he'd left in his wake... *Jesus.*

His hearing returned in time for the tail end of his father's remark: "—company that discovered those Rubens forgeries."

"I heard the Art Institute almost closed down after the Rubens scandal," Francine said.

Devon pulled himself together, focusing on three details. Based on the name of the company, Hannah didn't just work for a restoration firm; she owned part of it. Second, he'd heard about that forgery scandal at some exhibit Nicole had dragged him to. The well-respected Art Institute of Chicago had unknowingly hung three forged paintings, and the discovery sent the staid art world into a frenzy of paranoid speculation over their own works. Third, his father had unwittingly hired Devon's high school sweetheart yesterday. Harrison had never met her; Devon had gone to great lengths all senior year to make sure of it.

"The restoration firm is gaining a remarkable reputation," Harrison said. "Next subject."

Devon sank into the cushion, a warmth settling in him at Hannah's accomplishments. Followed instantly by the warmer memory of her soft lips, perfecting the art of French kissing. He inhaled unsteadily. *What the hell?* He was engaged. All that grand passion, roller-coaster crap was well left to his teens.

A discreet cough captured everyone's attention. Joseph stood in the doorway holding a white, frosted cake piled high with strawberries. "Don't sing," Harrison ordered, and nobody did.

Devon reluctantly shook off the remaining Hannah-daze as his father's girlfriend cut and plated the perfectly proportioned wedges. Honey had the kind of finishing school grace even Nicole and her aristocratic friends couldn't pull off. An aura of mystery surrounded her— someone so flawless suddenly appearing in his family. He made a mental note to Google her, because although he shouldn't care whether she'd snagged a sugar daddy, and Harrison was gullible enough to fall for it, something wasn't right. The father he'd left behind wasn't that stupid.

Honey passed Devon his slice, and although Harrison didn't make eye contact, the old man smiled grimly. This wasn't an innocent cake choice on his father's part, and they both knew it. Harrison had been aware a month ago that Devon would arrive on *their* birthday to sign the requisite papers; the Wickham executive secretary had even insisted Devon stay for the small dinner party. And yet eating even one of the strawberries would cause Devon's throat to swell up. Part of him felt the intended insult like a shank to the gut, while another side was amused at the calculated lengths Harrison had gone to tonight to ensure his complete discomfort. *So much for the sapling olive branch.*

With scalpel-like precision, Devon separated the berries and any frosting that even remotely came into contact with them, keeping his expression carefully blank. He was certifiable to even engage in this double dog dare to eat the cake, but he wasn't going to give his father the satisfaction of refusing the slice. Besides, he'd been so busy working throughout the private flight, he was freaking ravenous. He waited for Honey to lower the cake knife and raise her fork, and then all but shoveled the dessert into his mouth. And felt no remorse helping himself to seconds while his father opened presents.

When Harrison lowered the Jag XKR keys Honey had given him back into the little heart-shaped box, Devon shot a look at George Fallow, who had his briefcase by the clawed leg of his armchair. *Good.* Devon swallowed the last bite and slid the plate onto the cocktail table.

"I have several announcements," Harrison's said, his cup hitting the saucer with a clinking flourish, "which will cumulatively affect everyone here."

Rick jerked like a puppet on strings, almost spilling the new glass of wine he'd poured. The birdlike clutch returned to Devon's arm, and when he glanced at his sister, her profile was a study in dread. He frowned at his siblings and redirected his attention to the supremely smug man across from him. What the hell was his father up to?

Harrison smiled at Honey as his gnarled hand reached for hers. Her return smile held the contentment of a purring cat. "First, Honey has agreed to become my wife."

Devon blinked at the pair. The simmering gut reaction of something not being right boiled over. Why the rush? Jesus, if he had another half-sibling on the way... But maybe he was looking at this all wrong. Maybe he should feel sorry for Honey. *Welcome to the circus, wife number four.*

As he added his congratulations to the subdued chorus, he covered Frannie's hand and squeezed.

"Second," Harrison continued, "she'll inherit all the cash, stock, and property I own except for the trust I set up for my grandson." His gaze flicked to his fiancée, before focusing on Francine. "Provided you both remain under this roof until you finalize that disastrous divorce."

At her audible inhale, Devon clenched his jaw and stared into the crackling fire. Clearly Harrison was still a smothering control freak with Frannie. It was one thing when their mother died, but his sister was an adult with her own child. To force her and Todd to live here with the soon-to-be newlyweds was downright offensive.

"Third, I plan to retire immediately. Wesley here will be promoted to CEO of the Wickham Corporation tomorrow." Pretty Boy gasped. "Fourth. Once I'm gone, the entire empire is his to run. None of my three children has ever shown the slightest interest in my businesses anyway."

Devon heard Rick's weight shift on the creaky floorboards, somewhere behind him. "Why?" his brother sputtered. "Why would you disinherit us?"

Those arctic eyes focused like laser beams over Devon's shoulder. "It's time for you to make your own way in this world, son. It's time for you to stop gambling on every sport game or horse race, and using *my* money to pay off your debt. Your credit cards are one big bar tab. You want to engage in those debasing activities, fine. Pay for it yourself." Harrison sipped coffee without breaking eye contact with Rick. He set the cup in the saucer. "You're welcome to stay in this house while you make other arrangements, but by our wedding date…when is it again, sweetheart?"

"A week from Saturday."

He kissed Honey's hand, his demeanor relaxing. "I expect you to find a job and vacate the premises."

Rick didn't respond. The fingers on Devon's arm had him in a death grip now. He hurt for Frannie, even poor Rick. God knew he recalled the shock and terror this speech evoked. That his father would repeat it now with his last two children, when the old man was the richest son of a bitch in Chicago, was infuriating. Surely the old man could spare *some* change for his offspring. Honey wouldn't be able to spend a fraction of it, even if she lived fifty lifetimes.

"George is here to amend the will tonight." Harrison picked up his coffee cup. "Thank you for the presents. You're all excused."

"Come to bed soon," Honey said in a sultry tone, kissing Harrison's withered cheek. As inappropriate as the thought was, Devon caught himself wondering how the old man hadn't died of a coronary already.

It took the others several seconds to rise, and once upright, they moved stiffly, like sleepwalkers, except for old George, who lugged his briefcase as if it held gold bricks. Devon stepped forward, the offer to carry it on his lips, mentally running through room options where they could go to sign over the trust.

"Stay behind. I need to speak to you in private," Harrison said, and for a moment Devon assumed it was directed at George. But no, his father looked right at him.

"I have to meet with George. I'll return when I'm through."

"You'll sit down." The old man cocked an eyebrow. Devon was prepared to ignore him and follow George out, except for the warning on the lawyer's face. He was not prepared to defy Harrison and work on Devon's rightful inheritance tonight after all.

At the door, a teary-eyed Frannie threw Devon a troubled look, and he winked. The decision on his eighteenth birthday to change his last name had been the catalyst for getting tossed out on his ear. No announcement could possibly apply to him, unless his father was about to extend the olive branch after all and put him *back* in the will.

How fast could he get out of here and make sure she was all right? She needed to buck up until they could figure out how to get her out from under Harrison's thumb. Her smile was tremulous, and then the door clicked shut. He sucked in a breath and spun around. "What's up?"

"I'm surprised you haven't heard." And that was how fast his father could switch from wrecking ball to cat-and-mouse.

Devon glanced at his watch. "I've wasted enough time watching you play these twisted mind games. Just blurt it out."

Harrison shrugged, smiling slyly. "You're right. It's late and there's too much to go over. Profit and loss statements, marketing forecasts... I'd like to get an early start tomorrow. Eight o'clock, my home office."

Devon frowned. "What?"

"Late this afternoon, the Wickham Corporation tendered an offer to acquire Ashby Enterprises. At a surprisingly low cost—I didn't know your assets were so tied up until I looked into the situation."

Tendered an offer? Getting the privately held company's financial information? "Wait a minute." What an imbecile, letting his father get him all worked up like this. "Eric and I hold fifty-one percent—"

"*Held* fifty-one percent." As Harrison took a leisurely sip of coffee, Devon fought the impulse to snatch the delicate cup and hurl it into the fireplace. This was just a psych-out, and he wasn't going to take the bait.

"Meaning?"

Harrison gestured with his cup. "Did you even *think* to draw up a contract between the two of you?"

"We have a contract."

The   hard   stare   was   so   familiar—part

condescension, part questioning how his offspring could possibly be this stupid. "And you didn't stipulate an agreement giving each of you first rights to any liquidated shares?"

Moisture beaded Devon's lip. No. He hadn't. This was Eric Ashby, his cousin on his mother's side, his best friend...soon to be his best man. He was *family*, for Christ's sake! Surely Eric, the CFO, would have told him if he'd sold shares. "You're bluffing."

"Am I?" Nothing in those hardened features indicated so.

Devon kept tight control of his expression, aware that any shock or panic was an added bonus for the bastard. "Aren't you getting ahead of yourself, old man? My board and major shareholders are loyal friends. They'll never accept your offer."

"Wesley is expediting the deal and assures me your *friends* are quite unhappy with your leadership. I expect to own your company before my wedding. Thank you for the birthday gift; I'm sorry I have none in return."

Devon gripped the back of the loveseat as the icy reality of his failed night of triumph cut through him. All the blood, sweat, and toil that had gone into creating his company... Just to be snatched by Harrison, who had as many international irons in the fire as Donald Trump. Christ, there was no way Devon could return to Manhattan and face Nicole with this news. "Why are you doing this? To any of us?"

"How tediously dramatic. If you'll excuse me, I have a fiancée waiting."

Yes. This was how he could get his father to see reason. "I have three words for you: Anna Nicole Smith."

Harrison stiffened and set his cup down hard. "Honey's an heiress in her own right."

Scoffing would be too immature. If only Nicole

were here, sporting "that look." No man could stand up to her frosty disbelief and derision. Devon spread his hands, willing his voice calm. "Then why disinherit Frannie and Rick? You didn't during your other engagements. Why is wife number four winning the lottery? And what if, a year down the road, this marriage ends in the dumpster like your last two? Please tell me you had her sign a prenup."

Harrison's lips quivered into a snarl. "How dare you speak to me like this."

"How dare you force Frannie to live here."

"That's none of your goddamned business—"

"How dare you give Rick a week to find a job and a place to live—"

"You presume to come into *my* house and tell me how to run it?"

"And you presume to take over Ashby Enterprises?" Their volume had grown louder with each exchange. Devon clenched his jaw. This was beneath him. "You're not getting my company, old man," he said softly. "All you did was declare war."

Was it his imagination, or did his father's hand tremble ever so slightly? When he refocused on the gnarled fingers, Harrison clenched his fist, but the illusion of invincibility was broken. His father suddenly resembled exactly what he was: a seventy-year-old man, trying desperately to remain the fire-breathing dragon in a broken-down castle.

Devon spun on his heel, suddenly ill with shock or the lack of food followed by a ton of sugar. He had to get out of here while he could still stand.

He stalked the length of the room but hesitated when he reached the door. He swung around and met Harrison's glower. The question he'd ignored for so long resurfaced with the blinding intensity of a neon light. He didn't *care*; he just wanted to know—ever since he'd been a small boy. "What did I do to make you hate me this much?"

The glare turned to disdain rather than surprise or shock. "Let's start with you dropping your God-given name like you were ashamed of it. If you didn't want to be a Wickham, then you weren't getting a Wickham cent. And you damn sure weren't living under *my* roof."

"Frannie and Rick *want* to be Wickhams, yet they got the same treatment tonight, so I call bullshit." Devon groped blindly for the doorknob, blood boiling. "And you know exactly why I'm an Ashby. I'll *never* share a name with the man who murdered my mother."

Harrison huffed a breath. "I expected the histrionics when you were nine, but I didn't tolerate them twelve years ago, and I won't now. Your mother committed suicide. Grow up."

A haunting sense of powerlessness sagged Devon's shoulders. "You're lying." But the words were barely audible and steeped in resignation. Harrison had been powerful enough even back then to shut down the investigation and get a suicide ruling. Devon would go to his grave knowing his mother had loved her children too much to take her own life. But he'd never be able to prove it.

CHAPTER 2

DEVON SLIPPED INTO his mother's old painting studio, which was now a drab sitting area, stuffed with more grandiose relics and artifacts. No lingering scent of oil paints or turpentine remained. He closed the door softly behind him and dug out his cell phone, his fingers shaking so hard it took several tries to scroll down and tap Eric's number.

"Tell me the good news, Renegade," his cousin greeted cheerfully, and the pop of a champagne cork followed.

"Did you sell shares?" Devon said through clenched teeth. The background sitcom laughter stopped abruptly, the ensuing silence a yawning pit of hell. He groped for the nearest marble statue as disbelief threatened to take him down.

"A few. Why?"

"And you didn't think to tell me? Or give me first offer?"

"This was totally temporary, Dev. I sold last week, and I'm about to purchase them back. What the hell's going on?"

Devon wiped the sweat from his upper lip. "We no longer hold the majority of shares, and somehow my father just launched a hostile takeover. We're officially at DEFCON 1."

"Wait...takeover? I'm the damn CFO. I haven't heard anything. Why? How?"

"I don't know." He paced to the window, the whole evening blitzing through his mind. Something wasn't right. The timing was too odd. Too convenient. "I know my old man, Eric. He'd have figured out a way to destroy me long ago, when we were a fledgling upstart. This isn't his idea. I want to know who's behind it and why." He started for the door. "Wake up a damn private investigator. Get as much information as you can on a Honey Hartlett and a Wesley O'Brien."

"Will do. Did you sign for the trust at least?"

"No." He stopped in his tracks. "Jesus fucking Christ. It's already pledged to secure the bank deal. What happens to my money if we're taken over?"

The abrupt silence on the other end was his answer. He'd just lost millions. He'd left twelve years ago, penniless and unemployed, and in the space of twelve minutes tonight his father had done it to him again. Devon's breath came in short bursts. His shirt clung to his back.

"I'll check with our lawyers," Eric finally answered. "Surely they can try to find a loophole to get some of it back." The words held hope, but the tone didn't. "What are you going to tell Nicole?"

Devon closed his eyes. *Shit.* She'd said she'd wait up by the phone, and he doubted it was with any semblance of patience. Nicole was the kind of woman who rewarded brilliant business acumen. They both had high expectations of each other and were well on their way to staggering influence. Or had been. What could he possibly say to her about tonight? She didn't suffer failure, and despised excuses. Until now, it'd never been a problem. He wasn't ready to watch his demise in her esteemed regard; there were too many unanswered questions.

"I'll text her that the birthday reunion is turning into a late one, and I'll call her in the morning."

His cousin's grunt held a distinct warning, which Devon ignored. He could handle Nicole; it wasn't any of Eric's business. He ended the call and made his way upstairs and over to his sister's wing. Outside her door, he took a couple of deep breaths and refocused on her problems. Harrison rolled over others without mercy, and she'd never stood up to the old man like he had. She'd never hardened through their torturous childhood, so if tonight had been a shellshock for him, it must have been an atomic bomb for her.

He knocked softly, and Frannie answered in seconds, blotting her puffy eyes with a tissue.

"Hey." He drew her into a bear hug. "I came as soon as I could."

"What did he say to you?"

"Nothing important." He'd come to talk her into defying the old man's blackmail, not burden her with more horror. "You got a raw deal, Frannie—"

"At least she isn't homeless like me," Rick called, sinking onto the floral sofa in the suite's living room. He tilted his wine glass and finished the last drop.

Devon bit back a harsh reply at the pity party. Twelve years ago he'd left for New York that very night and never looked back. Granted, he'd smashed Hannah's heart in the process, and the guilt sometimes still rendered him sleepless… But he hadn't sat moping, even when he was dirt broke and sleeping on Eric's springless sofa. "Put the glass down and sober up," he said. "I'm here to help you guys figure something out."

"There's nothing to figure out, Dev. We're disinherited." Frannie teared up again. "But you sure made it look easier than this."

"Stop letting him win, Frannie. You don't have to stay." He winced at his outburst, but her waterworks meant surrender, which was abhorrent.

"Defying him means robbing my son of his trust fund."

"You know he wouldn't disinherit Todd. Call his bluff."

"I can't risk it." She sobbed, and although he gave her his shoulder, he stood too stiffly, patted her back too mechanically. Everything in his life was neat and clean and lacked messy emotions. There was something to be said for compartmentalizing. Crying wasn't problem-solving. It was a wasted reaction, something he couldn't deal with and hadn't since...jeez. Since Hannah. Funny how everything kept coming back to her tonight.

"What about me?" Rick interrupted. He spread his arm to encompass the living room. "At least she has a roof over her head. I have nothing."

Devon hesitated. "Isn't your mother still alive?"

"I'm not living in Phoenix!"

Devon frowned down at his sister. "It's not the weather," she whispered, sniffing. "Susanna is a surgical nurse."

So no middle-class living for Rick. New York would shake the entitled attitude right out of him. "You went to Northwestern, right?"

Rick nodded.

"What was your major?"

"Econ."

Devon shrugged. "Come out to Manhattan. I have a lot of connections, and you can stay with me until you get on your feet." He checked himself. Even though he and Nicole didn't live together, she'd have a problem with a slacker brother underfoot indefinitely. "I mean, at least through the winter while you get your bearings."

Rick's lips twisted. "Maybe." His gaze went to the bottle, although he didn't reach for it.

Yeah, Nicole would have his hide for this impulsive

invitation. She had little tolerance for anyone who wasn't grimly ambitious and rock steady in climbing to the top of the social scene. It was what they loved about each other. They knew what they wanted in life and had found the best partner to get there. Rick would be a serious speed bump along that road, but Devon wasn't going to take it back if his brother needed him. Eric had once offered him a leg up from homelessness, and Devon would pay it forward too.

"You're limiting your choices, Rick, and you're in no position to do so. Cut the pity party, man up, and both of you fight for what you want."

"I want to stay here." His brother crossed his arms.

"That's no longer an option. Rearrange the world until it's something else you want."

"Easy for you to say—getting a massive trust fund."

Devon opened his mouth to snarl an obscenity, but Frannie waved him off. "We only have each other. Let's not say anything we'll regret in the morning."

He scrubbed a palm over his jaw. They were going around in a circle, and he had his own problems to deal with. Besides, Frannie was right; they needed to band together. "How long has Harrison been dating Honey?"

"Six weeks, give or take," she said softly.

Stupefying. "How did they meet?"

"I think some charity auction. She moved into his adjoining suite within three weeks."

"I still can't believe this," Rick spat, his face flushed crimson. "Blonde hair, big boobs, and she gets all my money. I'm so mad I could fucking smash something."

Or set the house on fire? Devon frowned. "Either of you know anything about the fire?"

Rick shrugged and looked away.

"We all evacuated the house Tuesday just before midnight," Frannie said. "Firefighters put it out easily enough, but something makes them think it's arson."

Devon was quiet a moment. "Harrison didn't seem too concerned that someone had tried to torch his house."

"He's adamant it's something electrical."

Honey, the fire… When did his father get so old he was blind to the glaringly obvious? "Who discovered the fire?"

"Joseph."

Joseph? What was the old butler doing up that late and in that section of the mansion? And why withhold the detail tonight in the foyer? A sense of foreboding stiffened Devon's spine. "Anything else going on I should know about?"

His siblings looked at each other and shook their heads.

"I have a crucial meeting in the morning, and then need to reschedule George, but I'll bump my flight back a little and help you guys figure out what to do."

"Have breakfast with Todd and me," Frannie said. "I want you to meet my son." They agreed on a time, and he hugged her once more. As he walked to the door, he purposely ignored her telltale sniff. He could solve problems until the sun came up, but was clueless when it came to emoting empathy or comforting tears—a negligible flaw once he'd surrounded himself with people who were the exact same way.

He unknotted his tie as he roamed toward the other end of the house. Industrial fans grew louder with every step. This wasn't anywhere close to his mother's old room, where he'd sleep, but he needed to know something he couldn't bring himself to ask his siblings. After crossing through the first editions library, which linked the east and west wings, he turned the corner and stopped. A haze lingered down the long hallway, even though the fans in the theater now sounded like turbo engines. Inside the gallery, a few sooty paintings still hung on the walls. He grinned and turned away. Question answered: Hannah would be back tomorrow

.

CHAPTER 3

HANNAH MOORE GRATEFULLY took the mug of coffee Gretchen Allen handed her, and sat in one of the plastic orange chairs in Moore and Morrow Restoration's break room. Thankfully, no one else had arrived for work yet. She had no energy for the cheerful-boss mask, and with Gretch, she didn't have to. Once her personal trainer, Gretchen's energetic, positive outlook had catapulted her from a weekend Starbucks buddy, to best friend, and now Moore and Morrow's office manager.

"Let's see it," Gretch ordered, looking darling in a black spandex onesie with anatomically correct skeletal bones glued on. Halloween was her high holiday. No one else in the office would bother dressing up today. After all, Halloween wasn't until Tuesday.

Hannah reached into her purse and slid the red eviction notice across the Formica table. "Thirty days," she said, even though their hours-long phone call last night had covered that in the first sentence.

Her friend scanned the information and shook her head. Not a strand in her spiky blonde hair moved, although her skeleton earrings jingled as they danced. "How can they tear down an entire block? We need to call the local news. Get some neighborhood protests started."

Hannah fingered her mug handle. She had no time to march with a sign when the project of a lifetime had just fallen in her lap. She didn't even have time to find another apartment. "I looked up some realty links after we talked. The majority of places I can afford are either in unsafe neighborhoods or too much of a commute."

"How'd your aunt take it?"

"She was up half the night. So agitated that even *with* the oxygen tank, she had one of her episodes. I don't think her health can take the stress of a move. I mean, she's eighty-seven. She's lived there since before I was born."

"It says here they're holding a meeting tonight." Gretch underlined the sentence with her finger as she read aloud. "'To assist with alternate housing possibilities and answer any tenant questions, as your welfare and transition to new living arrangements is our utmost concern.' What a bunch of bull." She glanced up, slitting her espresso-brown eyes. "We're going, and we're fighting this."

"I don't have time to make a fuss."

"No, you don't *want* to make a fuss. Embrace conflict! Take a stand." She jabbed the notice in Hannah's direction like a saber, the bones attached to her forearm making it look like two emphatic people. "Meet me at Bakers Square at five; we'll have dinner, and I'll go with you."

The potential in-your-face conflict made Hannah's stomach churn. "Why waste the energy? There won't be anything we can do; the sale and teardown are legal." She nodded to her open briefcase, where apartment leads were neatly paper-clipped together. "I have thirty days to find a place, pack for both of us, move, and still coordinate an expedited restoration of the Wickham art." She petered out and sipped some caffeine, fighting the cloud of doom.

"Breathe from your gut." Gretch morphed into her commanding personal-trainer mode. "You'll get through this. Give me some of those leads, and I'll call in between doing payroll and receivables."

"Thanks. I'll really owe you." Hannah handed over a third of the stack, but her relief was short-lived. Shoving any of her work onto someone else, even her best friend, was proof she was drowning. She'd been brought up to finish her chores, fix her own problems, and never complain. Period. "Any place that's wheelchair accessible and takes Boots." She should be ashamed that at the ripe old age of thirty, she was bunking with her maternal great-aunt and Aunt Milly's ancient tabby, but Moore and Morrow Restoration was still in its infancy. Every penny that didn't go toward Milly's meds and in-home care went straight back into the company. The Wickham project took precedence over protests and media interviews.

As if reading her mind, Gretch tossed the red notice back. "How did it go over at the Wickhams' yesterday?"

"I told you. We won't know the full extent of damages until we clean the soot off."

Gretch folded her impressively toned arms, quite a feat with the clunky bones. "I'll rephrase. How did *it* go?"

Damn the curse that made redheads blush this easily. It all came down to Devon and those ten months of soul-encompassing love soooo long ago. Why did that moment and that man still haunt her? "It was weird," she admitted. Simply walking into his house had brought back a tsunami of memories she'd buried long ago, and they'd kept her on edge all day. Even after eight hours of hauling art from the smoke-filled gallery down to a sitting room they'd used to pack and crate, the jumbled emotions had kept her tossing and turning last night as much as the eviction notice.

"Was there any sign of your guy?"

"Devon. And he's not my guy." For Pete's sake, it was eons ago and she was well, *well* over him. But her heart stuttered over the phrase *my guy* and she tapped her foot rapidly. "There's no trace of his existence in that mansion, which is no surprise." And was actually a relief. If she'd come upon a photograph or gone into the family gallery to see whether his portrait still hung there, she'd have been unable to function. And dealing with Harrison Wickham had required every professional brain cell.

"Did you run into anyone besides the father? *Someone* knows how Devon is and what he's doing."

"I honestly don't care, Gretch." Immediately her palms prickled, and Hannah pretended to fix her ponytail to rub them against her wide plastic barrette. No way was she going to admit she Google-stalked Devon regularly and knew he was a hotshot private equity CEO about to marry the heiress of Tucker's Fine Chocolates in seven months. And two days. And approximately nine hours, given the time difference.

Gretch stirred her coffee thoughtfully. "Do you think he came back for that party the servants were setting up?"

Hannah smiled at the thought. "He won't ever come back to Chicago. Not even if the house *had* burned down. Or if Harrison had died in the fire that burned the house down." She'd seen the last of Devon on that stormy night when he'd stood on her mom's porch steps, soaking wet and spewing hateful words about his father and the final argument that had gotten him kicked out.

Then he'd tugged her hand and insisted she go with him on a Greyhound to New York. Knowing her mom had end-stage ovarian cancer. He'd refused to consider staying in Chicago, getting a job—even for a week or a month. Who gave that kind of ultimatum? "Let's talk about something else," she said sharply, desperate to dissolve the image of his stricken face when she'd chosen her mother. Of his sudden realization that he literally had no home, no family, no money, and no love of his life. "How did it go here yesterday?"

"Walter's on a tear about Bernice again. Told me to tell you she started the Matisse project using beeswax and resin as the backing."

Hannah swallowed her dread. "I'll handle it on my way out."

The skeleton earrings jingled again. "He's furious. He wants you to fire her."

Hannah stood and rinsed her mug without answering. There was no way she was going to fire Bernice, and Gretch knew it. Even if Bernice had screwed up and used some 1970s restoration technique that was proven to tighten over a decade and cause the paint to crackle.

"I'll handle Walter," she murmured, returning to the table and her briefcase. "I have to get to the Wickham estate before the team arrives. Oh, and make sure Walter gets these." She slid yesterday's restoration summaries, art measurements, and crating supply needs across to Gretchen. "And I'll need releases faxed to Mr. Wickham before I can begin transporting his paintings."

"Got it."

She pointed to the tiny red heart Gretch had glued under her left breast. "Adorable, by the way."

"I'm going to use it again when I'm Grinch at the Christmas party."

Despite herself, Hannah laughed. "We don't dress up for Christmas parties, dummy."

Gretch quirked an eyebrow. "Have you checked the employee suggestion box lately?"

Still snickering, Hannah stopped by Bernice's lab, which was dark and empty. Humor morphed into relief.

Thank God she's not here yet. Hannah jotted a note ordering the Matisse backing to be stripped and redone using mulberry tissue. Then, not leaving anything to chance, she also recommended applying the tissue with a boar's-head brush. An elementary choice and probably insulting to Bernice, but Walter was the *Morrow* in Moore and Morrow Restoration, and Bernice was on wafer-thin ice. Maybe today would be one of her good days and the project would be a snap.

Anxiety ate at Hannah as she trudged out into the bright, chilly morning. Eventually she'd have to deal with Bernice. Using the Wickham project and her hunt for housing as authentic excuses would hopefully mollify Walter, for now.

Once on the El, crowded with jostling commuters, she held on to an overhead pole and texted him that the Bernice situation was under control. Walter was born for sales and schmoozing clients. No doubt he'd find a way to tell Bob Schmidt—probably over golf or cocktails—that his Matisse would not be restored by the original promised date.

Hannah pocketed her cell phone and focused on the day ahead. Not the custom crating of priceless art or dealing with Harrison Wickham. More like drumming up the courage to step back into that mansion and deal with those body jitters again.

She'd stupidly peeked into the smoke-filled theater after the fire chief had left. Even through the haze, those ruby-velvet seats had caused her heart to squeeze painfully. The years had vanished in an instant, and she'd half expected Devon to magically appear, striding out of the smoke with that crooked, suggestive grin. They'd spent so much time in this dark hideaway, groping each other with the urgency of dumb, young lovers. Oh, the many nights they missed "seeing" the movie.

It was a crying disgrace—a professional restorer in the midst of a project of a lifetime, frozen at the entrance of a theater like a lovesick teen. But then again, the last time she'd been in there, she *had* been a teen. And lovesick. The visceral memory of Devon's delicious mouth and the slinky feel of worn velvet on bare skin was as real as if it'd happened the day before.

But today would be different. The memories wouldn't be so stark, she'd avoid the theater at all costs, and, like she'd told Gretch, there was no speck of evidence Devon had ever lived in that mansion. He'd probably be relieved to hear it. She exited the train, smiling at Gretch's absurd suggestion that Devon would ever come home.

CHAPTER 4

DEVON RAISED THE dainty china cup to his lips as he stared absently through the solarium window at the Poseidon fountain again. The searing coffee and deceptively warm sun slanting in helped burn off some of the fog that still clung to his sleep-deprived brain. Where was his razor-sharp focus? For some reason, his talent of compartmentalizing a business emergency from the emotional fallout hadn't automatically kicked in. He couldn't move past the shock.

Last night had been a train wreck. Completely avoidable, but instead he'd helped his father by tying himself to the damn tracks. Discovering Harrison was poised to take over Ashby Enterprises would have stung no matter what, but hearing about it long-distance might've saved some dignity, or at least taken the personal drama out of it. Devon massaged his tense jaw, his coarse whiskers rasping under his fingertips. How the hell could he save his company and the huge development project that he'd guaranteed with his trust?

Movement in his peripheral vision interrupted his line of thought. Honey and Joseph walked in. She murmured in a sultry tone, ticking items off her slender fingers while the butler nodded after each one.

Devon checked himself before his jaw sagged, but

he had no control over the scowl that emerged. His father's fiancée wore a pink dress that barely covered her ass, and matching kitten heels. For someone about to oversee an enormous house of wealth, servants, and status, it seemed inconceivable she was this clueless. Unless she wasn't, and this display in front of Joseph and any servant about to pass by was deliberate.

"May I speak with you a moment?" Devon interrupted with exaggerated politeness, as he stepped into her path.

She was a foot smaller yet still managed to look down her nose. "I'm afraid now isn't a good time."

Not the right answer, Honey. "It'll only take a sec," he said, mostly to reassure the gentle old man who hovered uncomfortably, clearly knowing his presence was still required by the mistress's demands, but not wanting to be at hand for this exchange. "It's about the hostile takeover."

Honey blinked those long eyelashes. "I have no idea what you're talking about."

"I think you do."

"You should probably speak to your father."

Devon stretched his lips into a wide smile. He stuck his free hand into his slacks, maintaining a relaxed stance. "I'm speaking to you. And I'm not leaving here without some answers."

At the issued challenge, Honey tilted her head a fraction and smiled thinly. "Well then, Joseph, see that Devon gets a mattress. Evidently he's sleeping in here tonight."

As she glided by, fury coursed through him. She knew something. Hell, she was probably behind it! "You'll be sorry you ever messed with my company."

Besides Joseph's eyebrows rising almost to his hairline, the only reaction Devon caught was the slight stiffening of her spine. At a small intake of breath, he spun around. Two housekeepers with dust rags stood out in the foyer, and from the looks on their faces, they hadn't missed a syllable. One nudged the other and they sidled off. Seconds later, Honey began to tick orders off her fingers again as if the whole exchange hadn't happened, and they disappeared through the swinging doors that led to the kitchen.

Christ, you just threatened a woman. What's next? Drop-kicking a baby? His cell phone rang, and he pulled it out, answering absently.

"Darling. You never called last night." The chiding voice of his fiancée did what the coffee and sun couldn't—snapped him back to the powerbroker with his eye on the throne. The corporate persona slid into place. Confident, dominant, a lion among lambs.

"The night went to hell in a handbasket. It was too late to call."

"You didn't get your inheritance?" A cool tone threaded her words, one she'd adopted only recently.

And the question made him pause. He mentally shook himself. Of course she'd ask that; it was the sole reason he'd gotten on the plane yesterday afternoon. "No, the lawyer was busy changing my father's will to disinherit my siblings." When she didn't respond, he added, "I'll make an appointment to sign the papers this morning."

"Wonderful. What time will you pick me up?" It took him a moment to recall the engagement party Chickie and Todd were throwing them at Daniel this evening. A party made up of pure A-list friends—a virtual who's who of Manhattan's wealthy elite. Nicole had insisted on authorizing Chickie's guest list.

"I'll stop by at six."

"I won't be dressed by then," she said.

"That's my point." Even though they scheduled sex on Saturday afternoons, he needed to burn off some of this stress. A vision of her slim curves and perfectly spray-tanned skin on those white silk sheets rose before him.

She laughed. "Darling, I'm having a spa day. I'll have just come from the salon; I can't possibly mess up one of Phillipe's creations. Come for a cocktail at seven. And wear the Armani tux, not the Hugo Boss."

He murmured his assent, mentally replacing "black, not gray" for the designer names.

Their strength as a couple was their synergy: Devon as a major player in the Manhattan financial district and Nicole in the social scene. She added the class, her father's cronies, and a cutthroat determination for their combined success. So even though sex had been shot down, his mood brightened. Within hours, he'd have dealt with his father, signed for his inheritance, and be on a plane, resuming life as he knew it.

They discussed the party a bit more, and he soaked in her resolve and confidence. When the call ended, he felt like himself for the first time since getting out of the car last night. He left a voicemail for George Fallow, asking to reschedule later this morning, and stuck the phone back in his pocket. Of utmost importance was not shaking the bank's expectation of forthcoming monies while he fought this takeover.

"Sir."

Devon swung around and again greeted Joseph, who apparently could still enter rooms without a sound. The butler's eyes held pity and compassion, no doubt for the ass Devon had made out of himself with Honey. "Your father was called downtown for an unexpected meeting. He left instructions to notify you of the delay and has rearranged his schedule to see you in his home office at one o'clock sharp."

How diplomatic of Joseph to make it sound like Harrison was moving heaven and earth to accommodate his son. Devon made sure not one facial muscle twitched. "Thank you, Joseph. And could you hunt down a razor? I forgot to pack mine."

"Of course, sir. I'll have it delivered to your room."

As the butler slipped out, Devon poured more coffee down his throat, turning back to the window as he processed his father's strategy—making himself purposely unavailable, thereby letting his adversary squirm like hooked bait. He squinted at the sunlight shimmering off the cascading water. Too bad Harrison had forgotten how much he'd taught his son. The delay was actually perfect. An afternoon meeting meant additional time to contact the board and major shareholders. It gave Eric that much more time to investigate what brought this on.

Devon called his secretary and had her switch the corporate jet to four o'clock; he'd land in Teterboro at six thirty. The engagement party started at eight. It'd be tight, but Sally assured him the weather report for New York was clear. He texted Nicole the change in plans.

"Dev," Francine said quietly from the doorway. He looked over and suppressed a grunt as he faced a younger version of himself standing beside her. The resemblance hadn't been as apparent in pictures or flashes of him walking past during video calls. Faced with direct eye contact, the boy glanced at the rug. "This is my son, Todd."

"Hey, Todd." Devon automatically stepped forward, hand outstretched.

"This is your Uncle Devon." Small hairs rose on the back of his neck. *Uncle.*

The grip that shook his was apathetic at best, and the moment Devon let go, the boy stuck his palm into his jeans pocket. He had yet to look up from the rug, and Devon cast about for a subject universally interesting to eleven-year-olds. "So what's your take on the Bears this year?"

Even as Todd shrugged, Francine rolled her eyes and shook her head. Huh. Maybe the boy was one of those nerdy, straight-A types. "What grade are you in now?"

"Fifth."

"You go to Washburne?"

Todd nodded and shifted his weight.

"I went there too. Back in the age of dinosaurs." Again the faint nod. Devon began to perspire. How hard could it be to engage a preteen for a few minutes? What else interested them?

"You both have something huge in common," Frannie said, and he threw her a grateful look. "Your strawberry allergy."

He glanced at Todd in surprise and sympathy. "Were you hospitalized too?"

The boy shook his head and finally lifted his gaze. "I just get hives everywhere."

"My throat closes." A nod, but no effort to continue the pragmatics of responding. Did preteens grasp the extreme awkwardness of this kind of silence? "You uh...play Grand Theft Auto?" he asked almost desperately.

A grin broke out on Todd's face. "GTA Five, yeah. I'm at one hundred percent completion on most of the missions."

"Sweet." Devon hoped he sounded legitimately impressed, given he had no clue what that meant. Meaning he had no further response, which Todd seemed to realize. The glow died from his smile, and after one more poor-postured shrug, the boy wandered to the side buffet and looked under silver lids at the breakfast spread.

"Hurry, dear. You'll be late for school." Francine watched her son help himself to sausage. There were dark crescents under her red-rimmed eyes. It wasn't likely any of the Wickham siblings had slept much last night. He'd spent hours on the phone with Eric, with very little insight into how to fight a Goliath company from swallowing them whole. But, truthfully, this was even more personal for his sister. She now faced an ugly divorce, a custody standoff, *and* being stuck here like some fairy-tale princess in a tower.

"I've thought more about your situation," he said. "The offer to Rick applies to you guys as well. New York has Grand Theft Auto too, you know."

Her smile didn't reach her eyes. "Brady's shark of a lawyer made sure there'll be hell to pay if I take Todd out of state. Even on vacation." She sighed. "I wish you could stay longer and get to know him."

"Chicago will never be big enou—"

"I know, I know. And after last night, I finally understand your reaction twelve years ago. I just never thought he'd..." She swallowed and blinked rapidly. Devon braced himself for the flood of tears, but after another hard swallow, her expression softened. "I heard about the takeover."

It was on the tip of his tongue to ask how the gossip could have reached her when Todd tilted his plate, reaching for a cinnamon roll, and a bunch of sausage links bounced onto the ancient rug. Frannie instantly headed over to diagnose the grease stains, clucking and scolding as she sank to her knees and rubbed the area with a linen napkin. So weird to see her as a mother. She'd gotten pregnant a year after he'd left. At seventeen. And the asshole who'd assured her that he'd pull out became her husband. No doubt Harrison had orchestrated the solution to that scandalous fiasco—statutory rape versus young lovers and a grandson. But if Devon had stayed in Chicago, Brady Goff would've never gotten to first base with his sister.

He glanced at Todd again then swigged his remaining coffee. He needed to continue exchanging ideas with Eric, conference in the corporate lawyer, maybe even hire a consultant. After refilling his cup, he headed out.

"Wait," his sister called. "I thought you were having breakfast with us."

He halted mid-stride. *Shit. The breakfast.* That promise seemed to have been made a decade ago instead of last night. It'd really hurt her if he admitted he'd completely forgotten about meeting Todd and had already eaten what amounted to a feast after surviving on two slices of cake last night. He turned. "Aw, Frannie, I'm sorry. I don't have the time..."

"Who doesn't have time to eat?"

"I've got so much work to do..." He petered out as his sister sat back, napkin dangling, lips pressed together in disappointment. "I *am* sorry, Frannie."

"Where will you be?"

He ran through the multiple room options like a Las Vegas card shuffler. He only needed a place with a desk, but top priority was choosing a room that gave him silence and absolute privacy. "First editions," he said, referring to the largest of the three libraries, the one that held his father's rare book collection. As children, just touching one of those books had been tantamount to crayoning a priceless canvas, resulting in corporal punishment severe enough to warrant a visit from Child Protective Services today. Like touching a hot stove, avoiding that library had become visceral instinct. It'd be the last place anyone would expect to find him.

Clearly his nephew and sister thought so too, given their widening eyes. After a quick salute to Todd, Devon strode out and bolted up the grand staircase. As he wound down hall after familiar hall, he resolutely kept the childhood memories of scavenger hunts and hide-

and-seek at bay. Despite his father's strict, museum-like rules for comporting oneself throughout the mansion, his mother had encouraged whatever fanciful activity their imaginations concocted. But he needed to stay sharply focused. Reminders of his mother had no place on a Friday morning twenty-one years later, when vultures circled his company.

He turned in to the massive library and crossed to the far corner, halting at the leather-topped executive desk, a masterfully crafted piece but, to his knowledge, merely decorative. Harrison collected beautiful things; he didn't enjoy or share them. Devon glanced around at the two-story shelves of priceless first-edition books and the brass ladder on rollers. Although both ends of the room opened into hallways leading to the east and west wings, no one would use this room as an access point. It was perfect for some private conversations, and the whir of industrial fans over in the west wing made it even more insulated.

He settled into the wide leather desk chair and scrolled through the emails on his phone. *Urgent* caught his attention, and he opened a note from Peter O'Callaghan, the Chicago developer for Ashby Enterprises' newest project—the one his trust fund was guaranteeing. O'Callaghan requested a video call as soon as possible, and Devon grinned. Now that Harrison had blown him off, his morning was wide open. Besides, the developer was accepting construction bids, and Devon was eager to hear the results in person. After securing a ten o'clock appointment, he resumed scrolling through emails until a whisper of sound caught his attention.

He raised his head in time to see an ethereal form glide into the room. His lungs ceased to function. *Hannah*. Older, curvier, but still emanating that inner radiance. It was what had first drawn him to her their senior year, and now, even with her on the other side of this enormous room, it left him dumbstruck. Her corkscrew curls had darkened to auburn and were tightly bound into a thick ponytail that fell to mid-waist. Just like always. He'd loved unbinding that hair. Feeling those silky coils bounce free and flow across his skin.

A stabbing pain in his lungs and his heart beating too fast drew his attention inward. He still hadn't breathed. He gulped a ragged inhale, certain she'd heard too, but no. She surveyed the floor-to-ceiling shelves, smiling like a kid facing mountains of candy. The mesmerized profile was the adult version of the cute teen curled up on her mother's sofa, nose buried in a novel. He opened his mouth in greeting and hesitated. As much as he'd looked forward to seeing her today, an internal warning suddenly flickered, like the lights in an execution chamber. He had no business waking up the past.

Regret constricted his chest again. He stayed perfectly still, deep in the corner of the vast room, capturing every gliding step she took toward the west wing like the f-stop shutter mode on a camera. Three more steps and she'd leave his life all over again, only this time she'd never even know it. Goose bumps pebbled his skin as a renewed need to blurt a greeting bubbled up. He couldn't just let her go like this.

Ringing pierced the air, as jarring as a scream. They jumped simultaneously, and she spun around. Her deep green eyes widened. Even this far, their expressiveness was like a sucker punch. He'd forgotten how she could hold whole conversations with her eyes alone.

His cell phone rang again. He rose slowly from the chair, unsure his knees would hold him. She squinted as if he were a mirage, and then her mouth fell open. He had to speak, yet his vocal cords locked up, and his lips were unable to form a single, stupid syllable. A third ring. If it was Eric, he had to take the call. He should really glance at caller ID.

"*Devon?*" She spoke his name breathlessly, and his mind flew back to the erotic things he'd done to make her call out his name like that. He gripped the desk. "H—happy belated birthday," she said. Even from over here, her trembling was visible.

"Thank you." He cleared the gruffness from his voice. A fourth ring. If he ignored it, there was no fifth. The caller would roll into voicemail. Instinctively he glanced at the screen. *Eric. Shit.* Maybe he had information on how Ashby Enterprises could survive, how to save the trust fund, how to ensure the development... "I, uh—I have to take this." His words sounded genuinely regretful but lame nonetheless. "I'll catch up with you in a bit."

He tapped the green Talk icon but never got the phone to his ear, because something flashed across her face. Sadness? Regret? Utter lack of surprise that the first sentence out of his mouth after twelve years was a blow-off? Whatever it was squeezed the oxygen right back out of his lungs. She disappeared into the west hall without a backward glance.

"Seriously," he called after her. "I'll be right there." *So fucking lame.* He cringed and forced his thoughts back to his crisis. "Hey," he said curtly into the phone. "What'd you find out?"

"There's definitely been some stealthy stock movement over the last quarter."

"How did we not pick this up?" he asked sharply, his emphasis on *we*—meaning solely his cousin, the damn CFO. The guru who'd taught him everything there was to know about being a financial genius.

"It was stealthy, Dev. The accumulation of shares was small enough and over such a long duration, it didn't trigger anything on our radar."

"Why not?"

"If someone bought a huge chunk of our stock all at once, it would set off alarm bells. We'd check into who's behind it and what their motivation is for the buy. But small day-to-day buying and selling—hell, we don't bat an eye."

"So you're saying my father isn't behind this accumulation?"

"I'm saying the stock wasn't bought by the Wickham Corporation. The purchasing company is Bryant Incorporated. Ever heard of them?"

Devon thought hard. Something about the word Bryant poked him. Something long ago. Maybe the name of a high school friend? A Cubs outfielder when he was Todd's age? Damn. Anxiety kept his mind blank. "No," he said, "but it's obviously an offshoot of my father's."

"I can't trace it back to Wickham Corp. The business address is the Cayman Islands, but the area code is local, two-one-two. Goes to"—a keyboard tapped—"Greenspan and Schmidt, LLP."

Devon glanced at his watch. Just after nine on the East Coast. "Did you call?"

"Yep. Secretary's evasive enough for the FBI, and bitchy enough to be my ex. I doubt I'll get any returned calls."

"Did you sell to Bryant?"

"Hell no. I sold to Allison Corporation, who agreed to sell them back next week. Besides, Bryant doesn't have nearly enough to take us out. Between the shares you, me, and the board still own, I don't see how a hostile offer could go through."

Harrison's words flitted through Devon's mind. *Your friends are quite unhappy with your leadership.* Who had sold to Bryant? He rubbed his jaw. "All right. Keep trying. I'll call you as soon as I meet with my father."

"Don't you want to conference me in? I can get Frank here in a heartbeat."

"Not for this particular meeting. Having the CFO and corporate lawyer on the line is admitting we're running scared."

"We *are* running scared, Dev. This isn't the time to let your pride interf—"

"I know my father," he snapped. "This cat-and-mouse game is just beginning. There's no reason to look like we're surrendering, or compromising, or even taking his threat seriously."

"Shouldn't we at least call some board members? Like Ken Tucker?"

Dread washed over Devon. "Not yet," he responded carefully. "The bastard doesn't think I'm good enough for his daughter as it is. If I lose the company..." He could go no further. He'd lose more than his life's work. And his fiancée's respect. Her incredibly high standard of living. And his mother's inheritance. Chills turned to sweat as the potential fallout hit him. The job losses. The dishonor. And the satisfaction on Harrison's face. "Let me see if I can talk some sense into my father. He could be blowing smoke up my ass for all our personal shit."

Twelve years later.

"The stealth that Bryant used to accumulate this much stock doesn't look like smoke, Dev. If this *is* Wickham, tread carefully."

"Just keep checking into the Bryant end," he ordered. "And did you hire a PI to look into Honey and O'Brien's backgrounds?"

"Just about to. The workday *did* just start, dude."

The tone brought Devon up short. He'd thrown all of this into Eric's lap in the wee hours of this morning. He didn't need to vent the fury he held for his old man onto his cousin, the closest friend he'd ever known.

Selling a few shares wasn't a crime. "Sorry. Just keep me in the loop."

"Same goes for you, Dev."

He tapped End and stared blindly at his surroundings. How his life could've gone from a relatively boring routine yesterday morning to *so* far off the grid boggled his mind. His frustrated gaze landed on the threshold that led to Hannah. Unbidden, her fleeting expression replayed. Hurt, maybe? Was it possible she still held feelings for him? Naw. Not the way he'd left their relationship DOA on her mother's doorstep. Should he go get reacquainted like he'd promised? At least apologize for his behavior back then? He hadn't been man enough to do it amid his heartbroken stupor when he'd disembarked in New York, and once he'd matured enough to realize just how in the wrong he'd been, the timeframe for apologies seemed long gone. But the words were still owed.

He glanced at his unread emails on the phone's small screen and mentally listed all the tasks he needed to do before his ten o'clock meeting with O'Callaghan and one o'clock meeting with Harrison. Number one was getting back on George Fallow's schedule. Signing for his inheritance. Shaving. Hannah's expression flashed through again, distracting him. He clicked open another urgent email. He'd problem-solve this one, then go find her and appease his curiosity. Five minutes of catching up. Definitely an apology. Maybe a quick hug goodbye for closure. What could it hurt?

CHAPTER 5

*Y*OU'RE TOO QUIET." *Devon shifted closer to Hannah on her mother's sofa and clasped her hand. "What's wrong?"*

She shrugged to give herself time. Conflict made her yearn to crawl inside herself like a turtle—with anyone, even the bullies in school. Until Devon. On the outside, he was this gorgeous, popular athlete, and no one seemed to get that he had this really gentle spirit. And the way he looked at her with unconditional love, as if he were the one lucky to be dating her, always gave her the courage to open up. Until today, with this mother of relationship conflicts. She couldn't answer. If she put words to her emotions, she'd cry, which would make it all so much worse. If only she could outright lie about her morose mood, but her palms would itch, and he knew the tell.

Still, he waited patiently. She had to think of something... Another incident today had been expected but was still a blow. It would do. "I didn't get the Denison scholarship."

He snagged a strand of her hair and coiled it slowly around his finger. "You were like this in trig. Before you got today's mail." His long-lashed eyes searched hers for a long moment. He always looked at her like this. Like he had a high-def view into her soul. "Tell me."

She glanced away. This was so hard. Even after six months together, even knowing he loved her...she couldn't say this out loud. Dread pitted her stomach. She couldn't bear the fallout. She changed the subject. "Why do you like me?"

"Not this again."

"I'm serious, Devon. You know it's what everyone whispers about when we're together. You belong with Amber or one of her cheerleader friends."

"Amber's interested in how far dating me can get her. I'm a prize, not a boyfriend, and I'm tired of shallow people. I want you."

The chronic insecurity of how she'd captured his love only took deeper hold. He'd answered why he wasn't dating Amber. "But why me?"

His eyebrows rose comically, and his face lightened. "Because you always let me have the last slice of pizza?"

Despite herself, she laughed. Ask Devon to sort through his feelings and he turned into a slippery goofball. She gestured to the cocktail table where the greasy box lay open with one lonely pepperoni slice left. "Help yourself."

"See? I love you." He shoved a third of the slice in. He chewed for a few seconds and then shrugged loosely. "I love how different you are." It came out garbled, the reason too vague, but at least he was trying. He chewed even quicker and waved a hand between them. "We both have one parent who's a pain in the ass, but somehow you let it roll off you. I don't know how you stay positive, but it makes you...special." He finally swallowed without spitting any food out. "I keep hoping some of your sweetness rubs off on me."

"I think I'm pregnant," she said, and promptly burst into tears.

His eyes widened, an electrifying blue in his

suddenly pale face. The slice sagged limply in his hand as he held deathly still. Hannah sniffled and wiped her eyes on her sweatshirt sleeve. God, she'd do anything to curl up in a ball and wish this all away. "I'm sorry. I've suspected for a few days and was too afraid to say something."

He opened his mouth and closed it. Emotions flitted across his face, none of them joy, which she hadn't expected—but now, faced with everything she feared, she palmed her face and sobbed in loud, jagged heaves. What would she do without him in her life? What would she do with this damn baby? Her mother would probably kill her, which would solve everything.

"Hey." He pulled one of her trembling hands away and held it in his damp, hot one. "Hey." He pressed her fingers gently until she reluctantly raised her head. "We're in this together, Han." His voice shook a little. That was the only emotion she was going to get. "I meant what I said—you and I belong together. I can't live without this." He motioned between them, taking her hand with. "Not even five minutes. We're soul mates. Tell me what happens next, and I'll be there for you. Forever."

The sooty residue from the Wickham paintings stung Hannah's eyes. She blinked rapidly. Impatiently. The tender moment and Devon's young, earnest face dissolved.

There were certainties in life. The sun rose in the east, green was a combination of blue and yellow, and Devon would never come back to Chicago. But there he'd stood—an older, chiseled version of the ridiculously handsome boy who'd walked away, like her love meant nothing. His emphatic promises a product of nothing but the pregnancy scare.

She peered at the geometric details barely visible in an oily Vermeer, but in her head she was still in the first editions library, locking eyes with Devon. The intensity in his cobalt stare had altered time to slow motion. Her brain had promptly ground to a halt. God, he looked incredible. As a teen, he'd always sported a trim, athletic body, and the years had hardened it to pure muscle— from the etched hollows beneath his lean cheekbones to the sleek torso in that black knit sweater. The only unaltered part of him was the rebel. The unshaven jaw. Those fierce brows. And the fact that he'd chosen to make calls in the one room she remembered was strictly off-limits. Sweet baby Jesus, that irresistible side of him left every molecule in her quaking.

She sank weakly into a Queen Anne chair, glaring at her traitorous limbs. How could he still have this much effect on her? She'd had the strongest urge to run to him as if the years hadn't passed. As if he hadn't left her with a heart so smashed she had yet to meet a man with the patience or skill to mend it. How was it possible for her inner scars to vanish so completely? Only his curt dismissal had saved her from making a bigger fool of herself than standing there gaping like a star-struck groupie.

The stark truth she'd avoided for twelve years swamped her, and she bent forward, clammy palms pressed to fiery cheeks. His love, his "soul mates" declaration—everything she'd swallowed hook, line, and sinker—had been one-sided after all. All these wasted years believing that maybe he was gazing at the moon, wondering whether she was too. Or that he sent out a happy birthday wish to the cosmos, like she had yesterday. What a stupid daydreamer. He'd chosen New York over her, made a success of himself, and was now so busy he *couldn't even say hi*. Well, that was that, right? Message received. Maybe she could finally, *finally*, put him behind her.

She bolted out of the chair, filling her lungs with

acrid oxygen, and resolutely shoved him from her thoughts. She snatched the list of tasks the team needed to accomplish from her briefcase and attached it to a clipboard. She and Sean could handle retrieving the remaining art from the smoky gallery. And she wouldn't be surprised if Robbie called in sick, so she hurriedly prepared backup assignments for everyone just in case. During her lunch break, she'd tackle the stack of apartments and—

"What a mess."

Hannah whirled around clutching the clipboard to her chest. "Frannie! You startled me." The house was over a century old; the floorboards creaked and groaned with every footstep. It hadn't occurred to her that the industrial fans in the theater could cover someone's arrival so completely. "It's good to see you again." Another sibling who'd grown up to be über-toned, although awfully thin.

"I saw you yesterday, but you guys looked way too busy to say hi."

Hannah nodded. "There was no way we could work in the gallery." The remnant smoke had been too thick for her employees, a testament to the amount of art that needed cleaning and maybe restoring. It'd taken her team most of yesterday just to transfer the paintings down the hall to this sitting room.

Frannie shook her head as she studied the filth. "This damn house has an eighty-year-old electrical system. Hard to believe the fire department suspects arson."

Hannah stiffened. Frannie had naturally been a de facto acquaintance, but she'd also been two years behind Devon and Hannah, so they hadn't hung out with her at school, and Hannah hadn't seen her too often here. Still, it wasn't like the quiet loner she remembered to gossip about arson. "Well, uh—it wouldn't have been to destroy your father's paintings," she said. "The gallery had its own state-of-the-art ventilation system and a reinforced wall between the theater."

"Then explain this." Frannie fluttered a hand at the black canvases.

"A hole burned through the gallery ceiling, which let in the smoke, and in the case of your dad's van Huessens, water damage raining in from the hose."

Frannie opened her mouth and then hesitated. "You *do* know Dev is back," she said bluntly.

Hannah fought the newest blush and lost. She couldn't discuss running into him. "Yeah." She waved the list like a white flag. "I'd love to talk, but I'm so busy and all—"

"Of course." Frannie backed up a few steps. "I'm actually looking for Honey. You haven't seen a gorgeous blonde wandering around?"

Hannah shook her head, her mood sinking even lower. Devon must've brought his fiancée; no wonder he'd brushed her off so quickly. *Honey?* She'd Googled pictures of the engaged couple; the woman was a stunning, statuesque blonde. Odd that a New York socialite named Nicole Tucker would call herself something as frivolous as Honey. "Devon's in first editions. He'll probably know."

Francine raised a shapely brow. "I highly doubt it. Anyway, if you spot someone who belongs in a beauty contest, let her know the caterer's here."

"Okay." Caterer? Had Devon and his dad made up? The girl inside found it hard to believe, and yet so many years had passed. Maybe incinerated ash could be built into a bridge.

Francine sighed as she headed for the door. "You'd think my father would haul this house into the twenty-first century and install an intercom system."

And a sprinkler system. Hannah finished jotting in

team names, trying not to think about Devon mere yards away. Or someone deliberately setting fire to the theater. Not a minute passed before a male said, "I can't believe this sight didn't bring the old man to his knees."

She jumped once again, pulse fluttering. Looming in the threshold was an overweight man, hair the color of fine yellow ochre, wearing saggy jeans and a rumpled T-shirt that said: *I'm Jealous of Me Too.*

Cripes! "Ricky?"

"In the flesh. Although I go by Rick now. You were Devon's girlfriend when I was, like, nine, right?"

"I guess so." She'd never paid much attention to the boy—hadn't thought he liked her because he'd always wanted to hang with Devon, and her presence interfered. In fact, her only vague memory of the chubby boy was his sulky scowl whenever he saw her. "Hard to believe you're so grown up." Just another reminder of all the wasted years, pining for Devon to come home and beg for her love.

Rick wandered closer, smelling strongly of cigarettes and minty mouthwash, neither of which covered the pungent whiff of alcohol. Pillow wrinkles crosshatched his cheek, and when he turned to survey the art again, he displayed a serious case of bed-head. Why would he come straight to the gallery project? "Did you...have a question about the paintings?"

"Nope." He looked around like his sister had. Was Mr. Wickham sending in his children to keep a close eye on her? She bristled.

"The team should finish crating and transporting by Monday at the latest," she said stiffly.

He grinned. A kinder version of Harrison's robin's-egg blue eyes twinkled mischievously. "I don't care."

"Oh." Her cheeks heated, as usual. "Sorry, it's...been a weird morning."

"Mornings are always weird. I try to avoid them

completely."

"Aren't you in the family business?"

"Can't—health hazard. I'm allergic to boredom." Although he attempted a boyish grin, it didn't reach his eyes. Matter of fact, he looked a little pasty. Maybe the hangover had finally caught up with him. He stuck his hands in his pockets and shifted his weight. "Say, any chance you'd be able to clean a painting I gave my dad last night?"

"Of course. That's what we do." She dug in her lab coat for a business card. Out came a crumpled Kleenex. Flustered, she looked in her other pocket. Two pens and lint. *Way to look professional, Hannah.* "I should be able to call you with a cost estimation and delivery date in a day or two."

"Naw, don't bother. Clean it up and bring it back whenev—"

"Stop flirting with Hannah and let her get back to work."

Frigid chills blanketed her, followed by a flash of heat that knocked out her equilibrium. It took enormous effort to turn with casual disinterest toward the familiar tenor, but she pulled it off. Devon stood close enough that the overpowering stench of ash changed to coffee and something unique she'd forgotten until now—a kind of pheromone that reminded her of warmth or sunshine... Eyes the color of lapis lazuli squinted as he smiled, which slanted those wide, sexy brows further.

Presto change-o, her knees weakened to noodles. She tore her gaze back to his brother. Had she known Devon would be in Chicago, she would never have taken this project, lucrative as it was. That's how much she couldn't handle seeing him again. That's how utterly un-grown-up she really was.

"I wasn't flirting, big brother." Rick winked at her, obviously to taunt him. Which was sweet, given Devon was engaged.

"Beat it," Devon ordered, his warm gaze still on her. "I want to talk to her in private."

His brother saluted and sauntered out, whistling the K-I-S-S-I-N-G nursery rhyme. Even though she knew Devon's fiancée was lost somewhere in the mansion maze, Hannah's blush burned.

Devon, however, didn't react as he wandered a few feet past her and surveyed the paintings like his siblings had before him. He stuck his hands in the pockets of his charcoal pants, which bunched the muscles of his back and triceps. She studied the hard curves with the same attention she gave a Bernini sculpture. When she glanced lower, at seriously tight curvature, her blood turned to liquid heat. There was a time she wouldn't have thought twice about stepping behind him and cupping that.

Hannah mentally slapped herself. He'd delivered his message loud and clear in the library. Why was he here? She exhaled audibly, but he remained motionless, those luscious muscles still taut. She tap-tapped her pen on the clipboard. Instead of clueing in, he reached down and grabbed a can of expandable spray foam and read the label. She cleared her throat. "Is there something you need?"

He swiveled around, nailing her with *the* stare. The one that used to precede a long, lazy kiss. Her breath hitched, and, as if he'd read her thoughts, his mouth formed the ghost of a crooked grin. He put down the can. "Yeah, Hannah, there's something I need. To come say a decent hello."

She nodded like that were a rational sentence. What was a decent hello from someone who'd once meant the moon and stars? A handshake? A brief, one-armed hug where most of her body avoided contact with his?

While she debated, he closed the distance, and suddenly she was smothered in a bear hug like in the olden days, only formidably more powerful than an eighteen-year-old boy's. Now the front of him was unyielding rock encased in cashmere, his arms defined steel. He palmed her head, burying his nose in the curve of her neck. She almost shivered at the intimacy of his touch. "You still smell like peaches and vanilla, Han."

She closed her eyes and tried to capture this memory, then realized she stood there stiff as a surfboard in his embrace.

He drew back, his stubble pulling several strands of her hair. "Sorry," he murmured, looking anything but, as he scraped them off his cheek and tucked them behind her ear.

She caught his curling fingers and stepped clear of him. "The caterer is waiting to speak to you," she bleated, much too loudly.

He blinked. "Me?"

"Well, you and Honey. Frannie's looking for her, although I told her she's probably with you." Was she babbling now? Clearly yes, because he studied her like she was that pinned frog in their biology class. "You *are* engaged." It wasn't a question. What game was he playing?

More seconds of frozen silence lapsed. His knotted brows rose. Then he threw back his head and laughed, the sound rich and deep. Long cords strained along his stubble-covered neck, and his Adam's apple bobbed up and down. She stared greedily, but it ended all too soon.

"Jeez, Han, I'd forgotten your sweetness," he said, and the warmth of his gaze overpowered her curiosity at his strange remark. He was looking at her like he used to, as if he saw all of her, not just the mask she showed the world. He pressed her fingers and sobered. "If you only knew how sor—" He broke off, glancing over her shoulder.

She snatched her hand back and spun around. In

trooped her team: too-cool-for-school Sean; Tina, who was too young to be that world-weary; and their skinny intern Robbie, whose allergies had kicked into high gear yesterday with all the smoke and soot. He stood in the doorway rubbing his nose. At least he'd shown up.

Hannah nodded at them and smoothed her lab jacket, face heating unfairly at the close call of almost being caught wrapped in Devon's arms. Besides Gretch, no one at Moore and Morrow knew of her past with this man, and she didn't need the gossip or questions. She stuck out her hand and shook Devon's in a brisk, hard grip. "Thank you for stopping in," she said formally, as if it were Joseph or Mr. Wickham. He quirked a brow but shook back with the same pressure. Thrusting the clipboard of itemized lists at Sean, she followed Devon to the doorway, her nosiness screaming at her until her lips formed the words. "I don't understand why you laughed so hard."

He glanced back, his face splitting into an easy grin, and for a second he was young Devon again, who'd brighten up like this every time he laid eyes on her. "Honey is my father's fiancée. But thanks for the chuckle. I really needed that."

At the threshold, he stopped abruptly and bent over a small, framed painting. She hadn't noticed it before, probably because it hung obscurely behind a lamp on an antique writing desk. Had she not been standing so close, she'd have missed his soft grunt. "Well, whaddaya know," he murmured. "My father didn't throw everything out."

He left without a backward glance. She numbly turned, answered Tina's question about crating, and handed Robbie a packet of tissues from her briefcase, desperate to go see what was in the frame. Finally, as her team began focusing on their tasks, she inched her way over.

The scene was painted in watercolors and clearly the work of a child. A summer landscape with emerald lawns dropped to a stretch of beach the color of Cheerios. In the distance, a Caribbean-blue lake shimmered, or else the globs of white were rippling waves. Bobbing in the center of the scene was a disproportionately large sailboat. A shiver ran down her spine at the scrawled signature. He must have painted it before he was nine. The scene was an exact replica of the back of this property, even the willow tree at the edge of the cliff, although this one leaned like Pisa.

Devon had taken her out back only once. He'd stood her at the precipice, where the lawn abruptly disappeared, and they'd stared at the thirty-foot drop to the sand below. Even the rough stone steps to the right looked too dangerous and narrow to descend to the beach safely.

The palm clamping hers had been damp, his body rigid. He'd told her tonelessly this was the exact spot where his father had pushed his mother. And that it'd been Devon, aged nine, who found her twisted body below.

CHAPTER 6

"YOU THINK WE can't see through your little game, Honey?"

Devon halted abruptly outside the dining room door, recognizing his brother's bluster.

"Shouldn't you be finding a job? A place to live?"

Before Devon could palm the brass handle, he heard shattering glass.

"I'd be real careful if I were you," Rick said in a low voice, as Devon lunged into the room. They both turned in surprise.

"Oh." She tilted her head. "I see you made it out of the solarium. So much for your scary ultimatums."

He ignored her and glanced at the ugly flush on his brother's face, then the crystal goblet that lay in pieces at the foot of an antique breakfront. Orange juice puddled in the shards, and an indentation marred the wood three feet up.

"Don't you have somewhere else to be?" he asked Rick curtly. The last thing either sibling needed was for Harrison to come down even harder on their heads.

"Like reading the want ads?" Honey said.

Devon spun toward her. "I don't need your help."

"She's ruining all our lives, and no one's saying the obvious—"

"Let it go, Rick. There's nothing you can do."

"Fuck that. I can." His brother's large hands fisted.

"And I will!"

Honey's lips curled without the smile entering her eyes. She raised her own juice glass and sipped delicately, her bearing like the Queen of England. When she swallowed, she tilted her head, glancing up between her lashes at Devon. "What? No more defending me?" Her sugary purr ratcheted the tight muscles in his back. This was a woman confident in her ability to play men against each other for her own amusement. How was Harrison blind to this?

"Come on, Rick." He didn't bother to keep the disgust from his tone as he turned away. "I have an appointment downtown; I'll drop you somewhere." *Anywhere. Out of this house, until you get your shit together.*

"Are you two running away from me?" He wouldn't turn back. Wouldn't take the bait, although she probably stood there in a provocative stance, with a smile guaranteed to egg a man on.

"Yeah," Rick said, "that's right. We're running from a fu—"

"Stop!" Devon yelled, and spun around. A kitchen maid had slipped in from the swinging doors. She stood poised for flight, eyes large as saucers. Rick's hands were still fisted at his sides, his eyes slits.

"Oh, please." Honey fluttered a hand and glanced between the maid and Rick. "Go ahead and finish. Especially now that we have a witness."

It was on the tip of Devon's tongue to warn his brother again, but the guy was an adult. Still, every muscle strained as he willed his brother to keep his mouth shut. Moments of silence passed where three of them looked like mannequins. Honey just sipped her juice with an arched brow. Jesus, she was cold.

"Let's go," Rick mumbled, and stalked past Devon, slapping the door open so violently the panel slammed against the foyer wall. "Fucking *bitch.*"

In the car, Devon kept the radio off, anticipating the inevitable explosion. He didn't have to wait long.

"It's just that she's ruining my life," Rick seethed, his hands balled in his lap, his face still an unhealthy shade of rage.

"You don't need to keep repeating that."

"But no one cares. She gets to waltz in and take our money and home—"

"Had she not waltzed in, Rick, what was your life plan? Bum around, mooching off Harrison?"

Rick faced the passenger window, his jaw clenched tight. "Pretty much. That money is my birthright."

"You remind me of that kid let off for being so spoiled he didn't know right from wrong."

"Bite me, asshole."

Devon headed south on Lakeshore Boulevard. "Where do you want to be dropped?"

"There's a twenty-four-hour bar downtown on North Clark Street."

"No."

Rick swung in his seat to face him. "Jesus, you're worse than the old man. Don't force me outta the house and then drive me somewhere I don't wanna go."

"Dude, the last thing you need is a drink. Why don't I let you off at an El station, and you can go to Northwestern. Find the alumni resource center."

"What don't you get?" Rick jabbed a thumb at himself. "I'm not getting a job. I'm going to fight that marriage."

"How?"

"Mind your own fucking business."

Devon glanced over. "Do you have money to hire a private eye and check into her background?" His brother stared out the front window. Devon waited a beat. "But you have money to drink."

Rick's fist thumped the dashboard. "Let me off here, fucker."

Devon was about to refuse, but he didn't need this added hassle. He'd gotten his brother out of the house before any more harm was done. He'd offered him a job and a home in Manhattan. Without Rick's willing participation, and a major attitude adjustment, there wasn't much else Devon could do. He pulled into the nearest El station and braked harder than necessary. "We may not know each other well, Rick, but I sure know Harrison. Don't fuck with Honey. Just get out of that godforsaken house as fast as you can and find a new life."

His brother bolted from the car, muttering a string of obscenities. Devon shook his head as he headed for the project manager's office to deal with whatever emergency had prompted the urgent email. Anything work-related was a thousand times better than the Wickham shitshow.

❦

TWENTY MINUTES LATER, he had a death grip on a Styrofoam cup. "It's just people blowing off steam," he said calmly, taking in O'Callaghan's linebacker build, almost cartoonishly large compared to the utilitarian desk he sat behind. "It isn't a big deal."

The developer thrust out his jaw. "It *is* a big deal, Mr. Ashby. I can deal with anger. But death threats? From *this* neighborhood? That's a whole different ball game."

Devon let a moment of silence go by, a negotiating tactic but also to defuse Peter's rising emotions. O'Callaghan pushed a stapler a few inches to the left and adjusted the angle of an acrylic picture frame. The harsh fluorescent lighting shone like a spotlight on the rosy flesh of his bald head. The way O'Callaghan fidgeted and avoided Devon's gaze was a good sign. In the corporate arena, it meant the person was undecided—reluctant to take the action they were threatening. Devon shifted in the uncomfortable chair and crossed an ankle over his knee.

"I don't want to make light of this, Peter," he said, "but anyone can say anything on social media and remain anonymous. We should've expected a backlash."

"No project is worth dealing with unbalanced people. It's a well-known fact that this neighborhood has its own watch because the police can't handle all the drugs and violence."

"Exactly how many people have threatened you?"

O'Callaghan finally looked up. "Six voicemail messages and fourteen emails."

"Did any of them state specifics, like: 'I'm going to shoot you in the parking lot tonight'?"

"No, just a bunch of obscenities and the phrase 'I'll kill you.'"

Shit. He planted the coffee cup on the desk between them. The Styrofoam was misshapen from the abuse. "Let them rant. They know you're not responsible for the teardown."

O'Callaghan swiped at the sheen on his very pink head. "I don't care. I'm still withdrawing from your project."

"You're under contract."

"Sue me."

Devon clenched his jaw and studied the multitude of fishing photographs that littered the walls. He had to negotiate today as if his company wasn't about to be taken over. He didn't know enough about his father's plan to shrug off this emergency. And he needed a better strategy, fast. Ashby Enterprises had no time to conduct the vetting process for another top-notch developer; the loan he'd personally guaranteed was not that generous. Besides, O'Callaghan was the best man to manage this project. He had a great rep with Teamsters and kept construction projects within budget—two miracles for Chicago. "Look, if you stay on, I'll raise your salary twenty percent." Eric would have his fucking hide.

O'Callaghan's slow blink was either a shrewd tactic, or he really was thoroughly insulted his life was worth such a pittance. "Fifty percent."

Devon held back the scoff and pretended to think about it. Even at twenty percent, all of this had to be presented to the board, if there was a board to even present to next week, but at the moment it was a shoot-now-ask-questions-later situation.

"Twenty percent and a fishing trip to Cabo after the project completion." He jerked his head stiffly toward the photographs. "Take your whole family for a week on us."

Wrinkles etched O'Callaghan's forehead. "Mr. Ashby, I've got two kids in high school. I want to be around when they get married and have kids of their own."

"Do you want me to hire a bodyguard? Or a PI to track down who's calling? The police?" His hands cramped from squeezing the thin arms of the chair. He spread his palms impatiently. "What?"

O'Callaghan shook his head. "It wouldn't make much difference. You're dealing with a volatile neighborhood here. This location could've been sold and redeveloped a long time ago. Even your father was interested at one time, but no one—"

"My father?"

"You are Harrison Wickham's son, aren't you?"

Devon planted both feet on the floor and leaned forward. "When was my father interested in the place?"

O'Callaghan shrugged. "Several years ago."

"Why?"

The manager looked at him like he was a lunatic. "I

don't know; you'll have to ask him. All I can say is he's been interested in most of Rogers Park, not just the parcels you have, and he's steadily bought them up."

Devon's heart drummed against his ribs. "What's he done with his land?"

"Torn down his old buildings. Built high-end condos and townhouses."

"Wait a minute...his old buildings?" Once again O'Callaghan shot him that look, like *how could the eldest son not know the business ventures of the father?* "Just give me the history on how my father connects with the area," Devon barked.

O'Callaghan shrugged. "The Wickham Corporation built Rogers Park back in the sixties, when the population was low income—so these houses were slapped up, and the neighborhood turned into one big melting pot of ethnic diversity. Fast-forward to the present, and all I know is that for the last several years, your father's been buying those same parcels, and trying to get zoning approval for upscale retail. I hear he plans to develop the next Magnificent Mile."

Similar to the Ashby Enterprises plan, only on a gigantic scale. Devon had just found the reason behind the hostile takeover: Ashby's set of parcels. "How much property has he bought so far?"

Peter scratched his forehead. "Most of the south and west. The fact that you purchased the northeast quadrant and have the lakefront and access to all the public beaches is a coup for you, but word is your father wants it at all costs."

"Yes," Devon answered shortly. "I'm aware of that." The lakefront benefits alone were worth all the inheritance money he'd sunk into buying the property, but hadn't his father ever heard of outbidding a competitor? Or offering the new owner an even higher price for the property—a price high enough that a small private equity company wouldn't refuse? "My father has many more city contacts than I do here. Why wasn't he able to, I don't know…"

"Pay someone under the table to refuse your bid?"

Devon reined in the urge to squirm. It wasn't every day you discussed your father's well-known cronyism and corruption with a semi-stranger. O'Callaghan leaned his arms on the desk, which creaked under the weight. "Word is, he's made enough enemies over the years that this time, and with this particular city hall director, it came around to bite him in the ass. Your deal was done before your father knew of it."

"Why didn't he start *out* buying the lakefront area?"

"And we've come full circle. Because of the reputation of this particular neighborhood. He probably figured once the other neighborhoods were gentrified, your renters would get the picture and start moving before it came time to snap up those blocks. Until you came along, no one else wanted it, so the Wickham Corp was in no hurry to buy it." He shook his head. "Believe me, if even half these apartment dwellers had left already, I could deal with this situation."

With the takeover mystery solved, Devon pushed his luck. "Does the word Bryant mean anything to you?"

O'Callaghan frowned and shook his head again. The secretary buzzed in, announcing an urgent call from Lincoln Park High School, and Devon sat back digesting the information while the developer took the call. It ended in seconds. O'Callaghan slammed the receiver down, his pate and face flushing an alarming beet red.

Devon took a wild guess. "Another threat?"

"Yes. Apparently they even know where my kids go to school."

Devon scraped his face with his palms, unable to find words of reassurance. How could he negotiate when kids were threatened? "Tell you what, Peter—give me two business days to come up with a plan. If I don't, then go ahead and bail on this project. Tuesday is all I ask."

O'Callaghan pulled at his lower lip, and Devon waited, his breath shallow. He was exhausted from the never-ending catastrophes, but keeping O'Callaghan was crucial. Seconds turned into minutes. Devon kept still, eyes on the man's face for any sign, but got nothing. O'Callaghan must be quite the poker player. Finally the other man cleared his throat, and Devon's gut seized in simultaneous dread and hope. "Mr. Ashby, I'll put up with the threats until Tuesday only if you agree to stand before the neighborhood at the community meeting tonight."

Devon forced his own face not to register alarm. "I can't," he said automatically. "I have a prior commitment." No one canceled on Nicole unless it involved a hospital visit on her part. This was their engagement party at the most exclusive restaurant in Manhattan.

"So it's okay for me to confront dozens of angry people as long as you aren't inconvenienced."

"I didn't mean for it to come out that way. Hire a security firm and bill Ashby Enterprises."

O'Callaghan slapped his desk and stood, a position of power. Startled at the man's sudden confidence, Devon rose quickly too. "Mr. Ashby, I'll accept your twenty percent raise, the fishing trip, and the additional security measures only if you face these people with me. You choose what's more important—this project or your *prior commitment*."

"Peter, this is ridiculous—"

"Is it, Mr. Ashby? I tell you I'm being threatened, you witness a call threatening my children, and you think a few incentives will mollify me? It doesn't matter if there are a hundred security people lining the walls.

You confront these people and *own* this teardown."

Devon set his jaw, trying to hold back his temper. "I'd be happy to if you can reschedule the meeting for another evening."

"The notices have gone out. The last thing I'm going to do is cancel or reschedule. That's just asking for a riot."

"Fine. I'll get my CFO to fly out here and stand beside you."

O'Callaghan folded his arms. "You, Mr. Ashby. I need to know how important this project and my well-being is to *you*."

"I appreciate your point—"

"Take it or leave it."

Devon walked to the door, his back ramrod straight. Now was not the time to make any impulsive decisions or remarks, although obscenities clogged his throat. "I'll be in contact."

"My secretary will text you the time and place."

Devon strode out into the sunny morning, a beautiful Indian summer day, but the synapses in his brain were firing so fast he barely noticed his surroundings. Cancel on Nicole? That would trigger unimaginable consequences. She still didn't know about the takeover, but her ability to sniff out losers long before they became a problem was epic. If someone in their circle had behaved the way any of his family had last night or this morning, she'd have cut them out of her life without a backward glance. It was a talent he was still trying to acquire. How would he explain this without revealing how far he'd sunk into his family's quagmire? She'd have little tolerance if he didn't sound completely authoritative while explaining how crucial it was to remain here. *In command. Efficiently solving this crisis. Remember the "love you."*

Once inside the car, Devon hesitated over the green

icon on the phone's screen. *Shit*. There was no way. He had to go back in and tell O'Callaghan to shove it. Blackmailing the CEO of Ashby Enterprises just to prove a point? Let the developer find another fucking project; Ashby Enterprises would suffer through the consequences.

No. O'Callaghan had the weight of his reputation and mega Chicago influence. It was in his power to make finding another developer very difficult, and Ashby didn't have the leeway for a long-haul delay. No way could Devon afford to lose the man's crucial union contacts just to attend a party that could also be rescheduled. He needed to channel Nicole's ruthlessness at staying the course and ignoring the emotional upheaval inside.

The call immediately clicked to voicemail. *Oh yeah. She booked a spa day*. He wiped the sweat from his brow as he listened to the clipped message. A short beep followed. He opened his mouth, heart hammering. Which decision was right? Out tumbled the words… "I'm sorry…emergency just cropped up…doubt I'll get home in time." He hung up and looked at the cell phone. Apparently his subconscious had decided for him, but he'd sure as hell sounded pathetic.

Driving back to his childhood home, Devon dragged his attention to the next crisis: the upcoming meeting with his father. The mystery of Harrison wanting Ashby Enterprises had something to do with the sixties. Why else would Wickham Corp be so cutthroat in wanting to buy up that property again? Maybe it'd been the site of a toxic waste dump and his father was avoiding a class-action lawsuit. Or buried skeletons. Probably the latter. But hopefully this was enough to bluff the old man to back the hell off. Devon exhaled harshly.

At the next traffic light, he put in a call to Eric, who

answered in one ring. "How'd it go?"

"Everything's on schedule." Devon skipped over the details. He'd tell Eric about the concessions later, after he knew where he stood with his father. "If there are no delays with union negotiations, we could get the project underway before the holidays."

"Excellent. I'll call the board."

Devon caught him up on Wickham's odd repurchasing of property they'd held in the sixties. "Hopefully this info will be the negotiating tool we've been looking for."

"If it is, I'm buying the first round of drinks at your engagement party."

Devon paused, dread pulsing through his veins. "I just canceled that. O'Callaghan needs a babysitter when he confronts the Rogers Park neighborhood tonight."

A moment of silence. Then, "Want me to Google whether ass transplants are successful? Because Nicole will shred yours."

Devon grunted as the light turned green and he waited for the car in front of him to clue in and drive. "So how many shares did you sell?" A question that should have been asked last night. Information he should have learned the day it happened. His hands tightened on the wheel.

"Not enough for anyone to threaten us, Dev. I wanted to jump into the commodities and currency market; those traders are raking in the profits. I just needed some seed money."

Eric was the kind of guy who shared too much information: explicit descriptions of his sexual escapades with bar hookups, the mole on his toe that had three hairs growing from it, hell—even the frequency and descriptions of his bowel movements. That he'd held on to this side hobby was peculiar, to say the least. "When exactly did you sell?" Devon finally asked.

"Last Tuesday. This should *not* be what we're focusing on."

Devon bit back a caustic reply. Had the sale not happened, they wouldn't be in this mess. "Have you gotten any info on Honey and Wesley?"

"I hired an ex-NSA employee, name is Kevin Houghton. He's working on them, plus anything he can come up with on Bryant. We should have a buttload of info by this afternoon. It's costing us a ton."

"It'll be worth it."

TWENTY MINUTES LATER, Devon parked between the fire marshal's sedan and a white van whose sides were custom-painted with *Moore and Morrow Art Restoration*. On instinct, he glanced around for a long auburn ponytail, but only saw a couple of skinny guys hammering two-by-fours into crates. He nodded as he passed, his mood brightening with each step. He had fodder on Harrison, had kept O'Callaghan on the job, and had just scheduled a midafternoon appointment to sign over his mother's trust. The fallout when he heard from Nicole would be bad, but she also understood corporate life. In the end, she'd agree his decision to stay in Chicago tonight was crucial.

He let himself into the Wickham foyer, starkly dim after the bright sunshine. Joseph appeared as he shrugged off his overcoat. "Lunch will be served in the dining room in five minutes, sir."

Devon tensed at the innocent statement. If the past had taught him anything, it was to enter that dragon's den calm and indifferent. He couldn't choke down food and dodge precisely aimed barbs with Harrison an hour before his meeting.

A flash of movement on the landing caught his eye. Hannah descended the stairs, her steps light, her attention completely fixated on the musty, old tapestry curving along the wall. Once again her expression was entranced. She clutched a paper lunch sack in her left fist. A brief memory of how she gripped him— *Enough.* "I won't be dining with the family today, Joseph," he said, without taking his eyes off the ethereal woman. "Please have Mrs. Farlow prepare a picnic for two and send it out to the gazebo."

"Right away, sir."

Devon crossed the foyer and stood at the bottom step. He hadn't made it through the apology in the sitting room; this would be the perfect time. He waited for her to notice him.

Back in high school, Hannah, who'd transferred in their senior year, had immediately hung with the book nerds. That fatal flaw, combined with being taller than most guys and her perpetual blush, had made her an easy target for the bullies. *Why the blush, Stork—did you just fart?* That remark was the first time he'd really noticed her, because the jerk sauntering past while yelling it was Brady Goff, the asshole linebacker who eventually became his brother-in-law. Amid the cruel laughter in the crowded hall, Devon had impulsively stuck out his foot. The thug had gone down like a redwood.

Immediately the milling students had redirected their laughter, which Devon had barely registered because the sudden eye contact with Hannah had squeezed something in his chest. Her face grew redder, deepening the green of her eyes to emerald, and he'd zeroed in on the tortured vulnerability filling them. Protectiveness had swelled inside him, and when she'd gifted him with a faint smile, the hall noise faded dead away. Before he could emerge from the weird catatonic state, she'd disappeared into the girls' room. And that was it. He'd even waited past the late bell, but she never came out.

For two weeks, he'd impatiently sought her out—

how hard could it be to find a tall redhead? Not a glimpse. It was almost like she was avoiding *him*, the All-American shortstop, captain of the baseball team, and generally considered the most popular guy. There wasn't another girl in the three surrounding school districts who hadn't made it perfectly clear she'd put out even before he reversed out of her father's driveway.

He'd finally caught a clue and went on reconnaissance through the library, and there she'd been, tucked in a far back corner cubicle. It'd taken every ounce of charm he possessed to get her to agree to a movie, but the whole process wasn't the smooth, assured invite he was used to. In fact, it was so awkward he'd stuttered and matched her blush for blush.

One thing hadn't changed in all these years: Hannah's inattention to the real world around her. Even when they were dating, a part of her had always been off somewhere in her head, her thoughts usually eliciting that secret half-smile. The harder he'd tried to capture all of her, the more it seemed like trying to capture a wisp of smoke. And in the end, he'd walked away with a shredded heart.

He blinked the memories away, but a glimmer of the teenage indignation remained. With five steps to go, how could she be this close and not be as drawn to him as he was to her? *Hypocrite.* He'd just canceled on his fiancée—what was he doing mooning over Hannah and her secret smile? In fact, lunch with her suddenly seemed like a terrible idea.

The second the thought flitted through his head, she turned from the tapestry, and they locked eyes. His heart thrummed in response. She inhaled sharply, and yep, there was the blush, creeping up her neck. That strange surge of protectiveness rose within him again, throwing him completely off guard. She paused on the step, almost shyly. He should say something, but nothing came to mind. Where was Renegade, who worked a room like a politician? He hadn't felt this off-kilter since asking her for that first date. And this wouldn't be a date. What the hell was the matter with him? *Don't ask her to lunch. Just say hi and walk away!*

"Is—is something wrong?"

He realized he was scowling up at her, and forced out a grin. "Caught up in crazy thoughts."

Footsteps rang down the long hall, and he glanced right. *Damn!* Harrison and some minion were a hundred feet away. The old man was engrossed in barking out an order and scrawling his signature on the top sheet of a thick binder. Devon had seconds to get the hell out of here before he was tagged, bagged, and dragged to the dining room.

"Let's go," he said, and snatched her hand. Or tried to. Because of her sack lunch, he grabbed more wrist than palm. Ignoring her shocked *oh*, he pulled her from the last step and speed-walked around the corner into the small parlor, out the other side, and across the sunroom. At the French doors overlooking the back lawn, he halted abruptly, pulse thumping as he listened for footsteps or voices.

"What on earth are you doing, Devon?"

He gazed down at Hannah's wary face. Her pink lips were open and slightly breathless. Those deep green eyes, ringed with warm amber, blinked once as if in slow motion. Two glaring certainties struck him: he'd be perfectly content to spend the next hour standing here staring into them, and, on a gentlemanly level, he stood way too close. Just like when he'd hugged her way too intimately in the sitting room.

He should back off, but his limbs wouldn't budge. As if his soul had never splintered, some primitive side of him was blindly pulled to her.

This was wrong. He was engaged. He drew in a

deep breath, which resulted in the heady scent of summer peaches, and forced himself to release her wrist. Easing back, he searched for the commanding businessman, but the blustering high schooler grinned sheepishly. "I'm inviting you to lunch."

A faint smile lit her face. "You mean kidnapping?"

He swept a hand around them. "I was giving you a quick tour first."

Her smile grew; that dimple forming on her right cheek. He chanted Nicole's name in his mind.

"Seriously, why did we race through the house like that?" Hannah glanced at the pink imprint of his grip still marking her skin.

He caught himself before he reached out to caress it, and gestured at the back lawns instead. "It's such a nice day, and I hate eating alone—"

"Liar," she scoffed. "I'd bet my paycheck you're trying to avoid your father."

He winced. After all this time, she still read him too easily. "Having lunch with an old friend came in a close second." *Jesus!* Could he have found a more insulting way to describe what she'd meant to him?

An awkward moment hung between them until she held up her sack lunch. "Thanks, but I was heading out to sit out by Poseidon. I've got a bunch of calls to make, and my team's crating out there. I should go check—"

"They're fine; I just saw them. Come on, Han. I haven't seen you in twelve years. Let me have this one hour." He motioned toward the gazebo to the far left of the property.

The unease that flashed across her face mirrored the warning buzz inside his brain. But after a slight hesitation, she stepped out into the warm afternoon.

CHAPTER 7

HANNAH HAD TWO options: continue trembling like a teenage imbecile, or completely ignore the familiar stranger striding on her right. She gazed left, where a thick forest of ancient oaks and maples blocked the mansion next door, and concentrated on how the trees swayed in the cheerful afternoon breeze. Leaves of scarlet, sienna, and sunburst fluttered like colorful rain onto the vast lawn. Ahead was a large gazebo right out of *The Sound of Music*, intimately secluded with twining vines of dark ivy. Beyond, like the backdrop to a vibrant painting, Lake Michigan sparkled in ever-changing hues of blues, the darkest of which reminded her of Devon's eyes. She should've insisted on eating lunch by Poseidon.

Abruptly, Devon halted. "You know what? Let's eat down by the boathouse."

She glanced over. *Boathouse?* She hadn't known one existed. A muscle tensed along his prickly jaw, and she followed his gaze toward the cliff. Although she murmured an assent, and they changed directions, her confusion grew with each step that led them closer to the place where his mother had died.

Instinct told her this bizarre second meeting—third, counting the blow-off in the library—had something to do with Harrison. By the curt way Devon had said his father's name in the sitting room this morning, the rift between them was as wide and engulfing as ever. But what was her role here? Devon may be engaged, but every minute she spent in his presence brought her heart that much closer to danger. Why didn't she have the survival instinct to walk out front and join her team?

They slowed at the estate border, where a row of pine trees and the graceful weeping willow camouflaged the steep, rocky ledge. Even after all these years, the abrupt drop-off to the beach made her dizzy, and she fought the instinct to step back. She inhaled deeply and concentrated on anything that could be a boathouse. All she saw was the lake, sand, and rocky cliff. "I think it washed away."

Devon pointed past the willow brushing the top of the steep stone steps. "Halfway down, there's an alcove built into the cliff. My great-grandfather carved out a boathouse."

Goose bumps prickled her skin at the thought of descending the cliff for any reason. "Why are we here, Dev? Why are you doing this?" A moment of silence stretched long enough that she figured he wouldn't answer. She wasn't a part of his life. She'd only been commandeered here so he could avoid his father. And she'd followed willingly, like a devoted puppy. Pathetic.

He turned from the softly lapping waves. "I wanted to be alone with you. Somewhere no one can find us. And I want to apologize for being such an ass twelve years ago."

As hard as she tried, she couldn't stop her mouth from falling open. The words she'd waited so long to hear. Her heart swelled, and her throat squeezed. Just before she completely embarrassed herself by tearing up, he looked over her shoulder and waved. A maid with a picnic basket was on the far lawn, crossing toward the gazebo.

"Don't climb down those steps without me." He

loped away in that lithe, athletic jog she remembered so clearly. She bit the inside of her cheek, seeing him that final night, drenched and unwilling to climb her mother's porch stairs to shelter. Those five steps the figurative impasse as she stood at the top, dry and sobbing at his ultimatum.

"She's not dying, Han. She was just diagnosed."

"It's metastasized to her lymph nodes."

"And she'll have surgery and then go through treatment and recover. You being here or being in New York won't change what's happening in her body. It's me who can't live without you."

A bolt of lightning descended like an exclamation point. Her desperate attempt to hold off hyperventilating, and using the roar of thunder to claw for oxygen. "Why can't you wait, Devon? Why does it have to be tonight?"

He swept the plastered hair from his forehead. "Because the sonofabitch just kicked me out tonight!"

"You can stay here."

"I'll never set foot in Chicago again." He patted his jacket pocket. "I have two tickets on a Greyhound bus, fifty-three dollars, and you. That's all I need."

"Where would we go? How would we live?"

"My cousin lives in Brooklyn. He said we could flop with him."

"But how would I get home to visit Mom?"

Silence.

Devon accepted the picnic basket and said something to cause the maid to smile shyly. Hannah stared overtly at the man he'd become: self-assured, hotter than fire, and sporting a physique worthy of a men's magazine. On occasional sleepless nights, she imagined the life she'd be living had she chosen him. After her father had been shot writing a speeding ticket, her mother had either been too wrapped up in her grief to notice Hannah or worse—noticed and actively disliked her. From age five on, life had been miserable because of her mom's bipolar disorder. But cancer was a game changer, and Hannah had sacrificed the love of her life to be at her mother's bedside until the last anguished breath.

At the time the decision was easy, because she'd fully expected Devon to return for her. But the years had slipped past. Time healed the grief for her mother, but the what-ifs for Devon had sharpened to razor wire, slicing her each time her thoughts skimmed close.

Devon strode back; his crooked grin causing butterflies to shimmer and swoop in her stomach. He reached her side and held out his hand. "Turn sideways and take it slow. The stairs can be slippery."

When she clasped his warm palm, he immediately linked fingers. The intimate contact tasered every nerve in her body. He misunderstood her hesitation and squeezed her hand, anchoring her with his braced bicep. "I've got you."

She descended the first step. The worn stone was so narrow that the outer part of her shoe was suspended in midair. Sweat broke out on her brow. She glanced at the sand far below, huffing out a breath. It'd be so easy to fall... "Holy baby—"

"Let's go to the gazebo," he said quickly, and she immediately shook her head.

"I—I've got this." Ten geriatric steps farther, the boathouse came into view. It had indeed been carved into the side of the cliff. The façade, created by giant stones and grout, resembled a miniature castle. The arched wooden carriage doors were framed by stone turrets on each side. Best of all, the entire area was set back ten feet, which gave them room to step onto wide flagstones. Immediately her shoulders loosened.

"This is...charming," she breathed, allowing a

glimmer of regret to surface. She'd dated him for ten months and never been to this place. Never even explored the whole mansion.

"Looks like no one's been here in ages," he murmured, and it was then that she noted small patches of rot in splintered russet doors that had clearly once been fire-engine red. The majestic brass doorknockers were covered by a pale green patina. Dandelions and clover weeds flourished between the flagstones at their feet. Except for the soft whoosh of waves rolling ashore, life down here stood timeless and still, a relic of the family's happier days.

He handed her the basket and yanked on the metal rings. The doors squeaked and lumbered on rusted tracks; the dark interior releasing strong odors of dust and mildew. He coughed. "Maybe this wasn't such a hot idea."

"Oh no, this is wonderful." She peered into the depths, where the bow of a tarp-covered speedboat loomed out at them. "But how do you get the boat down to the lake?"

He showed her the slots where metal rails were housed. "We had to manually haul these rails out, hook them to the boathouse, and use a winch to raise and lower the boat. About a year before I left, the old man had it all remote-controlled." And yet by the looks of it, the boat and beach toys were now rarely used. Before she could remark on that, he muttered, "There used to be a little table and some chairs in here."

He disappeared into the musty boathouse and returned almost immediately with wrought-iron furniture, gritty with disuse. After dusting the chairs with an old T-shirt he found hanging on a hook, he held the back of one and gestured for her to be seated.

Hannah placed her bag lunch at her feet and emptied the picnic basket that could easily have fed ten.

The oddly comforting smells of Lake Michigan in Indian summer—warm seaweed and dead fish—mingled with freshly baked bread and tangy slaw. Yet instead of the growls of hunger she'd endured earlier, her stomach kept flip-flopping. Any minute now they'd talk about *that night*, and suddenly she wanted to put it off as long as possible. The words she'd needed to hear might give her closure, but what would life be like afterward, when he returned to his fiancée? Or maybe it was the fear he'd say the wrong words. Justify his behavior. What if she'd wasted her life mooning over a boy who grew up to be an asshole? Jeez, how could she delay this until she psyched herself up? "Why *did* you come back, Devon?"

The serving spoon he'd picked up hovered over the coleslaw. "I had some papers to sign." He gestured with the utensil. "Technically I could've done it through express mail and notaries, but I had some idiotic idea of returning in triumph." He stabbed the spoon into the slaw. "You know, show the family I'd done well? Even hold out an olive branch, adult to adult." He emptied an enormous serving onto her plate. "It didn't go as planned." The hard glint in his eyes almost made her shiver.

"When are you leaving?"

"Are you married, Hannah? Kids?"

The question stung on many levels. Either her question was unimportant, or the answer she sought was none of her business. The fact he even asked meant that he clearly hadn't cared enough to Google-stalk her. She shook her head.

"Dating anyone?"

"I'm too busy with the company." Which was true. And more face-saving than admitting that her rare Internet dates ranged from dismal to colossal failures.

"It's beyond amazing running into you here of all places," he remarked.

"Right back at you." They laughed, but the awkwardness persisted. She rubbed a corner of the coral linen napkin in her lap and frantically searched for something to fill the silence. "Your father's secretary called us on Wednesday, after the insurance adjusters toured the gallery and provided a quote he thought was insulting. He's made it clear our documentation of the damage and restoration cost will probably be used in a civil suit against them. Of course, we're thrilled at this opportunity to work in his private galleries. Our bread and butter is actually conservation, not restoration. We're one of the vendors that serve the Chicago Art Institute." Jeez, she sounded like a company brochure!

He nodded. "I heard your company discovered the Rubens forgeries."

"*I* discovered them." Ah, the price of defensiveness. Here came the blush.

"I forgot how easily you do that." His eyes gentled, which only turned her flush up a notch. "How'd you find out they were forged?" He kept up the eye contact as he stuffed half a thick sandwich in his mouth and bit down.

She picked up her own and put it back down, wishing she could delve into her lunch sack for her carrot sticks and apple. This heavy food would make the afternoon drag. "The red ochre Rubens is known for was not the right hue. And there were hesitation brushstrokes in the tiny details. You wouldn't see that in a Rubens." She leaned forward. "As a matter of fact, he copied other masters himself."

A wide brow quirked. "You're saying Rubens was a forger?"

"Gosh, no. He was commissioned to copy other artists or repair their damaged works. He was proud of how authentic his copies looked."

"Fascinating." He spoke the word as if to himself. They ate a few bites in silence, but Devon wasn't looking at his forkful of slaw or the lake or anything else in this serene setting. He was looking at her. Raptly. With that deep, all-consuming, you're-the-only-person-in-the-universe intensity.

Hannah's stomach clenched. "Do you like art, Devon?"

"Hate it."

The emphatic tone startled her. "But the little picture you painted—"

"I was a kid, Hannah. These days, I work. That's my passion. If I go to a MoMA exhibit, I can assure you it's because I'm being dragged there."

Her opening! "Tell me about your fiancée." Hearing him gush about Nicole Tucker meant Hannah would finally *know* that the love of her life had found the love of his. No more hope. No more fantasizing. It would be over. Sweet baby Jesus, how many nails could you drive into a coffin before it finally sealed?

He twisted the cap off an Orange Crush—the soda his great-grandfather had invented, the start of their epic family wealth, and, naturally, the Wickham drink of choice. "I'd rather keep talking about you," he said. "How'd you get into this...art thing?"

She pressed her lips. So vintage Devon—automatically deflecting any personal questions that involved feelings. He hated art, but would rather talk about it than his personal life. Maybe he hadn't changed after all. She'd answer him, but she'd keep it short and turn the subject back to him, damn it.

"I majored in graphic art at Northwestern," she said in a clipped tone. "My junior year, I interned at Mannix Conservation and Restoration lab, and something just ignited in me. There's power in restoring a damaged piece to its full beauty."

"But when I left, you were waiting tables at Bakers Square. You weren't even considering colleges." The implication hung in the air like skunk spray. *You were too poor.*

"During the last months of Mom's life, her best friend, Bernice, moved in and took care of us. When Mom passed, I got a healthy sum from her life insurance. Bernice convinced me to use it toward college. She's also the one who got me the internship. She was a conservationist there. Now she works for me." *And now she's ill, too.*

"When did your mom pass away?"

"Seven months after you left." *Crap.* She bit the inside of her lip. She'd emphasized the last word too harshly. And now they were right smack in the middle of the topic she wanted to avoid. Her stomach churned as he studied her, his eyes a deep cerulean blue in this bright light.

"I'm sorry," he said bluntly. "The stuff I said that night...the way I left things. I was a complete shithead."

She waited for more—like how it'd taken years to get over her, how he still thought of her once in a while...

But no, he was done. Her hope for emotional maturity fizzled. Some things never changed. Genuine regret showed in his warm eyes, though, and damn if a little part of her torn heart didn't start stitching up. *So stupid.* She nodded her acknowledgment and searched for surer footing. "So how is *your* company doing?"

"It's all good." His expression didn't mirror the statement.

"How did you go from fifty-two dollars to"—she gestured at him up and down—"someone who has the world at his feet?"

A grin split his face, broadening those wide brows and etching grooves in the sexy brackets around his mouth. "Fifty-three dollars." He sipped his soda, but good-natured resignation remained, and when he put the can down, he said, "Remember that cousin I used to talk about like he was a rock star?"

She nodded, afraid any interruption would shut down the sharing.

"He was rising through the ranks at Langton Investments and took me on as his assistant. I learned everything I know about business, finance, sales, and work ethic during those years. No one works harder than him. No one plays harder either." He laughed, and she studied his beautiful mouth, the even, white teeth. *Dear God.* If only her stomach would settle down. "Guy will turn impulsive on a dime, invite a few girls to a suite in the Bahamas, and stay up for days."

"So..." She blinked to attention. "You didn't go to college?"

"Took some night courses. Mainly focused on clawing my way up the ladder."

"How did you meet your fiancée?"

He hesitated, and she smoothed the napkin, as if it were Boots on her lap. She had a right to know. Something shifted in his face, surrendered. "Eric took me to a country club he was thinking about joining, and she was coming off the golf course with her father. Eric knew him and introduced us..."

He stuffed in another giant mouthful, and she folded her arms, waiting for him to swallow and provide just a tad more information. Instead, he swigged the soda, his stubbled throat working up and down. Through the gaps in the wrought-iron tabletop, it was hard to ignore that rigidly flat stomach, and how he spread his thighs with such innate masculine confidence. "Come sit on my lap," he used to say, with a smoking-hot look in his eyes. And he hadn't meant sidesaddle.

She mentally shook herself. This wasn't helping. "How long will you be in Chicago?"

He swallowed the enormous bite. "I have a meeting

tonight. I'll head out afterwards."

As he spoke, Hannah caught sight of a stunning woman over his shoulder. She stepped down the same stairs that had terrified Hannah and onto the wide flagstones as lithely and soundlessly as a cat.

"Oh, hello," the woman said.

❧

DEVON JERKED AT the smoky voice, twisting around in his seat. *Honey.* He squeezed the wrought-iron arms of the chair as his teeth instinctively clenched.

She shifted her weight, thrusting a hip out like a runway pose, as if they might miss the stupendous body in a barely there white bikini.

He purposefully ignored the skin and curves and frowned at her wide straw hat, matching beach bag, and two-inch, bling-covered flip-flops. *Really? In October?* "The pool is that way." He pointed up and to the left.

"I prefer the beach." She lowered her oversized sunglasses halfway down her nose and perused him. "Your father has every servant in the house looking for you," she said in a syrupy tone. "Evidently you were to meet him half an hour ago?"

Shit. There was no way it could be that late. To hide his shock, Devon made a show of sitting back in his chair as if he had another half-hour to kill. "The cook, a maid, and Joseph all know I'm out here," he said over his shoulder, "but thanks for delivering the message." He missed Honey's reaction, but the dismissal in his voice sure straightened Hannah's spine. She looked back and forth between them, brows knitted.

"Is *this* your fiancée?" Honey asked.

The false disbelief brought him up short. She knew last night that Nicole wasn't here, and no doubt she'd seen Hannah working in the house. What game was she playing?

"Of course not," he responded curtly. Hannah's

fork clattered off the china and bounced onto the flagstone. The racket echoed in the tense silence. As she bent to retrieve it, his words and tone caught up with him and he bit back the surging apology. No way was he giving his father's fiancée any ammunition on the teenage love affair. "This is Hannah Moore, the art expert," he said calmly when she sat back up, her face in flames. "Harrison hired her company after the fire." *As I'm sure you know.*

"So you're having lunch with the help? How delightful."

He tossed his napkin onto the plate and glanced up in warning. A predatory gleam filled Honey's eyes as she studied his high school sweetheart. One thing about Honey: she wasn't dumb. She'd want to uncover the reason behind this little picnic.

Before Hannah could introduce herself and offer up their past like a stuffed Christmas goose, he said hastily, "Hannah, this is Honey Hartlett. My future stepmother." His lips felt so stiff, it was a wonder the words weren't slurred.

Hannah's smile conveyed her utter confusion, but also that disarming friendliness. A strong wave of nostalgia pulled at him like a riptide. Some things never changed, like her inability to make snap judgments about people with obvious ulterior motives. That openly pleasant face still held naïve friendship. If anything, the woman she'd grown into had an increased belief in the goodness of people. He couldn't fault her for the very essence he'd clung to during those dark days living under this roof. Like she was the sliver of warmth and light in his isolation cell. He both adored her for it and wanted to shout a warning as she held out her hand. Whether deliberate or not, Honey was already turning away, pointing down to the sand.

"Didn't your mother commit suicide down there?"

she asked.

Through ringing ears, he heard Hannah's gasp. It took all his will to rein in his expression. Seconds passed where no one spoke and no one moved. He wouldn't have been able to if he tried. Peripherally, he caught Hannah's pitying expression, which further fueled his fury. She knew all about his mom. They had no secrets between them back then, but a covered-up murder staged to look like a suicide should *not* evoke sympathy. It meant Hannah had never really believed him.

Devon gathered his wits about him, drilling Honey with his coldest stare. "Anything else?" His voice came out gravelly.

Completely unaffected by his reaction, or too stupid to realize the danger she faced, her lips curled upward as she flashed her cell phone. "I'd be happy to call your father about your little date, so no one bothers you further."

"That's not necessary. We were just leaving."

Honey shrugged and turned back to the stairs, descending the treacherous steps with fearless grace.

She was something else.

Devon sat back rigidly. The tension in his jaw spiked a shaft of pain behind his right eye. Of course time had flown too fast; it always had when he was with Hannah. But the pleasure of listening to her accomplishments and this impromptu reconnection was so tainted he could taste it. Without looking at Hannah, he scraped his chair back. "We better get back to the house."

"Shouldn't we"—she pointed to the table—"clean up? Put the furniture back?"

He glanced at the picnic items impatiently, torn between the betrayal of her pitying expression moments ago and the desire to hug her for those absurd questions. Her personality was so alien in the world he'd grown up in, and now built for himself. And yet it was that difference—her love of family, the brave resolve in the face of high school taunting, her perpetual kindness toward the disrespectful restaurant patrons she'd served—that had drawn him like a moth to a bonfire. He gestured for her to go ahead of him. "We're at the Wickham house," he said as gently as he could. "We don't clear tables. Someone will come for it."

She slipped by him, but he caught her stunned expression. Clearly she'd forgotten the ways of the Wickhams. Although, come to think of it, they'd spent most of their time at her house. Her mother had worked two jobs and rarely been there.

Their journey across the lawn and into the sunroom remained wordless. Which was stupid. He had so much left to say. He'd completely botched the apology, the whole point of lunch. His sentence would've been fine if he'd spilled milk or sworn rudely twelve years ago, but it didn't come close to covering the Godzilla number he'd done on their relationship. He'd started off all right, but the remorse for what could have been had choked the words in his throat. And now they were out of time, and worse, Honey had wrecked the final moments of their tenuous reunion.

They halted in the foyer. He glanced left, down the long hall to where his father's office lay. The tension in his muscles felt like radioactive waves. He'd take all this anger and smash his father's plans to bits. Fucking seek and destroy. He took a deep breath and refocused on her. She'd collected her little lunch sack and still clutched it tightly. "You hardly ate anything," he remarked.

"I wasn't hungry."

"I still have so much to apologize for—"

"Never mind." Her eyes flitted away. "It was so long ago. Who even thinks about silly teenage stuff?" She scraped the nails of her free hand over her palm. So even as a grownup she had that same tell. She followed his line of sight and clenched her fist, blushing. "Well," she straightened her shoulders, "I need to check on my team and get to work on your father's second gallery."

Her words registered through all the crazed thoughts. "Wait. That gallery is all the way down the hall. The smoke reached that far?"

"No. While we're here, your father asked us to check it for conservation purposes. Anyway—it was great seeing you again." She tilted her head and smiled. The kind of smile that didn't trigger her dimple or reach her eyes. The kind that would have made him crawl on his knees and beg for forgiveness back in the day.

He stuck his hands deep into his pockets because the dumbass urge to embrace her again reared its desperate head. "Yeah. You too, Hannah."

He stared unabashedly as she glided with ballerina-like grace out the front door. Somewhere in all the agitation inside, he recognized haunting regret. They wouldn't meet again. They'd chosen different paths long ago. But seeing her, talking to her, had been the single blissful fragment these last two days.

He probably should have told her that too.

CHAPTER 8

DEVON GLANCED AT his watch. He was seriously late, and payback would be a bitch. The lunch he'd wolfed down turned to lead in his roiling stomach. With one last glance at the front door, he stalked down the hall, passing the open doors to the formal parlor, gentlemen's room, and music room. All boasted large windows showcasing the lawn and sparkling lake, and in each view he watched the progress of a servant carefully descending the stone steps to the beach, precariously balancing a tray of iced tea.

"Didn't your mother commit suicide down there?"

That lancing pain stabbed him behind his eye again. He halted, shutting them tight—a catastrophic mistake. In a heartbeat, he'd jumped back in time.

His nine-year-old self racing across the summer lawn, thrilled at the cloudless sky and calm water—a waterskier's dream. Skipping down the treacherous steps to gather the equipment from the boathouse, determined to slalom without falling. Then catching sight of his mother lying far below, fully clothed and without a towel. Why wasn't she in a swimsuit?

Calling to her, even as a frozen part of his mind wondered about the odd angle of her neck and how it didn't look like her. She looked plastic, and her wide eyes were scary. Calling more sharply—why wasn't she moving?

Then his mind unfreezing. His mother—dead. Horribly mangled dead, like in the horror movie he'd seen the month before. Then his screams, the paralysis in his limbs. He couldn't climb the stairs to get help. His inability to look away from her twisted neck and glazed eyes. And finally the dozens of faces peering over the ledge—every one of them unable to help her too. Then Joseph's arms carrying him up, up…

The flashback shut down as fast as it'd come, but the emotional overload he'd fought since descending the stone steps with Hannah detonated. He drew in a ragged breath, barely hearing it above the roaring in his ears. "Don't," he whispered through clenched teeth. There was no time for this weak stuff right now.

"Uncle Devon, are you all right?"

He blinked several times, and the roaring noise faded. With relief, he raised his head. Cold sweat trickled down his temple. Todd stood a few feet away, an alarmed expression on his young face.

"Yeah." Was that feeble voice his? Devon straightened and rubbed his forehead with his sleeve. "Just a killer headache." The sharp pain had matured into a rhythmic throb, the kind that would last for hours, no matter what. "What are you doing out of school?"

"Half-day. Parent-teacher conference." Todd shifted his weight. "Grandfather's been asking if anyone's seen you. He's…uh, real mad."

Devon shook off the vestiges of his past. He lifted a weary shoulder. "He's always mad at something, kid. Shouldn't let it worry you."

"When Grandfather's pissed, everyone worries."

Despite himself, Devon barked out a laugh. "I guess I've been away too long, then." He jerked his head for Todd to accompany him, and they walked toward the office. "I used to head the counterinsurgency in this house. It got to the point where my father's anger was as regular and expected as the tide."

"Really?" His nephew jogged a couple of steps to keep up, eyes shining. "What kind of stuff did you do?"

"Anything noisy. Holding neighborhood tryouts for Olympic track and field down the halls. Tossing my little brother down the laundry chute—"

"Uncle Ricky?"

"Yeah. It was all fun and games until he grew so chubby he got stuck. Fire department had to be called."

Todd laughed. The thick oak door of Harrison's office lay ten feet ahead. Devon's pulse jackhammered, even as his jaw cemented in determination.

"What else?"

He quelled the urge to brush the kid off. He needed to think, to psych himself up, dammit. But the brusque gesture was too reminiscent of the man behind the door, so he glanced at his nephew and rummaged in his memory. "I, uh, drove the Rolls down Sheridan Road when I was about your age."

"No way!"

"And convinced your mom to climb one of the apple trees in the orchard out front and see how many apples she could pitch into the koi pond. She could really throw."

"My *mom*?"

"Sure. And man, could she run! Faster than me. Tag was her favorite game. The neighborhood kids and I rarely played with her. It was no fun—she'd whip our butts." He slowed four feet from the door and took a bracing breath. "She was such a tough girl. Wonder what happened to my fearless little army."

"If you mean Mom and Uncle Ricky, they aren't like that anymore." Todd sounded sulky, as if he'd missed out on something.

"That's probably for the best."

The boy frowned. "Why isn't she like that now?

Why isn't she more like you? I mean, she never has fun. I can't remember the last time I saw her *smile*, even."

Back to this topic. Like it haunted the house.

Devon massaged his tense jaw, feeling the prickle of whiskers. Shit, he'd forgotten to go shave. His father would love this. "She changed a lot when our mom died," he said quietly. "I mean, it was hard on both of us, but Frannie changed the most." The champion apple pitcher, who'd often been the brains behind their childish pranks, had turned into a quiet, pathetic mouse. She'd come through once in a while, but more often just took the punishment for stuff she hadn't even participated in. In that stoic, silent way of hers. Used to drive him crazy. He shook his head. What was the subject again? "My point is—don't ever let that old man scare ya." He cuffed his nephew gently. "Listen, I gotta get in there."

Todd nodded and stepped aside, but as Devon reached for the door handle, he blurted out, "Would you eat dinner with me and Mom tonight? I mean, if you're still in town? We're going to Uno's."

Devon hid his wince. His evening was jam-packed, and the moment it let up, his plan was to jet back to Nicole, slip into bed, and make it up to her. "I can't…" The words died on his lips. The look of hero worship twisted something in his chest. Was this what having a son was like? Had he ever looked at his father this way? "I can't promise anything," he said in a gruff voice. "But I'll try." Maybe before the meeting.

Todd beamed. "Great. And Uncle Devon?" He flushed painfully. "Give him hell."

HARRISON'S HEAD WAS bowed, the phone stuck to his left ear as he scribbled on a pad of paper. There was no indication he'd heard the door open, but he definitely had. Devon stepped fully inside the office and closed the door with a loud click, which still elicited no reaction from across the room. He mentally snorted; it would take more than this to make him sweat.

The air wove expensive cigar smoke with rich leather, a combination that always evoked memories of his father and this office. So little had changed in here over the years. Polished walnut paneling gleamed in the sunlight streaming in from the wall-length window. Hunting prints in forest-green matting lined the walls on the opposite side of the room. And behind the massive mahogany desk, an oil painting still hung of a brown bear raised on hind legs, jaws open in a ferocious roar. Devon's mother, a lover of art, had hated that painting. Harrison had refused to take it down.

Devon strolled to the window where two gardeners on purring mowers crossed each other's path, cutting the grass in a precise diamond pattern. Off in the distance, the lake glistened serenely. Hannah's gaze had strayed to it throughout lunch. Her constant distraction had been just fine with him. He'd gotten to stare freely at her profile, wondering how anyone managed to get to adulthood so unjaded. Even thinking about her now eased some of the tension in his shoulders.

Harrison barked out a last order, and the phone hit the cradle hard. Devon ran a dry tongue around a drier mouth, shoved his hands in his pockets, and turned to absorb the full impact of the old man's glare. Harrison's gaze swept over his unshaven face, and Devon waited for the scathing comment with relish.

"You're over an hour late," he growled instead.

"I was detained."

"Any other employee would apologize."

Devon forced himself to smile. "I'm not your employee."

"Not yet, boy, but by God, things are going to change around here." The comment eerily echoed of lectures past, as if he'd been hauled in for one of the dumbass things he'd just described to Todd.

He frowned at the personal slant, prepared for an epic corporate war, not a paternal demand for respect. This meeting was about the takeover, the Ashby parcels, and Bryant stealthily buying up shares while hiding their identity with a Cayman Island address and New York phone number. Devon mustered a casual voice. "So who's Bryant?"

"Part of being a savvy executive is knowing your enemy."

"Part of being a savvy executive is answering direct questions. And bottom-lining a meeting so we aren't here all day." Devon waited a beat and bit out the words. "Who is Bryant?"

Harrison folded his arms, a tight smile crossing his face. "Let's assume I am."

"How interesting. And by that, I mean in a cheap, dirty trick way."

"Whatever it takes, Devon." The smile turned condescending. "And as a CEO, you really shouldn't act so surprised at stealth and aggression in the corporate world."

"Successful leaders don't need to rely on deception."

"It's how Troy was defeated."

"Here's how I see it." Devon kept his voice lethally soft. "After lording the weight of the mighty Wickham name over me all these years, you declare war by hiding behind another name. Sounds cowardly to me. I wonder why you went to the effort."

A hiss escaped his father's lips. Devon couldn't recall ever getting to his father this fast or this easily, but the first point went to him, and he strode confidently across the room and dropped into the chair across from the solid desk.

"Bryant is a code. It holds great meaning." Harrison snatched up the phone and held the receiver toward him. "Dial your office and get an emergency board meeting on the books. By the end of today, Bryant will have transferred their shares to the Wickham Corporation, and I've ordered a press release to hit on Monday."

Devon made sure his shrug came off bored. "Bryant is nowhere near acquiring a majority of shares."

"Just as Sparta could not have defeated Troy by itself."

The triumphant glint in Harrison's eyes stirred up sick misgivings. "Meaning?"

"Meaning Sparta brought Argos and Hellas to war. But majority only counted for half the strategy. The other half was trickery, traveling right through the city gates disguised in friendship."

Friendship? The old man had mentioned that last night. Icy fear trickled down his spine.

"I've convinced two of your major shareholders on your board, Devon—shareholders you view as friends—to join the Wickham Corporation in tendering an offer for your ragtag little company."

Blood thundered through his veins.

"After the purchase, we intend to divide Ashby among ourselves."

"You...son of a *bitch*."

"I won't stand for employees speaking to me that way!"

Devon exploded from the chair. "I will never be your employee."

"You will be, effective today, Friday, October twenty-seventh. At four o'clock Central Time."

He paced to the window, hands fisted at his sides. Jesus, who were the two board members? What could he do? His company was finished.

No, it wasn't. He just had to think. He turned back.

"What does building the Rogers Park neighborhood in the sixties have to do with grabbing my company now?"

His father blinked in surprise. "There's no connection."

"It's too convenient to be a coincidence. Toxic waste? Buried skeletons? What happened on my parcels that you're so eager to hide? You had no intention of a hostile takeover until we bought that land."

Harrison sputtered out a laugh. "Your perceptions have always been so narrow-minded and obstinate. You'd do well to look at the whole forest, not the veins on one leaf."

"And what the hell does *that* mean?"

Behind him, the door opened. What were the odds it was Joseph bringing refreshments?

Devon braced himself and looked over. Wesley carried in a stack of files, his smile smug. "I haven't been able to get through to your CFO. Get him on the phone, will you?"

Devon's lips curled into a snarl.

CHAPTER 9

"...THE BUTLER DID it." Robbie laughed. "How clitchie."

"Cliché?" At Sean's droll tone, Hannah bit her lip to keep a straight face, and turned in to the sitting room. Robbie and Sean were on their knees, carefully pressing a Renoir into the Styrofoam at the bottom of the custom crate. Ten paintings remained. Her team had kicked ass getting the art crated and loaded today.

"The butler did what?" she asked, and both guys glanced back in surprise. Those industrial fans made it a breeze to wander the creaky upstairs undetected.

"He started the fire." Robbie pointed in the general vicinity of the theater, as if she didn't know—quite intimately, in fact—where it was.

"Joseph?" She scoffed. "I don't think so."

"We overheard the arson investigator talking on his cell phone. He was near our van and didn't know we were inside. That's who he suspects."

"*What?*"

"He said the butler called it in, but couldn't come up with a reason why he was walking by the theater in the first place. That he acted very fidgety during the interview."

"It was near midnight," Sean added, almost sympathetically.

She glanced at him sharply, but his face gave

nothing away. Could her history with this place and these people somehow be telegraphed to her employees? Only Gretch knew about Devon, and she wouldn't blab it around the office. But it had been a tumultuous day, and Sean was remarkably observant of emotional undercurrents. He could easily have been a psychiatrist. Or an FBI profiler.

"Well, I don't believe it," she declared, which was idiotic, because it didn't really matter what she believed. "Have they arrested him?"

Robbie reached into his pocket for another tissue. His nose was crimson and raw-looking. "The arson investigator didn't take him. Just called someone and left."

"That's because it's a police matter now," Sean said quietly, turning back to gently press the painting into the Styrofoam. "Arson investigators turn the case over once they find the point of origin and evidence of ars—"

"What's your ETA on crating the rest of these?" she interrupted. It was imperative that they keep on task, especially since anyone could walk by and overhear them gossiping, and they'd never know it.

Sean threw Robbie a dark look.

"I miscalculated the wood we'd need." Her intern wiped his nose and winced. "We have enough to crate a small one—the Caravaggio or the Bellini."

"Aw, guys!" She glanced at her watch. Two thirty on a Friday afternoon. By the time her team crated the last one, it'd be too late to drive downtown, collect the appropriate supplies, and return. "Okay." Her shoulders fell as she re-counted the paintings around the room. "Before I leave, I'll tell Mr. Wickham we'll finish next week."

"Sorry, Hannah," Sean muttered. He was supervising Robbie and should've rechecked the supply list yesterday. He also knew from the few meetings with

Harrison what a bitch of a conversation she faced.

She acknowledged his words with a terse nod and stuffed her clipboard into her briefcase, glancing at the apartment listings that lay in there. She'd have to spend all weekend researching and touring, because decisions needed to be made, movers called, boxes packed...

The frantic schedule made her rub her chest. Between lunch with Devon, the upcoming confrontation with Harrison, and this news about Joseph, her heart hadn't stopped fluttering in hours. It was a wonder she hadn't descended into an anxiety attack.

She returned to the second gallery but gave up inspecting the paintings within twenty minutes. Her churning thoughts were stuck on Joseph.

Back in her teens, Joseph always had a knack for being in the right place at the right time. Almost like he kept track of the kids in this huge house. And he'd *always* had their backs.

There was that time she and Devon were in a frenzy of lust on a basement futon. The door at the top of the stairs had suddenly opened and the fluorescent light switched on, freezing them like rabbits. They could hear Harrison Wickham discussing the wine selection for a dinner party that evening, as two pairs of footsteps began descending. Neither she nor Devon would have been able to right their disheveled clothes in time. Within seconds, shiny black dress shoes were in sight. Joseph must've heard the scurrying sounds, and stopped in his tracks, immediately suffering from a full-blown coughing attack, which blocked Harrison from descending any farther.

As Hannah and Devon hurriedly re-dressed and tiptoed to the far door leading to the side lawn, they'd heard Joseph apologizing profusely and suggesting the basement dust had kicked up his allergies. This was the Wickham home. There was no dust.

Joseph would never have started that fire. But someone in this house did, and not only did he probably know whom—he was covering for them.

She moved like a sleepwalker back into the hall where the industrial fans sounded like propellers. Did Joseph know he was the target of the investigation? Should she find him and warn him? Or find Devon and tell him this news? It wouldn't hurt to ask a household member whether Joseph was on the premises. Five minutes tops, and she'd get back here and finish up.

The bedrooms were all on this second floor, on the other side of the house. She walked slowly, gawking at the artifacts she passed. When Moore and Morrow had more than a "they found Rubens forgeries" reputation, and were on more solid financial ground, Walter planned to expand their services to include conserving and restoring artifacts too. The items in this house could keep them in business for years. Not that the art and antiques she passed were in disrepair, but Mr. Wickham's joy seemed to come from acquiring beautiful things, not necessarily in their conservation and upkeep.

She turned the last corner toward the bedroom wing. The noise from the fans and the clinging stench of smoke was replaced by a general smell of mothballs and ancient days gone by. Now her footsteps creaked loudly on the threadbare Persian runner. Instinctively, she moved closer to the wall and tried to be lighter on her feet. Not that she was tiptoeing or creeping up on anyone. More to lessen the eerie sound in this deathly silent part of the house.

A few steps later, she heard strains of classical music and the snapping hiss of a fireplace. At the threshold of the room, she discovered another, more informal library, shelves jammed with paperback books, some stuffed horizontally on top of vertical rows. Open magazines and newspapers littered the rose-colored carpet. Above the dark wood mantel hung an elaborate coat of arms, and flanking the fireplace were two faded tapestry high-back chairs. Someone sat in the one that faced the windows. All Hannah could see was the corner of a raised newspaper. On the accent table was a highball glass of what looked like water and a yellow plastic prescription bottle lying open on its side. Crumpled tissues littered the floor by the chair's clawed feet. She strained to hear—it sounded like the person was muttering to himself, but it was too faint over the music and snapping fire. She knocked lightly. "Excuse me?"

The newspaper crumpled. Seconds later, Frannie poked her head around the side of the chair, her eyes puffy slits. Just seeing the confusion on her face jumpstarted Hannah's blush. What was she thinking, sticking her nose in the business of this household? She was hired to do a job!

"Hannah?" Frannie leaned over the arm of the chair. "Are you lost?" Her words sounded nasally.

It was on the tip of Hannah's tongue to say yes and leave the poor woman to deal with whatever crisis she obviously faced, but something made her walk forward.

The room was sweltering from the substantial fire. Outside, the October afternoon was warm and beautiful, and yet Frannie sat mere feet from the flames in a thick Irish-knit sweater. Maybe she was coming down with a cold. Hannah picked her way through the books, magazines, and crumpled tissues to the opposite chair, glancing at the empty prescription bottle as she passed. Seroquel XR. And not a generic, hard-to-pronounce version. The small hairs on the nape of Hannah's neck tickled. It had been prescribed to her mother, who rarely took it. A medication well known for treating people suffering from bipolar issues.

Hannah stepped closer. The Apartment Rental page was open, and Frannie clutched a ballpoint pen in her left hand.

Appalled at the personal scene she'd stumbled upon, Hannah blurted, "I'm sorry to interrupt. It's just that..." God, what was she doing here? She inhaled and started again. "Joseph might be in trouble, and—"

"Joseph?"

"My crew overheard the arson investigator finger him as the suspect."

Frannie's grasp on the newspaper slackened. "Where's Joseph now?"

"I haven't seen him. I just wanted someone in the family to..." To what? Spread gossip? Race to his defense? Be as outraged as she was? "Check it out," she finished lamely.

"You must have misheard." Frannie's tone held none of the familiarity of this morning.

Between the smothering heat in the room and her humiliation, perspiration popped out on Hannah's forehead. "I hope I did. I should get back." She started for the door.

The paper fell in floating sheets as Frannie grabbed her wrist. Her fingers were frigid, the grip surprisingly strong. "Wait." Frannie released her. "I'm the one who's sorry. It's been a horrible couple of days. I seem to be snapping at everyone."

Hannah knew the feeling. "It looks like you're moving."

Frannie glanced at the apartment section. The same section Hannah should've been reading during lunch. "Just fantasizing. I'm almost twenty-nine, a mother, and trapped here until my divorce goes through."

"Trapped?"

"My father thinks I'll be happier here."

"But if *you* don't want to be here, just move."

Frannie's smile was bitter. "No one defies my father. Well, except Devon."

Hannah frowned. Frannie still bent to Harrison's whims? Surely she had her own money. "What do you do for a living?"

"I was a housewife until that national website offering discreet affairs was hacked and published my husband's name."

Hannah sucked in a breath. She really had no business being here. "I'm...I'm sorry." She glanced around, aware of wasting valuable time when she could have finished inspecting the second gallery. "I just wanted to make sure Joseph was okay." She slipped past. "I hope everything works out for you and your son."

Frannie never replied.

Hannah wound her way back down corridors, still half hoping to run into a maid. But aside from her own creaking steps, this wing held the eerie emptiness of the hotel in *The Shining*. Her cell phone rang, and she muffled a scream. "Hello?" she croaked.

"How's it going over there?" Walter asked crisply.

Her goose bumps didn't die down. She knew that tone. He was hugely pissed. Did he know they were short on supplies?

She bit the bullet and told him, and no, he hadn't known. *Great.* "So, I'll finish the other gallery," she said with mustered authority, "and then go tell Mr. Wickham the team will complete the transporting on Monday."

"Tell Wickham we'll finish everything on Monday, and get back here."

Uh oh. "What's going on?"

"We need to discuss this in person." He hung up before she could say good-bye, and she groaned. *Please don't let it be about Bernice.*

❧

HANNAH PAUSED IN front of Mr. Wickham's office. "The gates of hell," she'd laughingly told Walter after their initial appointment with him.

In high school, Devon had made sure she'd never met his father. She'd taken the gesture personally, as if he were ashamed of dating a girl without wealth or family connections. Yesterday's meeting proved how grossly mistaken she'd been. Devon had been protecting her.

Not that Harrison hadn't been cordial, but the discussion had been strictly to the point, and without any gesture on Harrison's part to make them feel comfortable. They'd stood in the office while he sat behind his desk like he was holding court.

Bracing herself, Hannah raised her knuckles to knock just as voices on the other side rose sharply. "You'll take orders from Wesley as if they came from me."

"I take orders from nobody, old man. This is my company!"

Hannah froze. The anger and desperation made his tone deeper, but oh, how well she knew that tenor.

"In twenty minutes, I'll control Ashby Enterprises."

"Over my dead body."

She heard striding footsteps just as a third, closer voice drawled, "I want your profit and loss emailed to me today. Before market closes."

"Shut the fuck up, Wesley." The seething reply came directly from the other side of the door.

Hannah gasped and stepped back. Too late. The door was wrenched open, and she stood nose to chest with sheer muscle and blistering fury. Midnight eyes, electrified with rage, glared at her like she was a stranger. Time stopped as the intensity of Devon's wrath washed over her, leaving her mute, fist still raised to knock.

In the next heartbeat, his face shuttered into an expressionless mask. "Excuse me, Hannah," he murmured, and brushed by her. The brief contact jolted her insides, as if she'd just fired back a double espresso. His long-legged stride ate up the hallway, his shoulders bunched as if warding off a blow. A cell phone rang, and he stuck his hand in his pocket. Before he turned the corner, his biting tone floated back to her: "I know I'm in deep shit, Nicole, but I can't talk right now…"

Hearing him say his fiancée's name drove a knife through her heart.

"May I help you?"

She turned back and faced a dead ringer for Robert Redford, circa 1970. Under his appreciative sweeping glance, her cheeks heated. "Oh," she sputtered, "uh…"

"Come in, miss," Mr. Wickham called impatiently from across the room, and the Jay Gatsby lookalike stepped aside, his slow smile an embossed invitation to sleep with him. She didn't return it. Like she needed her life complicated any more than it already was.

Hannah crossed to Mr. Wickham on wobbly legs. The testosterone still reverberating in here was almost palpable. What was up with him taking over Devon's company? Why wouldn't Devon have told her something this explosive at lunch? Maybe he hadn't known. What a crappy time to tell Mr. Wickham the project was a day behind. She halted in front of his desk, quaking as if this was an encounter with the school principal. Or a king rattler.

He looked over her shoulder and barked, "Make sure everything is in order to take that firm today. It *must* be today!"

Jay Gatsby nodded and lifted his cell phone, and then Harrison directed that high-voltage, ice-blue stare at her. "How are my paintings?"

"The, uh…project is coming along, sir. I was hoping to be through today, but barring any unforeseen circumstances, we'll finish the crating and transporting on Monday."

"You mean tomorrow."

She hesitated. Did he not know it was Friday? "Moore and Morrow conducts business on weekdays, Mr. Wickham."

"Not on my project."

She bit the inside of her cheek. She couldn't take on one more thing. But she'd have to; her employees were salaried. Maybe if she asked Sean to help her bang out the remaining nine paintings, and pad the Wickham bill to cover a weekend bonus for him. A tricky situation she'd hand over to Walter. But when would she have the time to look for apartments?

Harrison was already reaching for the phone without waiting for a response. The arrogance of his dismissal stung. She owned a company that had doubled in size last year; who was he to tell her how to run it? She raised her chin, and opened her mouth to reason with him. Under his withering glance, she slowly closed it.

"Will there be anything else?" he asked, his tone answering his own question.

She remembered the painting Ricky had asked her to clean. "We've also taken the art your son gave you last night. We'll send an estimate and delivery date to you by Wednesday."

"Keep it."

"Excuse me?"

"I'd be the laughingstock of Chicago if anyone ever saw that piece of trash in my possession. Donate it to some old people's home or something."

She managed a nod and walked woodenly to the door. She finally understood Devon's drastic decision to leave that rainy night, and how much of an impact her words must've had. No wonder Devon had never contacted her again.

Her choice to stay with her mother was a no-brainer. But to a boy who'd lost his mother so violently and then experienced nothing but this kind of dismissal and disdain from his father, her decision not to run away with him must have been the cruelest rejection of all.

CHAPTER 10

DEVON'S TREMBLING THUMB skimmed past Eric's number for the second time. *Jesus!* He needed to calm the hell down. The extremely short, rage-filled call from Nicole still rang in his ears. Canceling tonight had put their relationship on shaky turf, for the first time ever. It was also the first time their synergistic goals had parted ways. Keeping O'Callaghan happy meant retaining Chicago's best project manager, a brilliant strategy if Devon could also save his company from his father's clutches. To Nicole, no reason excused the social embarrassment. He'd expected her to be angry, but the extent of her wrath and her blistering words dumbfounded him. Where had her even-keeled, rational side gone? She always had her eye on the goal, and the goal was wealth and power, not a dinner party. Of course, she'd just gotten the message, which didn't give her a lot of time to cancel the extensive list of guests.

Devon glanced at his watch and his heart lurched. *Shit*. Because he'd been late to meet Harrison, he'd now blown through the will appointment with George Fallow. He gritted his teeth, compartmentalizing that issue. Why sign for the funds when they'd disappear if he didn't fix this problem? He rolled his shoulders and took a couple of bracing breaths, then pushed the video call icon for Eric. "Hey," he muttered, heading out to the privacy of the back patio.

"It's about time! How'd it go?" The anxiety on Eric's face was unmistakable.

"Before market closes, two of our board members will mutiny over to Bryant, aka my father. The three of them will hold a majority share of our company."

Eric looked down. His breath woofed out as though he'd just been punched in the gut. "Christ, I'm so *sorry*, man."

Devon hesitated. Anger at his cousin wouldn't solve the problem, and they only had seventeen minutes left. "We need to figure out which two; maybe we can talk one of them out of it."

"I wouldn't know where to start, Dev."

"Westcott almost staged a coup of his own over the Rogers Park acquisition."

Eric pursed his lips. Shook his head. "Naw. Granted, he's got the most conservative views, but I can't see him selling. Wickham Corp is an even bigger risk-taker than we are."

"But they have the available capital," Devon pointed out. "Westcott doesn't have faith the development can be pulled off in this economy. It's why he went ballistic when we voted him down."

"Okay, let's say he's one. Who's the other?"

Devon shrugged as he sat on the warm flagstone step. The late-afternoon shade was cooling the day considerably. "I can tell you who it isn't. You, me, and Ken Tucker." Silence and the blank look on his cousin's face were the last things he expected. Had the video call frozen? "Eric?"

His cousin blinked. "He's a shark."

"He's Nicole's father."

"He'd cut off your nut sac if it meant doubling his profits."

"And then stroll his daughter down the aisle toward

a penniless chump?" Devon forced humor into his voice. "Not to mention a eunuch?" Again, that expressionless, the awful silence. It spoke volumes, but volumes of what? "Talk to me, asshole."

Eric blew out another long breath. "Every woman in Manhattan knows the Wickham name rhymes with *cha-ching*. And you are, after all, the eldest son."

"And disinherited."

Eric quirked an eyebrow. "Does Nicole know that?"

Did she? He'd never talked about his past, because discussing childhood scars, unfulfilled needs, and broken hearts was navel-gazing and a waste of time. Their focus was purely on the future. Besides, not once in the four years of dating had she brought up the subject of money. Or glanced at a price tag. It was beneath her. "She's so wealthy, I doubt she cares."

Eric laughed and shook his head. "Ken Tucker cares. He made you, and he's the one who can break you."

Get in line, Devon almost said, but then his cousin's words registered. "He didn't make me. You taught me finance and tax shelters, and everything after that has been my own blood, sweat, and tears."

His cousin snorted. "I was with you at that country club the first time you met them, remember? She stood next to her father, ogling you like you were a Tiffany jewel no one could afford. And by God, Daddy bought it for her."

Devon stared at him in disbelief. "What the *fuck* are you talking about?"

"Dude, he bought our stock two days after that. He instantly became our largest shareholder. You never asked yourself why? And when we were invited out to the family compound in the Hamptons that summer, the whole weekend was mother, father, and darling daughter devoted to one thing—hooking you."

This was just stupid. "You're insane."

"I was there."

Devon jerked a thumb at himself. "I had control. I chased her, I seduced her, and I proposed to her."

"No ya didn't, Dev." Eric's smile was as condescending as Harrison's had been a short while ago. "They just let you think that. And not to sound vain, but I'm the one with the looks and the law degree. And we both know I have a hell of a lot better personality. So why would they choose you? Not even choose—*buy*."

"You're an asshole."

"Think about it, Dev. I'll wait."

Devon rubbed at the headache behind his eyelid, speechless. His recall of those early days was just a blur of energy, excitement, and feeling like he had the whole damn world within his grasp. He had *the* New York debutante on his arm, and new investors lining up with their fists full of cash. The adrenaline high of each new deal—a fracking company in Pennsylvania, a natural gas processing plant in North Dakota, high-rise developments in Jersey, Houston, and L.A. And just like that, the struggling company grew, tripling profits and exploding into new markets within two years, thanks to Tucker bringing his cronies onboard... *Cronies...* "Oh *shit*." The truth hit him so hard he felt his brain jolt.

Eric nodded. "I agree. Do you think he'd have put in the money and effort if he knew you were disinherited?"

Devon gazed off, his thoughts scattering like all the fluttering leaves around this vast landscape. His attention snapped back to the screen. "Wait a minute. I went by Devon Ashby the moment I left Chicago."

His cousin slapped his forehead. "It's like I'm talkin' to a newborn! Tucker doesn't allow anyone to speak to his daughter without a full-blown background check." He pointed at Devon. "You were vetted, right down to the size of your sphincter. Count on it."

"Nice." Devon put his chin in his palm. He still hadn't shaved. He couldn't remember a time in the last twelve years when he'd let himself go unkempt. It signified a lack of control, which he didn't tolerate. The emotional upheaval at every turn today had upended his steadfast routines. He scrubbed his jaw as if he could rub the sloppy evidence off. "You've argued yourself right out of your point, Eric. If he picked me for Nicole, that's all the more reason he's not the other investor."

"Every time I've seen him these last few weeks, Jason Deel has been at his side. I didn't think anything of it until this mess, but I wonder if Tucker has decided on another candidate."

Devon scowled. "You of all people know Nicole has a mind of her own. A formidable one." Her irate words still clung like toxic smog. "And she loves me."

"She loves her daddy more."

"This is pure conjecture." Devon glanced at his watch again. "We have fourteen minutes."

"Stick with me, Junior. Think about the timing."

Devon rolled his eyes. *Junior* was the nickname Eric used when Devon had first arrived in Manhattan, and an authority only on sports-related topics. His cousin had patiently taught him everything, until he'd not only mastered the subjects but had also started Ashby Enterprises. Devon had hoped his *Junior* days were behind him. "Go ahead," he said wearily.

"Bryant, aka Harrison, began buying up small amounts of Ashby several weeks ago, right? What if, during that time, your father called Tucker, our biggest shareholder? What if Tucker thought all this time that you'd inherit your father's estate, but found out during the call that you're nothing but a pauper in your father and Tucker's world? What if they *did* agree to buy out our company? Naturally Tucker would also begin shopping for a new fiancé for Princess, hence all his recent fawning over Jason."

The stabbing behind Devon's eye throbbed in time with his rapid heartbeat. He pressed his eyelid and saw stars. Was Eric right? There was the oddly cool attitude Nicole had displayed earlier this week, and her interest in whether he'd signed over the trust fund. Two separate events he wouldn't have thought twice about until Eric's *what-if* game. "What the fuck am I gonna do?" He stared at his cousin.

He waited for mental or physical pain at this potential relationship bombshell, but faced an apathetic void. It must be shock. Or denial. Or Eric was dead wrong, and Nicole's coolness was just the stress of planning a wedding. Her interest in the reason for his Chicago visit the sign of a loving fiancée.

Eric's expression morphed into the older cousin, brilliant mentor role. "You deal with your relationship, Dev. Why don't I call the board and ask each one outright?" His tone held the kind of gentleness people used on the infirm. It was exactly what Devon needed to ignite an afterburn.

What the fuck am I going to do? Those whiny words weren't part of the commanding CEO persona he'd cultivated all these years. He was Renegade, for fuck's sake. "Call everyone but Westcott and Tucker," he said. "They're mine."

"Dev—"

"Do it." He ended the call and squeezed the cell in his palm. He muttered an oath and scanned down his contact list, highlighting Westcott's personal number. It took one ring before the man picked up and greeted him by name.

"Sounds like you were expecting my call," Devon said.

"I presumed you'd figure everything out in time, so

yes, your call was not unexpected."

How tediously Westcott of you, he wanted to say, using that same bored tone right back. "Define 'figure everything out'?" he asked instead, keeping tight control over his pleasant monotone.

"Ah, the proverbial cat-and-mouse game. I will simply respond that I seek new leadership. Find your answers elsewhere."

Devon rubbed his bristles rhythmically. "You do realize Bryant is a dummy name? You're actually jumping into bed with the Wickham conglomerate."

"Of course I'm aware." Westcott's sharp tone held an edge of warning.

Devon waited a beat. Over by the willow, Honey ascended back onto land. "Is this because of the Rogers Park purchase?" He kept an eye on her but she held her head high, looked straight ahead, and did the runway catwalk toward the far side of the house.

"The majority of my decision was based on that, yes," Westcott said in his tinny voice. "I have no interest in being on the board or even invested in a company made up of naïve gamblers."

Devon cut his gaze to the flagstones at his feet. "How much is my father offering for your shares?"

"Since I know you can't afford to engage in an auction, I will simply respond that it is none of your business."

And I will simply respond, "Fuck you." Devon clenched and unclenched his fist, desperately seeking a new avenue to convince the old fart to stop the sale. It wasn't a secret Harrison Wickham's ruthless arrogance in the corporate world often meant dealing in or cutting out partners. Maybe the way to get through to Westcott was planting seeds of doubt. Play to his overly cautious side. And adopting some of that snooty Westcott-speak wouldn't hurt either. Neither would groveling.

"We may not see eye to eye on many issues, Boyd, but I've always respected your cautious judgment. That's why I'm surprised you aren't considering all the angles of Harrison's power play." He held his breath.

"What angles?" The alarm in Westcott's voice was microscopic, but it was there.

"I met with Harrison this afternoon, and let's just say it would behoove you not to act in haste." The silence had to be a good sign. Devon pressed his point: "Wouldn't it be prudent to contemplate all the options on the table?"

Westcott sighed. "All right, Ashby, you have my attention. What angles, what options, and what information do you have?"

"I'm extremely uncomfortable discussing this over the phone. I plan to be back in New York late tonight; we'll meet at the club tomorrow for breakfast. But I need your word that you'll withdraw the transfer today."

The next few seconds were the longest of Devon's life. He was vaguely aware of his rapid-fire heartbeat as he watched whitecaps appear and disappear—there one second, gone the next. Thriving and then dying.

Westcott cleared his throat. "You have my word, Ashby. I'll meet you at eight sharp. But you better not be bluffing."

"Thank you, Boyd." Devon gulped in a lungful of lake air as he hung up. Of course he was bluffing. But he'd just bought some time to figure out this insanity.

One down. He stood on cramped legs and paced around the patio, rehearsing several confident phrases before he highlighted the next name.

"Ken Tucker's office."

He strode faster. "Hi, Donna. Devon Ashby. Is he in?"

"He's playing golf this afternoon, Mr. Ashby."

"Okay, I'll call his cell."

"He left instructions not to be interrupted."

He chuckled, pleased it sounded natural. "He won't mind. I'm almost his son-in-law."

"Actually"—Donna's voice rose about two octaves—"he specifically mentioned you were not to interrupt."

Goose bumps prickled along his skin. Eric was right. His soon-to-be father-in-law was involved, and it had happened right under Devon's nose. Somehow he managed to thank the secretary and hang up, then instantly tapped Tucker's cell number. The son of a bitch was not going to hide from such epic betrayal. Voicemail clicked in immediately, and he stared at the phone in disbelief. He played golf with Tucker twice a week—the man's phone was always on. Multimillion-dollar deals had been struck in sand bunkers. Devon left a curt request for a call back.

Out of energy and lacking ideas, he sat back on the flagstone step and stared at the glimmering lake. At least with Westcott out of the picture, Harrison wouldn't have fifty-one percent by the end of today. Devon had the weekend to persuade his future father-in-law to drop the buyout. And convince his daughter she'd be deliriously happy in her marriage. He highlighted Nicole's number. It also clicked straight to voicemail.

"Hey, babe, I'm sorry again about this evening. Hell, I'm sorry about a whole bunch of stuff. I'm coming home tonight, I promise, and tomorrow we'll talk and shop and party, and anything else you want to do. All weekend, okay? I'm all yours. Call me."

Truthfully, the last thing he wanted to do was take his mind off his business. Shopping and partying at a time like this was tantamount to playing the violin on the deck of the *Titanic*. But he owed her. And he truly regretted not being at her side on what was supposed to be their night of social glory.

Shit. He slapped the phone against his forehead. *Forgot to say "I love you."* Aw hell, he'd say it in person in less than six hours. Over and over, and in front of her father, too, sometime tomorrow.

He texted the two Judases' names to Eric so his cousin wouldn't call and needlessly alarm anyone else on the board. Then he called George Fallow to apologize and see whether he could possibly squeeze in an appointment right now, but the first available was next Wednesday. He thanked the old lawyer and told him to express the papers to his office; Devon would get the necessary notaries there and send the packet back. He hung up with a sigh. The big symbolic gesture of coming home with the olive branch and gaining his mother's inheritance had finally and truly flat-lined.

He stretched his arms above his head and worked the kinks out of his back with a grunt. All he had to do was get through the shouting renters and go home. His last call confirmed his flight time with the private pilot for eight thirty, at the Chicago Executive Airport. He stared out at the lake. In a little over four hours, he'd be out of this godforsaken city.

"Hey, Uncle Devon."

He twisted and found Todd lurking in a shadow. "Hey, dude." His nephew shuffled forward, hovering awkwardly until Devon patted the step beside him. "How long you been standing there?"

"I just wanted to find out how it went with Grandfather. Did you give him hell like old times?"

Devon let out a dry laugh. "You bet I did. Ended up having my ass handed to me, but I gave it all I had."

Todd looked like he wanted to say more, but stuffed his fists into his jeans and squinted out at the lawn.

Devon mindlessly scrolled to Tucker's cell number again. Why would he sell? There was no broken engagement. Not even a hint. Nicole wouldn't rock this perfect boat they rowed together. Her priorities matched Devon's. With his business acumen and her social intuition and influence, Ashby Enterprises would continue its sensational growth until he was as formidable as both of their fathers.

"I wish Mom would stand up to my dad like you do to Grandfather," Todd said quietly.

Devon palmed his cell and redirected his attention. "What do you mean?"

His nephew shrugged, red spots appearing on his cheeks. "I dunno. I wish she'd say something back sometimes. Dad's mean to her a lot. Usually after he thinks I'm asleep."

Devon's jaw clenched for the umpteenth time today as the age-old animosity flooded back. In high school, his brother-in-law, nicknamed Brady the Bull, had been a brawler with a hair-trigger temper and a chip on his shoulder. Both personality flaws were ideal for a linebacker. His success on the football team and his good looks made him as popular as the quarterback.

Devon had played baseball, so he and Brady floated in different hemispheres. Passing in hallways generally meant ignoring the other, the teenage sign of grudging respect. Until their senior year, when Brady was an English lit test away from flunking out. The school counselor recommended a student tutor, which was how Brady the Bull happened upon Frannie, a mousy sophomore in granny glasses. A month later, when he slow-danced with her during the last song at homecoming, it drew more buzz than that day's winning touchdown. And no one had watched the warped pairing with more misgivings than Devon.

Eight months after he'd moved to New York, he got her sobbing phone call. Pregnant at seventeen; Harrison pushing for a quick marriage. Devon slept poorly for years because nighttime was when self-blame and questions could no longer be shoved down. If he'd stayed, like Hannah had begged him to, would he have headed Brady off at the pass during Frannie's junior year? Would his sister be in this messy divorce now?

"If I was as brave as you," Todd continued, his voice barely above a mumble, "I'd help her fight back so she'd stop hurting."

Devon clawed his hair off his forehead. "Todd, I'm not brave. I just fight for what I think is right, and it doesn't always mean I win. It doesn't mean I don't hurt people, either." Hannah's young, tear-stained face popped up, and he shut it down. "As a matter of fact, I may be losing two very important things in New York real soon, but the point is you stand back up and figure out what to do next. Always." Such easy words to say.

"Okay," Todd said, as if an important decision had just been made.

Devon slapped him on the back. "Gotta go shave, my friend."

"Are you still in the first editions library?"

Devon grunted out a confirmation and was halfway through the open French doors when his nephew muttered, "That is so *cool*."

CHAPTER 11

YOU'RE GOING TO have to fire Bernice," Walter said crisply. "I'm done with the delays and excuses."

A dozen justifications filled Hannah's mouth. Her compulsion to avoid conflict at any cost would not be denied. "I left her a note with specific instructions this morning, Walter."

"Which she managed *not* to follow."

Hannah winced. The Matisse... Two botched restoration attempts. The company couldn't afford the fury of a wealthy man with vast contacts. "What happened?"

"There are bubbles all over the backing. Someone else will have to redo it on Monday."

"I'll do it myself this weekend," she said hastily.

"This has to take priority over the Wickham project."

"Of course." These priorities shifting into her apartment-hunting time made her stomach cramp. There was no way she could take a weekday off, so losing these precious two days meant she was down to three weekends—six total days to look, find, pack, and move.

"This doesn't absolve you from firing Bernice."

In desperation, she brought out the big gun. "She has leukemia, Walter. On her good days, you know she's a competent restorer."

"Yes, but she won't tell us when she's having a *bad*

day. Like she has to prove something. And you assigned her the Matisse."

Because you insisted on giving Bob Schmidt a delivery date that forced me to choose her. Hannah bit her lip. What was she going to do? The whole company stood behind Bernice as she faced the battle of her life, and although it was true that Walter had given her many more chances than a healthy employee would've had, he also held performance expectations that were hard for them all to live up to. Like the quick turnaround time on the Matisse. Bernice would never have been able to handle the physical lifting and packing required on the Wickham project, so she was the only employee left in the workroom to meet Walter's imposed deadline.

"I know you secretly want me to take this burden off you," Walter said in a more compassionate tone, "but you manage the employees."

"I know. I can do this." *I can't, I can't, I can't.* Of all of them, Bernice needed a salary and health benefits. And she'd told Hannah many times that working, even during the times she felt rotten, beat sitting around her house, thinking about her illness. Who would hire her now? The stomach sensation turned into noisy churning.

"I warned you against loading the staff with personal friends."

Hannah nodded miserably. Bernice was more than a "personal friend." She was the woman who'd swooped in to care for Hannah's mother and her all those months. Who'd comforted Hannah when her world had crumbled. Bernice had been the catalyst in directing her into conservation and restoration in the first place, even buying a cheap painting from a flea market and showing Hannah the basics.

"It's past time," Walter said.

Throat thickening with unshed tears, Hannah nodded and stood. To hide her devastation, she pretended to glance at her watch as she left his office. The actual time gave her a start. She'd agreed to meet Gretch at Bakers Square for an early dinner before the eviction meeting. There was no way she could go. She needed to find somewhere to live.

DEVON DESCENDED THE main staircase, spying Todd and Frannie putting coats on by the front door. His sister smiled up at him. "Oh good, you're right on time."

He halted on the last step. "For what?"

"For Uno's?" Todd said. "Remember you said you'd eat dinner with us?"

"Yeah." Vaguely. "About that—"

"Aw, Dev." Frannie slapped her hands on her hips. "You did this at breakfast!"

"I'd love to...but I have to meet the developer across town, and traffic will be a...bear." He avoided looking at the boy's crestfallen face.

"But this is your last night in Chicago."

"Frannie." He held up his palms. "I'm sorry. I can't." Although he was entirely to blame for this misunderstanding, the number of people needing his presence during the same hours this evening was wearing thin. "My company's going down the drain. I just don't have the time. I'm sorry."

She twisted her lips into a fake smile and ruffled her son's hair. "Well, go say good-bye to your uncle, sweetie. I'll meet you in the car."

Todd loped over, and Devon clapped him on the shoulder, not knowing how to say good-bye to a virtual stranger without hypocrisy or awkwardness. If only the boy had reminded him out on the patio, maybe they could've gone to an early dinner. "Take care, Todd."

"I'm going to be just like you," his nephew blurted in a low voice, and then flushed so painfully Devon winced. He squeezed the kid's bony shoulder, and then

Todd left them behind.

"Frannie, seriously. I *am* sorry."

She snorted. "Forget about getting to know your nephew, forget about having one last dinner with your sister… It's all about money and power, isn't it?" She waved at the front door Todd had left open. "*Business over family.* You know what's funny, Dev? You left us for dead, and as hard as that was for me, I understood. You ran off so you wouldn't end up like Father. But guess what? That's exactly who you've turned into." She spun on her heel and marched stiffly toward the door.

Turned into his father? "Do me a favor, Frannie. Next time, use your fists."

She didn't even bother to turn around. "What next time?"

His lips had formed a reply when his cell rang. *Eric.* He caught his sister's I-told-you-so sneer before the door slammed. Never let it be said his sister didn't have strength. That mammoth door was as heavy as a vault. He hit the Talk icon. "Go."

"What's up with you?"

"Just the regular family shitshow. It's amazing how they can still push your buttons." Devon pinched the bridge of his nose. He really needed to find some aspirin.

"Got your text about Tucker and Westcott."

"Still working on Tucker." He shifted the phone and walked slowly over to the door, tugging it open. The taillights of his sister's SUV faded up the tree-lined drive as he headed for his rental car. For the first time in his life, he felt old. Tired. Defeated. He was a real shit to have let his nephew down. "What about you?"

"Just got the ex-NSA guy's findings on that chick you asked about—Honey Hartlett. I haven't read it yet."

Devon's breathing stilled. "Break it down for me." He turned the key in the ignition, waiting impatiently for Eric to pick out the meat.

"Holy shit, Dev. She was born Holly Howell. Her Honey Hartlett life is so tightly woven, Kevin said it's foolproof for anyone making discreet inquiries."

Devon switched to his Bluetooth earpiece and sped up the drive.

"It took him all day to pick apart one thread," Eric said. The sound of pages turning filtered through the earpiece. "The fake 'Honey' was born in Houston; went to all the right private schools, Oxford for art history. Her wealth is inherited through her oil baron father, deceased four years ago."

Devon hung a left and gunned it. He was already late to this meeting too. "And Holly?"

"Let's see… Both are thirty years old, by the way. She didn't lie about that. Born and raised in Fairfax, Virginia, as quite the little beauty queen. And I mean since the age of five. She won a bunch of titles, including Miss Virginia, runner-up Miss USA…went to William and Mary on a beauty pageant scholarship, where she majored in fashion merchandising and minored in art history."

Scholarship? "What's the source of her family's wealth?"

"Father owns a local auto dealership."

Devon almost missed the stop sign. "She's not an heiress?"

"Not according to this. Upper middle-class for sure, but nothing that parallels your family."

"Previous marriages?"

"None, although her Honey name is linked with a few wealthy men. Mostly European, nothing long-term."

Devon rapped his fingers on the wheel, adrenalin pumping through him. "Other aliases?"

"He's uncovered three so far," Eric said.

"Has anyone she's linked with ended up dead?"

Eric sighed. "I'll have to get back to you."

"Drop everything. I need to get to the bottom of who she is and what her plans are for my family." He'd come to terms with his mother's murderer never paying for the crime or cover-up. Whatever Honey had up her sleeve for Harrison was goddamn karma. But Frannie and Rick being rendered penniless was a game changer. The least he could do was save their inheritance.

"Maybe your dad bought us as a wedding gift. He's gonna turn around and toss her this company like a dog bone."

Devon grinned as he stopped for a light. "She strikes me as an authority on nail polish colors, not strategic marketing analyses—"

"I'm just relaying the facts. Now what?"

"Email me Kevin's findings. You and I are gonna go on like the business is still ours. Because it is— Westcott didn't sell his shares."

"Are you going to confront Honey-Holly?"

Devon paused. He'd relish the confrontation but had to get out of this hellhole, fly home, and fix things with Nicole tonight, and Westcott tomorrow. "Supporting O'Callaghan is more important," he said.

"You're the boss." After they hung up, Devon drove on, clenching and unclenching the wheel. He may not have time to confront Honey, but he had to tell his father. Frannie and Rick would stay in the will and continue on with their lives.

He pulled over to make the call. This conversation would take all his focus. Rick answered. "Put Harrison on the phone," Devon ordered.

"You'd get a lot farther if you'd call him Dad."

"Farther like you have? Have you found an apartment or a job?" He sucked a breath in the stunned silence. "I apologize. Just go get *Dad*," he said in a monotone. The word was alien and awful, and he had the urge to spit. A minute later, Harrison's curt voice straightened his spine—a visceral reaction since childhood. Devon shook his head in disgust. "I've been investigating your fiancée," he blurted. *Smooth, Dev.*

"Then you've wasted your time. You think I'm so smitten I didn't have her checked out?"

Perfect setup. He smiled cruelly in the flashing glow of the hazard lights. "And you found out she's an oil baron's daughter from Houston?"

"Of course. We even checked the father out."

Devon leaned forward for the kill, as if he were in the same room as Harrison. "Maybe there is an oil baron with a daughter named Honey, but she isn't your fiancée. Her fake background is nailed down tight, unless you do some creative digging." He proceeded to spill out the facts, and then offered to forward the emailed proof that had dinged in his cell phone seconds after speaking with Eric.

When he finished, he found himself oddly out of breath. He inhaled through his mouth in the silence. Then more silence. His father had to be humiliated beyond belief. The old man had always thought of himself as virile. Receiving a clean background check on über-wealthy Honey meant she really loved him. Now the woman he'd rejected his children for was just another user. And that all this information came from the son he hated?

"Hello?" Devon finally said.

The phone line clicked. He stared open-mouthed at a streetlamp. His goddamn father had hung up on him. *Of all the fu—*

He grasped the earbud when he heard a distinct second click.

CHAPTER 12

I CANCELED DINNER because I'm too busy, not because I'm afraid." Hannah stood beside Gretch outside the RP Community Center, shivering in the cool evening after such a warm day.

"You're scratching your palms, so try again."

"I don't have the energy to protest." She glanced at the slutty black boots and silver glitter leggings visible beneath Gretch's purple faux-fur coat. "And you're not dressed for this."

"It's strategic, thank you very much. If we're taking a stand, we make it difficult for them to ignore us."

Hannah stomach tightened. An angry mob of neighbors within that building against a greedy corporation. So much raw negativity. And she was about to march in there with a very noticeable, very fearless friend. Why make a scene? Wasn't it easier to just accept the inevitable? Hannah gave it a last-ditch effort. "I'd rather look through more apartment listings."

"And I promise we'll do that right after." Gretch linked arms and hauled her forward.

The center was a dingy clapboard structure of reddish-brown wood, adjacent to an abandoned, rusty playground. In her neighborhood, it was known as the Drug Store, a place for meth-heads, dope deals, and gangs—a place Hannah had never set foot in. She looked around, wide-eyed, at the sea of people and cacophony of voices. The strong scent of disinfectant barely masked the underlying odors of pot, urine, and God-knew-what-else.

"I have peeps saving seats for us," Gretch said as they passed a cluster of security guards inside the entrance.

"Peeps? You don't know anyone in my neighborhood." They pushed their way through the standing throng at the back of the noisy room. Metal folding chairs were lined up in tight rows with an aisle down the middle, like a mock church, and the place was overly warm and humid from bodies packed so closely together. Everywhere Hannah looked, familiar and unfamiliar faces turned toward one another nodding, talking, frowning. The knot in her stomach loosened in this atmosphere of reasonable concern. It would be all right. How sad that it took a neighborhood eviction to achieve this supportive community.

"There." Gretch elbowed her and pointed toward the front. Before Hannah saw more than a hand waving in the air, she was yanked along behind her friend, who chanted "excuse us" through the crowd. In no time, they stood at the third row. Clothing draped two empty seats, and beside them sat Sean, frowning, and Bernice, in her umber paisley headscarf. Hannah's mouth fell open.

Gretch turned to her with a wide grin. "Surprise."

"Where've you two been?" Sean snapped. "We almost had to strip down to keep these seats." He snatched two coats, a striped sweater, a Hogwarts scarf, and a thick book off the seats. "Some very rude people in your neighborhood, Hannah."

"What are you doing here?" For the umpteenth time today, her dumbfounded brain clocked out.

Bernice's pale, gaunt face was wreathed in smiles. "Gretchen told us what you and Milly are going through, and we're here to add our voices." She stretched out a hand and Hannah leaned in and gently squeezed it. Based on the second Matisse screw-up, Bernice had had a bad day health-wise. The fact that she'd hauled herself here to support Hannah brought tears to her eyes. "Thank you," she whispered to her mother's best friend.

"Now, none of that." Bernice waved her to the aisle seat. "Here, I made a poster."

"Oh God." Hannah glanced around. No one had protest signs, and no one seemed to have a posse. "That's not necessary," she said, pleading to Sean, because Bernice was bent over, grabbing something underneath her seat. "Please stop her." Sean murmured something, and Bernice straightened without the poster.

Hannah studied Sean, her too-cool-for-school employee—brilliant at restoring ancient artifacts, wit like an X-ACTO knife, but rarely giving anyone a passing notice. He couldn't possibly be here for support. They didn't have that kind of relationship. He wasn't "nice" in the traditional sense. "Do you live here too?"

"Hell no." There was the old Sean, lip curled into a dismissive snort.

"We were going to surprise you at Bakers Square until you canceled," Gretch muttered, pushing past her. "I'm not sure why Sean thought reading was involved." She plopped down next to him. "Kind of nerdy, if you ask me."

"You should try it sometime, princess."

Shushing them, Hannah took the aisle seat. *War and Peace* lay on his lap. *Jeez.* "Well, thanks for coming." Three of her employees, who didn't need to spend their evening this way, were patiently waiting for the meeting to start, and here she was, searching for the closest fire exit. *Buck up. You don't have to talk or yell or protest.* She squirmed out of her coat in the tight space.

Sean opened his book, ignoring them; Bernice turned in her seat to people-watch; and Gretch winked.

"The guy already looks scared."

Hannah tucked her coat underneath her and turned her attention to the front of the room. A thickset man in a rumpled gray suit sat on a metal chair on a dais, clutching a mic and scanning some papers. He'd have been indistinguishable except for the dichotomy of his imposing size and the amount of fear coming off him. Sweat glistened on his broad forehead, and the pages in his hand trembled. Every few seconds, he glanced around the room, where it was obvious by the increasingly agitated tones that the crowd's mood was growing ugly.

Undeserved empathy flooded through Hannah. He was the enemy! But she couldn't help putting herself in his place—on stage in front of an angry mob. She shuddered. The overly warm room was stifling and she huffed out a breath, fanning herself.

He cleared his throat and stood with the reluctance of a prisoner about to head to his execution. "Excuse me," he said into the microphone, which squealed. A collective groan went up, along with a few muttered curses. "Sorry. May I have everyone's attention?" At once the crowd fell silent, and he darted an uneasy look around. His chest rose and fell rapidly under the suit jacket. "I, uh, appreciate everyone coming out here tonight, and apologize for our late start. I've been wai—"

"Just get on with it!" a man shouted from the back. Murmurs rose.

He cleared his throat again, and the noise died back down. "Anyway." With a frown, he straightened his shoulders and read from the papers. "Allow me to introduce myself, as I know you have concerns—"

"That's right we have concerns," a woman shrieked nearby. Hannah flinched. "And you better lawyer up, mister. This has class-action suit written all over it, no doubt about it!"

Shouts of agreement erupted. Over the noise, Sean chuckled, muttering, "No. It doesn't."

Did he know something about property law? Was that why Gretch brought him? Hannah searched her memory for his résumé details, but brain fatigue rolled in like fog. Her food intake had consisted of half an English muffin for breakfast, a lunch with Devon she'd barely choked down, and skipping dinner to tour one apartment. She was tired and dizzy and just wanted this to be over.

"Please." The sweaty man held up a palm. "I'd appreciate it if you held all your questions and comments until we've had a chance to present our offer."

Gretch glanced around. "We?"

"It's the royal 'we.' You should recognize that," Sean murmured then grunted at the elbow sinking into his side.

Hannah shushed them again. Were they dating, and her best friend hadn't told her? She frowned at Gretch, who simply shrugged. Bernice was talking to an Indian woman on her other side. "...I shop there." How could Walter want to fire her? This generous woman who'd given so much of herself to Hannah, who struck up conversations with total strangers and never complained about the pain and sickness—God knew she must hurt something awful. Yet here she was.

"Oh..." The man's expression of relief seemed so sudden and out of character the room quieted, although the silence remained heavy with anger and suspicion. He spoke to someone at the back. "I was afraid you'd canceled..."

Behind Hannah, bodies shuffled and footsteps rang aggressively down the aisle. She was too tired to turn in her seat, but Gretch squeezed around and sighed her approval. "Mmmm, evict me, hottie," she murmured. "After you've given me all I can take."

"Gretch!"

He strode past their aisle, and Hannah wearily glanced up at the well-defined back in a fitted black sweater and charcoal slacks. His raven hair was a bit too long and newly finger-raked. "Oh, dear God," she breathed, filled with that combustible mix of boiling hot and freezing cold from this morning.

"I *know*." Gretch sat taller, angling for a better view.

It can't be. Please be hallucinating. Hannah's pulse reached a crescendo as he turned and faced them. *Devon.* Clean-shaven, brutally handsome, and completely at ease. This couldn't be happening.

"What are you doing back?" "When are you leaving?" If he'd answered any of her questions at lunch, she'd have put it together. Her breath sawed unevenly.

He stood before them on the dais, legs spread, scanning the room like a pirate captain surveying his prisoners. Without glancing at his partner, he held out a palm for the microphone. Hannah waited, lightheaded, as it was laid in his hand.

"Good evening. I'm Devon Ashby, chief executive officer of Ashby Enterprises, a privately held venture capital firm based in Manhattan."

Gretch gasped at his name and swiveled to stare at Hannah. Even Sean frowned. He must have recognized Devon from this morning. She didn't want to hear her friend gushing or asking about him. There was no way she'd acknowledge Sean's questioning glance. Without taking her eyes off Devon, Hannah shook her head. She wanted to hear every word that came out of the bastard's mouth. Her fists squeezed painfully.

"My company recently hired Peter O'Callaghan

here as project manager for an extensive and elaborate multimillion-dollar renovation project." That lush tone she'd wanted to drown in all day now sounded authoritative and clipped, the silence around her deafening. Maybe everyone was as thunderstruck as she.

"This is your home. You have a right to be angry. However, I'm here to offer each of you a chance to invest in staying in this neighborhood." He paused; his take-no-prisoners glare scanning the audience as he let his sympathy sink in.

What a colossal fraud. Gretch emitted a dreamy sigh. O'Callaghan's folding chair squeaked under his weight. The action and noise elicited zero acknowledgment from Devon, who remained ramrod straight and icy calm, like he owned the place, which technically he did.

This was not the man who'd gripped her hand tightly down the cliff steps. The guy who'd wiped off a dusty wrought-iron chair and held it out for her with twinkling eyes. This corporate persona was the epitome of Mr. Wickham: tone, body language, and that awesome fearlessness in the face of confrontation.

"You'll be given priority rights to purchase one of the future townhomes or condo units before the presale opens to the public, and I'm offering each buyer here a ten percent discount."

"Let me get this straight," Sean piped up, languishing in his chair. "You're kicking these people out of their apartments, then turning around and selling them right back?"

Applause and hoots exploded throughout the room. Devon zoomed in on the speaker and Hannah sat frozen, waiting for him to notice her two seats away. *Her.* Just another one of the neighborhood riffraff the rich man was evicting to become richer. Her nails bit farther into her palms.

Sean's question was the kind her aunt would've asked, had she been healthy enough to attend tonight. She'd have stoked this crowd into a riot. No one went up against Aunt Milly's whiplash tongue and walked away unscathed. But the outrage and worry over the eviction notice had deteriorated her already fragile health. Her oxygen level had sunk too low to risk coming. Hannah had promised to tell her every detail about the meeting. But how would she explain this? *So, the guy I lost my heart to is behind our uprooting.*

The noise died down. "Yes." Devon quirked an eyebrow at Sean. "It's legal for any company to buy and redevelop land. I'm simply extending an offer to invest with us."

"Invest?" Hannah sputtered. Sweet baby Jesus, she'd said it out loud! Those piercing blue eyes landed on her. Shock flickered once before the corporate mask slid back into place. Her cheeks flushed hotly but somehow her mouth kept moving. "Most of us live paycheck to paycheck—we can barely afford the rent. Your offer is meaningless."

More applause. He waited for the grumbling agreement to subside, maintaining that scorching stare-down, and she'd burn in hell before she blinked first. Gretch squeezed her arm. Maybe because she'd spoken up. More likely the intensity of his gaze.

What was he thinking under that icy veneer? Did he care at all about these displaced people, or was this just another humdrum meeting? Did he regret his Rogers Park purchase just the teeniest bit now that he knew a face in the crowd, or was he up there trying to decide between a juicy strip or rib eye for dinner?

When he had everyone's attention again, he answered her, his voice gentle, as though he were explaining something to a child. "The banks are loaning again, and they're eager for customers. I can't imagine condo payments being very much more than what you pay in rent right now, Miss Moore."

Her cheeks burned hotter at the formal title. Behind her, the crowd's murmuring took on a few positive tones. He was swaying them with so little effort.

"Where would we go while all this is being built?" someone on the left side asked.

Hannah lost his answer as Gretch nudged her firmly and whispered, "I can see why your Internet dates are doomed. Who can live up to that?"

"This is my neighborhood," she whispered back, finally as outraged as Aunt Milly. As eager to fight as the neighbors in this room. She glanced at the rolled-up poster under Bernice's chair.

"Seriously. He belongs in a magazine hawking watches or cologne." Gretch paused. "Or a little Parisian swimsuit."

"He belongs in hell." She said it quietly enough, but Devon paused in the middle of his sentence and threw her a hard frown.

Gretch whispered to Sean, who whispered something back. "Sean suggests selling one of the Wickham paintings so you can afford whatever he builds near the lakefront." This was definitely said loud enough for Devon to hear, and Hannah focused on the fists in her lap as an even hotter blush covered the one already there. Her blouse clung wetly to her back in the uncomfortably hot room. You didn't goof around about art theft in front of a Wickham. Jesus, what if it got back to Harrison? Moore and Morrow would be wiped off the map.

Someone directly behind her asked about timelines, and Hannah caught corporate-speak like "six-phase rollout" and "union issues," but her mind was in turmoil, and she hadn't stopped trembling since catching sight of him. She *had* to get out of here, or she'd go ballistic on his ass. The stifling humidity, his surreptitious glances at her, the air of impatience emanating off Gretchen to hear the details of this train wreck in her life... She was suffocating. "Let's go. I've heard enough," she muttered, rising from the chair an inch to retrieve her coat.

Gretch yanked her back down. "No way. See how he keeps looking at you? He's totally coming over here after this. Damn, he's hot. I can't believe you dated him."

"Gretch, he's engaged—"

Devon cleared his throat, drowning out the last word. "If there are any further questions, please feel free to call or email Peter. We have handouts by the door with our numbered phases, and I believe his contact information is there too." He glanced at Peter, who nodded once.

"Meet you outside," Hannah said under her breath, and darted up the aisle, ignoring the grunts and "hey!"s as she pushed through the mass standing in back.

She'd cleared the door and ten feet of grassless playground when strong fingers gripped her upper arm and whirled her around. Her thick ponytail whipped in her face, and she clawed it back. Her panting breath misted the evening air as she glared at Devon. Once again he stood way too close, darkly handsome, and furious in the moonlight. She yanked her arm free and stepped away, fighting the primitive urge to beat her fists against his chest.

He leaned right back in, head cocked. "I belong in *hell*?"

"The seventh fucking circle," she spat. *Cripes!* When she dropped the f–bomb, she was seriously out of control. He waved off someone behind her, and she glanced over her shoulder. A security guard. The man stood uncertainly, and Hannah almost laughed that someone considered her a threat.

"It's okay, I know her," Devon called, then crossed his arms and studied her under knotted brows. "I didn't know you were a tenant," he said in a low voice.

"Fourteen A, Kraft Street. Would it've made a difference?"

"Not in the long run. But we could have talked it through at lunch."

"Yes!" She puffed out a fake laugh and threw her arms up. "Instead, we shadowboxed around every subject about you. You've never been able to communicate, Devon."

He raked a hand through his hair. Several disheveled tufts stayed up, infuriatingly adorable. "I'm trying to communicate right now, and you're running away."

"I'm not running! I'm tired, and I'm going home."

"Even your friends think so."

Hannah heard them jogging up behind her. She was their boss; she had to act like one. She stiffened her spine. "All right, Devon. What do you want to say?"

A screech of tires peeling down the block stopped his reply, and he glanced over at the noise. In the dull streetlight, his chiseled profile looked exhausted and strained. He swiveled back with a sigh. "Look, Hannah, it's been a rough day for both of us. Would you like to get a drink with me before I head to the airport?"

Airport? Her heart betrayed her by squeezing painfully. She ignored it and held on to her anger. *Good riddance!* He was the corporate giant behind all her problems. A man with boatloads of money, probably a huge place to live, and that still wasn't enough. "No. I would not like to get a drink with you."

"And by no," Gretch said brightly, "she means yes."

"I mean no. I'm too busy finding a place to live."

Those beautiful brows locked even tighter.

Gretchen exhaled one short, harsh breath—friend-speak for "you're an idiot." Bernice was just arriving, out of breath. Oddly, Smart-mouth Sean stood off to the side, looking on in silence. The vise around her heart tightened as Devon stepped back. He stuffed his hands in his pockets. "I'm sorry about all this, Hannah. It's just business."

"So tossing people out on the street is just business?"

He paused a second too long. "In the real world."

Her upper lip quivered from the effort of holding in her emotions. It stilted her retort. "You've turned into quite a corporate monster."

"Oh, for fuck's sake—"

"Do you know your sister is on meds for serious depression and mumbles to herself?" she yelled. "Do you know Joseph is being blamed for the fire? Do you care about any of us at all?"

His jaw tightened and he glared down at her. "I cared enough to just invite you for a drink, Hannah. Your move."

She couldn't go. Sweet Jesus, how she wanted to. Have the last glimpse of him be the charming Devon from lunch. But she needed to hold on to this fury. He was about to walk out of her life again, and only rage would stop her from crumbling into a sobbing heap. Stupefying that her heart adored him while her mind despised him. God, she was so tired!

His lips shaped a syllable, then flattened back out as he shook his head. Shrugged. "It was a real pleasure reconnecting again."

Her mouth slackened. While her heart had raced all day, even when she wasn't with him, this was just "reconnecting." *A real pleasure. Just business.*

"What?" His tone resembled a plea.

If she uttered a word she'd burst into tears, so she

shrugged too. The man she wanted, the man she'd waited years for, was only in her fantasies. So stupid. So much wasted time.

He glanced at her friends, as if trying to find help there. Finally he lifted a hand in a weary wave and turned away.

He made it three yards before she found her backbone. She spoke softly to the boy she'd once known, the line she would've said that rainy night if she'd had an ounce of maturity and benevolence. "I hope you find happiness, Dev."

Amid all the noise of departing neighbors, he couldn't possibly have heard, but he halted mid-stride; his breath streamed out in a long mist. She gripped herself around the waist, silently pleading for him to turn around. To hug her good-bye and reassure her she still had a home.

She counted two more misty breaths before he began walking again. She tracked his long, even stride until he disappeared in the crowd. Salty tears blurred her vision. Too many emotions pummeled her, too fast to sort through, except for the familiar heartache; staying furious hadn't kept it at bay. Like déjà vu, she felt the devastation as deeply as a love-struck teen.

"Tomorrow night," Gretchen hissed, "when you're listening to some dweeb Internet date blather on, I hope you remember how tonight could've ended."

Hannah swallowed a lump the size of a grapefruit. She swiped her wet cheeks with the back of her hand and swiveled to face them. "He's engaged, Gretch." She shrugged, like it didn't matter. Because it didn't.

"Bullshit," Sean retorted.

"What?"

"He's not engaged."

Her mouth hung open at the audacity in his tone. "Google it, Sean."

"Then his future wife has a real problem on her hands. No guy looks at a woman the way he looked at you, and loves someone else."

"I agree." Bernice thrust the rolled-up poster at Hannah. "Here. A souvenir for your night of triumph."

"Bernice, this was far from triumph." Hannah's voice cracked on the last word.

"You spoke up, sweetie. You said your piece."

Oh, Bernice, how will I ever fire you?

Sean nodded in the direction Devon had disappeared. "You should've gone for that drink." He flashed the back of two fingers—half salute, half gang sign. "Come on, Bernice. I'll take you home." Within seconds, they blended into the crowd as well.

"Convince me not to fire that guy."

Gretch slipped her arm through Hannah's. "You don't let anyone go—that's your problem. Besides, he's our best employee, and I may have a crush on him. I haven't made up my mind." She pulled gently. "Let's go to your place and drink lots of wine while you tell me everything."

Hannah bonelessly let herself be pulled through the playground. As they crossed the street, up reared that odd twist of emotions again. She loved Devon, and hated him. She wished she'd never met him, and wished she'd said yes to that drink. Mostly she wished this godforsaken day would end.

CHAPTER 13

I JUST WANT this fucking day over with," Devon barked, bouncing through a pothole at the entrance to the tiny Chicago Executive Airport. He scanned the area for a car return sign.

Through the Bluetooth earbud, Eric grunted an acknowledgment. "How'd the community gathering go?"

Devon opened his mouth. *I hope you find happiness, Dev.* The look on Hannah's face. Her *anger*. If she'd slapped him, he'd have been less surprised. Hannah didn't get angry. She hated conflict. And he was fifty shades of shit to have been so stirred by those snapping green eyes, and how that tilted chin arched her slim neck. Her red-hot intensity had burned straight to his soul, stoking a need he'd thought he'd put out long ago. He shook his head. Christ, he could have handled their good-bye with so much more dignity than his pathetic plea to get a *drink*.

"It went fine," he lied. It was one of the worst meetings he'd ever conducted. Once he realized Hannah was there, his attention had strayed back to her again and again. Gawking. Stunned. Enthralled.

His thumbs drummed the steering wheel. Men who were engaged to the perfect woman didn't obsess over their high school sweethearts. "I got there late," he continued, shutting the preoccupation down. "It was spiraling into a bloodbath. O'Callaghan was all but pissing in his pants."

"Hmm. That'll teach you to leave him alone for thirty seconds. Listen, Kevin came through on Wesley O'Brien."

Finally. Something to refocus him. "And?"

"Typical Ivy League background. The right connections from Daddy landed him a junior VP position with Wickham Corporation seven years ago. How he climbed the ladder to the point where your father is grooming him to take control is beyond Kevin or me, but bottom line, there's nothing suspicious there."

Devon parked in the empty rental return lot. His head throbbed. "Every angle is a dead end."

"Focusing on your father's motivation is a complete waste of time. How do we stop this takeover?"

"By understanding Harrison's mind games," he answered impatiently. "He uses his wealth to shove people around their own lives like chess pieces."

A hundred yards away, the sleek Gulfstream sat on the tarmac, cockpit door open, golden light spilling out into the night. Manhattan was just a few hours away. He should be more relieved. But deep in his gut, no matter what he felt for his father, a part of him wanted to return to the mansion.

Joseph being blamed for arson? Frannie on pills? Mumbling? He frowned. Was she spiraling back into that dangerous depression from her teen years? And how did Hannah know all this? Her project had started three days ago. He'd been back for two. "I don't know," he said hesitantly. "Maybe I should stay."

"And how will that help us?" Eric sounded just as tired and impatient. "Just get back here and deal with Westcott and Tucker face to face."

Devon stayed inside the running car without replying. Something urged him to turn around; he couldn't put a finger on it. His mind flashed on the anguish in Hannah's accusing eyes. No, that wasn't it.

"Dude. Tell me you're at the airport and getting on the plane."

Devon heaved a sigh and killed the engine. "I'm at the airport and getting on the plane."

⁓

"CHEESE 'N' RICE...that makes me so mad," Aunt Milly yelled, as loudly as an eighty-seven-year-old could with emphysema and a whooshing nasal cannula in her nostrils.

Gretch pressed her lips together, shoulders shaking, and Hannah threw her a warning glance. She'd have been amused by the "swearing" too, if she wasn't so worried about how anger compromised her great-aunt's breathing.

"Gretch grabbed some of the handouts," she said quickly, pointing to the papers next to the almost empty bottle of chardonnay. "Between the discount Ashby Enterprises is offering and the places I printed out from the Internet, we'll be fine." Her palms began to prick, and she clasped both sides of her cool glass. It was important to sound optimistic.

"If I'd been there...I'd have marched...right up to...that corporate...know-it-all and—"

"Aunt Milly, take a deep breath—"

"That know-it-all dated Hannah," Gretch said, followed by whooshing oxygen as Aunt Milly stared at Hannah and Hannah stared at Gretch.

"Well, God bless America," Aunt Milly said calmly, and the banding up the back of Hannah's neck relaxed a fraction.

"I dated him in high school. It's not like I have any pull." Hannah swallowed an unladylike gulp of wine and reached for the bottle.

"But you did date him, and he did invite you for a

drink," Gretch pointed out. "And you're working for his father. Surely you have some pull somewhere."

"He doesn't get along with his fa—"

"You mean the Wickham boy?" Aunt Milly asked.

The bottle hovered over her glass as Hannah frowned. "I'd forgotten you'd met him." It had been one of the first times she'd invited Devon to her house—a barbecue celebrating her aunt's seventy-fifth birthday. The starkest memories of that day were how embarrassed she'd been by the minuscule patch of backyard, the radio wedged in the kitchen window blaring music, and the amazingly raunchy gifts Aunt Milly's friends had given her.

"I even remember Francesca."

Hannah glanced up, tilted bottle forgotten. It had never occurred to her to talk about Devon's mother with Aunt Milly, but she'd worked in the gift shop at the Museum of Contemporary Art. No doubt she'd seen Harrison's wife.

"She was very active in Chicago's art culture." Milly stopped for breath. "She often wandered through the shop with her two children. Spoke to all of us as if we were colleagues, which, believe me, is unusual for the rich."

"What…" Hannah had so many questions she didn't know where to start. "What was she like?"

"A fiery Italian beauty—"

"Italian?" Devon had never mentioned that.

"Her father was American, but she grew up in Italy. Harrison Wickham met her on a business trip to Florence."

Hannah took a microscopic breath. "So then…you know how she died."

"Everyone in greater Chicago back then knew how she died." Her aunt's voice sounded like chipped ice.

"Do you think it was suicide?" Hannah asked. The

wine bottle was still hovering, but she couldn't seem to tilt her wrist farther. Gretch, for once, remained silent and wide-eyed.

"The police ruled it a suicide. Both the *Sun-Times* and *Tribune* went along with the theory." Milly pursed her lips as she rattled out an exhale. "No one in the gift shop believed it. She loved life...loved those two little children. They came with her often and were so well behaved."

Devon? Behaved?

"What was he like?" Hannah asked wistfully.

"Quite an art know-it all." When had he turned his back on it? Milly laughed at the look on Hannah's face. "In a sweet way. And such a handsome boy, even then. The three of them were always so happy. I remember wanting to say something to him during the barbecue."

"The Wickham boy who'd lost his mother" pretty much summed up everything. Besides being gobsmacked by his looks, it was his tragedy that had initially drawn Hannah in high school—they'd both lost a parent, although only wispy memories of her father remained. His booming laugh; clasping his bright red hair as he galloped her around the house. And after he was gone, how instinctive it was to stay quiet and still during her mother's long, dark moods. She poured the rest of the wine into her glass. "Well, Aunt Milly, it turns out that boy is a corporate shark."

"We're Googling this right now," Gretch said firmly, scooting onto the chair in front of Hannah's computer. "Francesca Wickham, Chicago, date...?"

"Gre—"

"Ninety-five," Aunt Milly murmured. "I'll never forget it."

Gretch tapped the keys. A list popped up, and Hannah, although tipsy, fortified herself with another large sip of chardonnay. There was something tasteless and macabre about searching for these gory details. Google-stalking Devon to stay connected was one thing. But probing into his theory that his mother was murdered?

"Oh my God," Gretch whispered. "She was so beautiful."

Hannah leaped off the sofa, wine sloshing down her hand. She crossed the room in four steps.

"Yes. She was." Aunt Milly hauled herself laboriously to her feet. "The whole ordeal was a tragic waste. I'm off to bed, girls."

They chorused their good-nights without turning from the archived *Tribune* page filling the screen. The black-and-white photo captured Francesca mid-laugh—her even, white teeth and joyous expression enchanting. There was a strong resemblance between mother and son; a stronger similarity in how, even in one dimension, their charismatic personalities almost overpowered the viewer.

"What does it say?" Hannah whispered.

Gretch scrolled down. "Francesca Ashby Wickham, thirty-four, was found dead yesterday morning by her nine-year-old son. Initial indications reveal the death was a result of a thirty-foot fall, and police believe no foul play was involved. The fatal fall was alleged to have occurred in the early hours of Saturday morning on the Wickham property. The victim was unable to be revived. Winnetka police declined to comment further. Anonymous sources close to the family say husband Harrison, CEO of Wickham Corporation, is devastated and in seclusion. Francesca leaves behind two young children."

"Devastated and in seclusion?" Hannah's legs were so weak, she plopped at Gretchen's feet; wine sloshing again, chilling her fingers. Boots sauntered over and struggled to climb in her lap. "Devon is so sure that

Harrison murdered her." Her comment went unanswered as Gretch busied herself clicking the next Google link and scanning it.

"This is a week later… Medical examiner said there was no evidence of homicide…friends close to the family, all anonymous, say the marriage had been in trouble…" She clicked some more. "Ah, here… After weeks of investigation, Winnetka PD have ruled the death of Francesca Wickham a suicide. Although to date, no note has been found, police interviews with friends and staff indicate she had been unhappy over marital difficulties, and some claim she'd been contemplating divorce."

"Choosing suicide over divorce?" Hannah asked.

"Maybe the nineties were different."

"Not that different. Now it smacks of murder again."

Gretch turned and swung her arm over the back of the chair. "Did he ever talk about her?"

"When we were first dating, in that exchange-of-information kind of way—I did, too, about my dad being shot during a routine traffic stop." Hannah stroked Boots absently. "And that one time Dev showed me where he found her." She fought the shiver. Why wouldn't Harrison or the grandfather have built a fence along that cliff? Were the rich so arrogant they ignored safety for a pristine view?

Gretch nestled her chin on her forearm, her smile similar to Boots after a saucer of whole milk. "How did you capture that magnificent beast?"

Wine buzzed happy vibes through Hannah. "The hell if I know. I saw him the first day I transferred in, standing near his locker, laughing with a friend…so tall and handsome. So confident… I literally couldn't feel my limbs." She smiled to herself. "And what's weird is he was completely unaware of this gaggle of girls walking slowly by, then finding a reason to turn and walk back. He never had a clue. What great-looking guy doesn't know the effect he has on us?"

She glanced up at Gretch, who grinned, probably because of the dopey look on her face. "Anyway. A few weeks later, some jock was making fun of me, and Devon took the guy down. Effortlessly. Then he looked over at me—really looked, Gretch—right into my shy, awkward soul. And I felt this...spark." The giddiness of that moment tremored through her. She inhaled deeply. "Then I fled into the nearest bathroom and sobbed."

"Sobbed? Sir Galahad had just rescued you."

Hannah shrugged. She stroked Boots, who didn't seem to mind her wine-wet palm. "I was embarrassed. Relieved. Awestruck. My reaction was to hide. He asked me out a few weeks later and—" She snapped her fingers. Boots's tail twitched in annoyance. "We were inseparable. All ten months, he treated me like this priceless treasure. And always looked at me like that first time...like he saw *me*, spastic flaws and all. For a long time, I waited for the other shoe to drop." She gestured wildly. "Why was someone so blessed—a DNA lottery winner, the richest guy in class, this super-popular, smart, genuinely funny, *nice* guy—going out with me?"

"You're an idiot if you have to ask that."

"Gretch, I'm still your boss." Hannah giggled, because Gretch totally ran the show with her ex-personal trainer enthusiasm and iron hand. Yep, way too much wine on an empty stomach.

"Good lover?"

"So far no one's come close." Hannah blushed, grinning. "Actually, in any category. Making me feel special, wanted, unconditionally loved. I've never felt that spark with another guy. I'll go to my grave knowing Devon was my soul mate."

"You should have gone for that drink."

The grin died. "I know."

Gretch turned back to the computer and read in silence while Hannah stretched out on the carpet with an exhausted grunt. Boots realigned his obese body against her torso, immediately purring his contentment. The soothing sound and rumbling warmth were like invisible massage fingers, and as her muscles unwound, she closed her eyes.

Up popped snapshot moments of exquisite happiness with Devon lounging across the wrought-iron table, etched grooves bracketing that smiling mouth, muscles rippling every time he moved, his expression captivated despite her chattering about nothing.

She'd only ever known that tender side of Devon. This other Devon, who'd spat condo options into a mic, was a stranger. What had happened in New York to close that gentle side off from the world?

CHAPTER 14

W E'RE READY TO go, sir," the pilot said, and Devon
nodded his acknowledgment. He tossed back the
rest of the Crown Royal, set the crystal glass in
the deep cup holder, and sank into the butter-smooth
leather headrest. Seconds later, the jet rolled down the
tarmac.

Maybe it was the burning whisky or the fact that he
was leaving the worst of his day behind, but as the
Gulfstream taxied, his spirits lifted, and by the time it
soared in the air, his confidence was restored. He'd meet
Westcott for breakfast and convince him not to sell his
shares, even if he had to bluff or outright lie. He'd make
up with Nicole the second he got home tonight, and
together they'd arrange dinner for her family tomorrow.
Their united front would prove he was much more suited
to marry Nicole than that suck-up Jason Deel. End of
nightmarish week.

Outside the window, the downtown lights shrunk to
microscopic dots. Such a beautiful city, but Chicago
meant Harrison, and being around the old man brought
out a hateful side of Devon—a side that even on his
worst day in Manhattan, he didn't recognize. Eric would
have to take over the Rogers Park project; Devon was
never setting foot in this city or that damn house again,
no matter what.

Turning from the vanishing skyline, he grabbed the

heavy decanter and poured himself another Crown. *You ran off so you wouldn't end up like Father. But guess what? That's exactly who you've turned into. It's all about money and power. Business over family.* Shit, that still hurt. Was Frannie right?

No! There was not one aspect of Harrison he liked or respected, especially the cutthroat boardroom tactics and laying waste to honest, hardworking people.

So tossing people out is just business? A vision of Hannah's shell-shocked face filled his mind, and he tried to drown it with half the whisky. He wasn't like Harrison, goddamn it! The Rogers Park project was an upscale, multi-use development that would benefit the city and its people.

Shit, the line sounded smarmy even to him. Hannah must hate his guts. *I hope you find happiness, Dev.* What kind of remark was that? All he wanted was an orderly, efficient life. No gooey feelings and trip-hammering pulses. Hannah needed to stay in his past, in an adolescent time where love meant everything.

He rubbed his eyelids hard, fighting the lingering headache and the way his thoughts still stuck on her like some annoying advertising jingle. *Fuck it.* He finished off the whisky and checked his email, texting replies until his eyelids felt like ten-ton boulders. He'd had a total of four hours of sleep in the last two days. Dozing the last hour home was more important than this request from a Houston marketing director to fire a slacker named Tim Barnaby.

Grudgingly, he slipped off his seat belt, too tired to even hit the head, but nature called. He swung the door open mid-yawn.

"Hi, Uncle Devon."

His heart stopped. When it started again, it thundered in his ears. "Holy shit." He stared at the boy sitting casually on top of the toilet lid, playing some PSP game and looking suspiciously delighted with himself.

"Holy shit," he said again, because that was the only thought still screaming through his brain. He mentally slapped himself and inhaled a gallon of oxygen. "What are you doing here?"

"I took your advice and did what I wanted to do, instead of always doing what other people want all the time."

Devon swallowed dust. "I don't think I said that." He was vaguely surprised his tone sounded so offhand, because his now very alert brain was stuck in primal scream mode. So loud and persistent, in fact, that he couldn't problem-solve this.

The boy thumbed a couple of buttons, stood, and stuck the device in his back pocket. "I'm kinda thirsty."

"How long have you been in there?"

"Dunno. Awhile."

Devon stood aside, and his nephew headed down the aisle and chose a seat. The plush, spacious club chair was meant for beefy business types, and Todd seemed to drown in the vastness, reminding Devon, just in case he'd forgotten, that he had a child on board.

He snapped the tab on a Coke and handed it to the boy, then eyed the decanter of Crown wistfully. He needed a clear head. With a grunt, he threw himself in the opposite chair. "How did you get on board?" If the pilot had anything to do with this, there'd be hell to pay. As in: lawsuit hell.

"I did what you did. Told Mom I was going to my room, then snuck out and drove Grandfather's Bentley." Todd's beam held such blatant pride that despite himself, Devon's mouth quirked up.

"You drove? By yourself?"

"Sure. My dad's let me drive a couple of times."

"All the way to the airport?" Todd blushed. Even barely knowing his nephew, Devon's stomach lurched at the thought. Thank God the little airport was all surface streets from Winnetka, not the freeway. "Go on," he said gently. "What happened after you got there?"

"I watched the pilot walk around the plane a couple of times and check some stuff on a clipboard, and when he went into the building, I just climbed in."

As the shock passed, a tiny part of Devon gave his nephew kudos for having the balls to pull this off. It sure as hell beat any of his stunts. But once that thought flitted past, Devon nailed him with his boardroom stare. "Did you leave a note for your mom?" Todd shook his head, and Devon's gut flip-flopped expensive whisky. "Why not? She's probably worried sick."

"I was afraid she'd find it, and come and get me before we took off."

Devon rubbed his eyelids, hard. Maybe there was aspirin in the john. "Well, here's the bad news: you're in—*we* are in a lot of trouble." He took out his cell phone. The battery was low, but he could get in one fast call.

"I don't want to go back! I want to stay with you."

How did parents deal with outbursts like this? Devon fumbled around in his mind for words, and finally went for frank honesty. "You can't stay with me, Todd. You're a kid. You're Francine's kid. I can't take care of you."

"Why not?"

"What do you mean, 'why not'?" He couldn't imagine the albatross of someone depending on him.

"I won't be much trouble, I swear. We get along, and I'm happy when I'm around you. My parents"—Todd spread his hands—"all they do is yell...at me, at each other. Maybe if I left, they'd get along. At least they'd stop arguing over me all the time."

Christ, the kid was blaming himself for the custody fight. "Todd, I'm sorry. I wish I could."

The boy teared up, and he swallowed hard a few times. "It's just that, well, there's another reason I can't go back."

Fucking Christ. "What?"

Another gulp. "I—I'm the one who started the fire."

Devon squinted at the boy. Could the searing pain behind his eye be a stroke?

"It was an accident, I swear! I can't go back, don't you see? Grandfather's bound to find out. I want to puke every time I see the arson guy wandering around upstairs." The Coke can trembled in his hands. "I'll be in so much trouble."

Devon leaned his elbows on his knees, which put him at Todd's height. He forced his expression to remain calm. "What happened?"

Todd sniffed. "I was, you know, trying to figure out how to smoke."

"Cigarettes?"

"Yes. But Grandfather's going to kill me."

As Devon gazed into the boy's pleading eyes, pity surged through him. He remembered the horror of anticipating Harrison's wrath like it was yesterday. But apparently Joseph was being fingered for the fire, and if Devon could do nothing else to fix the chaos of his visit, he could do this. "All right, look. We're almost to New York. How about if you stay the weekend, but that's all. And when you get home, the first thing you do is face your grandfather like a man and tell the truth."

"But Unc—"

"Take it or leave it, Todd."

The boy pouted. "I'll take it."

"And never smoke again. That's the other condition."

"Okay." He shrugged. "It wasn't fun anyhow."

"Your mom's probably called the police by now." As he scrolled through his cell phone for her number,

Todd ducked his head, but not before Devon saw the tears shining in his eyes.

The call was answered in half a ring. "OhmyGodDevon, he's gone." Her hysterical shriek must've been heard across the row, because Todd stiffened.

"He's with me. He snuck onboard."

"OhmyGod." There was a fumbling sound. "Put him on the goddamn phone."

Across from him, Todd paled. "He's...asleep."

"I'm leaving for the airport right now. When will you be landing?"

His phone beeped a low battery warning. "I'll let him stay for the weeke—"

"No!" She screamed the word so loud he and Todd straightened in their seats.

"Jesus Christ, shut up! You'll wake the whole house."

"I'm in my car. I've just been to Brady's looking for him. He caught me peeking in the window. It was awful." She sobbed. "You can't believe what I've just been through. Just bring him home."

He couldn't. There was too much at stake. He had to get to New York. "Okay. He'll be on the next commercial flight back—"

"Noooo! He's not allowed out of state!" Her words were hard to understand, given the hysterical crying. "Putting him on a flight will be proof. His name will be in the computer. Turn around now!"

"I can't—"

"Forget your company for once! He's all I have left!"

Devon sucked in a breath. His headache had picked up the rhythm of his pounding heart, and his stomach protested the whisky. "It's not just about my company, Francine. The pilot still has to get to Tucson for an early pickup tomorrow. He can't turn back to Chicago and still take me to New York." Which was true. Ashby Enterprises only rented hours with this company; they had no pull whatsoever.

The hiccupping sobs sounded far away, as if she'd dropped the phone. His cell beeped insistently, and his mouth dried up. He prayed the battery lasted. Having her think he'd hung up would seriously suck. "Frannie," he said loudly, hoping she'd hear his voice. "Frannie!"

"Brady was awful... They're going to take Todd...my baby."

Another jagged round of crying, and he tried to shout his message over her sobs. Whether she heard or not, he was left midway through his sentence holding a dead phone.

"Fuck." He threw it on the seat next to him, then realized all over again that he was in the presence of a kid. "Sorry."

"I didn't mean to worry her this much." Todd looked so forlorn that there was no doubt Devon was about to have another crier on his hands. He quickly patted Todd's knee.

"I don't think she's upset with you as much as having to go to your dad's to look for you. It didn't sound like that went too well." Hell, she just handed Brady a buttload of ammunition for the custody battle. And wait till the bastard found out about his son driving on suburban streets and stowing away in an airplane toilet.

Devon stared at his nephew, whose eyelids drooped. The poor kid was stuck in the middle of a vicious divorce and had tried to figure a way out of it. Instead, his dumb stunt had set off a shitstorm. If Devon went against Frannie's wishes and kept Todd for the weekend or stuck him on the next flight home, she'd be lucky to end up with supervised visitation rights. But if he instructed the pilot to turn around, drop them off, and head to Tucson for his next passenger—and who knew if that was even feasible—breakfast with Westcott was a nonstarter.

And he'd be breaking another promise to Nicole.

CHAPTER 15

HANNAH BRUSHED THE toast crumbs from her fingers and typed an apologetic text, canceling her Internet date. Besides having way too much work to do, in the end Gretch was right: Hannah would compare everything about the poor guy to Devon. The fact that she was furious with Dev, that he was no longer in town, and that she *should* go on this date didn't matter. Her heart wouldn't have it.

She tossed the phone in her purse and picked up the four apartment listings she hoped to tour sometime today. All but one had longer commute times to get to work, but they were affordable, had two bedrooms, and took cats.

"You don't look so good, dear. Did you drink too much wine last night?" Aunt Milly said from the other side of the table.

Yes. "No. I just slept badly." Which was true. Between her hangover and a second night of tossing and turning, her mood was sour. And today stretched bleakly before her: crate the remaining nine paintings with Sean, race to the office and finish the Matisse, then visit these apartments. She should probably schedule some moving company quotes too.

She glanced at her aunt's kitschy clock, a black-and-white cat's head, whose eyes glanced left and right in conjunction with the ticking seconds. Seven o'clock.

The annual Chicago Halloween Gathering Parade was this morning, smack in the middle of the direct route from her office to Winnetka. No doubt there were road closures already, but she'd better leave now to pick up the company van and Sean before traffic and crowds widened the detour.

"I probably won't be home for dinner." She rinsed out her plate and coffee cup, then grabbed her purse and kissed her aunt's withered cheek. "Don't forget, the new home health aide comes at nine thirty. Try not to run this one off."

"I don't mind a bit of exercise. I draw the line at training for the Olympics."

Hannah pressed her lips to keep from smiling; it only egged her aunt on. "Walking to and from the bus stop twice is hardly the Olympics," she said over her shoulder, heading into the living room.

"Walking?" As Hannah gathered her coat and headed to the door, Aunt Milly was still muttering. "...I may have even hurdled something."

Hannah hurried down the windy street, juggling the pros and cons of efficient routes past the parade, but paused as she neared the center's playground. Day one of life after Devon. *Again.* Thank God he was gone. After last night, she couldn't deal with facing him. A part of her still wanted to verbally rip him to shreds. In reality, the tiny amount of outrage she'd displayed horrified her. So much for confrontation, or as Bernice put it: triumph. He'd hate her forever. The fact that she even cared was damn pathetic. Hannah climbed the stairs to the El platform. From this second on, she was going to be as jaded as her mother during her dark days.

A few minutes to midnight. Hannah tiptoed past the open door of her mom's bedroom, holding her sandals, and her breath. Please God, let Mom be asleep! *Or not back from her own date yet. It was way past curfew, but whenever Hannah was with Devon, time ceased to exist.*

Her lips felt singed by his fervent kissing, and her insides still tingled with frustrated desire. If only they could just go off somewhere—anywhere, just the two of them. A place of their own where her mom and his dad didn't ruin things—

"You're grounded." The words floated out into the hall, and Hannah's breath whooshed out at the tone. Mom's recent "up" ride was over. Even though the manic energy was hard to take, it was so much better than the depressive slide that would enclose this place in days of darkness. Worse, nothing from now until the next up cycle could come out of Hannah's mouth without it being considered talking back. Protesting being grounded was suicide.

"I'm going to the kitchen. Can I get you anything, Mom?" she asked timidly. What she wanted to say was, "Act like an adult and take your meds." Why were Mom's highs so great she risked this very thing—the basement of moods instead of living an even-keeled life?

A whisper of movement and then her mother was in the doorway, her dress disheveled, mascara smeared. A partially filled highball quivered in her hand. "You seem to be confused which one of us is the mother and which is the child. I said eleven."

Dread scurried up Hannah's spine. Mom on a slide and drunk and wanting to pick a fight. It never ended well for Hannah. Not ever. Her tongue tangled around all the words she wanted to say. Words she would say one of these days when she grew a backbone.

"I'm sorry I'm late." Clutching her dangling sandals in her fist, she focused on her door at the end of the short hall.

"And by grounded, I mean the next three weekends."

Hannah spun around with a shriek.

"I warned you—"

"I'm only an hour late," she sputtered. "We had car trouble."

Mom swayed slightly. "If you're going to lie, I'll take away your phone privileges next."

"I'm sorry you're upset with whatever happened on your date tonight, but don't take it out on me!" Hannah's breath stilled. She'd blurted it without thinking.

A long moment of excruciating silence. Then her mother turned and drifted back into her room. "Call Devon in the morning and tell him you won't be at prom."

Hannah stumbled to her room, tears blinding her. She slammed the door with all her strength and fell to her knees. "I hate you!" she whispered, despising the cowardly inability to scream it at the top of her lungs. "I fucking hate you. I wish you were dead!"

⤳

DEVON JERKED AWAKE at the distant gong of a doorbell. What day was it? His eyes felt gritty, and his mouth tasted like rotten whisky. Where the hell was he? He rolled over with a groan, surveying his surroundings in the dim light streaming through a crack in the curtains.

His mother's room? *Oh, shit!* By the time he'd carried a soundly sleeping Todd upstairs to a still weeping Francine, he'd been so damn tired he must not have been thinking straight. If he'd turned right around and driven to O'Hare, he'd have been on the first flight out. Instead he'd come in here, plugged in his cell phone, left emails and voicemails at three in the morning, and promptly fallen asleep.

He sat up stiffly and squinted at his watch. Seven forty-five. *Shit, shit, shit.* Emitting a long sigh, he rubbed his bristled jaw. Hopefully the stowaway excuse would wash with Eric, Nicole, and Westcott. He'd instructed Eric to take the meeting at the club and provided a few talking points to sway the stodgy old man not to sell so quickly. Anything to delay him until Devon got home. It was eight forty-five in New York. They ought to be in the middle of the discussion. *Please let it go well.*

He went over to the frilly drapes and parted one side a few inches. The lake looked like a rippling mirror, the sky baby blue. A breeze ruffled the giant willow by the cliff, which swept the lawn in graceful laziness. Beds of boxwoods and thick flowers in burnt autumn colors bordered the massive backyard. Three gardeners were already trudging toward them with wheelbarrows of supplies and piles of moist black soil. Just another beautiful fall morning at the Wickham estate. He let the curtain drop and grabbed the shaving kit from the overnight bag.

As he padded across the white-tiled bathroom, he mentally listed the additional calls to make, the excuses to give. Muffled voices passed by out in the hall, a guy's and a lyrical response sounding a lot like Hannah. His heartbeat jacked to an insane rhythm, and some primitive instinct urged him to burst into the hall. He quickly turned on the crystal taps until the rushing water drowned out any sound. After last night, she was the last person he wanted to run into. Opposites may attract, but they were not compatible as life partners. He needed to get back to Nicole and the ideal life they'd been building before the wheels had come off the cart with this godforsaken trip.

Within minutes, Devon repacked his belongings and headed for the door. He made it three steps down the grand staircase when he heard a scream from the backyard. The panic in it catapulted him down to the landing, where the giant bay windows overlooked the lawns and lake.

One of the landscapers tore toward the house, red-faced and waving his hat, as if he were chasing down the last city bus in a dangerous part of town. He hollered repeatedly as he ran. Devon turned abruptly from the window, but instinct held him immobile as the patio door slammed and the man yelled again in rapid-fire Spanish. The only word Devon understood was *muerta*. *Dead? Jesus Christ... Frannie? Todd?*

He swiveled to race downstairs when Joseph's commanding voice cut through the stream of Spanish. "What's going on here?"

"Sir." This came from a shrill female. "Pedro says it's Miss Honey. She must have fallen off the cliff."

Devon froze mid-step. *Honey—dead?*

"Oh dear God in heaven, not again," Joseph said.

A ringing started in Devon's ears amid the bursts of Spanish and English, now out-shouting each other as everyone in the house seemed to have rushed to the foyer. He backed up slowly until he bumped into the wall of the landing.

Honey was dead...twisted on the beach like his mother, with her broken neck and glazed eyes, and she wouldn't move even though he kept calling to her. Sweat dampened Devon's forehead, and bile rose in his throat. He opened his mouth and panted, but couldn't get enough oxygen. The horrifying sight his nine-year-old self regurgitated threatened to drop him where he stood.

Then a sharp British accent forced its way through his daze. Mrs. Farlow, the cook. "Where's Mr. Wickham?"

"He left early." That from Joseph, in his everyone-calm-down voice. "He had a meeting."

"On a Saturday?" More unfamiliar voices rose up the stairwell.

"Has anyone called nine-one-one?"

"I will."

Ice water couldn't have snapped Devon out of his paralysis faster. *The police!* Honey had clearly been murdered. He knew her real identity, his father knew, and so did the person eavesdropping on the line. Rick? He was the one who'd answered last night. And both his father and his half-brother had undeniable motives to kill her.

You'll be sorry you ever messed with Ashby Enterprises. Joseph and two maids had witnessed him threatening her. Devon had seen enough TV to know he'd be a suspect too. She'd died while he was under this roof. Even without a cause of death, his presence in this house, on this property, was not a good thing. Once the cops began crawling all over the estate, they'd detain everyone to get statements, and he'd never get back to New York.

He screwed his eyes shut. *So much for putting family first. I'm fucked!* He had to see Nicole this morning, first thing upon landing. He had to know they were solid. How would he get out of here unseen? *Think!* He glanced around the empty landing and clear passage back to his mother's room.

Wait a minute. No one except Frannie had seen him set foot in here last night, and he'd left her sitting at Todd's bedside over in the south wing. For all she knew, he'd simply walked back out into the predawn night.

He drew in a steady breath, mentally mapping out the pathway to freedom. He could take rarely used passageways to the east side, get down to the basement through the tiny servants' staircase, then slip out the side entrance that let out by the garages. With everyone clustered in the foyer, this'd be a piece of cake. He eased soundlessly up the carpeted steps and turned the corner, his back hugging the wall.

CHAPTER 16

HANNAH'S MOOD DIDN'T get any better when they walked into the sitting room and Sean realized Robbie hadn't left the toolbox as instructed. "Sean, you gotta supervise him better than this," she snapped.

"Sorry, boss." He'd never called her "boss" before, and she scowled at him. Giving him an involuntary peek at her personal life last night hadn't done her any favors. As it was, the team knew she couldn't reprimand or fire anyone if her life depended on it, and now Sean got to see the dumb, lovesick side. *You should've gone for that drink.* Relationship advice from Sean, who equaled Gretch when it came to fear of intimacy.

With a start, she realized he was still speaking. "...like I'm starting to think he's an idiot savant. He can't follow basic instructions, but on his first try, he'll choose a color hue to match the exact palette an artist used centuries ago."

"Well..." She blew out a breath. "I guess we better ask Mr. Wickham for a power drill and screws." Really. Could this day get any worse?

Sean swept a hand through his dark-brown hair. "No. I'll text Robbie and find out where he put the toolbox. I'll go back and get it."

"That parade already delayed us. This'll put us back hours," she protested. "I don't have the time." Even without this delay, it'd be a late night.

"Then I'll go ask Wickham. It's my fault."

She almost said yes. She would've, had he not seen the side of her last night that stood there passively while her high school sweetheart destroyed her. It was time to grow a backbone. "He doesn't know who you are. Besides, if I can hunt down Joseph, he'll find some tools, and our unprofessionalism will never reach Harrison's ears."

Sean looked at her oddly. "Sure, if you think he hasn't been arrested yet."

She wound her way down the hall, anxiety building. Had Joseph been arrested? She'd given up trying to find him yesterday afternoon, wimping out in the face of Frannie's drug-induced dismissal, and Harrison's innate intimidation. Joseph hadn't greeted them at the front door this morning, and he'd always seemed omnipresent. If he was down at the station, she'd never forgive herself.

She gnawed on her lower lip as she crossed through the enormous first editions library. Her gaze swept to the far corner and the majestic desk where Devon had sat, blowing her off to take a phone call. How had she missed seeing him as a corporate shark? What a perfect career for someone so emotionally withdrawn.

No doubt he was just waking up in his Manhattan condo. Making love to his fiancée. A stabbing sensation left her breathless. Maybe they were breakfasting in robes out on their private balcony overlooking Central Park. Why did she care? She was *over* him. *Jaded.* She no longer believed in a happily-ever-after.

The hug in the sitting room yesterday popped into her mind. The familiarity of his embrace had tumbled her back in time, like the vortex at the beginning of *The Twilight Zone.* As if no years and no heartbreak had come between them. What if the team hadn't walked in a moment later? What if she'd pressed her lips to his boldly—with years of built-up emotion?

"Oh, knock it off," she whispered. She turned the corner and ran smack into a body so concrete her teeth clicked.

"Christ!"

She gasped at the familiar tone. He gripped her arms and separated her, just barely, from his warm chest. "Devon?"

"Hannah!" The powerful grip on her upper arms tightened. He smelled of toothpaste and shaving cream, and his face was shockingly pale, those long-lashed eyes bloodshot. The burn of his gaze and violent slash of brows caused her to sag in his arms like a rag doll. "Hannah," he said again in soft anguish.

His eyes dropped to her mouth, and her lips parted on instinct. She pressed a trembling hand to his chest, feeling the thud of his heart. He angled his head, his breath hot and close. The nanosecond of suspended time, of pooling need, went on forever.

Kiss me!

He exhaled roughly and pushed her upright and away from him. Her hand dropped lifelessly to her side. "You never saw me," he rasped, his lips white with tension. He shook her gently. "Did you hear me, Hannah? No matter what, you never saw me today."

"Huh," she said. Relief cleared the fierceness in his haggard features, and he released her. She almost stumbled at the sudden freedom and gulped in oxygen. How long had she gone without inhaling? Long enough for her knees to quiver.

He leaned down and grabbed an overnight bag. When he straightened, his expression blended tenderness with pain. "Do you ever wonder what our lives would've been like if you'd gone with me that night?" His Adam's apple bobbed up and down hard. "I spent years hoping you'd follow me."

He brushed past while she stood like a zombie. *Years*. What was happening? Why this sudden, intimate glimpse? She spun around, but he'd already disappeared—without so much as eliciting the teeniest creak from any of these old floorboards.

Many voices, far off, reached her. The collective hysteria was evident even from here, in a distant hall, where she'd accidentally bumped into someone clearly on the run.

HE COULD TRUST Hannah. Devon slipped down the back passageway, his stride swift and noiseless. Even as his mind pointed out that the moment union negotiations ended he'd be tearing down her apartment, his gut trusted her blindly. Hannah wouldn't tell the police she'd run into him. No one would know he'd been in this house or even on these grounds today.

He crept down the ancient wood stairs, spiraling past the kitchen until he reached the door to the basement—or fallout shelter, depending on the decade. He made his way carefully down those steps in the darkness, one hand on the cool concrete wall to his right. The scents of moist earth and mold clung to the insides of his nostrils. He halted, eyes straining to make out the obscure shadows. The silence was so complete that the rapid thumping of his pulse and short breathing cycle seemed to echo. Once his eyes adjusted, he pushed off from the bottom stair, stepping cautiously, in case childhood toys like Rollerblades still lay strewn around.

Finally his palm brushed over the molding around the far basement door, then the bolt, and he unlocked it. He fumbled with the door handle. *Please don't be locked*. He had no key and no plan B. Slowly he turned the cool metal handle. The door squeaked shrilly as it opened. A thread of sunlight and fresh air slipped in. He exhaled heavily, opening the door a fraction at a time on its rusty hinges.

Slipping outside, he glanced left, at the white stucco wall of garages ten feet away. Except for twittering birds, he was out here alone. If only he could grab the Bentley he'd driven Todd home in and blitz to an airport. But that wasn't an option if he wanted to remain invisible. As a teenager, he used to sneak through the forest between this property line and the Dawsons' next door, until he was close enough to Sheridan Road. That could still work. He'd slip out onto the Dawsons' driveway; no one in that house would be able to see that far. On Sheridan, he'd grab the bus to the El and ride it to Midway or O'Hare.

He relaxed his death grip on the overnight bag and breathed in the chilly morning air. Confidence soaring, he strode toward the trees. The crunch of gravel on the drive and purr of an engine came from his left. Instinctively he ducked, sprinting for the side of the garage. He slammed his back up against the stucco, skin prickling with unease. Of all the damn luck! The only people with the authority to drive any of the expensive cars were his father, the chauffeur, Rick, or Frannie. Three out of the four, Devon absolutely had to avoid.

Rattling glass and squealing joints rent the morning air, jolting him before he realized it was only the ancient carriage door opening. The one closest to where he stood. All he had to do was stay still for the next few minutes and wait until whoever it was went into the house. The probability of anyone walking around the corner of the garage to an obscure part of the side lawn was nil.

The distinct sound of sirens wailed in the distance. Sweat trickled down his temple. A car door shut a few feet away, then seconds later another.

"Thank you, Evan." *Harrison. Shit!* Devon molded further into the wall, if that was even possible. His heart tripped off rhythm. "I won't need you again until this evening. Ms. Hartlett and I have tickets to the symphony at eight. We'll be dining afterward."

"Very good, sir. I'll have the Rolls ready at seven."

So, either his father didn't know she was dead, or he was creating nice details in a tight alibi by still planning to take her out this evening. The answer was obvious, given Harrison knew she was a fraud. Sirens shrieked closer. Two pairs of footsteps crunched on the gravel. In about five seconds, Devon would be clear to bolt.

The vibration in his pants pocket started a second before the shrill ring of his cell phone. *Shit! Shit! Shit!*

The footsteps halted in the gravel. "What in the hell…?"

"I don't know, sir."

Devon jammed his hand into his pocket. As he pulled the phone out, his clumsy grasp hit the Talk icon. Caller ID: Nicole. The line was live.

Sorry, babe. He winced as he hit the End button and disconnected her.

"Hey!" The outrage of the chauffeur's shout a few feet away was nowhere close to the tone his father used calling his name. Devon tilted his face to the cloudless sky. *So goddamn close.* Then Harrison stood before him, annoyed and suspicious.

"What are you doing here?" The sirens shrieked in decibels that could no longer be ignored. Confusion washed over Harrison. He spun around as a squad of black-and-silver Winnetka police cars careened into the circle, screeching to a halt with a slide of gravel, right out of some movie action sequence.

The old man faced him squarely again. In a voice ringing with blame and promising punishment—a voice carved into Devon's memories—he shouted, "What the hell's going on around here, goddamn it?"

CHAPTER 17

"WHAT HAPPENED?" HANNAH asked.

The nearest woman in the frenzied crowd whipped around. "Miss Hartlett's dead," she said, eyes widening in fresh horror.

Hannah opened her mouth to reply, but although the name sounded familiar, she wasn't sure who Miss Hartlett was.

"Mr. Wickham's fiancée," the maid supplied in a disbelieving tone.

Honey. Goose bumps chilled Hannah from the inside out. Screaming sirens arriving outside hurt her ears. "Wha—what happened?"

"The gardener says she fell off the cliff."

Just like Francesca… It was beyond a freakish coincidence. How could two women have plunged to their deaths this way? Her breath stilled. *Oh God. Devon!* The panic on his face. *No matter what, you never saw me today.* The stealthy way he'd disappeared. Hannah twisted her fingers together, searching the crowd of shocked faces in the hope she was mistaken. He was long gone.

She licked parched lips with a dry tongue. Maybe she was jumping to conclusions. Those cliff steps were so narrow and slippery. And yesterday, Honey had worn heeled flip-flops. If she'd returned later wearing ridiculous shoes, who knew what could've happened?

Hannah would never have tried those stairs in heels *or* by herself. "Did the gardener see her fall?"

"No, when he went to rake the sand. Her neck's broken."

Hannah shuddered. The sirens abruptly stopped, and she went rigid with anticipation. What was she doing? She quickly texted Walter and Sean a one-sentence explanation, with a strong suggestion that they cancel the rest of the day. She and Sean did not need to be trekking through the house with crated paintings in the middle of this.

Car doors slammed, effectively silencing the crowd around her. She slid past a few servants to go stand near the bottom of the staircase and wait for Sean, but the staff around her jostled and parted like the Red Sea, their bodies effectively closing her in their ranks. Suddenly Joseph strode right past her down the cleared passage, smoothing his cravat as though he was on his way to greet any old visitor. He was still here! She almost smiled but caught herself in time.

The moment he opened the door, Harrison Wickham swept in, his stride imperial, his face a thundercloud of rage. A step behind, sporting a deer-in-the-headlights stare, was a young blond man in a black suit. Devon followed, eyes exhausted and mouth set in a rebellious line. Hannah swallowed hard, staring at him. He couldn't be responsible for the heinous murder. She bit the inside of her cheek squeezing her biceps, exactly where his strong fingers had held her captive.

Half a dozen officers trooped in after the three men, some immediately sizing up the staff as if they were suspects, while others stared at the grandness of the foyer. Harrison stopped just short of the clustered staff and opened his mouth to speak. When he hesitated and frowned, Hannah followed his gaze behind her.

Francine descended the red-carpeted steps, hair in

disarray, thin body swimming in overlarge sweats as wrinkled as Devon's clothes. She blinked in surprise at the family, staff, and police in the foyer. Silently, everyone stared back. "What's going on?" she asked absently, glancing around. "Why didn't someone answer the phone?" She held up a cordless phone. "It's the caterer. Honey's not answering her cell."

FRANNIE'S STATEMENT RAISED the cacophony echoing in the foyer. Devon closed his eyes. How could she not have heard the commotion—the news? Frannie's bedroom in the south wing was far, but not that far.

"Silence!" Harrison roared. His command was abruptly obeyed, but the frenzied energy remained in the flushed faces and shifting weight of the onlookers. "Someone tell me what's going on."

Devon edged toward the bronze statue of Zeus and leaned a shoulder against it. He'd refused to answer his father out in the driveway, which had only ratcheted up the old man's temper. But Devon had no intention of either playing along, if his father was establishing an alibi, or being the one to impart the news if he wasn't.

Joseph stepped forward. "Sir, I attempted to notify you on your cell—"

"Yes, yes, I was on an international call. Now what's happened?"

"I'm Sergeant Wilson." An officer with a third-trimester paunch stepped forward, unconsciously palming his holstered gun like a child checking for the presence of his security blanket. "There's been a report of a fatality on the premises."

Harrison blinked once then scanned the faces in the foyer. "Where's Honey?" he demanded in a low voice, and Francine, still halfway down the stairs, wiggled the phone.

This was fucking surreal.

"She's passed on, sir," Joseph said. "I'm sorry. I tried to call."

Except for the dual *thunks* as Frannie dropped the cordless and sank abruptly on the step, the hall remained hushed. Devon watched his father closely. Harrison passed a trembling palm over his mouth and swallowed hard.

Was this how he'd reacted twenty-one years ago? Was he about to get away with his second murder?

"How?" he whispered.

"The cliff, sir."

Harrison pitched forward as if an invisible force had just punched him in the stomach. His face drained of color. A murmur swept through the spectators, and Joseph stepped closer.

"Mrs. Farlow, a brandy, if you please," he ordered, gently clasping Harrison's elbow. "This way, sir." He escorted Harrison into the parlor and closed the door firmly behind them.

Mrs. Farlow motioned to one of her staff, who scurried away, then marched up to Sergeant Wilson. "I'm Mrs. Farlow, the head cook for the Wickhams. I'll show you the way to...the body."

Wilson nodded to an associate, and then gestured for half the police force to follow him and Mrs. Farlow toward the patio doors, while the associate requested everyone else stay where they were. The remaining cops rummaged for notepads or organized a line for the staff to stand in. Devon caught one by the sleeve as he walked by. "Excuse me, Officer. I have a flight I'm very late for. Could you collect whatever it is you need from me first, so I can head to the airport?"

The cop looked him up and down, his expression surly. No doubt the wrinkled clothes didn't scream high-income CEO. "Who are you?"

"I'm Devon Ashby...Wickham. I'm Harrison's

eldest son." Prickles crawled over his skin at trading in on something that normally shamed him.

Instantly the officer straightened. "I can take your information, but until Sergeant Wilson says otherwise, no one is leaving this hall."

And just like that, Devon was stuck in this godforsaken house. He mentally screamed a string of curse words as more commotion began on the stairs. Two maids crouched on either side of Frannie, who'd collapsed into a sobbing ball. Another death involving the cliff. If her memories were as haunted as his, he hoped she had some Valium.

"I'll need your contact information—" the cop began, but Devon held up his hand.

"Excuse me, Officer. I need to get my sister out of here."

"Sir, no one is to leave."

"We aren't leaving," he snapped. "I'm taking her to her bedroom."

"I mean no one can leave this entry hall."

Devon clenched his jaw. "Watch me." He shouldered his way through the milling staff not yet in line and caught sight of Hannah hovering at the edge of the chaos. She stared at him in such horror it knocked the breath from his lungs. Without a thought, he veered her way. She stiffened and glanced around for the nearest cop, and he quickened his steps. As she held up a hand to flag one down, he lunged the remaining few feet. "Hannah." He kept his voice low and calm. "For God's sake, it's not what you think." He instinctively reached out, but she shied away.

"*Don't.*"

"Just listen to me—"

Her gaze strayed over his shoulder, and she nodded to someone. He glanced back in paranoia. No cop. One of the guys from her company stood on the landing, surveying the shitshow. "I need to go talk to him." Her voice sounded cool and detached, and the second she finished speaking, her mouth formed a grim line.

"I had nothing to do with her death, I swear. I just wanted to get out of here before"—he motioned around them—"this."

She threw him a do-I-look-that-stupid frown, and then a maid was at his side asking for help with Frannie. Panic edged out reason. He leaned in again, close enough so the peach scent of her rich auburn hair became his oxygen. He hovered a second longer than necessary, surprised she stayed put. "Look at me, Hannah." He waited in torture until she lifted her chin and stared dispassionately into his eyes. The complete absence of her sweet inner light shook him. "I was only trying to get home. That's all."

The second he finished the last word, she studied the black-and-white tiles at her feet, her face giving nothing away. The maid tugged his sleeve again, and he helplessly followed the woman to the stairwell, where a keening Frannie was now surrounded by four female staff, all murmuring to her at once.

"Come on, kiddo." He picked her up effortlessly and hugged her to his chest. As he climbed the stairs, he looked over his shoulder. Hannah watched his progress openly. At least her expression held resignation now, which was better than accusation. But the starry-eyed, joyful soul he'd reconnected with two days ago was long gone. Just another casualty poisoned simply by setting foot in this house. The triumphant Devon who'd stridden in here thinking the world lay within his grasp had imploded too.

"I can't take any more," his sister said through her sobs, clinging to him as he got to the bay-windowed landing. Cops descended the ledge cautiously, each disappearing from view. He shielded his sister from the sight and rounded the curve, murmuring words of comfort. Taking the remaining stairs two at a time, he strode toward the south wing, shocked at how bony she felt in his arms. Todd had been much heavier. Come to think of it, he hadn't seen his nephew in the foyer with the others. And Rick was missing, too.

"Where's Todd?" he asked gently.

The question effectively turned off the waterworks as the maternal side emerged. "He's still asleep. It's why I grabbed the damn phone when it started ringing." She turned her wet and exhausted face to his. "He's been through so much lately. I don't know how to tell him this."

Devon didn't answer. He and Frannie had suffered a massive shock when they were kids, but without a comforting parent like Frannie to turn to. His father might have remained in this house during the tumultuous days and weeks after their mother died, but Harrison had locked himself in his office until long after they were in bed.

"What should I do, Dev?"

He swallowed a thick lump and focused on his sister's tear-ravaged face once more. "Here's what you're gonna do," he said with authority. "First you're going to wipe off all the snot running down your face." He absorbed the whack on his arm. "I mean, that's just gross." Another whack, but mission accomplished. Already the tension in her muscles began to ebb. "Then you're going to wake him up, and tell him the truth. There's been a horrible accident, and Honey's dead."

"This was no accident."

"We don't know anything yet. Let it be the truth for now."

"I think he had a crush on her." Her eyes watered again.

"She was a beautiful woman." He shut down the

avalanche of other, completely inappropriate adjectives to describe the newly deceased.

"What do you think Father will do now? With his will, I mean?"

Devon shook his head, disguising a frown as puzzlement. *Talk about wrong timing, sis.* "I don't have a clue. I don't recommend you ask anyone else, either." He stopped outside Todd's closed door and gently lowered her to her feet. "You gonna be okay?"

She nodded and wiped her face with the sweatshirt sleeve. "Thanks again for last night, Dev. I know it was inconvenient to come all the way back here." He swallowed his reply. "Did you tell anyone?" Her fingers scrunched the long sleeves. "About Todd?"

"No." He stopped himself before adding how insulted he was that she'd even ask.

"And you won't, right? Not anyone. Not even Father."

"Frannie. It's *me*."

"I just"—and here came the tears—"don't know who to trust anymore. Getting custody is all I have left. If anyone finds out he got on that plane..."

"I promise never to tell a soul." He shifted his weight impatiently. Efficient problem-solving skills were never her strong suit, so he nodded toward the west side. "Just tell Brady you finally found him asleep in the billiards room."

She gulped and sniffed and wiped and nodded. "Okay." He turned to go. "Wait, Dev." She looked so tiny and helpless in that enormous sweatshirt. He'd forgotten how defenselessly feminine she always appeared, bringing out an overwhelming surge of protectiveness in any man, when really, she was all lean muscle in that thin frame. "I'm sorry you're stuck in this mess with the rest of us."

He nodded. "That makes two of us. Which reminds

me, where the hell's Rick?" For sure, he had to get to the bottom of whether his half-brother was behind the second hang-up.

"Check his bedroom," Frannie said. "If it's still morning, he's still in an alcohol-induced coma."

❧

DEVON BARGED INTO his half-brother's room, lit by the morning sun because the shades were still up. Rick lay on his back, his open-mouthed snores all but rattling the windowpane. "Hey."

Not even a muscle twitched. Rick was out cold. Kind of an odd reaction if you'd murdered someone only hours previously. But then again, Devon's bet was still on his father.

He glanced around his brother's room. Bears, Bulls, and Cubs paraphernalia littered most of the shelves and dresser surfaces. Clothes were flung in wrinkled heaps, and it smelled distinctly like dirty socks. He leaned down and shook Rick's shoulder. "Get up."

"Shove it." An arm swatted air.

"Rick, Honey's been murdered." Why pretend it was an accident? Too many people had means, motive, and opportunity. Startled eyes blinked up at him. A moment passed, and Devon watched closely for any expression of guilt.

"Good," his brother said.

Couldn't get colder than that. "Did you do it?"

"I sure thought about it." He yawned and scratched his head. "All the fucking time. What're you still doing here?"

"It's complicated. Where were you last night?"

Rick quirked a brow. "You pretending to be a cop?"

"Just answer me."

He sat up slowly with another yawn. "Down at Joe's. Watching the Bulls play the Mavericks." He wore the same T-shirt as yesterday, which had a dried mustard stain now, but nothing that looked like blood. "How'd she die?"

Devon told him, adding quickly, "When did you get home?"

"One twenty, and no, I didn't see Honey or hear anything suspicious, all right?"

"Did you see *anyone*?"

"Frannie. Crying her eyes out."

"I mean anyone else."

Rick shook his head and rubbed his eyes hard with the heels of his hands. There was a deep scratch on his inner left wrist, scabbed but still fresh-looking. After a beat, he lowered his hands. "Wait a minute. You think Frannie did it?"

Devon let out a mirthless laugh. "She was too busy. How'd you get that?" He pointed to the gouge.

"Picked up some chick last night who had a cat." He glanced at the wound in disgust. "'Bout the only action I got."

"Do you know anyone in this house who'd have a motive to kill Honey?" Besides their father.

Rick's mouth turned down in thought, but he shook his head. "Honey didn't win over any fans with the staff, but it's hard to see one of them offing her."

"You may want to bone up on appropriate phrases for the dead, kid."

Rick rested his back against the mahogany headboard. "And be a hypocrite like you?"

Devon's muscles braced. "Really? How so?"

"Who leaves this"—Rick gestured around his messy room—"because they hate the Wickham name and all it stands for, just to go imitate it all in New York as an Ashby?"

Devon filtered through obscenities, sarcasm, and protest. He shouldn't care what his half-brother thought of him. Hell, Rick was probably right in his own distorted way, because Devon hadn't made any effort to maintain the sibling ties to give him any other point of view. But after hearing versions of this from Frannie and Hannah last night, the accusation was wearing thin. "Now that you're back in the will, you still gonna get a job?"

His brother shrugged. "Don't see a need to."

Devon wandered to the window, taking stock of the busy activity by the cliff. "So your life plan is mooch off Harrison, sleep until noon, and watch sports at Joe's Bar?"

Rick sighed. "Mind leaving? I'm tired of holding this fart in."

Devon turned to face him, folding his arms. "Quit being a smartass. This is serious."

"So's the gas buildup." Rick rubbed his stomach, grinning. "Great having this brotherly chat, though. Thanks for stopping by."

Devon headed toward the door. "Did you eavesdrop on my phone conversation with Dad last night?"

"Hell no. I've got better things to do than listen to you two bicker like old women." Rick threw off the covers. "This is your last warning."

Devon turned the doorknob. "The cops are downstairs interviewing the household. I suggest you clean up quick." He shut the door on the explosive noise and shook his head, trudging to the stairs. Would he have been this crass and spoiled if he'd stayed here? They'd both had privileged upbringings by a cold and distant father, but Devon had fallen far from grace. Nothing like barely living above the poverty line to be motivated to never end up in that vulnerable state again.

"*Ken Tucker cares. He made you, and he's the one who can break you.*" Eric's words yesterday brought him up short. Jesus, he'd hung up on Nicole an hour ago, and hadn't called to explain why yet.

He got as far as yanking out his cell phone when Joseph intercepted him. "Sir, the sergeant is requesting your immediate presence in your father's office. Unfortunately, two housekeepers overheard you threatening Honey in the dining room yesterday morning."

He exhaled wearily and stuffed the phone back. "That didn't take long. Will you check on Frannie? She's not taking this...situation well."

"I was just on my way to do so." The butler gave a half bow. Given Frannie's mood swings and Harrison's tendency to chase the almighty buck, Joseph had often stepped in as the adult who'd consoled Frannie.

Devon spun around. "Joseph, did you know she's on medication?"

A guarded look came over Joseph's face. "Yes, sir."

Of course he'd know. There wasn't much that escaped the gentle butler's notice. "And you know who set the fire." When Joseph remained stoically expressionless, Devon held up a hand. "It's all right. Todd confessed last night."

Without seeming to move a muscle, Joseph physically relaxed. "Yes, sir. I'd overheard him tell a friend he was going to try smoking, and kept a careful eye on his whereabouts Tuesday evening. I was on my way to his wing one last time before retiring when I passed the theater. The fire had started, and by the time I got him out and ran for an extinguisher, it had grown out of control."

"Does my father know any of this?"

"I don't keep secrets from him."

No wonder Harrison had spoken of the event so calmly on Thursday. He'd known all along it wasn't arson.

"Todd doesn't know that Harrison knows," Devon said quietly. "I think it would build character for him to get up the courage and confess. He's agreed to it."

"Very good, sir." Joseph hesitated. "The sergeant…"

"Yeah, I'm going. Thanks, Joseph. For everything you do around here." Without waiting for a reply, Devon trudged down the staircase. How was Eric doing with Westcott? How furious was Nicole? Should he try to call Tucker again? What he wouldn't do to go back in time and spend the night at O'Hare. Or go farther back and never have come to Chicago in the first place. Goddamn good intentions and olive branches—he was a modern-day Don Quixote.

He reached the foyer, nodded to the cop who'd initially told him to remain in the hall, and headed toward his father's office. Yeah, he hadn't pushed Honey, but given his total lack of control over his life, and two witnesses establishing his motive, his stomach roiled ominously.

CHAPTER 18

ONCE HANNAH AND Sean gave their information to the officer, he released them from the foyer crowd with a warning to remain on the premises until further notice. Which was fine—they could still build crates outside. But unless there was a mass exodus of people, bringing the pieces down would be unprofessional and unsafe.

"Let's go find some tools," she murmured to Sean, studying the dismissed servants still loitering. It suddenly struck her that Devon hadn't come back down from carrying his sister. She bit her lip. As heroic and gentle as he'd been with Frannie, Hannah couldn't chance running into him again. She needed time to sort through the mudslide of feelings.

She pointed to a man in overalls—maybe a gardener or mechanic. "Go ask him. I'm going out to the patio to call Walter." She discreetly threaded her way to the back of the house and slipped out onto the flagstones. The air was chilly in the long morning shadows, but it was the grisly reality of the scene a hundred yards away that evoked a full-body shiver.

Swarms of uniforms: cops and EMS worked in clusters... Two men in sport coats with badges around their necks rounded the side of the house, walking toward the cliff. She'd seen enough TV to know they were homicide. If she looked close enough, the mayor and commissioner would probably be traipsing around near the fluttering crime scene tape too. No doubt the Wickham name brought in the big guns.

Everyone was so focused on their work that no one spotted her. Hannah stayed in the shadows and sat on a concrete Roman bench adjacent to the house, partially hidden by the thick limbs of a scarlet maple.

Ignoring the phone clutched in her fingers, Hannah watched the activity in morbid fascination. They were all too far away to hear any discussions, but their expressions were somber, the atmosphere energized. Enough cops ambled to the ledge and peered over that Honey's body must still be down there. Large sections of the lawn had been lined with yellow tape, and uniforms combed each segment of grass, almost blade by blade. One official, carrying a long-lensed camera, stumbled over a tangle of branches from the weeping willow and swiped at them in agitation.

Hannah hugged herself in the chilly breeze, her imagination of the horror below running roughshod over her. The detectives negotiated the stairs slowly and disappeared from view. Naturally the scene was being treated as a homicide. Who killed herself just before marrying the richest man in Chicago?

She drew in a long breath of crisp air and her jumbled thoughts calmed. There was no way Devon murdered Honey, even though Hannah had witnessed the clear hostility between them at the boathouse yesterday. Besides disliking her, what was his motive? And yet, why skulk through hallways looking for a back way out? And why hadn't he left last night? She exhaled slowly and tapped her cell phone screen. The monumental list she needed to accomplish today didn't include obsessing over Devon or spying on the crime scene. She scrolled down to Walter's number.

"How dare you, you son of a bitch!"

Hannah shot to her feet at Harrison's shout. She glanced around wildly. *Oh crap!* Behind the maple, a hand-cranked windowpane stood ajar. *Harrison's office.* Goose bumps skittered along her arms. His tone held the same animosity as yesterday. She sidled to the thick trunk and studied her surroundings again. The warning hadn't carried far enough to capture the attention of the police across the lawn. Blushing at the needless risk but unable to ignore the compulsion, she tiptoed forward, avoiding the few crisp leaves scattered on the ground, until she stood within inches of the window.

"...will have to ask you to leave if there's one more outburst, sir," said an official voice.

"This is my house, Sergeant, so stop with the threats and get back to questioning him."

A pause and a sigh, then: "Mr. Ashby, where were you around nine o'clock last night?"

Hannah tensed in anticipation.

"On a Gulfstream heading to New York."

So he did get on board. She frowned.

"Why nine?" Harrison barked.

"So far that appears to be the last time anyone saw Miss Hartlett."

Silence. Hannah envisioned the officer waiting for permission to go ahead with the questioning from the man truly in charge. His next question was hard to hear, as if he'd moved farther away. "Why are you still in Chicago, then?"

She strained forward.

"I was forced to return."

"Why?"

"A reason beyond my control. But it had nothing to do with Honey."

A longer pause. Her nails bit into her palms, and she flexed her fingers.

"What did you do upon returning to Chicago?" the

sergeant asked.

"I…came back here."

"Why?"

"To bring something back."

Hannah frowned again. None of this made sense.

"So now you're stealing from me? What did you take?" The sound of movement and the sergeant murmuring. "Fine," Harrison shouted. "Just get on with it."

The sergeant cleared his throat. "What item did you return to this residence?"

"I'm not at liberty to elaborate." Devon sounded strained. And very aware of the inadequacies of his answer.

Silence.

"What time did you enter the residence with the item?"

"Just after two."

"Did you see Miss Hartlett or anyone else when you returned?"

Hannah stilled, waiting for the answer. A prolonged pause.

"No."

"Liar!"

"Mr. Wickham, I'm going to have to ask you to leave."

"I want him arrested."

"On what charge, Father? There's no ruling of a homicide. For all we know, she committed suicide."

"Get this son of a bitch out of my house!"

Hannah clapped a hand over her mouth. How could Devon have grown up with this constant animosity?

"Or maybe you killed her after I called you," Devon replied softly, his tone baiting.

Her eyes widened. What conversation could lead to murder?

"I won't even dignify that with an answer."

"Mr. Ashby," the sergeant said, "would you mind—"

"What were you doing hiding behind my garage, then? Still figuring out a way to return my stolen item?"

"Mr. Wick—"

"My Honey is dead!" A tremor encased the last word, followed by an audible inhale and exhale. "You haven't even asked him if he pushed her."

"Seriously?" Devon's voice sounded cool and collected compared to Harrison's shouts. "What was my motive?"

"To pay me back for taking your company."

"Oh, I plan on that, old man, but it'll be a lot more creative than this. Her death saved this family, and you know it, so cut the fake grieving."

"Mr. Ashby, this arguing isn't conducive to our investigation. I'll need you to come downtown and answer the remaining questions."

"What other questions?" Panic threaded his words. "I returned...the item, I fell asleep in my mother's room, I woke up an hour ago. That's *all*."

A fist banged a desk. "You were sneaking off. I saw it with my own eye—"

"Why were you over by the garages?" the sergeant interrupted.

"Because I overheard the staff spreading the news, and didn't want to get caught up in all of this. I'm desperate to get to New York, sir."

Movement appeared in the little window, and Hannah froze. Devon's pale face registered a split second before his gaze landed on her. An expression flashed; if she didn't know better, she'd have labeled it tenderness, or a sense of calm in seeing her again. The impact almost knocked her off her feet. She spun away and hurried across the flagstones, chased by confusion and searing embarrassment at being caught. Lord, if it'd been either of the other men, Moore and Morrow would've spent their last minutes on this project. What had she been thinking?

She slipped through the patio door and wound her way to the foyer. A few staff loitered around, still looking shell-shocked and talking in low tones. The front door opened. One of the homicide detectives walked in. Down the hall, the three men came out of Mr. Wickham's office. Devon argued urgently, palms up, expression fierce as the sergeant nodded and kept his gaze on the tiles before him. On the sergeant's other side, Harrison stalked stiffly, his face an unhealthy crimson. She wrapped her quivering arms around her waist, heartbeat thundering in her ears.

Soon, they were close enough for everyone to hear. The underlying panic was still plain in Devon's voice. "It's imperative I leave at once. I can be available by phone. I can return in a few days."

The detective halted near Hannah and stared at Devon intently.

"Don't let him leave Chicago, Sergeant," Harrison growled. "You'll never see him again."

"You'd love for me to stay—a hostile takeover would be so much easier if I'm tied up with the police. Hell, maybe that's your strategy. Kill her and frame me."

Harrison surged forward, swinging wildly. The sergeant plowed between them, arms spread. Out of nowhere, a handful of officers sped past her toward the threesome, soles slapping the marble, leather holsters creaking. The scuffle was over as fast as it started. Oddly, the detective remained as still as a panther, absorbing every detail of the interaction.

"You bastard," Harrison spat. "If you're so desperate to leave, it'll be my sole purpose on Earth to make sure you stay. Sergeant, I'm pressing charges for whatever it is he stole."

The sergeant glanced at the detective, clearly seeking help. Time seemed to hover as they somehow communicated without speaking. The sergeant turned to Devon. "I'm sorry, son. I'll need you to come to the station."

Alarm flashed across Devon's face. "I didn't *take* anything."

"You're not under arrest. I'll finish questioning you off-property."

"I want him arrested," Harrison ordered, hands still fisted.

"That decision is not up to you," the detective said quietly.

Harrison swung around and glared at the man like this would be his last day on the job. Standing so close to the detective, Hannah's skin seemed to shrink in the effort to turn invisible.

As Devon was led out the door, his gaze latched on to her. Instantly, his mouth softened and he double blinked. Back in the day, it used to be his special Morse code to reassure her of his utter indifference in the face of serious trouble. Not once had she ever believed the bravado. She squeezed her clammy fingers together as he walked out the door, posture ramrod straight, head held high.

CHAPTER 19

A N HOUR LATER, Devon fingered the carved obscenity on the wood table for the hundredth time.

On the way to the Winnetka PD, he'd considered calling a lawyer, just to expedite this waste of time, but Sergeant Wilson had assured him he was free to go, once he answered the same routine questions he'd have been asked back at the mansion. Halting the process while they waited for a lawyer would be more time wasted, so Devon cooperated and kept his replies to a bare minimum. Anything to get the hell on a plane.

The door opened, and he snapped to attention as the sergeant re-entered, holding a file. "Why am I still here? I answered your questions."

"You still haven't told us what you were doing at two in the morning that pertained to returning an item."

Devon clamped down on the urge to blurt out his nephew's name and be done with this shit. During the ride downtown, he'd called Francine to get her permission to revoke his promise, but she hadn't answered. Had he been facing jail time, all bets would have been off, but despite his need to get to Manhattan, hanging out at the PD answering the same questions over and over didn't qualify as enough of a reason to rat out her secret. He'd never forgive himself. "It has nothing to do with Honey's death or my father or his possessions. It was a personal reason. I'm not discussing it further."

"How well did you know Ms. Hartlett?"

Seriously? You guys didn't understand me the other twelve times? "I met her for the first time Thursday evening," he answered tonelessly.

"Was there any animosity between you?"

Was instant distrust animosity? Was finding out she was a fraud after his siblings' inheritance animosity? "No, sir."

"There were two maids—"

"They misunderstood."

The sergeant paused. "Your father was about to marry her next week and disinherit the lot of you."

Devon raised a brow. Guess the police had been digging while he'd sat here with his thumb up his ass. "My father disinherited me when I was eighteen, Sergeant. As for my brother and sister, I have to think their resentment was directed more at my father than Honey."

"What about your nephew?"

His muscles went rigid. "What about him?" he snapped.

"What was his relationship with Miss Hartlett?"

He raised his hands and let them thunk back on the table. "I haven't seen my family in twelve years. I can't answer these questions." Christ, if they were throwing Todd in the mix, he'd have no choice but to give up Frannie's secret to establish his nephew's alibi. He rubbed the tension in his jaw. "Why would an eleven-year-old have anything to do with this?"

The door reopened. A cop young enough to be in high school headed straight for Sergeant Wilson and handed over a single sheet of paper. "Definitely homicide, sir—perp's skin was found under her fingernails," he whispered, but Devon heard it as if it'd been shouted.

Shit. Ricky's damn scratch! Although Harrison had never taken off his overcoat after Joseph told him the news. Devon watched the sergeant for any facial cues, but got nothing.

After reading the sheet for what seemed like an eternity, the sergeant nodded and stuck it in the file. He turned to Devon. "Are you willing to give us a DNA sample?"

He'd seen enough police procedural shows. "You'll need a warrant."

Sergeant Wilson nodded slowly. "Yes, which is why I said 'willing.' Since you want to head out of town, it would work in your favor to let us swab your cheek before you leave the station."

It wasn't worth arguing further. He hadn't killed Honey and hadn't given up Francine's secret. Devon screeched the metal chair away from the table and stood stiffly. Once he gave the requisite swab and found the nearest urinal, he headed out into the afternoon and ordered an Uber.

As the car headed to the mansion, Devon finally pulled up his voicemail. The first was from Nicole, recorded shortly after he'd hung up on her this morning. "It's over, pal. Ring's in the mail."

Devon pressed End and stared out the window. Lake Michigan glinted flat and gray far into the horizon. When he'd walked away from Hannah, it felt as though slivers of glass were lodged in his throat. The entire Greyhound ride, his chest had hurt like a boulder sat on it. That boulder had taken so long to disappear. So fucking long. He waited for the excruciating pressure to come again.

Nothing happened. Probably because he was older now, more in control. And also because Nicole hadn't reacted like Hannah. A detonating nuclear warhead wouldn't cause Nicole to mimic Hannah's devastation.

He knew his fiancée—uh, ex. Groveling or do-overs had the opposite effect. He had to strategize how to negotiate their make up before he called her. She'd listen to facts and reason, not emotional pleas and familial excuses. But frankly, the facts sucked. There was a high probability he'd lose his company, and likely his trust fund. He'd just supplied a DNA sample to rule him out as a murder suspect, and had somehow become ensnared in the epicenter of a combustible family drama.

He studied the gray sky. Her seven words replayed in his head, almost lyrically. No anger. No drama. No resonance in her voice like she was crying... That was so Nicole. The monotone could've been the weather report in the Big Apple: *Sunny and breezy, high of seventy. Pal.*

Maybe he was in shock, like how a car accident victim got up and wandered around the scene while blood gushed from his head. It had to be shock. He literally felt nothing except curiosity. Hanging up on her didn't warrant breaking off the engagement. It guaranteed a hellish backlash the next time they spoke, but canceling the wedding was too dramatic. And Nicole didn't do drama. Had Tucker convinced her the brilliant future she dreamed of could never be attained with a disinherited son, clawing his company from Wickham Corporation's clutches?

Surely she had faith in Devon's abilities. Whenever he hit a crisis, he always resolved it calmly and efficiently, and he was doing so now. Worst-case scenario: if he lost his company, he'd start over with that much more experience and a bigger network. She had more faith in him than this; they were partners with the same temperament and life goal. What had changed?

He reluctantly raised the phone and punched the next message, from Eric. "The meeting was a no-go. Westcott saw me across the dining room and left immediately. I even followed him to the parking lot. All he said was, 'If the CEO can't be bothered to get his ass in here, that's all I need to know about your company.' I don't know what we're gonna do from here, Dev. Call me."

Devon cut the call and tossed the phone on the seat beside him. He leaned against the headrest, weary resignation washing over him. Choosing Frannie and Todd's future had killed his own. The glorious life he'd worked like a demented man to achieve lay in ruins at his feet. On Monday, he'd lose his company to his father.

No. He wasn't going down this easily. He may have seriously messed up any arbitration strategy with his father this morning, but the pressing need to return to Manhattan was gone. If he stayed here, there was a glimmer of a chance he could get his father to listen to him. To find out the motivation behind the takeover. Devon straightened in his seat, inspiration pushing out the defeatist attitude. Time to jump back into the fray.

As he scrolled for Westcott's number, he told the driver, "I've changed my mind. Take me to the Drake Hotel." He didn't need to stop for his overnight bag. The hotel would supply toiletries, and he was wearing the only set of clothes besides the suit he'd worn on Thursday night. It was high time to buy something that didn't make him look as wrinkled as Rick.

He'd give Harrison some space. Tomorrow he'd have a better chance at rational conversation and get to the bottom of this. Rogers Park clearly had something to do with this sudden attack. But then again, the cryptic word *Bryant* still nudged something deep in his memory.

⁓

"NICOLE CALLED OFF the wedding," Devon said into the mouthpiece, rattling the ice in his whisky for emphasis. "Won't answer my calls or texts."

Eric grunted. In the prolonged silence, Devon shifted on the hotel bed so his back was up against the headboard. He waited for the outrage, the platitudes, even a blistering insult about his ex-fiancée... Nothing. "That's it?" he asked in disbelief.

"We're going to have to do some heavy brownnosing to keep Tucker onboard."

"Are you shitting me?"

"What?"

Eric sounded genuinely confused, which ratcheted up Devon's irritation. He gestured with his drink as if his cousin were in the room. "Shouldn't a buddy say something comforting right about now?"

"I would if I thought you were upset."

Tension pulsed through him. "What the hell is that supposed to mean?"

"Aw, never mind." Eric sighed impatiently. "I'm sorry for your loss."

"No. Say whatever it is, goddamn it!"

In the prolonged pause, Devon wiped the condensation off the glass with his thumb; his jaw clenching and unclenching.

"I've said it all before," Eric finally answered. "I saw it coming, and I don't think it's the end of the world, except for how it'll impact our company. And I'd bet a Benjamin you think so too."

Devon let the silence lengthen while he nursed the sting of the words. He hated it when his cousin saw past his bullshit to the shallow man inside. He slammed back the last of the whisky, savoring the burn in his throat. He *thunked* the glass down on the nightstand, hard.

"Are you saying I'm wrong?" Eric asked. "Do I need to alert the Chicago authorities a heartbroken man is locked in his hotel room about to harm himself in some way?"

Devon didn't answer. He wouldn't compound his

superficiality with lies. He *wasn't* heartbroken. The honest-to-God truth? For some reason, he felt lighter and freer than he had in a long, long time. It didn't make sense.

Nicole embodied everything he wanted for his future. She was success-driven and results-oriented, and she didn't stand for drama or emotions. You knew where you stood with her. Until now. Somehow in the last two days, he'd turned into a hothead who'd descended right into the middle of this circus. He never behaved this way in Manhattan, and without the benefit of the doubt, she'd wrapped a tourniquet around their love. But he wasn't *this* Chicago person, and he wasn't one to give up when options were still on the table. "Once I solve this thing with Harrison and get back home, I'll dog her until she listens to reason."

"That's so fucking cold I have no words."

Devon stiffened. "How so?"

"First, it's called apologizing, not listening to reason."

He ignored the condescending tone. "Not with Nicole. But if you're going to get hung up on semantics... I'll *apologize*. Grovel."

"You're only groveling to keep Daddy in Ashby Enterprises. I don't think you ever wanted to marry her. You're so fucked up on how you deal with women, dude. You treat them like they're business deals. Seriously, you should be on one of those talk shows where the audience gets to boo and throw things at you."

"Says the man who rarely goes out on a second date."

Eric snorted. "I ain't ashamed of that stat. I just haven't found the woman who'll keep me intrigued—"

Hannah popped into Devon's mind. Instinctively he tried to substitute Nicole—*she* was the one he wanted—but Hannah remained. Specifically the *ah-ha* look on her face when he'd glanced out the office window this morning. As if she'd finally understood something...or recognized something. And even though whatever it was couldn't be good, there'd been no derision. Devon snapped back to attention at his cousin's raised voice.

"—or can get through an evening without endlessly yakking about herself, or taking selfies, or Tweeting every fucking thought. Just once I'd like to meet someone who's halfway interested in me."

"We shadowboxed around every subject about you. You've never been able to communicate, Devon."

He expelled a long breath and debated grabbing another whisky out of the minibar. "Talk to me about Westcott, besides your cryptic 'no-go' text."

"There's nothing more to say. He's a write-off."

"I left him a message at three this morning letting him know I couldn't make it. I tried to call him twice after I left the police station. I'll keep trying. I know I can sway him."

"Doubtful, Dev. You should've seen his face."

He knocked his head against the headboard several times, hoping to shake loose a foolproof idea. Nothing. "I have to try. How else can we hold the majority of shares?"

"Go ahead. Anything to keep the company." Eric let out a harsh sigh. "Things are so fucked up."

"What did you find out about Rogers Park?"

"Nothing to explain why your father would steal your company to get his hands on it. Sounds to me like this really is paternal revenge."

Devon shook his head, frustration flooding through him. "Doesn't wash."

His cousin sighed. "I knew you'd say that. I already told Kevin to keep digging. I'll check email again when we're off."

"Take a break." Devon tried to lighten his tone.

"Any hot plans?"

"Still at the office."

"On a Saturday night?"

"This from the man drinking alone in his hotel room." They shared a bitter laugh and hung up.

Devon immediately dialed Westcott, not expecting an answer and not getting one.

He disconnected the call, tossed the phone on the bed, and scrubbed his face. He was finally moving through the numbness. Disgust and self-loathing threatened to drown him in a black rage. He'd chosen family over business, and look where it'd gotten him. Hell, each decision at every turn was catastrophically wrong—starting with coming to the damn birthday party in the first place.

He gazed around the quiet, luxurious room, then down at his watch. Just after nine. The night stretched endless and bleak before him. He swung his legs off the bed. Damn if he'd sit here drinking minibar whisky and playing the "if only" game. He needed to fix this shitstorm.

CHAPTER 20

"WHAT ABOUT THIS one?" Hannah swiped her cell phone screen and showed her great-aunt another picture. "Two bedrooms, one bath, a living room, and kitchenette. Exactly what we have now. It's perfectly adequate, and the neighbors seemed quiet."

"Those walls are dreary."

"We can paint them."

"*Humph.* Next."

Mentally rolling her eyes, Hannah read off the next description and swiped to the corresponding pictures. Her aunt stopped petting Boots to squint at the screen for a long moment. The oxygen tank hissed steadily at her side. She pursed her lips and shook her head. "Next."

"But it's five minutes away. You could still go to North Shore Baptist Church and lunch with the girls at Svea's."

Aunt Milly shook her head. "Next."

Hannah slumped in defeat. "These were the only two I toured." After the morning from hell, she'd banged these out and gone to the office to fix the Matisse. It was after nine o'clock, and the only part of the day she'd enjoyed had been luxuriating in the bath half an hour ago.

Aunt Milly patted her hand. "We'll find a place." She adjusted her nasal tubing and peered at the tank. "Is this thing on? I feel breathless."

"It's working fine." Hannah didn't look up from the cell phone. "I think we're both just nervous about moving." She clicked out of her photo files and the apartment-finder app and checked her email, skimming through listings Gretch had searched. The first two were in sketchier neighborhoods than this one. The next five were more than they could afford.

As much as her aunt's stubbornness drove her crazy, a secret part of Hannah agreed with her. These places were a lateral move, and she couldn't bear the thought of living on the fringes of safety anymore: the late-night sirens, the gunshots in the distance—infrequent, but still.

She rubbed her exhausted eyes. Reality finally weighed her down like an anchor. Walter would have to buy her out of their partnership. The thought made her sick to her stomach, but it was the only way to get out of this mess.

Right now, rent, utilities, and groceries came from three puny sources: the measly salary she paid herself, along with Aunt Milly's Social Security and her deceased husband's pension. Her great-aunt's funds by themselves would've landed her in a state nursing home long ago had Hannah not come over one day when her aunt complained about the lights not working. Even though this apartment was cheap, it had been evident from the pile of red-stickered bills that her aunt could no longer afford to live here. That was four years ago.

At the time, Hannah had been working at Mannix Restoration Lab, enjoying Internet-dating, membership at an exclusive gym, and living in an upscale one-bedroom. All her wages had gone into supporting her carefree lifestyle, so she'd had none to give her aunt. Once she'd realized the extent of her aunt's predicament, though, it was a no-brainer to move into the smaller of the two bedrooms. A month later, all the back bills were paid, and she'd begun to dream of owning her own restoration company with the money she'd been able to save.

When another Mannix employee, Walter Morrow, mentioned a similar goal, it took them two years to gather the capital, and weekends of scouring the city for a cheap but respectable place. Then they'd stalked eBay and going-out-of-business art and hobby shops for supplies before finally opening Moore and Morrow. They'd had enough clients defect from their former employer, including a few projects from the Art Institute, to squeak by with Gretch and Bernice the first year.

After their company was splashed all over the national news for the Rubens forgeries, business had exploded. Wealthy art collectors in general were insecure, and prone to both buyer's remorse and a healthy sense of paranoia. Many repeat clients suddenly brought in their newest purchase with its provenance for an authenticity re-inspection.

Hannah had no idea whether Walter had the funds to buy her share of the business. If he didn't, she'd have to find another investor. It was the only way Aunt Milly and she could afford an apartment that accepted sixteen-year-old, obese cats and was in a decent neighborhood close to her great-aunt's beloved church.

A heavy rap on the door echoed through the tiny living room. All three of them jerked, and Boots scrambled off her aunt's lap, waddling down the short hall that led to the bedrooms. Hannah frowned at the door. She knew Gretch's knock, and her aunt's friends were probably in bed.

"Who would visit at this hour?" Aunt Milly fumbled with her oxygen tank, a sure sign her anxiety was spiking. Hannah hurried over and peered through the cloudy peephole. Every nerve ending flared to life.

Devon leaned against the wall, darkly pensive in the dim hallway.

"Who is it, dear?"

"It's...an old friend," she said, the sudden tremble in her fingers rattling the chain. She paused and got a grip on herself. If her aunt clued in that the friend was Devon, aka Ashby Enterprises, the woman would sacrifice her ability to breathe just to bean him with her tank. After managing to release the chain and flip the three deadbolts, Hannah arranged her expression into cool detachment and cracked open the door. "Hi."

He straightened and stared at her as if he'd come to the wrong apartment. "Your hair's down." Her hand flew to the riot of curls, instinctively trying to smooth them down. "Don't," he murmured. His eyes, all the more blue because of the fitted cobalt shirt, held banked heat. His black hair was damp, the tips slightly curly, and he wore jeans that hugged his slim hips and outlined the long muscles of his thighs.

She hated the melty feeling flowing through her. This man was responsible for her having to sell her partnership. She gazed back poker-faced until she'd channeled enough anger. "How do you know where I live?" she asked curtly. If he had a printout of all the residents' private information, she'd slam the door in his face.

A corner of his luscious mouth lifted. "You spat out your address loud and clear last night." He jerked his head in the direction of the community center.

She had no recollection of that. Shouting, yes. Telling him where she lived? What had she been thinking?

He held up a bottle of wine. "May I come in?" he asked softly, with that mesmerizingly deep gaze she used to think made her special.

"Why?" she asked. He flinched like she'd slapped

him. "I mean…" She inhaled, her insides quivering. "Why are you here?"

He hesitated, and his sudden wariness startled her. "I had to see you." His solemn words and the vulnerability that flashed across his face punched her chest. This wasn't even remotely the hard-driving executive. He looked miserable. Lonely. Maybe without that forceful personality, she could sway him not to destroy so many lives. But it was imperative her aunt didn't find out who he was. This was going to be tricky.

She mutely opened the door and stood aside. He crossed the threshold; the scent of spicy aftershave and clean skin wafting past. Her knees almost gave out. *For the love of God, he's engaged! And the corporate enemy.*

She bolted the door and glanced at her aunt, who sat rigidly on the sofa as if she expected him to whip out a gun. "Aunt Milly, this is…an art dealer, David Ryder." He stiffened. "David"—she threw him a look of warning—"this is my great-aunt, Milly Seaver."

His beautiful eyebrows knitted in confusion. Seconds passed that felt like eternity. Finally he turned and nodded stiffly. "It's nice to meet you."

Her aunt squinted, and Hannah held her breath. Aunt Milly had met teenaged Devon once, and adult Devon sported many similar facial features as his mother. "An art dealer? What could you possibly want to talk to Hannah about at this hour, young man?"

"Aunt Milly!" Hannah turned to Devon, heat suffusing her cheeks. "It's…been a difficult night," she said softly. "We're looking for apartments."

"Oh." The quiet syllable held full understanding. He raised the bottle. "Would you care for some wine, ma'am?"

"She shouldn't drink," Hannah murmured.

"I'm not deaf!"

Yep, talking to Devon about the teardown would

definitely be a problem. "We can go out somewhere..." Hannah gestured helplessly in the direction of downtown.

"Don't bother," her aunt huffed. "I'm not blind, either. I'm obviously in the way."

"Oh, Aunt Milly, he's a *friend*. We just don't want to disturb you." It was no use. The old woman clutched the handle of the oxygen tank and began to haul herself off the sofa. Devon stepped forward, and Hannah grabbed his sleeve, shaking her head. Good hearing and great pride—those were her aunt's assets. Even as David Ryder, if Devon tried to help her off the sofa, he was liable to get a smack upside the head. Besides, when Aunt Milly got in one of her moods, even winning the Publishers Clearing House Sweepstakes wouldn't mollify her. "Art dealer," she muttered as she hobbled down the hall.

Devon wouldn't appreciate that, as slow as she walked, this was actually a sprint. Hannah bit her lip and stared after her. She'd go check her aunt's breathing and blood pressure in a few minutes. "Good night, Aunt Milly," she called.

The bedroom door banged closed.

She sighed. "Guess I didn't fool her. It's strange she didn't try her hapkido ninja moves on you, though." She glanced back in amusement and froze. She wore her ratty aqua bathrobe and the fuzzy bunny slippers with one of the ears torn off, all of which he was perusing at leisure.

"Niemen's?" he asked, the laugh lines around his eyes deepening. He slowly scanned back up, his gaze landing on her untamable hair. A muscle flexed along his jaw.

She wanted to bunch the thick strands into a tight twirl, but her hands refused to leave her sides. *Stop staring at me like that!*

He sobered. "What's that look for?"

"What look?"

He shifted his weight and tapped the bottle against his thigh. "Should I leave?"

She shook her head, forcing her shoulders to relax. "It's been a difficult day. And we rarely get a visitor this late." She smiled stiffly. "I'm still trying to remember giving you my address."

"I remember everything you've ever said, Hannah."

The rich undercurrent in his tone sent tingles through her. Why was he acting like this? He had a fiancée.

She frowned. "This is just a friendly drink, right?"

His eyes widened. "Of course."

He seemed so surprised that she wanted to drown in embarrassment. Had she imagined the attraction? She fluttered her hand toward the kitchen, trying to redirect his attention away from her flaming face. "There's a corkscrew in the drawer next to the sink, and juice glasses on the shelf above. Make yourself at home. I'll go change real quick."

He snorted a short laugh. "I've seen you naked, Han. I can handle the bathrobe." Maybe to prove his indifference, he walked off, all three feet, into the center of the living room and spun in a slow circle, absorbing her aunt's decor.

Hannah tried to see it from his wealthy eyes. The hand-crocheted afghan draped across the powder-blue sateen sofa with butt dents; a faux-Tiffany lamp on the card table in the corner, where her laptop screensaver displayed Renoir's *Dance in the City*; faded photographs in tarnished frames on every available surface; lace curtains, dusty with age. His gaze landed to her left and stayed. She didn't need to turn. He'd found the bookcase crowded with tchotchkes. Porcelain Dresden dolls, miniature spoons, ashtrays from national parks—Aunt

Milly's prized collections occupied every shelf. Quite a change after the first editions library.

She lifted her chin.

"Nice digs." He didn't sound facetious as he took in everything again. "And it sure beats a boring hotel room. Thanks."

She exhaled softly. "Have a seat. I'll be right back."

He nodded and headed into the kitchen. His stiff walk betrayed how ill at ease he really was. She bit her lip, her bunny slippers making scuffing noises on the beige carpet. He'd been arrested this morning and was still in Chicago tonight. What had he been through today to warrant that glimpse of vulnerability in the doorway? And how on earth could she get past her mind-melting attraction to convince a corporate shark to leave them all alone?

CHAPTER 21

GREAT TIMING, DEV. Invading her home when she'd clearly been dealing with the fallout from his company's project. As Hannah knocked faintly on her aunt's door, he twisted the corkscrew a final time and yanked with pent-up vigor. He should make an excuse and leave. And yet for the life of him he couldn't bear it. He'd been in the fight of his life since his birthday. He just needed this moment, needed her. And he needed to figure out why, with his world crashing down around him, she hadn't left his thoughts for very long all day.

They'd grown up to be totally incompatible, given her idealistic nature and passion for old paintings. He understood P&L statements and boardroom politics, and frankly he had no patience for art of any kind—something Nicole could never understand. It reminded him of his father's love of possessions over family. Even worse, it reminded him of his happy childhood, touring through art museums with his mom and Frannie. And Devon didn't look back.

Two long swallows of expensive Bordeaux from a juice glass gave him the courage to return to the doll-sized living room and wait. He placed the bottle and her filled glass on the cocktail table and wandered slowly, because there was so much to see. The place held a charm he couldn't pinpoint. Kitschy for sure, but somehow refreshing and unpretentious. Nothing of value, no one to impress, just sentimental treasures—he liked that. And he especially liked how the place smelled of Hannah: peaches and vanilla. And old-lady hairspray.

Wandering over to a round side table crowded with framed photos, he perused Aunt Milly's younger years. He held only a vague memory of the woman, but then again, his life had been one big absorption of anything and everything Hannah. Or fighting with his father until he wanted to choke the bastard. He sipped his wine. Truth be told, he'd probably been a little shit at eighteen.

He moved on to the card table with neat colored files and a laptop—Hannah's, obviously, given the screensaver. A ceramic picture frame was on the window ledge, almost hidden behind the laptop's open screen. He brought it into the light, and his heart skipped off beat. Hannah at eighteen, hair wild and free like tonight, sitting on his lap with her head cocked. Even now, her dimpled smile took his breath away.

He lowered himself into the ladder-back chair, memories flooding back. It'd been spring break. They'd stayed in town because of her waitressing job, and that day they'd gone to the zoo. The afternoon had been clear and beautiful, and they'd been in that dumb, teenagers-in-love period where they weren't as interested in seeking out animals as finding hidden alcoves to make out in. This picture had been taken on the park bench outside the monkey pavilion. It was the first time he'd said "I love you."

He peered at the photograph closely and smiled. Yep, you could still make out her red-rimmed eyes. A professional photographer roaming the grounds had dogged them throughout the day, and they'd finally sat for this. Devon had purchased the picture and this silly gorilla frame for her.

Nostalgia partnered with loss as he traced the photo

with his thumb. Her sweetness in high school had blossomed into grace, and innate generosity in the face of his blow-off in the library yesterday and Honey's snub at the boathouse. She'd been admirably modest talking about her achievements. In Manhattan, you blew your own horn—loudly. He shouldn't be surprised the Hannah he'd known had grown up to put herself through college, excel at her passion as a restorer, and care for her aunt with the same selflessness as when her mom had those depressive attacks.

Her naivety and dreaminess might annoy him to hell and back, but it was what had made her special. She didn't hold all this balled-up negativity inside. Being with her was like stepping into sunshine after weeks of rain.

The love he once held for her ignited fiercely in his chest, and he rubbed it as if he had heartburn. Christ, they'd been so innocent. The drama of their lives summed up by a catastrophic test score for her or losing a baseball game for him. Their passion had been off the charts, and their breakup had crippled him so severely, the only way to survive had been to decide never to look into the past again.

He put the picture back on the ledge, bumping the laptop in the process. The screensaver vanished, and a *Tribune* page filled the screen. *After weeks of investigation, Winnetka PD have ruled the death of Francesca Wickham a suicide...*

Devon stood so abruptly the chair thumped onto the carpet. He glanced behind him, listening. The only sounds were outside—repetitive bass from loud music down the block and a car alarm blaring in the distance. He righted the chair but remained standing, reading the entire article. His pulse pounded erratically at the lies, and the shock of finding this on her computer. Why would she Google his mother's death?

"I hope none of my neighbors saw you in the hall," she said from behind. He spun around, blocking the screen. "Especially old Mrs. Beckenstein. She owns a Glock." She flashed him a quick smile, dimple and all, and reached for her juice glass. "Cheers."

He watched her sip, still trying to pull himself together. She'd left her hair down and still wore those ridiculous bunny slippers, but had thrown on gray sweats and a well-worn men's white button-down. Somewhere in her past, she'd been in an intimate enough relationship to hang on to that shirt. Jealousy pumped hotly through his veins.

"What're you doing in my office?" Her dimple flashed again.

Unable to form words, he stepped sideways. Within seconds, her smile morphed into wide-eyed, red-faced dread. It helped feed his outrage. "Why?" he rasped.

Her mouth opened, but nothing came out. The wheels were spinning, though; he could see her frantic attempt to explain away something that was so obviously none of her business. "I'm so sorry, Dev. Gretch, my friend from last night, was curious about"—she nodded to the screen—"it."

"You're referring to my mother's murder as *it*?"

If anything, she blushed harder. "I figured saying either murder or suicide would set you off."

"Down at the boathouse, I could tell you thought it was suicide, too."

She held the little glass in both hands and shook her head. "I was never sure. But Aunt Milly knew your mom, and remembered the event."

His jaw dropped. "What did she say?"

"That it couldn't possibly have been suicide. Your mother loved you both too much."

He hadn't known his shoulders were so rigid until they relaxed with the same fatigue as when he worked out at the gym. "I knew I liked your aunt," he said lightly.

Hannah took a deep breath. He was pretty sure she wasn't wearing a bra, given the miniature peaks tenting the front of the oversized shirt. The tip of her pink tongue wet her lips and disappeared. Irritated as he was, blood dumped straight to his groin. He wanted to bend her over the cocktail table, slip down those sweats, and take her in one thrust. He'd never wanted Nicole with this kind of primitive lust. Sweat broke out on his forehead.

Her lips shaped words, and he dragged his mind out of the gutter. "—of our concern, and I'm sorry."

He nodded and finished his wine in one gulp. He would've walked over to the cocktail table and re-poured in a heartbeat except for two insurmountable problems: he didn't trust himself to get that close to her right now, and he sure as shit couldn't hold the bottle steady. His insides still buzzed from the jolt of reading the lies in that article. He never looked back, and yet this trip kept forcing him to do it. He'd thought more about his mother's death these last few days than in all the years since he'd left.

"Well," she said. "So much for me owning all the moral outrage tonight." She grinned, and he tried hard not to stare at that sweet mouth. Rampant nostalgia now fire-hosed through his system.

He scraped a hand through his hair. Coming here was a huge mistake—one of the biggest in the string of mistakes these last three days. Seeing her with her hair down and that picture of the zoo... It was as if twelve years hadn't passed at all.

His engagement had ended only hours ago; he should be morose and stone-faced drunk by now, yet he couldn't stop thinking about Hannah. Worse, wondering whether they had any kind of chance. They were complete opposites; his ladder of success required a partner with the same goals. He needed Nicole and the life they'd been building in Manhattan.

Grasping at a lifeline, he glanced at the screen again and sobered immediately. "I've never read any newspaper accounts about it before," he admitted.

"There were quite a few. They all back up your father's account."

That was the bucket of ice water he needed. "Why am I not surprised?"

She curled her hair behind her ear, and it bounced back out. "It's just...hard to believe your father could wield so much power over an investigation."

"Really?" He hardly recognized his harsh tone. "'Cause I spent a good chunk of today with Winnetka's finest."

Those breasts rose and fell sharply again. "What...happened down there?"

Evasive tactics filled his mind, but the memory of her expression from that little window in his father's office drove them off. He owed her, at the very least, for keeping him sane today. "Let's sit down," he said abruptly, and waited for her to get situated on the sofa before he claimed a seat next to her. But not too close.

He refilled his glass and topped hers off quickly, before peaches wafted his way. He used to hold her in his arms and just breathe in. No matter how crappy the day, or how intense the rage after a fight with Harrison, the combination of her optimism and the warm scent had calmed the beast within. He set the bottle down and inhaled. His shoulder blades settled into the sofa cushion right on cue. At her questioning glance, he bottom-lined the visit to the station in one sentence, adding the skin found under Honey's nails and his DNA swab. "I'm sure everyone in the household will be tested in the next few days."

"Your father seemed convinced it was you."

"By the look on your face this morning, you did too." Her expression hardened; she was obviously recalling the moment he'd slipped past her. "How can I convince you I had nothing to do with Honey's death?"

"I should think you'd be more concerned with convincing your father."

"I stopped trying that when I was nine."

Her index finger twirled a corkscrew curl, and again envy flash-banged through him. To lean in a few degrees and touch that hair... "Why did you come back to Chicago last night, Dev?"

He blinked. Swallowed. The indirect answer slipped out as smoothly as this morning. "To return something."

"Yes. It wasn't anything of your father's, yet you specifically brought it back to his house," she parroted monotonously, as if reciting a boring poem. "At two in the morning. You can understand why anyone hearing that would be confused."

Shit. That did sound damn suspicious.

A dimple shadowed her cheek. "Still avoiding talking about yourself, I see."

Instead of replying, he swigged his wine with one hand and snagged a strand of her hair with the other. He couldn't help it. She gulped oxygen through parted lips. They both watched the coil straighten as his fingers slowly slid down. He released his grasp, and it sprang back into a spiral. "It's still like satin," he murmured, meeting her sea-green eyes. They looked both vulnerable and guarded.

If he were even half a man, he'd get up right now and leave. He shouldn't be here. This was really, really stupid. And her aunt was thirty feet away, in an old apartment that no doubt had paper-thin walls. Compulsively, he reached for the strand again, captivated by the feel of it. Nicole's hair was short, stylish, and stiffly unforgiving. He swallowed more wine. "Ever have one of those days where nothing went right?"

"Yeah," she whispered.

The sadness in the word drilled through him.

He meant to say, "Me too." He meant to let the curl slip through his fingers. For some reason, he gently tugged it instead, forcing her face an inch closer. He leaned in and brushed open lips across hers, the barest of contact, catching the whispery hitch of her gasp. He backed off, slumping against the cushions, trying for the nonchalance he'd faked when she'd announced she was getting dressed. *Oscar contender.*

"How much longer will you be working for Harrison?" he asked in a perfectly normal voice, hyperaware of her knee a millimeter from his.

She blinked like she'd just awoken, and gulped some wine. Her hand trembled. "Depends on the extent of the damage. We should have an estimate by the end of next week." Her tone was professional and automatic, as if she'd been asked so often, she morphed right into the restoration manager role.

An uncomfortable moment of silence passed.

She trailed a finger around the rim of her glass. Her plump lower lip disappeared beneath her front teeth, then popped back out. "So I guess you're leaving for New York tomorrow?"

"Nope."

"Oh." She frowned.

And that topic was finished. He should probably tell her about Nicole, the reason he was suddenly in no hurry to race away from Chicago, but the words didn't come. He couldn't bear the emotional quicksand. Christ, he'd never felt so ill at ease around a woman, and this was *Hannah.* The girl who knew his boyhood secrets and dreams and how hard life had been in that house. He searched his frazzled mind, desperate for something witty to say. He wiped perspiration from his upper lip. "I checked in to the Drake, though. The mansion's way too small for egos the size of my father's and mine."

"I don't think you have a big ego, Devon. I never did."

His stomach flip-flopped at the gentleness in her eyes. Sweet Hannah. Instinctively he reached for her again, but she held up a palm.

"I...can't do that to your fiancée."

"She broke it off this morning."

They sat with that bomb between them for a while. Her finger orbited the glass a few more times. "Do you want to talk about it?" she finally asked.

"Nope."

Something died out in her eyes. "I didn't think so." She sighed. The tip of her tongue wet her lips again. He swallowed dust. "Remember when nothing was awkward between us?" she whispered.

Yes. He did. That was the problem. He stood at some kind of abyss and had never wanted to jump so badly in his life. He slid the glass from her grasp and clunked it blindly on the cocktail table alongside his. "Christ, Hannah, you still have this crazy hold over me."

He leaned in slowly, giving her ample time to throw up a red flag. Instead, her pupils dilated as she inhaled shallowly through barely parted lips. He sifted both hands through that amazing hair and cupped her head. Her eyes fluttered closed. And then he was kissing her, thoroughly, impatiently, sweeping his tongue along the seam of her lips.

She moaned softly as she let him in, and the sound rushed more blood to his groin. *Hannah.* She tasted of wine and a flavor so uniquely her. In high school, she'd been an exceptional kisser, and they'd spent hours perfecting their rhythm. But this woman—the slow, searching tease of her lips—shattered him. The longer they kissed, the more sparks reignited a blaze he hadn't felt in twelve years. He broke off raggedly, sliding his mouth along the slant of her cheekbone, the curve of her neck, the quivering hollow at the base of her throat. He wanted to drown in her peach scent.

She murmured his name, her palms sweeping up his shoulders and caressing his back. He was so far gone that everywhere she touched fed his hunger for more of her, dissolved his thin grasp of control.

He returned to her mouth in desperation and angled deeper, savoring her sweetness. At the tiniest pressure from her leaning in, he clasped her waist and lay back on the lumpy bottom cushion. Her satin hair cascaded like rain, forming a shelter around them, and the weight of her breasts pressed into his chest. She definitely wasn't wearing a bra. He groaned his appreciation and his balls tightened. In the far reaches of his memory, the image of her wanton willingness emerged. How her body flowed like an undulating wave under him; her fingers exploring, lips and tongue tasting, sighs and moans directing him where to linger. For so long, sex had been a silent, perfunctory task.

He skimmed his palms under the tails of her loose shirt, and caressed the smooth arch at the small of her back. Rather than feed the natural instinct to slide his fingertips downward, under the elastic of her sweats and panties, he languidly traced her spine up to her shoulder blades, filling his senses with all the scented, bare skin. He gently raked her back with his fingernails.

She broke the kiss with a soft *aaah*.

"I remember how you crave back scratches," he muttered, grinning, and treated her to a couple more swipes. She smiled blissfully after each one, her lips swollen, her eyes unfocused. He was struck with a sense of coming home, his heart suddenly so large and full it fluttered off rhythm. "I need you," he whispered urgently, primitive lust mainlining through his veins. He slipped beneath the elastic, gripped her bare ass, and ground her pelvis into his, rotating his hips.

Her breath caught. "Stop," she whispered, and he froze. The moment suspended as those liquid emerald eyes searched his. Their soft pants mingled. His arousal pulsed. She squirmed her beautiful ass out of his grip. "We shouldn't be doing this."

Of course. Her aunt was in the next room. He squeezed out a breath; his hard-on straining in outrage. She grabbed a large section of her hair and struggled off him. He hid his wince, hoisting her clear of sensitive areas. "What do you want to do?" His voice was hoarse; he cleared his throat roughly.

"I don't know." She sounded as breathless as he felt. "Talk?" She scooted back, claiming the far side of the sofa, and curled a leg underneath her. He almost smiled. She looked as frustrated as he felt.

He sat up with a half groan, half laugh. "It's like we're teenagers again."

"Adults talk."

"Not when they could be doing something else." He didn't bother to hide how insanely he needed her, and a matching fire flickered in her dark eyes. For a second, she wavered, her lips parting. Every muscle in his body stilled. Then she shook her head, the sexual light in her gaze fading.

"I'd like to talk about you for once. Please, Devon."

Trading the one thing he wanted to do for the one thing he despised drained some of the uncontrollable desire careening through his bloodstream. He tried for a good-natured smile. "All right, shoot."

"Why *did* you come back last night?"

Well, shit. He rubbed his face, debating his options. Did it matter if she knew of his stealthy return? Would telling her ever affect his sister and the custody case? Would it get them back to kissing faster? Maybe back to the Drake?

"Tell me," she whispered, and he knew how badly he'd fallen for her again, because out came the sordid story of the plane, and an eleven-year-old hiding in the head, and even the little guy's drive on the dark suburban streets.

She gasped in surprise or shuddered in horror in all the right places, and before he knew it, he'd launched into his sister's divorce proceedings and her jerkwad of a husband and the unfit-mother claims she fought.

"You could've told your father," Hannah pointed out. "He doesn't want to lose his grandson. Besides, he's the most powerful man in Chicago. I can't believe Frannie's even remotely afraid of losing custody."

He fought the scowl and lost. "First of all, it was Frannie's secret to tell, and secondly, I'm not surprised she kept it from him. He's old-school—survival of the fittest. He'll make sure he has rights to see his grandson, which undoubtedly will never come into question, since Todd's still in the will and my brother-in-law's a greedy sonofabitch. But Harrison doesn't stick up for his kids— never has."

"That doesn't make sense."

He shrugged. "Maybe he thought that's how we'd grow up strong."

She bit her lip and leaned against the back cushion, looking as sweet and fresh as if those twelve years had never happened. He had to be getting old to be drowning in teenage reminiscing like this.

"I know he treated you like that," she said, "but I don't remember you telling me he'd ever done anything cruel to Frannie."

She had him there. His father hadn't doted on Frannie, but in keeping with the grand lie that their mother had committed suicide, he'd been carefully affectionate around Frannie, as if her lapse into childhood depression and the emotionally unbalanced teen years might trigger the family suicide gene. Hence Harrison forcing her to live under his roof now, through the turbulent divorce. It was all such a fucked-up ruse. Now that Devon was sticking around Chicago, he'd double his efforts to help her gain independence.

Hannah reached for their glasses. Not the direction he wanted to go, but at least one of them had a level head. Her fingers still trembled, though, and knocked his empty glass onto the carpet beside him. Muttering an oath, she leaned down and snatched it, her heavy hair landing in his lap. He flashed back to her ministering to his needs so enthusiastically in high school, and his cock stiffened further.

All too soon she straightened up. In a heartbeat, she was in the kitchen. He leaned back, closing his eyes and breathing hard. His lips still pulsed from her kisses; her peach scent had somehow transferred onto him. He should probably call it a night, because this—being with her, smelling of her—was torture. Scuffing slipper footsteps neared, and then the sofa cushion shifted. More peach scent.

"I really don't know how to segue into this or even how to say it in corporate terms, but is there anything I can do to persuade you not to tear down our neighborhood?"

Shit. Even further in the wrong direction. He opened his eyes and looked over wearily. "I can't look for another property, Hannah. I bought this one."

"You're wealthy. Can't you just walk away from this?"

And there it was. Hannah the idealist. As a partner in her own company, it was stupefying she hadn't gone out of business. He searched for words that would preserve the tentative relationship they'd built tonight. "The art you restore looks nothing like the crap that's brought in, right?" She nodded. "So you of all people know not everything is what it seems on the surface."

A guarded look came over her face. "Yes?"

"We took an unprecedented risk because the property came at a dirt-cheap price and construction costs are still down."

"But if you had any idea of the hardships—"

"Enough with the hardships, Hannah," he snapped. She recoiled, and he held up a palm. "Sorry. I meant— I'm right there with you. Even before I landed in Chicago, I knew this development had a fifty-fifty chance of bankrupting us. It's fractured my board. And you stood outside my father's door yesterday—you must've heard he's about to swallow up my company. Hell, why are we even having this discussion? I won't be tearing down Rogers Park—*he* will."

She studied him, poker-faced. "What will you do if he takes your company?"

"Get back up and start over." *With a fucking vengeance.* Wallowing in pity was as abhorrent as wallowing in the past.

Silence descended, which he didn't mind. He'd made his point, the topic was over, and he could study her openly as she frowned at the threadbare carpet. Her hair was a tangled, erotic mess, high color stained her cheeks, and when she bit her kiss-swollen bottom lip, his balls tightened again, painfully this time. *Hurry up and process this, because you're going back to the Drake with me.*

"Just so you know," she said, "there's a ninety-nine percent chance I'll have to sell my half of the partnership to afford a two-bedroom someplace else."

Lust drained from him. Wine soured in his stomach. Her partnership? "Two-bedrooms aren't *that* expensive."

She hugged her knee, a gesture she used to do when she was upset and had to confront him instead of waving it away in that dreamy way of hers. "The rent we pay here is only comparable to places in unsafe neighborhoods or way too far of a commute."

"But surely you can afford an upgrade from"—he swept a hand toward the window—"this."

She shook her head. "It has to be this inexpensive to make ends meet. Aunt Milly never took out long-term health insurance, so her ongoing osteoporosis and emphysema have drained most of my savings."

"That's what Medicare is for."

"Only if she were to go to the hospital for three consecutive days, and she hasn't for over a year. So all the home health costs for her personal care or to drive her to physicians aren't covered. Nor is twenty percent of her medications, and those are freaking highway robbery."

He could find fifty ways to problem-solve this. With Herculean effort, he kept the frustration off his face, and asked in an even tone, "What about a nursing home?"

"First of all," she said, clearly mimicking him, "she's my great-aunt, and I would never do that to her. Second, she made me promise never to admit her, just in case I had any nefarious ideas. And third, that's even more out-of-pocket expense than home health."

Aside from admiring her long, elegant fingers as she ticked her points off, he didn't appreciate her condescending tone. "Not if Medicaid pays."

"She doesn't qualify."

He rubbed his jaw. "Then pay yourself more of a salary."

She frowned at his clipped response. "Walter and I structured a profit-sharing plan with the bank before her health progressed to this stage. We receive an adequate salary until our fiscal year ends and our profit sharing kicks in. But even then, the bank makes sure a good portion of the profits are kept in retained earnings. I can't touch that."

He was trying so hard to remain patient. He waited a beat and gestured with his palm. "You've got long- and short-term bank loans? You know the difference, right?"

She hugged her knee tighter. "I'm not an imbecile. I do own my own company."

He swallowed the retort. "Then increase your short-term capital loan and give yourself a raise that way."

"We signed a personal guarantee to shave off a half-percentage poi—"

"I know what a personal guarantee is and what it does," he snapped. His entire trust fund was about to vanish because of one.

Her chin tilted. "Then you know we're personally responsible for the *entire* debt if there's any default or business failure. There's no way I'm going to risk taking out more money; it's a slippery slope." She spread her hands. "I've thought it all through, Devon. The only way I can afford her increasing healthcare costs and a nice two-bedroom is to cash out of Moore and Morrow."

He exhaled harshly, owning the heartache displayed across her face. The differences between him and Harrison were dwindling. He had the same ability to demolish loved ones, in that same flippant manner. How could he answer her without sounding like Harrison? He fortified himself with a deep breath, leaned in, and cupped her cheek. "I *am* sorry, Hannah. I never meant to hurt you."

A sad smile appeared. "Which time?"

He should have seen it coming, but the lobbed grenade stunned him silent. So they were going back to that night after all. The quick, emotionless apology at lunch yesterday would not suffice, which was no surprise. He'd have to descend into feelings and heartache and relive the teenage tragedy that haunted him still. He slid his hand away and rubbed his mouth.

"Forget I said that," she said hastily.

How like her, running from confrontation.

"Oh no," he said emphatically, "it's time to clear the air." *Past time to let that night die.* He swallowed hard. "In that moment...on your mom's doorstep...the stuff I said...the solution to run away...was so obviously the right choice to me, it never occurred to me you'd say no." *Christ, that was lame.*

"You gave me two impossible choices."

A sliver of defensiveness knifed through him. "I offered to marry you, Hannah. That sounds like a decent choice to me."

"Only if I left my dying mother. You wouldn't wait. And you wanted to haul me off to a strange place when neither of us had money... What kind of choice was that?"

He sighed and raked his hair. "I was fueled by hate that night. I had to get out of here. And why *wouldn't* I think you'd go? All you did was talk about how much you couldn't stand your mom too. Why not both of us get the hell out of Dodge?"

She studied him like he was deranged. "Yeah, I bitched about her when she was healthy. I was a teen. But she was still my mom! And then *bang*, she gets cancer, and *bang*, you hold out two bus tickets. You knew she didn't have much longer. You could've gotten a job, even at McDonald's, and lived with us. But no— hating your father meant more than loving me."

That boulder pressure thing returned to his chest, and he had to breathe through his mouth. "That's not true, Hannah. You were my life."

"Then why didn't you write?" she asked softly. "Or

come back for me?"

"Because the honest-to-God truth…" He paused. He had to get this right. Her hands were clenched around both knees now. He wanted to reach out and tug them into his, but these words could not be said in comfort. "I realized during that nightmare bus ride that if I didn't stop loving you, I wouldn't survive in New York. I'd always be virtually here, completely absorbed with you. I had to cut the cord and never look back." Her eyes slanted in pain, but he owed her not to look away. "I found all kinds of immature reasons to hate you so I'd never be tempted to contact you again."

Her brows knit. "What kind of immature reasons?"

"I don't know. It was a long time ago."

"You know."

He flushed. These were ridiculous twelve years later. He dredged up the least offensive one. "That you'd only loved me for my money—once that was taken away, you wanted nothing to do with me."

She bolted to her feet, her beautiful eyes wide with shock. She opened her mouth but nothing came out. He used the time wisely. "I told you it was immature. I know it's not true."

"You should probably go." She fluttered her hand toward the door, her gaze watery and fixed on the carpet.

He'd done that to her. Twice now. He rubbed his chest again.

The words he sought burrowed deeper, like dozens of hot pokers. His time with Hannah had been the happiest in his life, and long after he'd started his fledgling company with Eric, he'd rarely dated. *Iceman*, his cousin—who loved nicknames—had teased. Maybe so, but instead of women, he immersed himself in learning the art of corporate negotiating and high-finance deals. The more he learned, the more he ensured no one would ever render him powerless again. Eventually his determination not to glance into the past callused the heartbreak. That was why he never came back for her. He'd ruthlessly trained himself *out* of love. By the time he met Nicole, she was everything he required— everything Hannah was not.

He stood, simmering with self-recrimination. He really was a loser when it came to women. He inflicted pain thoughtlessly, the way Harrison had on him.

"Okay," he said, because of all the words needed to undo the damage, this was the brilliant one that came out. He stuck his hands in his pockets and walked to the door. Silently she followed, slipped past him, and released the deadbolts, her back rigid, head high. It was all he could do not to pull her against him, wrap his arms around her belly, and beg to start the evening over. He kept his hands in his pocket.

As she opened the door, she faced him, hesitating. Hope surged—for what, he had no idea, but at least it wouldn't leave them like this—with so much hurt between them.

"A part of me wishes you luck keeping your company," she said softly, and she wasn't scratching her palms. "And another part of me hopes you lose it. Maybe your dad will leave our neighborhood alone."

Her words fell like sledgehammer blows. He waited until he could breathe, and managed to utter, "Good night, Hannah."

"Goodbye, Devon."

CHAPTER 22

THE MORNING DAWNED bleak and gray, fitting for Hannah's new outlook on life. She'd barely slept again, and the shadows under her eyes would've stood out starkly on her pale face if the puffy slits above hadn't stolen the show. She had no intention of encountering Aunt Milly and a boatload of nosy questions, so she turned from the mirror, tiptoed around, and dressed quickly in khakis and a brown sweater.

She still smelled Devon on her skin, remembered his taste and the unyielding muscles as she lay on him. His slow, thorough kisses had thrilled her, unfortunately reawakening her sexual hunger. The side that had never truly been satisfied by another man. And now she had a stark memory of exactly what she'd be living without. Again.

She glanced at the clock—seven twelve. On Sundays, Aunt Milly's friends took her to the nine o'clock service at the North Shore Baptist Church. Even the smallest task took her a great deal of time, so she often awoke just about now. Hannah slipped soundlessly into the bathroom they shared and brushed her teeth, patted freezing water on her eyelids, and pulled her hair back with a clasp at the nape of her neck and an elastic to hold the ends. In the living room, she grabbed the colored files from the card table and slipped out the door. She'd agreed to meet Sean at the office at nine, where they'd take the van loaded with yesterday's unused lumber back to the Wickham residence. It wouldn't hurt to go in early, check on the Matisse, and answer emails. Hopefully by the time Sean came in, she'd look human again, instead of like a sopping dishrag.

The second she stepped outside, Hannah's eyes teared from the brisk, windy air, which was fine—at least she could excuse her red lids now. But really! How typical of Chicago after the Indian summer warmth two days ago.

By the time she unlocked Moore and Morrow's nondescript wood door, Hannah's fingers shook from the cold. She closed the door and paused. The aroma of freshly brewed coffee filtered from the break room. Why would Sean be here this early? She rapidly blinked and wiped the raw skin on her nose. He'd witnessed enough incidents this week to lose all respect for her. Ducking into her office, she shed her jacket and dropped her files on her desk, then headed down to the break room, calling his name before she turned in.

She stopped short, heart lodging her throat. A magenta-scarved Bernice sat at the round table holding a royal-blue Moore and Morrow ceramic mug and the Sunday *Tribune*. "What are you doing here?" they both said at the same time.

Hannah smiled, hoping it didn't convey her dread at encountering the last person on Earth she wanted to see. Her soul was brittle enough without adding fired-a-family-friend-with-leukemia onto the heap. Maybe she could hold off, delay it day by day, because in less than a month this company wouldn't be hers to manage. It said something that this thought cheered her. "I'm meeting Sean. We're going to finish the Wickham transfer."

"Oh, that poor woman's death is all over the news."

"It was awful," Hannah admitted. "Why are you

here?"

"I wanted to check on the Matisse, but…"

Hannah sat across from her, heat already inflaming her cheeks. In all the chaos, she'd forgotten to tell Bernice she was taking over. "I redid it yesterday. Walter saw your second attempt and was…unsatisfied."

"Why didn't you just tell me? I'd have fixed it."

"Because…he…didn't want you working on it a third time."

"Oh." Her friend's eyes began to water, which immediately started Hannah's tears again.

"I'm so sorry, Bernice—"

"Why are you apologizing?" She took the napkin from under her mug and dabbed her eyes. "I've been screwing up so often, I don't know why you keep me here."

It was the perfect setup. As much as she didn't want to, Hannah could segue right into the termination, and the anxiety that had been clawing at her stomach whenever she thought about the confrontation would disappear. She opened her mouth. "Oh, Bernice. You're so valuable, what would we do without you?"

Shit! She fought the instant itch by squeezing her hands under the table.

Bernice smiled and dabbed her wet cheeks. "You and I both know I'm the worst technician you have here."

Hannah was so stupefied by her own exact-opposite outburst, and trying not to rub her prickling palms on her pants, that she had no comeback.

After a slight pause, a look of understanding came over Bernice. "Walter wants me gone, doesn't he?"

"You've had bad days; we all know it—" Hannah inhaled a shaky breath and shut up. Nothing she'd said had come out professional or supportive. They'd been platitudes and lies to make herself feel better. She went with honesty. "Yes, but I don't want you to leave." She broke down and covered her eyes. The tears eased the last of the itch.

Bernice reached out and grabbed Hannah's wrist. "You know what your problem is, dear?" Hannah shook her head miserably as Bernice squeezed the newly free hand. "You never let anyone in your life go," she said softly. "Not ever."

"I don't need to," Hannah squeaked. "They all leave me."

"Your father was shot in the line of duty. Your mother died of cancer. Neither chose to leave you."

"But they're gone. And Devon walked away. And Aunt Milly's emphysema is getting worse with this pending move, and now you..." She sobbed in ugly gasps, her shoulders shaking like pistons. "I'm tired of losing the people I love."

"We all leave one way or another. Of course I want to keep working, but I don't want to become a detriment to the company."

Hannah reached for a napkin and blew her nose. Bernice's self-awareness was confusing. "If you know that, why don't you quit?"

"Because you need to let me go. It's time for you to confront this, and know that you and I will both be okay afterward."

"I can't," she whispered.

"Try."

Hannah braced herself. Say the sentence really fast, and then it was out there: *I'm sorry, Bernice, but we have to terminate your employment.* Her heart pounded in fear. Maybe just the two words: *You're fired.* It wasn't as though this was coming as a surprise. She could do this. She opened her mouth and inhaled. Her vocal cords seized. *Christ!* Shaking her head, eyes screwed into leaky slits, Hannah gasped out a sobbing exhale.

"There, there, sweetie." Bernice scooted her chair around, enveloping her in a patchouli-scented hug. "Why are you making this so hard?"

Hannah couldn't speak. Confronting people had never gotten her what she wanted. She'd spat words of hate to her mother, and her mother got cancer. She'd stood up to Devon's stupid ultimatum, and he'd left her. And now Bernice. She wept for Bernice, for Devon, for the family she'd lost and the loved ones about to go. Why couldn't she hold on to time? Why couldn't she have a normal family who was there for graduations and weddings and babies? Why couldn't her true love have known it was true love in high school, and stayed for her?

She took in several rapid breaths, trying not to hyperventilate. Bernice cupped her head and patted, shushing her quietly, until eventually Hannah's sobs turned into childlike hitched breaths. For years, Bernice had been the strong motherly presence in her life, and that hadn't changed one bit during this leukemia fiasco. Or now. Who faced their own termination and comforted their boss? Hannah sat up and blew her nose noisily into a napkin. "I'm a disaster at managing. I shouldn't be in charge. I can't do this."

"It's not like you won't see me again." Bernice smiled.

"But you're ill. At least here I can check on you daily. And you need the healthcare."

"I can go on COBRA. I have two daughters. You and I can email daily. I'll be okay, Hannah. I want to hear you let me go."

"Okay." Hannah grabbed another napkin and pressed it to her eyes. Who was she to feel sorry for herself? "I can do this." Her voice was one big nasal twang. She straightened her shoulders and held Bernice's hand. "Here I go, for real." Despite herself, she laughed. "You don't need to look so excited about it."

"It's not every day I get to see one of my baby girls hurdle something huge."

"Something huge," Hannah muttered, and took another bracing breath. Heart hammering, she stammered out, "Bernice...you're fired." Moisture popped into Bernice's eyes, and Hannah clapped a hand over her mouth, tears already falling. "Oh no..."

But Bernice laughed as she cried. "You did it! Sweetie, I'm so *proud* of you." They both grabbed napkins, giggling, and when Bernice encouraged her to repeat it, she complied. "Louder," Bernice commanded.

Hannah inhaled and yelled at the top of her voice, mimicking Oprah, "You're fi-red!" They dissolved into more giggles. A throat cleared. Hannah gasped, whipping sideways in her chair.

Sean leaned in the doorframe, arms crossed and a wary look on his face. Wary as in: coming across a rabid animal or someone arguing with an imaginary enemy. "Ready to go, boss?"

DEVON STRODE ALONG the Magnificent Mile, glancing down westward-facing blocks, ready to head toward whichever Starbucks came into view first. He'd needed to escape the claustrophobic hotel room, and more coffee to work out the kinks in his sluggish mind. Most of all, he needed to obsess over his father to distract himself from thoughts of Hannah and how much he wanted her. Somehow, in all the talking and kissing and seeing that zoo photo, he'd broken his cardinal rule. He'd looked back. And his heart had jumped into the past with wild abandon. Even after Hannah had stood at her door, clearly rooting for the Wickham takeover, basically tossing his heart into a Cuisinart.

He turned down Chestnut Street toward the familiar

green insignia, immediately plunging into a pure Chicago wind tunnel. The buffeting arctic air triggered his tear ducts, and he buried himself deeper in his coat. It didn't matter what he felt about Hannah; they had no future. Even if she could forgive him for tearing her place down, and forcing her to sell the partnership, there was still the matter of location. She clearly wasn't moving to Manhattan, and he was done with this godforsaken city.

Devon's cell rang, and he yanked it out, sheltering in a doorway. He glanced at caller ID, and his gut clenched. What did the old man want now? Devon answered gruffly, relief spreading through him when he heard his brother's voice.

"Hey. You better get over here. Frannie's hysterical. She locked herself and Todd in the sunroom ten minutes ago."

"Why?"

"Dunno."

Devon plugged his other ear as a truck roared past. "Where's Harrison?"

"You mean *Dad*? At the funeral parlor."

Devon squeezed his eyes shut, shivering with cold. How often did Frannie lose it like this? Who would Rick have called if Devon was in New York? Why was he wasting time asking stupid questions? He turned and jogged back toward the hotel for a taxi. "On my way, but do me a favor—ask Joseph to have coffee waiting."

"Done."

"I should be there in twenty." He was about to hang up when a thought struck him. "Hey, did *Dad* ever mention the word Bryant around you?"

"No."

"Did he ever tell you he was buying up old neighborhoods that he'd built back in the sixties?"

"Dude, it's me, Rick the underachiever. He never

discusses business when I'm around. Why?"

"Trying to figure something out."

His brother blew out a breath. "Just hurry. She's a mess, and I don't know what to do."

The plea pulled Devon into a sprint, barely cognizant of the wind. It had been years since he'd felt needed, and as dysfunctional as his family was, they were his, and it was time he helped.

CHAPTER 23

I CAN'T BELIEVE the cops are still working in this weather," Sean remarked. He parked the van next to a squad car in the Wickham circular driveway.

Hannah didn't answer. Her head hurt, and her eyes, although no longer red—thank God—stung from all the crying. She just wanted to get this part of the project wrapped up and go take a nap until her depression lifted. Wishful thinking. She had three more apartments to tour, even though she could already tell from the website that they probably weren't suitable.

Sean cut the engine, and she jumped out, shivering as the north wind whipped her coat and ponytail. "It's too cold to construct the crates out here." He opened the back of the van and grabbed the toolbox next to the stacks of lumber.

"Well, we can't traipse through the house with all this. Or hammer and drill next to all his artifacts."

He glanced at her oddly. "I meant, we'll have to move all of the supplies out on the driveway and work in the shelter of the van."

Heat burned her face. Before she could apologize, he very kindly glanced at the sky, where dense clouds in battleship-gray hung low. On the horizon, angry purple-black clouds plowed ominously forward. "But we'd better haul ass."

The air felt damp, and instinct made her pause. "If it

rains, the wood will get wet." They stared at each other, and she knew his frustration at working on a Sunday and in such conditions was mirrored on her face. "It'd be safer to construct the crates in the basement. Let me go ask Mr. Wickham for permission."

She jogged up the front steps and rang the doorbell. A gust almost blew her off the front stoop. Unprofessional as it was, she hopped up and down, teeth chattering until the door opened.

Joseph greeted her, and Rick peered over his shoulder, only to turn away, frowning. "Good morning, Miss Moore," Joseph said kindly, ushering her inside. She almost brushed by him in her haste to be out of the cold.

"Weather sure changed fast," she gasped.

He nodded with a slight smile. In the four days she'd been on this project, he'd greeted her without a glimmer of recognition, and yet he'd been such a fixture in the times she'd spent here with Devon. Did she look that different, or had Devon brought home so many girls during his high school years that Joseph eventually paid no attention? Nothing used to get past him in this busy domain, and he'd known her name and spoken to her often back then. But it hurt to be treated like—well, a businesswoman. Hannah shook the idiotic thoughts from her mind and quickly explained the situation to him. "So if you could ask Mr. Wickham if we can construct the crates in the basement, I'd appreciate it."

"He's not expected back until afternoon, miss, but I think that's a splendid idea." He held out his arm. "The basement is—"

"I remember." She froze. If he hadn't known she'd been the disheveled girl with Devon down there one lazy Saturday afternoon, she'd just outed herself.

Merriment flickered in his eyes. He nodded. "Very well, miss. May I provide you with staff to assist in transporting the wood?"

"That'd be perfect. Thank you, Joseph."

❦

WHAT WAS THE Moore and Morrow van doing here? The massive front door opened, and Devon turned. Joseph stood in the doorway with a steaming mug of coffee on a small silver tray. Despite his miserable mood, Devon grinned. "You're a sight for sore eyes." Entering the warmth of the foyer, he almost groaned. "I'd forgotten how the weather turns in the blink of an eye."

"Yes, sir. We're expecting severe storms later this afternoon."

Ah, thunderstorms and this house. An epic combination. "Is Hannah working?"

"After you...*left* for the police department yesterday, she notified me she'd rather finish today."

"When does my father get home?" He swapped his coat for the coffee.

"We expect him closer to noon, sir."

Devon glanced at his watch. Over two hours. Good. He didn't need the added complication. Whatever Francine's problem was, she had to get over it before his father became even more overprotective. "Has my sister been like this before?"

"Not to my knowledge, sir. Miss Francine seems to have..." He tightened his lips, a sure sign he was uncomfortable gossiping about anyone. Devon nodded impatiently. "Been out of sorts since Miss Honey's death."

Since before that. Todd had left the house before nine o'clock, when Honey had last been seen, which meant Frannie must have been hysterical around six or seven. "Who was the last person to see Honey alive on Friday night?"

Again Joseph hesitated. "An upstairs maid saw your

father leaving her suite. Miss Hartlett was alive and well inside the room before he closed the door."

Devon sipped the coffee. He should be heading to his sister and her crisis, but he needed to lay out a timeline and motivations. His call to his father had occurred before the Rogers Park meeting at six. Someone else had been on the line and heard the facts about Honey conning his father to inherit the vast fortune. Then Harrison must have canceled their plans, no surprise, and no doubt visited her room at nine to kick her out of the house. Which was when the maid saw Harrison leave Honey's bedroom.

But what didn't make sense was the next morning Harrison told the chauffeur to have the car ready for another function he and Honey were to attend that night. Was that a lie, like Devon had originally suspected? Or had she said something in her room to convince Harrison she loved him, and their engagement was back on? "Joseph, did you see or hear anything out of the ordinary that night?"

"No, sir."

"When did you go to bed?"

"I retired at ten."

"Did you"—how to say this without sounding like an accusation?—"happen to overhear the conversation I had with Harrison over the phone that evening?"

Joseph, the ageless, stoic butler who'd been with them since before Devon was born, swallowed audibly. "Yes, sir. I saw the telephone off the hook in the parlor, and went to hang it up. I did overhear a bit by accident."

"Were you ever suspicious of her?"

"I'm uncomfortable answering, sir."

He opened his mouth to press Joseph but let it go. Frannie was the priority right now, not fishing for clues as to whether his father had committed a second murder. Devon nodded his thanks and wound his way to the back of the mansion.

Rick paced beside the closed paneled doors of the sunroom, hands deep in his pockets.

"I'm here. So what's the story?"

Rick glanced up, the worried expression instantly clearing. "Hey." His eyes were bloodshot, and he smelled like a brewery. He wore wrinkled olive khakis and an orange T-shirt that said: *You Wish*. "From what I've been able to gather, Brady's on his way over to take Todd."

A trickle of unease crept down Devon's spine. "What do you mean, 'take Todd'?"

"I don't know. But Frannie immediately locked herself and Todd in the sunroom, and won't come out or talk or anything. I've been knocking and calling for half an hour." Rick shook his head. "Ever since you came home, it's like she's gone around the bend."

"What's that supposed to mean?"

"Just an observation. I mean, she's been a mess since announcing the divorce and moving back here, but it was more hyper and energetic. In these last few days, it's like…she's cracked or something."

"It's called Honey being murdered, asshole. It's Frannie having to relive our own mother's death. Keep my visit out of the equation." Devon grazed his knuckles against the door. "Frannie? Open up."

"I already tried that, Batman."

They stared at the white, arched doors for thirty seconds before a lock clicked and the right panel flung open. Frannie launched into Devon's arms. He jerked the mug away and caught her, coffee scalding his hand. He winced, swallowing the howl of pain as he circled her thin body with his other arm.

"Thank God you came. I have no one else to turn to," she said, sobbing.

"Well, fuck me," Rick muttered, and walked off.

"So what's going on?"

Frannie squirmed out of his embrace, sniffing a very congested nose. "Get in here." She yanked his arm, and to keep the remaining coffee in his cup, Devon allowed himself to be pulled into the sunroom. She slammed the door and turned the old-fashioned key.

"I hear Brady's on his way."

"Todd told him what happened Friday night. He's gone to speak to his lawyer and threatened to come take my son right after. He said any court in the land would side with him."

Devon looked over at Todd, slouched miserably in the corner of the yellow-flowered sofa. "Dude, why'd you do that?"

His nephew shrugged. "He has a way of tricking you with his questions. I didn't mean to. I'm sorry, Mom."

"Help me," Frannie whispered. "If he takes him, I'll kill myself."

Devon's teeth clicked tight. "I don't want to ever hear that phrase come out of your mouth again." His sister glanced away, nodding and sniffling. "Have you called your lawyer?"

She shook her head helplessly. "He won't get here in time. He lives in Des Plaines."

"Do it," he snapped. He spun around and tried the door handle. The flimsy old panels rattled easily in his grip; this fortress would cave in with one kick. He glanced out the window to where three cops chatted over by the cliff, one drinking from a large Styrofoam cup. Yellow crime tape snapped in the wind. He swigged the remainder of his coffee as Frannie picked up the phone across the room.

"Hey, Todd. You ever been in our fallout shelter?" he asked quietly. When the boy shook his head, Devon motioned for him to follow. At Frannie's questioning glance, he held up a hand. "Be right back." He ushered Todd out of the room just as Joseph rounded the corner with a platter of donuts, the glaze still dripping.

"Mrs. Farlow heard you'd arrived and made these especially for you."

The sugary cake aroma enveloped him, and his stomach grumbled noisily on cue. "Tell her thank you and that I'll visit her shortly to propose." He took the platter without breaking his stride, ushering the boy down the same back hallways and old servants' stairs that he'd used yesterday, until they reached the basement door.

He handed the platter over and opened it, startled to find the fluorescent lights already on. They quickly descended. The path he'd taken to get out the side door yesterday was now blocked by a drop cloth and stacks of lumber. An open toolbox lay nearby, with colored files on top. The breath streamed out of him. He'd seen those colored files last night in Hannah's apartment.

"The art restoration staff must be working here," Devon said, "so when they come back, I need you to be extra quiet, okay?"

His nephew grunted, but the tone was high; he was clearly afraid.

Devon turned to him fully. "Don't worry, Todd. I'll straighten things out with your dad. And you've met Hannah, right? The red-haired woman dealing with your grandfather's art?" Todd shook his head. "Well, she's really nice, and she'll keep our secret, but it'd still be better if you stayed as quiet as possible."

The fingers gripping the platter were white. "Okay."

Devon scanned the enormous room, his body humming with energy. Hannah was somewhere nearby. Brady was on his way. Devon had to get back to Frannie. He put his coffee mug on the bottom stair.

Large boxes, stacked three high, covered most of the east wall. He tugged one of the middle stacks, which eventually slid out. There was enough room between the whole row and the wall for an eleven-year-old boy to hang out until Brady gave up his search and left.

"Get behind there. Here—" He gathered a canvas folding chair and a small box labeled *VHS Movies*. He placed the donuts on the box and handed over his cell phone. "I've got Angry Birds on there, but keep it on mute. Don't make a sound or come out unless it's your mom or me. Only. You hear?"

"But you will come back?" Todd's eyes were saucer round.

"You're damn right I will—you've got the donuts. Get in; I need to get back to your mom."

"Do you think she's going to kill herself like your mother?" The words came out through trembling lips.

Devon kept his expression blank with difficulty. The boy didn't know any better; he'd been brainwashed by his grandfather, probably since he was old enough to understand words. "Your mom will be fine. And my mother didn't kill herself."

"You think she was pushed?" Todd paled. "Like Honey?"

"Just get in there." Devon leaned in and grabbed a few donuts, then shouldered the stack of boxes back into place.

"You okay?" he called, and heard a muffled reply. Apparently a donut was already in his nephew's mouth. Devon stuffed one in too as he grabbed the coffee and mounted the steps two at a time, then closed the door softly. He paused and stopped chewing, listening for footsteps nearby. A part of him was dying to see Hannah again, despite the hurt. But all was silent.

When he returned to the sunroom, Frannie flew at him, looking seriously unhinged in her filthy sweats and snarled hair. "Where is he? What did you do with him?"

"Relax. In a house this size, no one will find him, and you can honestly tell Brady you don't know where he is."

"You'll stay, won't you?"

The doorbell chimed its ostentatious gong. "Of course. Sit down and take a couple of deep breaths. Are those yesterday's sweats?"

"This is a shitty time to be discussing fashion, Dev."

"It's more of a discussion on hygiene." She punched him hard, and he grinned, nodding his approval. "That's the spirit, sis. Let's do this."

CHAPTER 24

B RADY'S NOSE CRACKED under Devon's fist, an oddly satisfying feeling, which only fed his desire to hit the fucker again. He yanked his limp brother-in-law half off the floor by his bloodied collar. "And this is for what you just called my sister." He swung his fist back again. It was caught in an iron grasp and held there. He whipped his head around, snarling.

"No need to hit him again, son," a homicide detective said in a soft Southern accent. "He's about out cold."

Devon glared, panting, but the calm smile remained. It was the detective who'd stood up to his father yesterday. Devon nodded stiffly, releasing the shirt, and Brady's head thumped on the rug. Although the bastard's eyes were puffy gashes, they remained open and vacant. His linebacker heft had dissolved into a booze paunch, and it was clear by the guttural wheezing that he hadn't seen this much exercise in years. With immense effort, Devon regained control over the killer-rage instinct and straightened.

A crowd had gathered during the fight. Strange, he hadn't been aware of anything except going after Brady like some junkyard dog. Besides Joseph and Mrs. Farlow, he knew none of the house staff, and most stared at him with round, frightened eyes. Welcome to the Wickham Reality Show, folks. Starring the vicious patriarch, the violent son, and the batshit-crazy daughter. When his gaze swung back to Joseph, though, he could have sworn the old butler winked.

"I'm sorry," he gasped to everyone, and only then did the detective release his grip.

"Move along." Joseph fanned the air with his open palms. "Back to work, plenty to do."

Devon wiped his mouth with the back of his throbbing hand and sought out his sister. She cowered on the sofa, arms wrapped tightly around a pillow. If she were any paler, she'd be laid out on a slab. "You okay?"

She nodded and, of course, promptly burst into tears. Behind her, the patio door stood open, with two cops positioned in the threshold as if blocking an escape route. Gusting wind billowed the bright yellow curtains, and Devon only now felt the chill. How long had they been standing there? The shouting and crack of Brady smashing the antique cocktail table on his first trip down must've reached cliff-side.

"I apologize," he said again to the detective. "It's a fight that's been years in the making." *Since that homecoming dance with my sister.* At his feet, Brady stirred and groaned. It was all Devon could do to hold back a rib-cracking kick.

"Would someone mind telling me what's going on?"

Everyone swiveled toward the authoritative voice except Devon. *Home way too early, damn it.*

"I was just about to ask that myself," the detective said.

Harrison marched past the rapidly departing staff and looked pointedly from daughter to son to son-in-law. "Well?"

Devon remained silent; this was Frannie's story to tell. Even though Todd had blown it and the truth about the onboard stowaway adventure would come out, it wouldn't be from him.

"Brady came to take Todd away." Francine's words trembled with hate. "And Devon told him to go to hell, so Brady punched him."

Devon swallowed, tasting blood. Her verbal play-by-play sounded a lot less mature than the testosterone brawl that had just ended. The detective took out a notebook from his breast pocket.

"Why would he have cause to take Todd away?" Harrison asked. "Does it have something to do with Honey?"

Like yesterday, the tender way he spoke the dead woman's name squeezed the air from Devon's lungs. Either his father was giving a spectacular rendering of grief, or he actually had been deceived again by Honey, even after hearing the facts.

"No, Father." Tears dripped from Frannie's eyes, and she clamped her lips into a thin line. "He wants Todd because he thinks I'm an unfit mother."

"Out with it, Francine," Harrison ordered, but he said it gently.

He'd spoken to her like that after their mom died too. That didn't bode well. Did Harrison think Frannie was going around the bend?

Devon watched her closely. She was still pale, her eyes wide and wild. And that whole homeless look she had going on... But after a shaky inhale, she blurted out the story. Devon shifted his gaze to the spattered blood drying on the Persian rug, while his role as heroic uncle and sacrificial big brother unfolded. When she finally lapsed into silence, no one spoke. He waited, expectation clenching his gut so tight a bitter surge of coffee crept up his esophagus. Somehow his father would turn the tale on its head, and he'd become the villain.

"Where's Todd now?" Harrison asked.

Devon looked his father right in the eye. "He's

down in the basement. Behind the boxes marked Easter decorations." Francine bounced off the sofa and hurried across the room, her sweatpants sagging at the butt, her socks noiseless as she fled out the door. "I'll need my cell phone back," Devon called.

Harrison glared down at Brady, clearly conscious and clearly anticipating the old man's wrath. "Joseph, throw this man out of my house, and have him arrested if he ever trespasses on this property again."

"With pleasure, sir."

"And Detective," Harrison said, in the same mild-mannered tone, "arrest *that* man."

"Jesus." Devon shook his head. "Can we just talk about Rogers Park, Father?"

"Arrest your son, sir?"

"No, we cannot talk about Rogers Park, and yes, Detective, my son."

"On what charge?" Devon asked in resignation. "Protecting your grandson?" He balled his hands at his sides, immediately realizing his mistake when the detective and his father glanced at them. He flexed his fingers, but the simmering hate built, shaking him to his core.

"I don't care what you boys charge him with, but keep detaining him until you find the proof you need that he murdered my fiancée." Harrison spun on his heel and left. The detective stuffed his notebook in his breast pocket as Joseph assisted Brady off the floor and out of the room. Devon offered his wrists, psyching himself up to spend another few hours in that uncomfortable metal chair.

"I suggest you leave here lickety-split, son. I have no cause to take you downtown, but the longer you remain here, the more I'll be forced to find something."

Devon nodded. No doubt Harrison had his clutches deep inside the upper echelons of the WPD. "Thank you," he said, hearing the pitiful relief and not caring. He walked back to the foyer, massaging his hand, which sported minor bruises and red welts from the spilled coffee. Joseph opened the door and helped a stumbling Brady out. In the distance, thunder split into an ear-shattering boom.

Static energy shivered through Devon. If he didn't leave now, he'd be stuck here until the weather cleared. Storms over Lake Michigan were living beasts, surging waves that slammed into the cliff, shaking this ancient house to its foundation. Driving the curving suburban roads would be hazardous, flooding likely.

On the other hand, he was reluctant to follow Brady out this soon. He didn't trust himself in a second encounter; the need to unleash was still too near the surface. Should he ignore caution and dog his father for new insight on why Rogers Park warranted a takeover? No, the old man was fixated on having him arrested. He'd give Harrison some space, and hope for more evidence from the PI.

Lightning lit the foyer. He counted the seconds... Eighteen before more thunder cracked. Maybe he could find an excuse to return to the basement and shove himself into Hannah's life, because those invisible ties that had bound him to her so long ago had tangled around him again. She was right. He should never have walked off that night. It'd taken twelve goddamn years, but he got it now. He could've manned up and taken a job somewhere, found a buddy to let him bunk on a sofa. He debated going to tell her so she'd know with absolute certainty that he understood the depth of his mistake. *Aw, hell. Just leave her alone.*

The door opened, and Joseph stepped onto the threshold, his white hair billowing wildly. "I beg your pardon, sir."

The temperature seemed to have dropped another

ten degrees, and Devon bit back a shiver. He stood aside, and as the butler strode past, he watched Brady's red Porsche taking the long driveway at Mach 2.

"This came for you a short while ago."

Devon closed the door and turned. Joseph was picking up an express-mail envelope from the console. "Thank you."

"Will you be leaving, sir?"

"Soon."

"I'll collect your coat."

"Go update Ms. Farlow on all the drama." He grinned at the old man. "I can get my own coat." It was so easy to fall into a state of helplessness around here.

Once the butler disappeared into the breakfast room, he slit open the envelope. Wedged in the left corner was Nicole's diamond ring. Not packaged, or stuck inside a smaller envelope, or even wrapped in a tissue. Just the platinum-set, four-and-a-half-carat, ideal-cut, D-color solitaire winking up at him. *Ring's in the mail, pal.* So much for a figure of speech.

Should he be impressed or humiliated that she'd paid premium to make sure he got it on a Sunday? And it wasn't lost on him that his thoughts shifted immediately to the corporate fallout this would have. Tucker would pull out every last crony. It didn't matter whether Harrison stole the company. The final song on the *Titanic* was fading, and the lifeboats were long gone. There wasn't even a one percent chance Ashby Enterprises would survive all this. His inheritance would disappear in default. Several moments passed before he got his breath under control.

He put a call in to Eric, who didn't answer. *Shit.* He texted: *Call. It's urgent.* He peered down at the ring, luminous even wedged in cardboard. She should have kept it; he didn't want the damn thing.

Wait a minute. He turned the envelope over, and the

ring tumbled into his palm. Maybe he'd just found a legitimate reason to see Hannah again.

"Hey, Uncle Devon."

He turned and forced a grin at the boy lurking in the shadows. "Did you save any donuts?" The boy blushed, and Devon laughed. "No worries; I'd have done the same thing. Where's your mom?"

"Upstairs crying."

Jeez. Did Todd know Devon had just beaten Brady to a pulp? He shifted his weight, squeezing the ring in his fist. Just as he was about to utter a blanket apology for anything his nephew might or might not know, Todd brightened.

"You wanna play Grand Theft Auto Five?"

Devon kept the smile on his face as his mind screamed the instinctive answer. But he'd blown the guy off for two meals and returned him to a house he'd tried to run away from. The least he could do was look like an idiot playing someone with "a hundred percent completion," whatever the hell that meant.

"Lead the way," he said. "But get ready for an ass whooping."

"Yeah," Todd said. "Yours."

CHAPTER 25

WE'D BETTER STOP," Hannah yelled. Thunder boomed in surround sound, and a vicious squall slammed her into the Moore and Morrow van. She steadied her footing and shouted, "Hurry, it's getting too dangerous."

Sean nodded, eyes screwed against the flying foliage and twigs. Together they shoved the crated painting farther into the belly of the van, and she scrambled in to secure it to the custom rails with bungee cord. She hopped back out and stood clear as he body-slammed the doors. Each blast of wind ripped more strands from her ponytail to swirl like mini tornados. She futilely pushed her hair back from her face, her fingers shaking from the cold. Her cheeks felt raw and inflamed, and her teeth chattered uncontrollably.

"Get in," Sean hollered, even though he was only several feet away.

Hannah shook her head and gestured behind her. "I have to finish the second gallery. I'll order an Uber."

He nodded again and shoved his hands into his jeans, his lean body curling like a billowing sail against the wind as he made his way around to the driver's side. For an instant, she almost went after him. It was four in the afternoon, and they'd been delayed from carrying these to the van because of rain on and off. Why not quit for the day? To hell with the mess of packing paper and board strewn about the basement, or the second gallery barely inspected. She'd grab this ride while she had a chance—return bright and early tomorrow.

In two steps, she halted. This was the Wickham project. The profit would push them to a new tier of operating, and their swiftness and professionalism here would reverberate in the art industry for years. Even if she was no longer going to be a partner, responsibility forced her to wave good-bye to Sean.

As the van roared to life, she raced into the warm foyer. The wind sucked the doorknob from her grasp, and the massive door slammed shut, echoing like a sawed-off shotgun. Hannah cringed, glancing around for Joseph, or any staff. The great hall held the gloom of evening, the silence thick and creepy. Seconds passed. Where was everybody? It must be her imagination, but the house seemed to shudder. *What the hell?*

The dark foyer double-flashed blinding neon, followed by a roll of thunder reverberating so low, the hair on the back of her neck bristled. Shuddering, Hannah folded her jacket and laid it beside the statue of Zeus. She rubbed her cheeks until they warmed and glanced around again.

She'd been here half a week; not once had she stood in this main hall and not encountered a variety of servants crossing through it. The foyer lights were on long before it ever got this dark in here. Seriously, where was everyone?

Footsteps rang, swift and dominant. *Thank God.* She turned to apologize to Joseph for the racket, but it was Devon. Her mouth dropped open. *He's back?* Maybe it was the electric atmosphere, but tension emanated off him like a force field. He stalked closer, his long-legged stride stiff, his posture impossibly rigid. A brutal scowl marred his handsome face.

She frowned. Maybe she'd finally gone round the

bend, and he was just her imagination. Nothing could've brought him back here—he'd told her so last night. But the white buttoned-down shirt had fold lines. Part of one cuff was coffee-stained. The hand beneath red and swollen. She didn't daydream in such detail.

He was ten feet away and closing in fast. She stared up at that frown, pulse skittering. Another fucking confrontation. She'd gotten in the last word the night before, and he wasn't letting it go. She drew her shoulders back, mouth suddenly dust dry. She was sick of being afraid, of not sticking up for herself and her needs. She was going to give it to him with both barrels.

He halted in front of her, torso muscles rippling beneath the fitted shirt as though he was bracing himself for something. "Hi." His tone was low, his eyes a shocking blue with dark circles beneath.

"Why are you here?" It came out exasperated. Rude. A part of her was thrilled.

His scowl flickered to surprise. "Frannie had a problem."

"Don't tell me...that only you could solve?"

He studied her like she was an alien species. "Under the circumstances—yes. What's wrong with you?"

She clawed the mess of hair behind her shoulders, suddenly physically and emotionally drained. The upheaval with him last night and this morning with Bernice, then hammering crates for paintings, and struggling under their precious weight to transfer them into the van in this freezing weather... "It's been a shitty day." Lightning flashed, illuminating the stark angles of his handsome face.

"Try getting your ass handed to you by an eleven-year-old all afternoon," he muttered. The scowl flickered back, but then he grinned, and her heart fluttered up to her throat like a cartoon bird. She was so pathetic! "Sorry." He stuck a hand into the pocket of those formfitting jeans. "I'm sure your day was shittier than the video game from hell, but I'm about to make it better. I've found a way to solve your problem."

Maybe if she'd had more sleep or they'd parted on less hostile terms, she'd have come up with a pleasant response, but his tone drove an iron rod through her spine. "Which problem, Devon? Moving my chronically ill great-aunt? Selling my partnership? Finding out the guy I once thought roped the moon is a heartless corporate shark?" She threw her hands up and let them fall until they slapped her hips. The sound was lost in the rolling thunder.

He frowned, pulled his hand out, and opened his fingers. In the center of his palm lay a gargantuan diamond ring. Even in the dim hallway, it glittered like fire. "Take it." His voice was soft. When she didn't move, he picked up her hand and placed the beautiful ring onto her palm. She stared at it hypnotically. It shone like it was alive. It was so heavy! And huge. And...*beautiful*. The band was warm from being in his pocket, and her chilled fingers closed over it. She lifted her eyes. He was clearly waiting for a response.

Wait, a ring? Solving a problem? He was proposing? Her thoughts fragmented in a million directions. "Take it?" she whispered.

"It's yours if you want it."

She blinked. "That's...the worst proposal I've ever heard."

His brows rose close to his hairline. "It isn't a proposal, Han. Either my company or my father's is going to raze your neighborhood. That train has left the station, and no apology will ever be enough. Here's a solution so you don't have to sell your partnership." He nodded at the glittering gem in distaste. "Hock it. You need money, and I don't want it. Problem solved." His cell phone rang, and he reached into his pocket.

She blocked his arm. "*What?*"

"I've made your life miserable, and I'm fixing it. Take the emotions out of the gesture and think about this rationally." He pulled the phone out and glanced at the screen. "I'm sorry. I have to take this." He turned his back on her. "Yeah, hi, Eric."

He began walking away, as if the phone call was more important than...*this!* Giving her his fiancée's ring?

"Are you kidding me?" She whipped it at his broad back, and he stiffened on impact. The ring fell to the marble with a *tink*. "If you think you can assuage your guilt by bribing me with that, then you're stupider than I ever thought possible, you son of a bitch!" She spun around and fled up the grand staircase.

❧

"SO," ERIC SAID, "whoever the hell that was confirms you really are clinically retarded when it comes to the workings of a woman."

Devon muttered incoherently, scooping Nicole's ring off the black tile. He was at a complete loss. His plan was brilliant. Yeah, it was a used ring, but for fuck's sake, take the symbolism out of it, and it was a *solution*! He'd paid enough for it that Hannah would never have to worry about finances again. His pulse thumped wildly as her frozen expression stayed in his head. She'd thought *take it* was a proposal? He'd fucking botched this good. "What's going on at your end?"

"Back at the office, going through files."

Devon's gut seized. "What aren't you telling me, Eric?"

"Nothing. If Wickham Corp marches in on Monday, I don't want us to get caught with our pants down. I'm buried in stacks, making sure everything's in the right sequence and accounted for."

A flash of lightning almost blinded Devon. "Call Sally in to help."

"I know where everything is, and how to do it right. It'll take longer to explain my OCD methods than to just do it myself." Even with thunder booming through the foyer, Eric's voice sounded thin and exhausted.

Had he been at this since last night?

"Eric, seriously. Call Sally. You need to rest."

"Why'd you call?" His tone was brusquer than Devon had ever heard before. Eric was the jokester, the guy who impulsively told the staff to take off an hour early on a Friday and paid for their first round of drinks. Where Devon was the workaholic with the drive, the ideas, and the contacts, his cousin schmoozed investors' money from them and figured out how to double their profits. Eric choosing to work all weekend was as shocking as having a ring whipped at him, but to worry was a waste of time. There was nothing fishy on their books; the board would have caught it long before now.

Devon sighed. The last few days had been a disaster for both of them. "Just got Nicole's ring back," he said instead.

"Shit."

"I gotta find Harrison and finish this. Even if I did convince him to do a catch and release, Tucker's definitely pulling out, Westcott's flipped us off, and our shareholders are mostly made up of their cronies."

"We are so fucked," Eric mumbled.

Devon frowned. "You, of all people, taught me to never give up," he said sharply, "and to never take no as a final decision. Maybe I can turn this around and convince my father to be an investor instead, but you need to give me something to twist his arm. Did the investigator pull up any suspicious activity during the initial Rogers Park construction?"

"We've got nothing. No doubt Wickham Corp used

asbestos like everyone else, and although there are a bunch of class-action lawsuits for mesothelioma, it's directed at construction workers or insulation repairmen. Taking our land will make no difference."

Devon sighed his aggravation. "Keep me posted if anything changes." He hung up and slipped the cell phone in his pocket. It clinked against Nicole's ring. *Hannah.* A low burn ignited in his belly.

Outside, rain drummed on the driveway and blew in sheets against the rattling windows. Devon bolted up the main staircase, jaw set.

CHAPTER 26

"STUPID JERK," HANNAH muttered as she stormed through the first editions library. Her clenched fists began to cramp, and she shook out her hands, huffing a breath. Actually, Devon handing her his fiancée's ring was perfect, because she was done excusing his emotionally stunted behavior. Growing up with a father who didn't like children could only go so far. She turned left. The long hall stretched before her, and abruptly she slowed her pace. Icy fingers skittered along her spine as she tuned into the unusual silence up here too.

She hadn't passed anyone in the halls the whole way here: no music was playing, no voices in the distance—not even the roar of industrial fans. Someone had to be upstairs, though, because lights blazed throughout the second floor. Hannah walked right past the final few paintings in the sitting room and down more halls, her eyes peeled, ears straining. "Hello?" Only eerie silence inside and shrieking fury outside. Dread settled in her chest. As in: horror-movie, something-was-about-to-happen dread.

She reversed direction and headed back quickly, footsteps lost in the groaning of an ancient home under assault. *Forget this.* She'd finish picking up the sitting room and find Mr. Wickham to explain why the project had been interrupted again. A tremor rippled through her at the thought.

The rain grew more furious, sounding like rocks strafing the roof. Another wave collided into the cliff with a sonic boom, and the house shuddered. "Creepy-ass place." Hannah turned the final corner, nearing the sitting room again.

A door behind her clicked. "There you are."

She spun around, a scream high in her throat. Devon stood halfway out of the fire-damaged gallery. Really? He was the only other person in this house?

His hooded gaze swept over her. "I've been looking for you." Although the storm raged overhead, his soft words carried clearly.

Anger rose like a tidal wave. Her teeth clenched. "Go. Away."

He stepped fully into the hall, hands on his hips. The effect was breathtaking. Tall. Commanding. Savagely handsome. "Make me."

She squinted at the dichotomy. "Are you *kidding me*?"

He spread his arms, exposing the sleek lines of a defenseless torso, and jerked his chin, beckoning her. Weirdly, it didn't look like he was mocking her. The slash of those brows, the grimly set jaw... He looked as angry as she felt. When she made no move to punch him, he folded his arms, the shirt melding to his biceps. "That's what I thought." His tone was deep and deadly, like a lion speaking to a gazelle.

She snapped out of her daze. "What the hell were you hoping for? That we'd wrestle like we were kids again? That you'd make me forget what a Neanderthal you are?"

He gestured at the closed doors along the hall. "Or we can sit down and talk. Like adults."

It wasn't lost on her that he was tossing her own words back in her face. She sneered at his fuckery. "We have nothing more to say to each other, Devon," she warned. Her heart raced with the need to pummel...scratch...bite...*anything* that would cut through that cool layer and finally hurt him.

"Confront me, Hannah. Let's get this all out. Start with the ring."

She wanted to slap that insolence off his face.

He wanted an argument? He had *no* idea what she was about to unleash. "I don't want your goddamn ring. I don't need your pity." She marched over and stuck her index finger in his face. "You're a moron if you think after the history we've had, I'd hock a ring meant for the woman you love! What could possibly be going on inside your head that you believe it's even remotely acceptable behavior? I feel sorry for your ex. No, actually, I don't! I'm delighted for her. She broke your heart! I applaud her; she's a fucking genius."

One eyebrow quirked up. She couldn't tell whether he was amazed or about to laugh. "Are you done?" he asked quietly.

"No!" But any remaining words escaped her, and she stood there, panting, seething with unspoken snark, which made her even madder.

He blinked. Blinked again. "It sounds like you're done," he said cautiously.

That did it! She struck his chest, the impact almost snapping her wrist. *Jesus!* There was absolutely no give in his pecs, no hint he'd felt anything. Her other arm flew out, and suddenly, like a dam breaking loose, she pounded on that solid torso, shrieking obscenities. He stood there and took it; those deep-blue eyes watching her patiently, almost curiously, fueling her rage.

All too soon, her upper-body strength fizzled, and with one more double thump, she staggered back, shaking with fury and exhaustion. She gasped in oxygen. Thunder roared overhead.

"I never meant to insult you, Hannah. And God

knows I never, ever wanted to hurt you the way I did."

"And yet that's all you do," she wheezed, clasping her fury like a shield. Behind it, tears threatened to well up.

"So tell me what you want." The corners of his eyes crinkled in frustration. "Tell me what to do."

She grabbed the lapels of his button-down. "I want you to leave me the fuck alone!"

A muscle fluttered along his jaw. "No." His dark eyelashes lowered in warning. "Pick something else." Beneath her fists, his pecs coiled with tension, kick-starting a tremor that shivered through her. The tender teen she once knew now emanated raw masculinity and don't-fuck-with-me dominance.

She drew a shuddering breath. In this contest of wills, a primitive lust roared to life, joining forces with her wrath to create a crazy, combustible fuse. Sexual arousal shouldn't belong anywhere near her insane need to hurt him, and yet the pumping endorphins tingled completely inappropriate places within her. She was at some kind of crossroads here. Time to back the hell away from whatever this was. "There is nothing else," she said carefully.

"Sure there is." His intense gaze raked over her face, and settled on her mouth. "Think, Hannah."

Fuck it. She snatched fistfuls of his thick hair and yanked his head down, colliding into his mouth and body with such force that they slammed into the wall. Their teeth clicked on impact, and he grunted deep in his throat. She viciously thrust in a tongue, but he was ready and waiting, surging into her mouth, tasting wicked and delicious. His powerful arms snaked around her, dragging her impossibly closer. His kiss deepened to hot and dirty. He was hard, so incredibly stiff, that she paused. In that heartbeat, he took over, spinning them so she was pressed against the wall, on tiptoes.

She fought the fog of desire rolling in to shut down her brain. She had to stay in control here; she had to stay livid. She pushed him until he gave her a sliver of breathing room, then yanked open his shirt, gaining purchase as buttons popped and pinged at her. Warm flesh and smooth muscle and sinew met her trembling palms. *Sweet baby Jesus, the muscles!*

He broke off the kiss, his mouth hungrily trailing to her earlobe. "That was a new shirt." He didn't sound amused, which helped refuel the anger quickly losing out to lust in this bizarre love-wrestle match.

She wrenched her head back and looked him in the eye. "Buy another one, rich boy." She clasped the strong column of his throat and hesitated. Under her palm, he swallowed, his gaze scorching, waiting. Screw it; she could choke him later. She gripped his hard jaw; the rough evening stubble pricked her flesh. "Kiss me," she hissed.

His nostrils flared. "I gotta tell ya," he muttered through his barely mobile jaw, "I'm lovin' this angry, bossy side of you."

She sneered and hopped up, crossing her calves behind the small of his back, tightening her hold cruelly. He caught her butt, grinding her against his erection, mashing their bodies into the wall. She squirmed in annoyance and bliss, nipping his lips and scratching his scalp. Nothing deterred him. He was hell-bent on seduction, and that luscious tongue lapped up her anger until she was nothing but a trembling mass of crude desire.

He tipped his head back and gulped air. "Pick a door."

"What?"

He adjusted her weight impatiently. "Unless you want me to strip you down in this hallway."

"Yeah, right," she muttered breathlessly. She tried

for a grin and failed. She'd never seen him look so fierce, so on the brink of losing control, and that primal passion triggered delicious throbbing sensations. She squeezed her legs tighter, clamping their pelvises. Nothing could come of this; it was just good-bye sex, but it was *happening*. A thrill shot through her even as she shrugged like she was bored. "Whatever room you've been sleeping in this week."

"We'll never make it that far." He captured her lips again, and she closed her eyes, surrendering to the full-on assault. His hips ground inside her thighs as he walked them rapidly down the hall. The light softened, and she broke off the kiss and glanced around. Majestic shelves of the first editions library towered before her.

"Not here," she gasped. "Someone might come in."

"No one comes in here." His head slanted, but she averted her face so his tongue simply assaulted her earlobe. She squirmed and shivered as aural nerve endings flared. His steps slowed, and the cold metal of the brass ladder rail pressed against her spine. Instinctively, she lowered her legs, standing with the strength of a newborn calf. He tugged her sweater up.

"Devon, wait. Let's go in the gallery. The sitting room. A room that can lock."

"I need you, Hannah." His voice was a harsh rasp. "Right now." He released the clip and tore the elastic from her hair, snatching handfuls as he anchored her head. He bent in again and trapped her mouth, soft lips grinding out rough pressure. She met his hunger head-on. She'd spent so many years craving words never said, letters never written, fantasies that had never come true. Until now. He was here and real and wanted only her. She trailed her hands down solid, shifting biceps as his fingers snaked under her waistband. Her pants button popped open.

She jerked her mouth free once more. He was a

sorcerer. How could she keep forgetting this room connected the wings? "Behind the desk, then," she pleaded, as his teeth nipped a sharp trail from her neck to her clavicle, the bites erotic, electrifying. She arched in his embrace; her body shivering with awareness. A few more seconds and she'd accept all of him inside her, right here in the middle of the most prestigious, open room in the house. She moaned in desperation, her defenses crumbling. "Please, Devon." He slowly raised his head, a drugged look in his dark eyes. "Fuck me behind the desk," she whispered.

A deafening clap of thunder answered her. The lights flickered, casting the intensity on his face into something dark and dangerous. Every cell in her body stilled. A heartbeat of time that lasted an eternity passed as a battle raged across his features. With a grunt, he swept her legs out from under her and crossed to the farthest point in the room at an effortless speed she'd have had to sprint to achieve.

He kicked at the desk chair, which wheeled in a crazy zigzag until it bumped a shelf. Falling to his knees, he lowered her on her back then braced himself over her, searing her lips with an incinerating kiss. A shutter banged somewhere close.

She reached down and traced his thick cock along his jeans. He whispered an obscenity, and seconds later her khakis were unceremoniously whipped off, her sweater and bra shoved up, exposing her to the cool air. He rolled and nipped and tongued the jutting peaks until she squirmed, whimpering.

He eased back. His palms trailed down to her waist as his glazed eyes took stock of her various stages of undress. Two lower buttons were all that held his shirt together now; the rest gaped open, framing the firm contours of his chest and rigid abs. In one motion, he stripped the shirt off, rolled it into a ball, and stuck it under her head. "Lift up, Hannah." She raised her hips, and he whisked her panties off, pausing over her mostly naked form. "Jesus, I've missed you. I've missed these."

Wide palms skimmed up her hips and stomach, halting at her aching breasts. He molded and squeezed the sensitive flesh again, rolling the nipples between his thumbs and fingers until they resembled hard pebbles. Her head thrashed from side to side, the desire and agony in her moans drowned out by the torrential rain battering the roof.

"I have to taste you," he whispered. His gaze descended to her apex. The soft touch of his hands whispered to her inner thighs, parting her wide. Two fingers slid inside her wet heat, and his thumb flickered her. She cried out, bucking, but he'd already withdrawn, leaving her aching and unfulfilled. He knelt back on his heels and stuck the fingers in his mouth. His cheeks sucked inward. He groaned and closed his eyes.

"Devon…"

He leaned down until their faces were centimeters apart, his aroused gaze unfocused, and did it again. A swipe of her clit, then licking his fingers like a lollipop as he watched her closely. She spread her thighs wider, quivering. "For the love of God…"

"Complaints?"

"Nope," she gasped. "Just a polite request to move along."

He hovered over her, grinning like the devil. The banging shutter picked up its tempo, slamming as wildly as her heart. She wanted to scream. Her gaze traveled to his jeans, and the hard shape straining against the fabric. "Please fuck me."

He swirled the fingers in his mouth, brows knotted in contemplation.

She rolled her eyes. "Really? 'Cause you almost took me out in the hall."

Those deep-blue eyes burned through her. "You've driven me out of my mind for days, Han." He tugged her hips, sliding her a few inches along the scratchy Persian rug until her ass rested near his knees. "Let's call this payback."

Her breath hitched as he lowered his head until he was a hairsbreadth from touchdown. Seconds passed. His warm, moist exhales tickled her most sensitive spot; his gloriously broad shoulders spanned the width of her spread thighs. The anticipation was excruciating. She whispered his name, but it disappeared in the storm. In desperation, she wriggled, and he blinked as if he was coming to. He bent down the last centimeter, sealing his mouth on her. The gentle lick of his tongue sent a thousand volts pulsating through her. She bit back a shriek and squirmed. He shifted his weight and wrapped his hands firmly around her inner thighs. Then went to work.

Her eyes bulged at the searing intensity, and lightning promptly blinded her. She squeezed them shut, giving herself over to the feel of that clever tongue. When she thrashed from the intense pleasure, he tightened his grip, rendering her immobile. The pure helplessness only heightened her excitement. She moaned beneath him, raking her fingernails across his scalp and holding his head steady.

He studiously brought her closer to her peak with single-minded focus. As her cries intensified and her breath began to shudder, he withdrew, laving his tongue along her inner thigh like a paintbrush.

She gasped in outrage, straining for the simple touch of air on her throbbing button to hit her orgasm. *"Shit!"*

"That's for hoping my company goes under."

She let go of his scalp and reached for herself, but he snatched her wrists and pressed them on her spread thighs. "Oh, no, baby," he said thickly. "We've always been great at communicating this way. Let's keep talking. I've got a lot more on my mind."

Before a snarky reply popped to mind, he returned to his ministrations lightly, the contact and rhythm nowhere near the pressure she needed. She quaked with frustration. No doubt the ring-throwing incident, her screaming fit, and ripping his damn shirt would all be in the conversational lineup. She wouldn't survive it.

As he orchestrated the buildup again, she tried to steady her breath. If he didn't know she was about to peak, he'd keep up that wicked nibbling and sucking. And the intense effort of holding in her moans and restraining the natural instinct to move beneath him enhanced the exquisite pressure. The peak was near; she had this!

Just as her inner thighs quivered and her ass tensed, he withdrew again. She screeched filthy names and fought the viselike grip he had on her wrists. He knelt above her, stock-still and unsmiling as she lay splayed out, sweaty, and in utter anguish. "I hate you," she panted.

"Lies aren't going to get you there any faster."

"Okay, I don't hate you. Not at all."

A corner of his mouth tilted up mischievously. His lips were swollen and glistening from working her over. She wrenched her fists from his iron grasp and beat them against the rug. "Why are you doing this?"

"Because I never want you to forget this...us. Ever." The vulnerability in his eyes belied the dominance of his words and the wild force that had driven her to almost-orgasm. This was the look of a man who hadn't gotten over her either, and hadn't found the words to say so.

She breathed his name and pulled him up for a deep, searching kiss.

He relieved her of the sweater and bra, still bunched near her clavicle, then drew a nipple into his mouth, his fingers nimbly taunting the other one. He took his time roaming down her stomach, tasting every inch of her body, caressing her inner thighs as she squirmed with the need to feel him *there*. And when he finally landed, she almost sobbed at the slow, measured pressure of his tongue.

She wouldn't survive a third round, and he must have sensed it, because he worked faster, watching her intently, swirling and sucking until the buildup was excruciating. She reached her peak like a rocket launch, bucking beneath him as pleasure disintegrated her. Nerve endings pulsed and quivered, electrified. She clawed at his scalp, shrieking, holding nothing back, not caring if she screamed the house down. Either the lights flickered again or she went temporarily blind as the long crest peaked and sparks ebbed.

Her breath came in labored gasps as she floated back down.

When her world finally ricocheted onto its axis, she opened her eyes to find him nude, sheathed, and waiting. He smiled with supreme cockiness, and one of those handsome brows quirked up as he glanced at his watch. His arrogance was too much. She gave him the finger.

"Glad we're on the same page," he growled, bending his beautiful, muscled body over hers. He gripped himself at her entrance but held rigidly still above her until she met his eyes. A question lingered there.

"Yes," she breathed, "yes. Same page."

His grin was pure depravity. Powerful thighs spread hers wider than she thought possible. The rug scratched her bare backside, heightening her sensitivity, as did the wanton knowledge that she was stretched open, in a completely public room, in a house filled with people.

Hooded eyes, blue-black and fathomless, held her spellbound. In one swift thrust, Devon plowed into her, his grunt so primal she almost came again.

He braced himself on his forearms, unmoving until her muscles relaxed around him. "Christ, I remember this," he muttered, nuzzling her ear. "You're so fucking tight."

He shifted and rocked her knees up near her shoulders, propping her socked feet next to his neck. Sweat ran down his temple as he eased out. He pushed in with excruciating slowness this time, and she accepted him with an ecstatic groan. Her eyes drifted shut.

"No," he said gruffly, freezing his thrust. Her eyes flew open. "I want you watching. Don't you ever forget this."

She nodded, breathless. Granite biceps strained on either side of her and she ran her fingers over the bulges. Her gaze traveled to the intensity on his handsome face, down the solid lines of his chest, and brick-stacked abs, until it reached the apex where they were joined. He rewarded her with a sliding tempo, and when she made eye contact again, he was gazing at her with that all-encompassing absorption. He leisurely increased his rhythm, opting for powerful strokes over rapid friction. She twisted, as much as she could in her curled position, to meet his solid thrusts. Over and over he plunged— deeper, more forcefully—and she welcomed it, squeezing her muscles to hinder his retreat, opening herself wide to receive all of him. A droplet of his sweat fell on her neck.

"You feel so good," he grunted through his teeth, inserting a thumb between them and stroking her clit. "Christ, you're so tight. Come for me, Hannah. I want to feel it."

The uninhibited rawness of his passion was too much. She shattered beneath him, writhing as he ground into her faster and faster. Suddenly his eyes squeezed shut and those black brows slashed together. "Oh Christ," he said hoarsely, and his hips shuddered. Within seconds, his long thrusts weakened, and finally he collapsed, drenched and spent, his pulse thundering under her palms.

She drew oxygen in audible gulps, as if she'd broken through the surface of a fathomless ocean. Lowering her stiff hips, she encircled his coarsely haired thighs with her calves. His breathing slowed, and he mumbled something indecipherable. Too exhausted to respond, she simply laced fingers through his sweat-soaked hair, accepting the weight of him. She closed her eyes to capture her other senses: The taste of him in her mouth. His sinuous, damp muscles beneath her hands. And that warm summer scent, so unique to him. The storm raged in surround sound, and that damn shutter banged. Each pounding wave shocked the house—a symphony underscoring their violent lovemaking. And that's what it had ultimately been: lovemaking. *Because I'm in love with you. No matter what you do to my apartment or how soon you leave for New York. I'll never forget you or this moment.*

He braced his weight on his elbows without lifting off her. "I'm sorry," he murmured, kissing the corner of her mouth.

"Mmmm?"

"I was way too rough." He stroked the damp hair from her face and neck. "Are you all right?"

"Mmmm. I was pretty rough on you too." She traced the column of his throat, and he chuckled.

"I've never seen that side of you. I like it. A lot." His lips trailed along her temple, her eyelid, her cheekbone, then slanted over her mouth. The kiss was languid, his breathing deep and slow, as if he fought sleep. Eventually he broke off, slipped out of her, and snapped off the condom, tossing it in the wastebasket under the desk.

He stretched out on his side and pulled her to face him. His expression of utter contentment probably matched hers. The shutter banged, rain drummed savagely on the roof, and she'd never felt so safe and secure.

❧

GOD, HE STILL loved her. Everything about her. In this suspended time before reality crashed him back to earth, everything seemed possible—especially them staying together. She looked like he felt. This was doable; he'd problem-solve it later. He traced her lips, mesmerized by the glow on her smiling face, the flaming hair pillowing around them, and her sleek, glistening legs tangled in his. Someone should paint her just like this. Call the piece *Sated*. He could handle that kind of art.

"So what happened here?" she said softly, flicking a finger between them. "I threw a ring at you, called you an SOB, and you gave me the orgasms of a lifetime?"

He grinned. "You could've thrown Super Bowl tickets—my reaction would have been the same. These last few days—being around you again—I was done with the platonic shit."

"I was done with it Friday morning when I saw you in here." She twisted her head and studied the desk and the large room. "I don't know how we haven't been caught, though," she whispered, which was ridiculous, given how loud she'd been moments before.

He held back his laugh. "No one comes in here. Seriously."

"Even if they hear bloodcurdling screams?"

He let go of the chuckle. "Ever think of doing sound effects for horror movies?"

"Ha, ha." She stretched languidly and smiled. He couldn't help but kiss the dimple. "Thank God we were here, though. Aunt Milly has perfect hearing."

"Even over this storm?"

"Her ears could be classified as secret weapons."

"Sweet Aunt Milly," he murmured, tracing those lush, kiss-swollen lips again. "If she only knew what a tramp... *Ow!*"

"As glad as I am that we did this," she kissed the fingers she just bit, "why exactly *are* you in this house?" He traced her jaw, unable to stop the muscle clenching along his. "Don't shut me out, Devon."

The betrayal of Eric selling off shares, the final death knell of his company, the beatdown with his brother-in-law from hell, Frannie melting down by the second, Harrison ordering his second arrest... He couldn't tell her. If he started, he'd never stop.

She halted his hand from tracing her cheekbone. "Talk. And insert a feeling word."

He sighed, the sudden fatigue spreading through him almost debilitating. "I told you my father was trying to take my company, and...he'll have it tomorrow." Her expectant look reminded him of her last command. "I'm upset."

Her eyes softened. "No matter what I said last night, I am sorry to hear that, Dev."

He nodded. "My father plans to raze your neighborhood, too. Your problems haven't gone away. It's why I wanted you to have the damn ring."

She ruffled a hand through his hair. His scalp still tingled where she'd raked him repeatedly with her nails. "I'll find another way to afford an apartment, and hopefully keep my partnership too."

"Was that a horrible thing? Giving it to you to hock?"

She searched his eyes, her brows crinkling. "You have to ask?"

"I was trying to fix everything. Obviously I fucked

up, and I'm sorry."

"Sometimes good intentions aren't good enough."

He nodded. His fingers trailed along the curve of her waist and up over her hip. Her skin was moist and warm. "My cousin told me I don't know my way around women, and it's messing with my head."

"Well, physically you know your way around a woman. As in gold-medal skill."

"Hannah, I'm serious. How can I"—he scrubbed his face—"not be an ass around you? How can I convince you that the ring is worthless to me, and it would make me *happy*—I'm using a feeling word here—to help you?"

She was quiet for a while, her face troubled. "This is a good start, I guess. You're actually talking, not frantically solving a problem."

"There are people who talk and people who *do*. Every time I try to talk about meaningful stuff, I sound lame."

She leaned in and kissed him softly. "Lame is better than silent. If we'd been doing this twelve years ago, maybe we wouldn't have lost each other because of our last parent."

He rolled onto his back and folded her to him, resting his chin on the top of her head.

Their last parent. His had kicked him out, and he'd tried to force Hannah into that same miserable boat. If his mother had been alive and diagnosed with cancer, he wouldn't have considered leaving. Not for a second. He'd never thought about it that way; any thinking about his mother or Hannah was looking back.

As if on cue, she said softly, "Tell me about her." She caressed his bicep so lightly it tickled.

He stayed silent. He wasn't kidding about the lame comment. *Talking* meant something completely different to women, and he didn't know what it was. Fuck it;

couldn't go wrong with honesty. "She was a great mom. The best."

"Devon…"

Nope. Honesty wasn't going to cut it. "Help me out, Hannah. Ask a specific question so I know what it is you're looking for."

"Tell me something that made her great. Something unique that no one else could replace."

Well, shit. Road trip through the quagmire of memories. Like how Mom tiptoed into his room each morning and woke him with a kiss on the forehead. Or Cooking Day on Mrs. Farlow's day off each week, when she taught him and Frannie how to make homemade pasta and cannoli. The tears in her eyes when he formally presented another painting of her or the family or even the house and grounds. She'd had such love and pride in everything either of them did or said or gave her. Those were the only times he'd felt secure in this house.

"When I was young, I used to think she was magical," he said, but then laughed because that wasn't what he meant to say. *What the fuck?* "I mean, she was always happy, so everyone around her was happy."

"Aunt Milly said she loved life."

He nodded, his chin bobbing on her head. "I never saw anything get her down." He exhaled in a snort. "Except Harrison."

"Did you ever hear them fighting?"

"Near the end of her life. And not often. He always seemed to be at the office—either downtown or in this house. None of us were welcome in either place." He sifted a hand through her snarled hair, but his fingers snagged immediately. He cupped her head instead, adjusting his other arm tighter around her.

"Before that, was he a good father to you two?"

He shrugged. "He wasn't like he is now, but he

never had any interest in us, and we rarely did anything as a family. Most everything was just us and Mom. Then when I was nine, if I saw him at all, Mom was there and they were arguing."

"About what?"

He'd spent so much time *not* thinking about the past that it took several minutes to reach that far back and make sense of his childhood perceptions. "Something was happening with his company," he finally said. "He was always in a rage about it. I think my mom would try to soothe him or make him see the positive side, and he'd shout her down." He shook his head. "Something like that." But dormant memories stirred, broke free, floated upward.

"We have more money than we'll ever need."

"That's not the point, Francesca. He's stealing from me."

"But if he needs it that badly, just give it to him. Or turn a blind eye—"

"This is business! My reputation! I could go to jail for what Wilson did."

"Jesus!" Devon bolted upright, sending Hannah's face flying into his naked lap. He helped her sit up, kissed her temple, and scrambled to his feet, aware of her speaking but unable to hear words. Without her body heat, the air was chilly. Or maybe he was shivering in shock. *Bryant Wilson.* His father's old partner was behind this.

"Devon!" Hannah called, hugging her knees to her chest. "Answer me."

"I…I have to find Harrison." He picked up the wrinkled shirt her head had lain on only moments before. A few strands of hair clung to the fabric, and he didn't remove them. "I remembered something my parents fought about and…" He couldn't finish. This couldn't be true. He thrust his arms into the shirtsleeves and realized all over again only two buttons remained. *Shit.* He would have to tear around this house looking like Fabio. "Please stay here until I return. The moment I get some answers, I'll be right back. And when the storm lets up, I'm taking you to the Drake."

"Where you'll spend hours explaining this to me."

"Only after we run through a box of condoms."

Her eyes twinkled and a dimple appeared. "Ouch."

Pulse in overdrive, Devon thundered down the stairs and into his father's office. It was dark. He returned to the foyer. The sunroom. The dining room. All dark and empty. He swung through the doors to the kitchen—cold and dark. That stopped him short. Even in his earliest memories, something was always boiling on the stove or roasting in the oven. The place was spotless and deserted; no aroma of recent food lingered in the air.

Come to think of it, he hadn't seen anyone in hours. Not one staff or family member. He'd tried to find his father earlier, but was so hung up on Hannah and the ring-throwing incident he hadn't made the connection that they were probably in this house alone.

"Hello," he called. "Joseph? Mrs. Farlow?"

Was tonight Honey's wake? Funeral? That had to be it. He'd never in his life experienced this house empty, and the yawning quiet was unsettling. He flicked on the overhead light. Seconds later, a crack of lightning split through the howling storm, and the room went black. "Shit." He flicked the switch a couple of times and swore some more.

Rain slashed at the kitchen windows, and deafening thunder roared directly overhead. The storm had to be right on top of them. God knew how Hannah would fare in a creepy, unlit mansion. He needed to get back to her, quick. They could keep each other thoroughly busy and wait Harrison out. And then he'd get some goddamn answers!

Pushing through the doors to the dining room, Devon used the next flash of lightning to locate the candelabra centerpiece. He popped out two slim candles, returned to the kitchen, and stuck the wicks in the old stove's pilot light. When he passed the bar area, he grabbed a mostly full bottle of merlot and glasses with his other hand.

The load was awkward enough to make cupping the candles impossible, and the slightest speed caused the flames to flicker wildly, slowing his journey upstairs considerably. By the time he made it to the library, it felt as though an hour had passed. When this room was empty too, he considered drinking straight from the bottle. "Hannah?"

He crossed to the second gallery, then down to the first, with its lingering, acrid smoke tickling his throat. He stepped back into the hallway.

"Hannah?" he bellowed. She couldn't have gone far in the pitch black. No response. Foreboding crept down his spine. Why would she wander all alone in an empty, unlit mansion?

Only the relentless boom of the surf and the shudder of the house replied.

CHAPTER 27

"THANK GOD YOU heard me calling," Hannah said. "I was beginning to freak out."

"Yeah, the mansion gets pretty spooky during a storm. You're lucky I was on my way to fix myself a cup of tea. You'd have been lost for ages." Frannie laughed at her own joke, but the notes fell flat, and in the residual glow of the flashlight she carried, strain and exhaustion etched her face. The sweats she wore bagged around her, and her black hair looked like a Disney witch's.

Hannah self-consciously smoothed her snarled coils but let her arm drop. There was no hope. She hadn't found her hair clasp in the dark, or her cell phone, which must've fallen out of her pocket in the frenzy. Hell, it was enough that she'd found her clothes and dressed. Her mouth probably looked as if it'd been stung by a swarm of bees. Frannie wasn't stupid, although hopefully she hadn't heard them. Hannah's throat felt raw from all the screaming. She fought her smile of bliss.

"Where's Devon?" his sister asked.

Hannah cringed inwardly. If only she could've responded that she'd been diagnosing Harrison's gallery. "Off looking for your father."

"Hm. He'll be looking a long time."

"Where is everyone?"

"Honey's wake. Father gave them the afternoon and evening off—probably to ensure the funeral parlor was packed with mourners. Except for my son, Todd, I don't know anyone who would've gone to pay their respects of their own volition."

"Why didn't you go?"

She shrugged. "It would be too hypocritical. Our lives are a thousand times better off now that she's dead."

The flippancy of the remark caught Hannah off guard. "I was in the foyer yesterday, Frannie. You took the news very hard."

"It was the manner of her death," Frannie responded tightly. "It unleashed a bunch of repressed memories."

Of course. Hannah blushed. There was no way to get her foot out of her mouth.

Francine turned and flicked the beam down the long hallway. "Well, come on, let's get that tea."

"I—I've misplaced my phone." She bit her lip at the gaffe. She really didn't want Devon's sister helping her look around under the desk of the first editions library. Besides any other evidence of crazy-monkey sex, there was the damn used condom...

"Where did you leave it last?"

"Uh...maybe the basement where we were crating. Don't worry; I'll find it later." But as they fell into step, unease trickled down Hannah's spine. The emptiness was so eerie that it tainted all the beautiful artifacts. Francine's beam bounced off centuries-old paintings. They'd reached a row of baroque art—a family in a sitting room, a devout woman in prayer—but the scenes took on a sinister cast in the dim light or neon-blue lightning. "Why aren't we going down the main staircase?" Her voice sounded too high.

"It's actually faster this way."

Hannah nodded, but she didn't know these gaping, dark hallways. She really would be lost for days if Frannie took off right now. But why would she take off? They were just having tea. Damn it, where was Devon?

She shivered and tried to focus on her surroundings: the pattern on the Persian runner, the art that resembled the Wickham family ancestry now. With each step, a fluttery feeling persisted as the seam of her pants rubbed her, echoing the astonishing orgasms. She even took comfort in the raw rug-burn on her backside. Mentally she chanted his name, hoping some cosmic force would lead him to her. *Wait a minute!* "Did you bring your cell phone?" she asked Frannie. "Maybe we can call—"

But Frannie was already shaking her head. "Watch yourself on these steps." She swept the beam in an arc, lighting up a small threshold, beyond which a tight spiral staircase descended into dark nothingness.

Hannah froze. "Wait." The descent looked downright dangerous, the narrow wooden treads so worn that the centers were concave and scuffed a much lighter color. "Where are we?" Her voice shook, but she was past caring. She should have stayed in first editions. She didn't even like tea.

"In the olden days, this was the servants' staircase." Frannie flicked the beam this way and that. The cramped corkscrew steps resembled something from a Hitchcock thriller. "It lets out in the kitchen and also keeps going down to the basement."

"I don't think this is such a hot—"

"Come on, Hannah, don't be a scaredy-cat." She laughed, the sound distorting in the tight stairwell.

Hannah glanced furtively down the long hall she'd come from, one of many she'd have to negotiate in darkness to try to find her way back to Devon. And using the intermittent lightning to find her way through the maze was just as terrifying. She turned back with a sigh and descended the first step after Frannie and the dancing beam. They spiraled once, and the second-floor threshold disappeared; they were truly inside a descending tunnel now. Hannah's mouth dried up, and she all but piggybacked the other woman. She concentrated on the narrow beam and her breathing and the fact that each footstep brought her closer to the kitchen. Even the roaring surf and thunder seemed far away in here—muted, buried. She squeezed her hands into fists.

Frannie stopped abruptly, and Hannah flashed on some scenario where she'd say, "We're trapped," or "Stay here, I'll be right back." A scream lodged in her throat.

"This is the servants' door," Frannie said. She waved the beam across a worn door blending into the wooden wall. "In my grandparents' day, the help lived here. It's the only entrance to their quarters." Hannah managed a squeak of interest. "Once in a while, I go and sit in one of the empty bedrooms. I crave the silence."

"Where does Joseph live?" Hannah asked, not caring a flying fig, but hearing her voice, even quivering, lent a speck of normalcy. Two friends wandering to the kitchen for tea. Yeah, that's all this was.

"He and Mrs. Farlow live up the driveway a bit, past the garages." They continued circling down, and Hannah breathed faster. The oxygen seemed thinner now. They should have reached the ground floor long ago. Frannie hummed under her breath, and Hannah choked on her hysteria until one final turn dumped them out into the enormous kitchen, shadowed in the flashlight's beam, then lit like the Fourth of July by a split of lightning. The clear crack of thunder was the most comforting sound Hannah had heard in ages. Her chest loosened, and she sucked in several gulps of air.

"Have a seat over there." Frannie pointed to

barstools under the enormous marble-covered island. "Do you have a tea preference?"

"Whatever you're having." Her rock-steady tone surprised the hell out of her. Perspiration made her sweater cling to her back.

Frannie turned on the burner, and a burst of blue flame ignited beneath an old-fashioned aluminum kettle. She disappeared into the walk-in pantry, where her humming sounded discordant.

But at least they were in the kitchen. Hannah rubbed the goose bumps underneath her sweater. If only she'd found her cell phone, she could call or text Devon. He was probably looking for her now. And when he found her, he'd take her back to the Drake. Probably any minute.

Frannie placed a box of tea on the island, and Hannah consciously unclenched her shoulders and fists. "May I help with anything?"

"Nope. Water will be ready in a jiffy." Francine claimed the next stool and stood the flashlight on its end, lighting the ceiling.

Hannah tried to smile. What was wrong with her? This would be a perfectly normal half-hour if the sun shone or the electricity worked. "When, uh...do you think the service will be over?"

"No clue. It's an open house. By the way, I didn't want to say anything before, but since we'll probably be here when people start returning, your sweater is on inside-out."

"Jeez..." Hannah blushed and fingered the wool blend. Should she whip it off right now? Nah. If the lights came back on, she'd go into the pantry.

"You *do* know my brother is engaged?"

Hannah stiffened at the accusing tone. Frannie must not know the engagement was off, but even so, it was none of her business. "Well..." She lapsed into silence.

"Well what? It's a yes-or-no question."

Hannah rubbed damp palms on her pants and glanced at the kettle. The blue flames licked around the sides of the pot, and the water hissed in pre-boil. "I think their plans have changed. You'll have to ask him."

Frannie's eyes flared wildly, and for a second, she looked deranged. "He would've told me."

There was no way Hannah was gossiping about this. "I think it's very recent. He may not have seen you."

"He was with me most of this morning."

At her shrill tone, Hannah wanted to slap herself. This woman was on medication; she'd just relived her mother's death; her husband had been publically caught having an affair. Hannah veered into her childhood instinct. When Mom had gone into those dark moods, anything she'd said would be taken wrong. The solution was not talking. She spread her hands. "I'm sure he's looking for me right now. He'll tell you soon."

"So, you moved right in to fill the empty space."

It was an accusation, not a question. Hannah frowned. *Get her off this subject.* "Is everything all right, Frannie?"

"He'll go back to New York and leave you again. Leave me."

Hannah waited for the stab in her heart to subside. Of course he would. What happened upstairs was just what she'd expected. Sex without a relationship. She inhaled unsteadily. "Probably."

"You don't seem too upset for someone who adores him like I do."

"I'm just facing reality, Frannie."

"You don't know the first thing about facing reality."

Hannah bit the inside of her cheek. *Everything you say will egg her on.* "I'm sorry you feel that way."

Frannie huffed out a breath and stared fixedly at a point over her shoulder, almost trancelike. Except for the torrential patter of rain and rattling windows, the silence between them was fraught with hostility.

At the end of an eternity, the kettle whistled. Frannie slid off her stool, and when her back was turned, Hannah wiped the perspiration from her lip. She'd be better off negotiating this house in the inky blackness than drinking a beverage she didn't like with a woman who reminded her of Mom at her worst. Hannah straightened. She knew the way to the main stairs from here. As she opened her mouth to cancel her cup of tea, the hair pricked up the back of her neck. Although the storm raged loudly, Frannie was muttering to herself. The only words Hannah made out were "stupid slut." The kettle clanked back onto the burner, and cups rattled on the saucers.

Well, shit. She wasn't going to sit here and be insulted. She jumped off the stool just as Frannie turned with the filled cups. She shrieked at Hannah's abrupt movement; the teacups slipped from her grasp. China shattered, and boiling water splashed the tiles and her sweatpants. Another ear-piercing shriek, as water saturated the fabric. Frannie stared at the mess and slapped her hands over her mouth, oddly resembling a little girl. Her overly large sweatshirt sleeves slid to her elbows and Hannah gasped. Long scratches ran down Frannie's left forearm. Devon had given a DNA swab because of skin found under Honey's nails. Hannah's heart drummed so fast she couldn't catch her breath.

Frannie lowered her arms and kicked at the wreckage. She didn't seem to realize what she'd just exposed. "You startled me." Her voice was an accusing shrill. That creepy, vacant stare returned. "Look what you've done."

I didn't do it. Lightning blinded Hannah. She

should leave. Call out to Devon. Surely he'd heard the screams. "I was about to excuse myself." Her mouth was so dry, it was a wonder the words came out intelligibly. "I don't want tea anymore. I'm going to find Devon." She pointed at the doors that led to the dining room. "He'll help us clean up."

"I can't be alone when I get like this."

"Like what?" A metallic taste coated Hannah's mouth.

"When I'm not right."

"You're all right, Frannie." To get the itchy palms to stop, she added a bit of truth: "You just called me a stupid slut. I'd say you're fine."

"I said that about Honey."

"Honey's not here." Hannah's knees trembled so badly she gripped the corner of the island.

Tears spilled out of Frannie's eyes, the same beautiful blue as Devon's, but as fragile as the teacups on the floor. "Don't leave me."

Hannah shivered. "I...I'll stay a little longer. Take some deep breaths." All she had to do was make light conversation and babysit until Devon came to see what all the noise was about. Then she'd figure out a way to show him the gouges his sister hid under the thick sweatshirt. And maybe there was a perfectly good explanation. Frannie was unbalanced, but she seemed too wrapped up in her own problems to murder her father's fiancée. Hannah breathed calmly for the first time in minutes. She was reading way too much into all of this because of the whole creepiness factor.

"He didn't love me enough," Frannie mumbled, wiping her eyes on the cuffed sleeve. "No one does. And then fucking Honey walks into our lives..."

Sympathy flooded Hannah. "Your father would still love you if he'd married Honey," she said in the soothing voice she'd used to calm Mom in the bipolar lows and Aunt Milly during her anxiety attacks. "Honey could never have taken that."

The shrill laughter made her step back. The ping-pong moods were too much. "I'm not talking about my father. She was fucking my *husband*!" Frannie shrieked. "I saw them through the window when I was looking for Todd. She was going to marry my father, take my inheritance, my husband, *and* my son!"

"How could Honey have possibly known your husband?" Her voice sounded way too high.

"I found out she met him on a website guaranteeing discreet affairs with married men. Only she blackmailed them. Instead of giving her money, Brady turned her on to a bigger fish. Within six weeks, my father proposed."

Hannah bit her lip. Were these hallucinations? Fabrications? The story was so bizarre. "Did you...tell your father?"

"Punishing her was more important."

Fresh horror skittered down Hannah's spine. Where Honey had been tall and slim, Frannie had wiry strength. A fact Devon used to point out in high school. *Never underestimate my sister. She may look fragile, but she's faster than me and probably just as strong.*

"You think I killed her," Frannie said softly.

Hannah choked back a scream. Pretending to toss the mess of hair off her shoulders, she cast about the kitchen. A rolling pin was two feet away on the counter. She eased to the side. "Did you?" The squeak was so high, even she didn't hear it over the storm.

Frannie tilted her head, smiling. Only the smile was cold and calculated.

Hannah folded her arms nonchalantly, her fists clenched. She eased another step to the side.

"You'll never make it to the rolling pin, Hannah. Sit back down. I'll make us more tea."

The swinging door to the dining room pushed

inward. Joseph strode in with an industrial-strength flashlight, his white hair and black raincoat sopping. He paused in surprise when he spotted them. "Miss Francine. Miss Moore."

"I don't think Frannie is well," Hannah blurted, taking the final step and resting her hand on the rolling pin. "I think she stopped taking her meds a few days ago."

"Nonsense." Frannie waved a hand, and by God if she didn't look perfectly normal as she smiled up at the old man. "We were about to have tea." She raised an eyebrow at Hannah. "Right?"

Joseph gazed from one to the other, and then took in the watery shards littering the tiles.

Devon's voice shouting for her filtered through the storm. It gave Hannah the backbone she needed. "I think she pushed Honey."

Said aloud, the terror of the last half-hour crushed her. The adrenaline dump turned to bile in her throat. She trembled like an old woman, and her limbs tingled. It didn't matter. She was safe, and Joseph could take it from here. She let go of the rolling pin as the stoic carriage of the unflappable butler crumbled before her.

"Oh, Frannie," he said, sounding achingly old. "What have you done?"

CHAPTER 28

DEVON PIVOTED AT the quick footsteps. "Oh, it's you." He palmed the erratically flickering candles.

"I was in the kitchen." Frannie thumbed the dining room doors she'd just walked through. "Thought I heard you shouting." Her voice echoed hollowly around the foyer.

"Christ, it's like wandering around a haunted house. Where is everybody?"

"Wake. I couldn't face it, so Ricky took Todd. Nice shirt. Is that the latest fashion?" She swung her flashlight and hummed as she made her way toward him. Her eyes seemed wild and overly dilated above its beam.

The storm must have unhinged her a bit; it certainly had him. And God knew how poor Hannah was dealing with it. "Have you seen Hannah?"

"About ten minutes ago. I asked if she wanted tea, and she said no. She was in a hurry to get home."

"Home?" Devon walked in a circle, as if he could light up the far corners with his candles. She left? In the middle of this? Fear gnawed at him. Something wasn't right. At the next jag of lightning, he spied a dark lump at the base of Zeus and walked over, illuminating it. "She's still here. She wouldn't have left without her jacket."

Frannie looked around, blinking rapidly. "Huh. I don't know where she could've wandered off to then.

We were in the kitchen, and she said good-bye and headed out through the dining room."

Which leads straight to here. It wasn't like she could have gotten lost. Devon circled again, feeling like an idiot. Where could she be?

Frannie stepped closer. "I didn't know you two were on such intimate terms, what with your high-society wedding in May."

"Just help me find her," he snapped. "Hannah!" The front door pushed open, and they spun toward it. Frigid, damp wind whirled in, snuffing out Devon's candles. Harrison staggered into the foyer, his umbrella bent, his white hair like a mousse commercial gone horribly wrong. He slammed the door shut, the sound reverberating through the empty house.

"Father." His sister's voice sounded strange. "What are you doing home?"

Harrison leaned the ruined umbrella gently against the wall and breathed out a ragged sigh. When he straightened, the dead eyes and weary lines carving his face made him resemble a frail man every bit his seventy years. He attempted to smooth his hair. "I had Evan drive me home. I couldn't maintain the façade."

Frannie's mouth popped open.

She'd probably been left out of the loop on Honey's duplicity. That could wait. Bryant Wilson couldn't.

"We need to talk," Devon said shortly.

Harrison slid an exhausted gaze his way, pausing at the gaping, half-dressed look he had going on. "It's over. I didn't get your company in time."

In time? He was done with the games. "What about Bryant Wilson?" he asked through clenched teeth. His father's shoulders slumped. Something tugged inside Devon, but he ignored it. "I demand answers."

It was another moment before Harrison spoke. "All right. Come into my office."

"In two minutes. I need to find Hannah." At his father's confused look, he added, "The art lady. She was near your second gallery when the storm hit. Now she's lost somewhere in the house."

"Take the flashlight, Dev." Frannie held it out. "Go talk your big business deals. I'll relight your candles and make sure Hannah's safe. Take as long as you need."

Devon hesitated. He should really be looking with Frannie, because something was *off*. But his sister knew more hidey-holes around here than he ever had, and Harrison held answers he needed. *It's over. I didn't get your company in time.* What the hell did that mean? Harrison was dropping the takeover? And why would he have claimed he was Bryant on Friday? Curiosity and a thin ray of hope dragged Devon into the office.

Harrison gingerly lowered himself in the leather chair as if his body ached. He hadn't made eye contact since the foyer, and now gripped the edge of the colossal desk, staring at his white knuckles.

"What do time and your old partner have to do with you stealing my company?" Devon sat across the wide desk, glancing out the window at the next flash of lightning. The display was nature at its most savage. Trees bent at a frightening angle, and the lake rose like a dark beast, covered in furious, foaming white caps. All went dark. He shuddered and turned to his father. Although he wanted this confrontation to be all fire-and-brimstone fury for what he and Eric had been put through, he couldn't bring himself to even raise his voice in the face of this peculiar frailty. Thunder ripped overhead, the bass hurting his inner ears. Still he didn't press for an answer.

Harrison finally looked up. "What do you know about Bryant Wilson?"

Devon shrugged. More games? Harrison couldn't just explain outright why Bryant Wilson was helping steal Ashby? "You and Mom argued about him a lot. I think she sided with him, and you were always angry. Whether it was at him or her or both, I don't know. I was nine. It meant nothing to me. Why would he buy Eric's shares?"

"He didn't. He died of heart failure four years ago. And I hope the bastard is burning to a crisp."

Devon spread his arms. "So we're back to square one. You are Bryant."

"I took the name, yes."

"Why? He was your enemy."

"Not always." Harrison's shoulders slumped, the resignation on his face such a white flag of surrender that Devon's jaw slackened. "He was my closest friend at Yale. We both entered the Navy together, running the supply department aboard the *Princeton*. After Korea, we started a brokerage firm. Figured we'd marry a couple of babes, settle in the suburbs, have kids who'd also grow up as best friends."

Devon raked a hand over his still tender scalp. He wanted answers. He wanted to find Hannah and take her back to the Drake. He wanted to turn her back into the wanton vixen she'd been upstairs. This trip through his father's memory played no part in any of that.

"We named the company BryWick. Eight years in, we were making money hand over fist. Not a deal went wrong; not a contract fell through. Then one day we received a surprise visit from the Securities and Exchange Commission. Turns out Bryant had played fast and loose with investors' money. He'd dummy up statements, pay old investors with new investor money. Siphoned off millions no one ever found. He did this for years, right under my nose. Only he'd grown careless. The reports he issued were too good to be true, and it sparked the SEC's interest."

Harrison pressed his lips together and let more

silence linger. "Your mother had a naïve streak a mile wide. She never believed he'd do that, and the more evidence the commission uncovered, the more excuses she found. That was the reason for the arguments. Initially, because I suspected an affair"—he waved his hand before Devon could react—"which was a knee-jerk reaction. But her belief in him was a betrayal to me, because if he wasn't defrauding investors, then I was. And I may be a ruthless bastard, but I'd never cheat a client."

Devon folded his arms and leaned back. "Again— why call your takeover a name you despised?"

"Tomorrow, Tucker plans to file a complaint with the SEC against Ashby Enterprises."

A chill raced over Devon's skin. "What? Why?"

"For fraud. Is your cousin in the office this weekend scrambling over paperwork?"

"Yes. Due to your impending takeover."

"He's lying. He's in there covering as many tracks as he can."

"Wha…" The rest of the words stuck in his throat. Cold sweat covered the chills blanketing his skin.

"Eric has taken you to the cleaners, son. Your reported results are bogus. He's been siphoning off investors' money and misrepresenting your company's profits for months. The SEC will begin an investigation, and you'll probably face prison time. Just like I almost did."

Devon inhaled through his mouth. He still couldn't capture enough oxygen. There was no way Eric would do this to him. To them. "How do you know all this?" And how did he *not* know?

"What aren't you telling me, Eric?"

"Nothing. If Wickham Corp marches in on Monday, I don't want us to get caught with our pants down. I'm buried in stacks, making sure everything's in the right

sequence and accounted for."

"Call Sally in to help."

"I know where everything is, and how to do it right."

"Oh shit." He palmed his face. "Oh shit, shit, shit." *Why would Eric do this?* They'd been best friends since Devon had staggered off the damn Greyhound bus on Eighth Avenue… He'd taught Devon everything he knew, and together they'd taken their company into the stratosphere. Or they hadn't. It was all a fraud.

"Your future father-in-law sniffed it out first and called me," Harrison said, and Devon slumped back against the leather. "He had no idea I'd disinherited you, so naturally he still wanted the marriage to go through, and therefore, your reputation was as important to him as his own. I played along. We agreed if I purchased your firm, I could flush money back in to cover your cousin's greed. No other investor would need to know; no one would file a complaint. I tossed in a little money at a time as Bryant, and during that same period Tucker took a vast withdrawal for wedding expenses. And we watched the rat scurry. Eric began squeezing some investors for more money, and delayed paying out requests from others to fund Tucker's demands. Friday morning, your cousin had the bright idea to tell Tucker you'd been disinherited in an attempt to stem the cash withdrawals. Naturally, Tucker exploded and pulled out of our plan. He warned that if I didn't take your company by the end of the day and flush money back in, he'd immediately file a complaint with the SEC.

"But you managed to convince that little runt Westcott to hold off, so I didn't acquire you on Friday. And now Ken Tucker is out for blood."

Devon inhaled a shaky breath. "My fiancée called the wedding off on Saturday."

Harrison nodded. "No doubt Tucker was the

puppeteer behind that."

Probably not. Nicole, with that formidable talent of hers, must have seen through Devon's Manhattan persona, once she got a glimpse of his behavior these last few days. Trying to emulate her and her father's intimidating hold on social and financial power as the key to happiness was his biggest mistake. Second was the blind trust in his mentor and best friend. The thought was punctuated by another roar of thunder. The windows rattled at the reverberation. Had Frannie found Hannah yet? No doubt. He needed to focus and finish this.

The old man straightened in his chair. "Here were your two critical mistakes. Don't look at me like that; someone needs to tell you. First, not signing a partnership agreement so you'd get principal buying power. Second, personally guaranteeing your mother's inheritance to get the loan for Rogers Park. What a stupid risk."

"The property was a steal," Devon said through his teeth. "The inheritance was the only way to get the bank to green-light the loan that fast." His defensive tone annoyed him. His father was not his boss. He inhaled and started again. "I had it written into the shareholder agreement that I'd get a higher percentage of the profit for taking all the risk." Nope. No better.

Harrison studied him as a long roll of thunder roared overhead. The mansion shuddered and groaned as waves pounded relentlessly at the cliff. "Your project will be shut down during the investigation; no doubt the bank will call in the loan. Every penny of that trust fund is gone."

Devon swallowed a hard lump. "I knew that as soon as you decided to take Ashby from me. So why, after all these years, would you *save* me from…whatever's about to happen tomorrow?"

"Retribution for what Bryant did to me. Even after

years of trials and appeals, the bastard never faced jail time. I never found the money. Our company declared bankruptcy. Our reputations were ruined. I started Wickham Corp with nothing but cutthroat ambition. This time I vowed to catch your cousin in the act and throw him to the wolves." Harrison smiled without humor. "And the other reason was simple. You had a vulnerable company, and it was easy to take. I know you expect me to blather on about fatherly love and building a relationship from the ashes of twelve years ago, but kindness wasn't the motive."

Devon's jaw hurt from clenching his teeth. His father sat lost in thought while Devon absorbed the shock of Eric's betrayal, and his life's work collapsing like a sinkhole. His instinct had always been to seek options, implement solutions, formulate contingency plan A, and back it up with B and C, but his mind was struck dumb. All he could think about was revenge.

He grabbed the flashlight and slapped it lightly against his palm. The metal felt wet, and when he raised it, a splotch of blood smeared his palm. Weird. Frannie hadn't mentioned she'd cut herself. He glanced behind him at the door. She'd seemed fine in the foyer. He frowned at the smudge. Another strike of lightning. Another violent wave attacked the cliff, and the house shuddered once more.

"And then the unthinkable happened," his father said suddenly. He waited a beat for the thunder to roll on through. "You actually came home."

Devon rolled his eyes and wiped the blood on his jeans. This was going nowhere. He had to wrap this up and go search for Frannie and Hannah. He eased to the edge of the chair.

"Going somewhere?"

"I wanted to make sure Frannie's okay."

"She's fine. Sit."

With a sigh, Devon sat back, tapping a thumb on his jeans.

"I took one look at you striding into the living room, and your striking resemblance to your mother, and I knew I'd made a critical miscalculation."

"You didn't expect me to fight back?"

"I didn't expect to care. I'd get the company and that rat cousin of yours, and Tucker would get a son-in-law whose reputation was intact. It was purely business. I didn't anticipate the...regret."

"Regret? For helping me?" Why was he surprised? Why did it still hurt, like he was a kid craving his father's approval?

"No. For being such a horrible father."

A crack of thunder covered Devon's rush of breath. Surely he'd misheard. He stared at the old man's overly shiny eyes in the mostly dark room.

As the rumbling died away, his father chuckled softly. "I've never let emotions sway me, but there it is. Who'd have thought I'd get so old and sentimental?"

"Sentimental? You've been nothing but hostile. Hell, you've demanded my arrest twice."

"I had to be sure I could pull this off—an aggressive takeover, not a father bailing a son out. One is an advantageous business plan; the other is collusion." He waved a hand. "Initially, my plan was to take the whole thing over, full stop. Screw Tucker and his greedy belief that you'd inherit. But after you stood before me, so proud, so like your mother, I altered my plan. If I'd gotten control on Friday, I would have wrapped the whole thing up next week and handed it back to you. All I can offer now is a low-interest loan to flush money back in to cover the fraud, and keep you from going to jail. I know the CEO of the bank you guaranteed your inheritance to; I'll pull some strings and see if I can save any of it. But between the SEC investigation and

Tucker's wrath, there will be no hiding the news. Ashby Enterprises is a write-off."

Anguish filled Devon's chest, as piercing as a heart attack. His company. His partner. His inheritance. The potential of the Rogers Park development—all gone. The irony of his own role in fighting the takeover was not lost on him. Anger flooded in, as comfortable as an old blanket. His father may have attempted to help him avoid jail time, but the lies and deception these last few days had wasted valuable time. "Keep your sentiment and your money," he said evenly. "I'll figure a way out of this mess without you. We will never be friends, old man."

"Ah, now that's the son I raised." Harrison's mouth settled into grim regret. "You really have turned out like me. Don't wait until you're my age to realize life isn't about how large you grow your company or how influential you become. It's about family. Finding a wife who loves you, not your money."

The hypocrisy was too much. Devon waited until the urge to shout obscenities passed. "Says the man who proposed to Honey."

His father glanced away, shoulders almost bowing from the weight. Earlier in the week, Devon would've paid to see this, but now the tired, broken man he faced... Devon fought the foreign surge of pity. "Why would you make the oldest mistake in the book?"

"I—I was sure it was passionate love."

Devon frowned. "You're not that stupid."

After a pause, his father continued, his voice smaller somehow, and Devon leaned forward to hear over the storm. "Even before you uncovered who she was, I became suspicious at that party. What heiress squeezes your arm like that, hearing she'll inherit *more* money? I never did change my will—interesting in hindsight, don't you think?"

Devon placed the flashlight between them again, and folded his arms. "I didn't kill her. I don't care whether you believe me—they took my DNA."

"They've begun the process with the household; it's only a matter of time." Again his father emitted that dry chuckle. "There were so many motives for killing me after the birthday," he said. "I almost expected it, and, you know, my money would have been on Rick. But when Honey was killed, all I could think of was that only you had the motivation and the courage to take the most important thing from my life, the way I did to you."

The injustice of being force-fed the suicide lie flashed back. Devon squeezed his fists. "Are you talking about Ashby Enterprises, or are you finally confessing to my mother's murder?"

Harrison's residual smile turned haunted. His gaze flitted from Devon to the flashlight between them. A faraway look came into his eyes. "I *hated* you," he whispered. "It's a horrible thing for a father to say, but Francesca never looked at me with that much love."

Devon used every ounce of willpower to remain expressionless. After all these years of knowing... It shouldn't hurt this much to hear the words spoken.

His father folded his gnarled hands on the desk in front of him. "I was a bachelor when I laid eyes on her in Florence. She was twenty years younger, so fresh and beautiful. I fell for her and never stopped worshiping her." He shook his head. A bemused smile lit his lips. "You can't imagine how stunned I was when she agreed to marry me. So many men hovered around her—men much richer, much younger. More handsome.

"But she chose *me*, and it was so glorious in the beginning. I wanted to be the perfect husband, give her anything she ever wanted. And then you came along, and her love for you stunned me." As if chiming in, a wave boomed up the cliff.

"I buried myself in work," Harrison said, "because *I* could buy her things. But she only wanted to be with you children. And the more I stayed away and worked, the unhappier she got. And the unhappier she got, the more insecure I became. Clearly I wasn't providing enough, so I worked even harder. I had to be the best, own the best, buy her everything so she would never leave me."

Devon's breath streamed out. *Like me with Nicole.*

The lines on Harrison's face tightened, and his folded hands fisted. "The years passed, and she spent more and more time with you and Francine. I was bitterly resentful, especially of her special bond with you. I'm not proud of that, but there it is." Tears sparkled in his eyes. "And then came that horrible day…" Devon's breathing grew shallow. He didn't want to hear anymore. "She was gone," Harrison whispered. "Just like that."

Lightning lit the office like prison yard floodlights. Devon bolted from the chair and stumbled across the room. His eyes stung. It was too much: Eric's betrayal. The shocking change in his dragon of a father. And this final, mind-numbing blow. His mother had, in fact, committed suicide. She'd left him behind. Chosen death over her children.

His throat closed. No amount of swallowing relieved the pressure. He slumped his forehead against the rain-splattered window and stared into blurry blackness. The storm raged, and the surf roared. The house shuddered, and the window, cool against his fevered forehead, rattled. His father still spoke as thunder clapped, but it was difficult to hear the words. Devon couldn't turn. Wouldn't have been able to move even if the house burned down. The thunder rolled off in the distance.

"…and each of my marriages since has probably

been to capture some part of her. Susanna loved art and music; Renee had a fiery personality. Honey...such breathtaking beauty."

Another jagged bolt of lightning flashed, illuminating the lawn with its tattered crime scene tape and bending trees. A tall form staggered against the onslaught of rain, lugging something toward the cliff. All went black, leaving spots before his eyes.

"Jesus," Devon whispered. Thunder reverberated as his overloaded brain tried to process the nanosecond. The surf pounded, the foundation groaned, the window rattled.

"I know Honey didn't—"

"*Jesus fucking Christ!*" He tore out of the office and pounded down the hall.

"Devon?" Harrison called.

Ahead in the foyer, a few staff held dripping raincoats. Rick, coat still on, was walking out of the dining room with a full glass of wine.

"Call nine-one-one," Devon roared, racing past. The horrifying image played over and over. He closed in on the patio doors at a dead run.

The *something* being dragged had long hair whipping in the wind.

CHAPTER 29

HANNAH FOUGHT TO stay in the deep, dreamy warmth, but thousands of icy bees stung her cheeks, and her frosty skin sent panic signals that dragged her sluggishly back to the surface. She opened her eyes to more darkness, immediately squinting as freezing rain beat on her. Her head hurt so much she wanted to vomit, and every muscle shuddered from the onslaught of icy wind and soaking rain. The surf sounded like cannon fire. A few muddled seconds later, she realized a viselike grip dragged her backward. Whoever it was muttered unintelligibly. *Frannie.*

No—Joseph. Oh shit, she was being hauled toward the cliff! "Stop," she cried. "Somebody help me!" The words chattered unintelligibly from her numb lips, and her voice was so feeble she barely heard it above the fury Mother Nature unleashed. Her head pulsed from the wasted effort. "Joseph...for God's sake...stop." She dug in her heels, scratched at the raincoat-covered arms that held her. Her skull throbbed where Frannie had struck her with the flashlight when she'd tried to convince Joseph of the woman's insanity. The fact that she was well on her way to certain death meant Joseph was as crazy as Frannie.

Hannah renewed her struggles, wriggling her torso, slapping any part of his hold she could, but the movement only made her puke on Joseph's sleeves. He didn't react. Nothing halted the old man's slow, determined tug toward the sheer cliff and raging surf. "It's me, Joseph. Please—I don't want to die!"

Harsh breathing drew close to her right ear. "I'm sorry, Miss Hannah. It's the only way."

"I won't tell anyone," she gasped, thrashing violently. She shuddered through more rising bile. "I don't care if Frannie killed Honey."

"It's for the best this way."

Hannah sobbed, shivering uncontrollably. They traveled by inches through the soggy grass and mud, both gasping in their opposing efforts. Lightning lit the backyard and the imposing house. All went black.

Joseph began muttering again, and Hannah strained to make out the words. "You never meant to hurt anyone, did you, dear? I'll take care of everything. Just a few more steps now, that's it. It'll all be over soon, my good girl."

Did he think she was Frannie?

Another boom of the surf. Wind-whipped spray stung her. Christ, they were right at the ledge! She kicked and clawed in renewed frenzy. Suddenly the grip around her ribs slipped. She twisted violently and broke free, the right side of her face sinking into freezing muck. Endorphins burst through her. She was free! She reached up, clutched Joseph behind the knees, and yanked him to the ground. Thin whips slashed her. They were next to the weeping willow. It flogged them in a rage of its own.

She rose to her knees and began to crawl, but his hand snatched her ankle and clung. "You won't get away with this," she sputtered, falling flat. "You're crazy!" Her fingers clawed at mud for purchase. It was useless.

"I will not lose my Frannie," he yelled.

My Frannie? A thick cluster of willow branches whipped Hannah's cheeks, stinging her breathless. In that heartbeat of hesitation, Joseph grappled her and tugged her back into sitting position. His bony knee banged into the tender lump at the base of her skull. Pain exploded into a galaxy of stars.

Through the agonizing haze, she swung her arm, connecting to his cheek in a wet slap. She clawed her way down until her fingers found his throat, then squeezed with all her might. Her grip was too slick, her strength gone. Thousands of tiny lights still flashed behind her eyes. Her arm dropped, and her vision tunneled. This was it; she was going to die.

A calm settled over her. She was no longer in a freezing storm, no longer petrified or in pain. She was in the warmth of Devon's arms, basking in the light and love that shone from his eyes. Her dream was so real, she even heard him shouting her name far away. "I'm here," she whispered. "I love you."

∞

"HANNAH!" DEVON STREAKED across the soggy lawn, terror fueling adrenaline, but like some hideous nightmare, the more he pumped his arms and legs, the slower he progressed. Deep swaths of muck or slick grass hindered every step. Horizontal rain blinded him, so he raced straight at the sound of the booming surf. He was vaguely aware he was shouting, although except for her name, he couldn't comprehend his words.

A double fork of lightning streaked through the air. In the split second of light, he made out two forms at the cliff. He had thirty feet to go. Blinding dark returned, but at twenty feet, lightning struck again. Hannah, pale and bloody, lay collapsed on her side.

Joseph, grim-faced and focused, leaned over her and shoved.

Devon's brain blanked out in shock. In that split second of blue-white light, he experienced the thin line between life and death, felt the overwhelming power of love and hate.

Hannah reached for Joseph and grabbed only air as she disappeared over the edge.

"Hannah!"

CHAPTER 30

SOMEHOW HANNAH CLUNG to the narrow stone step protruding from the cliff. Her body swayed in the gust as her feet clawed for another step. She found it as an icy wave rammed her from behind, bashing her knees against the rock wall. Frigid water engulfed her and retreated with such violence, it sucked at her like a vortex. Her shaking fingers slipped a fraction. She cried out, clasping the step with all her might.

She'd seen Devon a split second before she went over. All she had to do was hang on. Could she? Her fingers cramped; the smooth step was so slippery. Willow branches whipped her head and neck mercilessly. A new wave slammed into her, and her fingers slipped another fraction. *Oh God, don't let me die!* Her breath came in rasping sobs, and her body shook with chilled convulsions. She clung for all she was worth.

At a sudden shout, she craned her neck. Rain beat into her eyes, but she made out hazy images of the two men grappling. Then a soaking-wet form peered over the edge, blocking the rain and taking the brunt of the willow whips. Lightning cut through the sky. Devon's frantic face morphed to shock as he spotted her a foot below.

"Hannah!" Steel fingers closed over her icy wrists, and she began to rise up the cliff face, lighter than air.

Another wave battered her into the rock; he swore and tightened his grip painfully. She tried to say his name, but her teeth chattered too hard, and her lips had frozen into a stiff grimace. Her torso rose above the cliff, and he laid her across the grass, dragging her dangling legs up and around. Dark figures spilled out of the mansion, holding flashlights. One had much more of a head start, streaking toward them, only yards away. The inert body of Joseph lay a few feet to her right.

"Are you all right?" Devon wiped the tangled hair from her face and cupped her cheeks. He remained bent over her, trying his best to shield her from the pelting rain and willow tree. "Can you understand me?"

She nodded. The only warmth in her frigid body came from the tears trickling into her hairline. She turned her head cautiously toward the house, and a blur of movement near the willow tree trunk caught her eye. The first of the help had arrived.

Frannie! The younger woman dragged a thick branch from the ground and stumbled through the sweeping, clawing branches toward them.

"N-n-n-n-no," Hannah chattered.

"It's okay, sweetheart. *Ouch*," Devon muttered as the willows slashed him.

"F-f-f-rrraaa..." She pointed, but her arm was down by her side, and his face was an inch from hers. He wouldn't look behind him in time.

Frannie raised the branch like an ax and swung with all her might, aiming right for the middle of Devon's back. A sickening thud and his grunt of surprise preceded him falling heavily onto her.

"D-d-devon," she sobbed, trying to twist out from under him and help him. Frannie flung the branch away and shoved him hard. He fell onto his side, groaning.

Lightning lit the sky, and Frannie, face distorted in rage, dropped to her knees in front of them.

She pushed Hannah backward, muttering obscenities, and once again Hannah struggled for all she was worth, clutching at slippery blades of grass and handfuls of mud. Devon stirred beside her. Flashlights bobbed faster, but they wouldn't be fast enough. She moaned as she clawed at Frannie's rain-slicked hands, tried to bite the wrist that held her.

In dreadful slow motion, Frannie rolled her backward. The surf roared up over the ledge, soaking her. Another bundle of willow branches slapped her. With one final push, she was slipping over the cliff again. Her fingers clawed for the steps, a jutted rock—anything—as another cluster of willow branches sliced down. Her fists closed over them. She hung on, praying the willow would hold her weight as once again her feet scrambled for purchase.

<hr>

DEVON SHOOK HIS head, hair splatting against his cheeks. The pain in his back was intense. What the hell had just happened?

"You're as bad as Brady," his sister screamed from behind. "You're engaged and carrying on with a whore, just like him!"

Hannah! She was gone. He jerked to his knees, and the twinge in his spine felt like the twist of a knife. No fingers clutched the cliff. He crawled to the edge, and his sister wrapped her hands around his throat from behind and squeezed.

"You bastard. You're all the same!"

He shrugged her off and leaned over the cliff, prepared to dive into the angry froth to either save Hannah or die with her. There she was, three feet down, clinging to branches, for fuck's sake. "Hannah," he shouted, scrambling to where she swung.

She twisted her head at the sound of his voice and opened her mouth just as a wave slammed her into the rock and crested over her head. A second later, it surged back out, sucking at her as she coughed and sputtered. He stretched over the cliff and grabbed her just above the elbows. Fists beat on the backs of his thighs.

"I've got you," he murmured, and clung tight as they rode out another ramming wave.

Her body strained away from him as the retreating swirl sucked her, but the second the lake retreated enough to release her, he grabbed flesh and clothes and hauled until he caught her about the waist. They waited out another wave so vicious he felt the strain of holding her stab through his injured back. He stilled, immobilized from agony.

"Oh no," she whispered in defeat, and he knew another injury was on the way. He held on to her as tightly as he could and braced himself. If they were going to die, at least he'd go out with his arms around her.

"Frannie!" Rick shouted.

"Enough!" his father roared in his dragon voice, and it seemed that even the storm paused in that split second. "Put it down!"

The blow never came. Devon hoisted Hannah slowly, rolling onto his side and dragging her up and across him. He closed his eyes against the battering raindrops and hugged her sobbing, breathless body.

"Francine. Drop it." Harrison used that gentle tone with her again, the one he'd used after Devon had beat up her husband...jeez, only hours ago. "That's a good girl."

Devon squinted through Hannah's soaking mass of hair. Harrison shined a light at Frannie's feet while she swayed, still holding a remarkably large tree branch. Rick crept up stealthily from behind. A shitload of cops and EMS stood frozen in action stances, while Harrison held up his other hand, like a puppeteer keeping them at bay.

"I have to kill her," Frannie said. "I have to."

"No, baby girl. Let's go inside. Right now." The tree branch slid from her grasp, and she sank to her knees. Harrison motioned to the cops, and suddenly flashlights and lanterns blazed, gurneys rolled forward, and medical personnel swarmed. Harrison waved them away from Frannie and helped her up.

Rick fell to his knees beside Devon seconds before the medical personnel. "Are you guys okay?"

"I don't think so, Rick." He tried to infuse ironic humor in his voice, but it came out as pained as he felt.

"It was an accident," Frannie sobbed. "I never meant to do it, Daddy. It was a terrible accident."

"I know, sweet girl." After cursory glances, first at Joseph, then Devon and Hannah, Harrison turned and led her toward the house. Two EMTs knelt over Joseph, blocking him from view.

Devon swiped blood from his nose without losing his grip on Hannah. Why would Joseph try to kill her? And Frannie try to finish the job? None of this made sense. He ignored the crowd hovering around him and clutched Hannah's shivering body, so miraculously alive and glued to his.

"She…she killed Honey," Hannah said. "It wasn't an accident."

"Shhh." He kissed her quivering cheek, and then three techs were gently probing, questioning, and prying them apart. He barely heard them, still trying to wrap his mind around Joseph and Frannie's actions. What had Hannah *ever* done to them?

"I'm fine," Hannah insisted, weakly brushing off the tech covering her with an aluminum blanket. Flashlights blazed around them. Lightning lit the sky.

"Ma'am, I need you to lie still—"

She slapped at his hands clumsily, and before

Devon could order her to cooperate, she staggered to her feet. By the look on her sheet-white face, she was going after his sister.

CHAPTER 31

HANNAH DIDN'T MAKE it four yards before she sank to the frigid ground and threw up, her humiliation complete when Devon knelt and held her heavy hair back while the techs waited. After vomiting until she dry-heaved, she was too dizzy to do more than wipe her mouth on her soggy sweater and groan. The throbbing in her head felt like a thousand gonging church bells.

"Come on, sweetheart. Let EMS take over now."

She allowed them to lay her on a gurney, and they all carefully made their way toward the mass of flashlights twirling like a laser show over by the patio. Even the beams drove shafts of pain through her skull, and she closed her eyes. When the rain suddenly stopped beating on her, she knew they'd reached the sunroom. The abrupt warmth felt like a pile of luxurious fur coats.

"Where's Frannie?" Devon asked someone, and she risked opening her eyes. The room was filled with more officials holding flashlights. It took her a moment to realize he'd spoken to his father, who stood near the arched doors with his arm around a deathly pale teenage boy, and that homicide detective scribbling in his notepad.

"She's upstairs changing." Devon's reaction must have caused Harrison to quickly add, "We have a female officer with her."

Hannah's gurney was wheeled through the house, Devon at her side, arguing with his father and the medical staff on why he didn't need to lie on one too. "It's a small bruise," he insisted, but the deep lines bracketing his mouth exposed the lie.

They loaded her up in the ambulance, and more arguing ensued as Devon insisted on riding with her to the hospital, and the techs gently refused. "There's no room. She'll be at Evanston Hospital, sir. We'll make sure the ER staff knows you're on your way."

"How about you ride in this other ambulance?" Another tech pointed at a third vehicle. "And get yourself checked out as well."

"I said I feel fine."

"I'll drive you, Dev." Rick sidled up to his brother, holding an extra-thick jacket and studying Hannah almost apologetically.

Devon waved the jacket off, his two-buttoned, tattered shirt glued to the chiseled torso. How could he not be shivering after all this? "Hannah, I'm going to change into some of Rick's clothes and grab some for you. I'll be right behind you, okay?"

She nodded weakly as a shout came from somewhere outside the vehicle. Using the last of her strength, she raised her head an inch off the thin pillow. Everyone outside the ambulance turned toward the house, where orders were barked, but she couldn't make them out. "Devon...what's happened?"

He held up a finger, still listening, his handsome profile shadowed outside the lighted ambulance. Rick shifted his weight, and as he leaned into the light, she saw his jaw drop and his eyes dart to Devon.

"Devon?" she said again, not sure he heard her over the noise of the storm, the diesel rumble of the ambulance, and the tech sitting next to her talking into a phone. Then both brothers faced her, their expressions stricken. "Frannie overpowered the police officer," Devon rasped. "She's disappeared somewhere in the house with the cop's Glock."

❧

DEVON DRAGGED HIS eyes from Hannah's battered, frightened face to his father standing on the threshold of the open front door. They shared a bleak moment. No one knew hiding places in the house like Frannie. There was no electricity. She had a gun. This would not end well, not if attempted murder and beating him with a tree branch was acceptable to her frame of mind. She'd suffered from depression, but nothing he'd ever considered severe, certainly nothing to warrant this psychotic break. But then, Hannah had mentioned seeing pills...

"Devon," Hannah said faintly for the third time, and he turned back, masking his panic. She beckoned him closer, and after the tech nodded and scooted over, he ducked inside the ambulance. Guilt thickened his throat as he crouched by the gurney. He ignored the shaft of pain down his spine and grasped her hand. Everything about her swollen, purple cheekbone, the welt lashes from the willow, and her inside-out sweater was his fault. She could've finished her job in the second gallery and been long gone from this godforsaken house, but he'd instigated a fight and manhandled her right out of her clothes. Why, of all of them, had she become the victim?

"I'm so sorry, Hannah." He kissed her knuckles and brushed a strand of hair off her forehead. "What in the hell happened between you and Joseph and Frannie?"

She squeezed his hand. "It'll take too long. Frannie led me down a tiny spiral staircase tonight." Her voice cracked a bit. "It opens into the far side of the kitchen." He nodded. "She showed me a door hidden in the wall... Said it used to be servants' quarters. She still goes there to be alone."

The four bedrooms tucked back there were from their hide-and-seek days. Frannie had returned there often in her dark teen years.

"Brilliant, thanks." He leaned in to kiss her gently, but she turned her head away.

"Don't go after her, Devon. She's already tried to kill you tonight too."

"I have to. I know how to talk to her." *I hope.*

Her eyes filled with tears. "Come with me," she whispered. "She has your whole family. I only have you."

His heart wrenched, the pain as excruciating as the throbbing in his back. In a distorted version of that stormy night, she was asking *him* to drop everything, turn his back on his family crisis, and go with her.

They'd both lost so much twelve years ago. He couldn't afford to make the mistake again. But this was different. She was loaded into a warm ambulance about to be cared for. The technician cleared his throat.

"I'll be there before you get through the admissions process." He kissed the non-swollen part of her face. "You'll be fine. My family needs me."

"*I* need you." Tears streamed down her cheeks.

He hesitated a few seconds, torn by the devastation in her gaze. But his decision was right. Sit around the hospital waiting room like a bump on a log, or stop his sister from harming anyone else? It was a no-brainer. "I'll be there soon, okay?"

She turned her face to the wall and closed her eyes. He was fucked, but he didn't know what else to do. He kissed her cheek once more and beat it out of the ambulance before he buckled under his need to stay. By the time he'd jogged back to the foyer, Rick had told his father and the officers where Frannie used to hide.

The homicide detective with the Southern accent

handed them flashlights and motioned for them to lead the way. In the crowded spiral stairwell, an argument in primitive sign language ensued, where the homicide detective initially didn't want any family to enter the servants' quarters. He finally acquiesced to Harrison's forceful headshake and pointed to Harrison, Devon, and one other cop, leaving Rick and a very youthful-looking uniform at the entrance.

If they'd hoped for stealth, the squeal of the rusty, old door ruined those plans. The stench of mold and dead rodents permeated the dusty air and twitched Devon's sinuses. He crept along the corridor, following the others step for step. The servants' hall was twenty feet long and had four closed doors, two on each side. The detective gestured with a series of hand signals, obviously demanding that father and son move out of the way and stay put. Harrison shook his head again and stood before the farthest door on the left. After a prolonged stare-down, the detective finally scowled and nodded. Once each man flattened himself up against the wall beside a door, he signaled a three-second countdown. On one, Devon rotated his doorknob and pushed. His flashlight encountered only white-sheeted furniture and the stink of even stronger mold and dust.

"I did you a favor, Father."

He spun toward his sister's voice across the hall. Over his father's shoulder, he had a clear view of Frannie, squeezed into the far corner of the room, knees up. She held the trembling Glock to her temple. In two strides, he was behind his father, and a second later, the cop was jostling him out of the way. Devon held firm and glared out a challenge.

"We can deal with the situation from here, sir," the detective said in his soft accent. "Y'all step back, please."

"Everyone stay where you are," Harrison

commanded. A few seconds of tense silence followed, but the cop stopped jostling. "Frannie. Put down the gun."

Frannie didn't obey, but she also didn't react when Harrison stepped farther into the room, waving the cops off without turning.

"I did you a favor. Honey didn't love you." She trembled visibly in her soaking clothes, but her voice was steady, almost conversational. "I had to kill her, don't you see? She was about to take *everything*."

"What do you mean you had to kill her?" Devon asked harshly. "Outside you said it was an accident."

"She wasn't referring to Honey," Harrison said, without taking his eyes off his daughter.

"What she did to Hannah was definitely no accident. You were there!"

"She's not talking about Hannah either, are you, baby girl?"

Devon's world tilted. His sister wept silently, rocking and hugging herself, the gun now loose and angled toward the floor. Devon was too thunderstruck to reach beyond his father and slip it from her grasp. He couldn't think straight.

"We were eating breakfast and arguing," she said, her voice high like a little girl's. "Devon wanted to water-ski, but I wanted to play tag. Mom said we'd water-ski first because the lake was like glass, and to hurry up and finish my breakfast." She sniffled and shivered, the brightness in her eyes feverish. "She always chose what Devon wanted. He laughed and ran upstairs to put on his swimsuit, and Mom went outside. Why wouldn't she wait until I finished my toast? I saw her walk to the cliff. Devon wasn't down yet, so we could play tag. Just Mom and me."

Tears streamed down his father's face. The lump in Devon's throat pulsed like a heartbeat.

"I ran to her," she whispered. "She didn't hear me coming—just stood there, looking out at the lake. I tagged her and yelled, 'You're it!' But she didn't turn around. Didn't say anything. She just...fell." Frannie blinked and glanced around like she'd just awoken to find herself in this room. She wiped her eyes as she gazed up at Harrison. "It was an accident. I just wanted to play tag... No one would play with me."

Harrison nodded and held out his arms. The gun clattered to the floor, and she launched herself at him, sobbing pitifully. Immediately the cop swept up the gun, and the detective positioned himself to take her into custody, although he made no move to touch her under Harrison's glare.

Weak as a newborn, Devon sank onto the dusty bed and stared up at the old man patting his sister's back.

The detective got up enough courage to clear his throat. "Sir, we need to take her now."

"I want her in dry clothes and with dry hair. You're not to question her until my lawyer and I arrive."

"Yes, sir."

Frannie was gently led away, her soaked sweatpants dripping in the dust. Once the outer door screeched closed and silence descended, Harrison faced him, eyes hollowed and haunted.

There was only one reason he would look like that. "You knew." Devon's voice scraped like sandpaper. "You've known this whole time."

His father nodded, lips pressed tight. "The forensics team informed me of a trace stain on the back of your mother's shirt. It was clearly a child's first two fingers and part of a palm."

Devon frowned. All the brutal years of living with his father's hatred. How he couldn't meet the old man's standards or find a way to earn his love. "Wait," he sputtered, "you thought that I...?"

"No, Devon." His father spoke in that gentle voice he'd used with Frannie. As if Devon were deranged. "The stains were strawberry jam."

"But..." He couldn't wrap his mind around this. "She could've touched Mom anytime that morning and transferred the jam."

Harrison nodded patiently, sitting on the other twin mattress. The mannerisms he'd shown in the office, stooped posture and fatigued expression, were back. Why did he only show this weak side around Devon? "I argued that exact point to shut the investigation down. But Joseph witnessed the accident. He ran into the house and called nine-one-one, so he never saw you heading across the lawn. You were the first to find her." His father waited a beat. "I've always been sorry about that."

Devon shook his head, still confused. "All these years...you and Joseph—"

"Have done everything in our power to protect my daughter." Although Harrison's familiar harsh tone returned, the loose skin around his jowls quivered. "I battled, bribed, or burned anyone in my way to shut that investigation down and keep it shut. I'd lost my wife. I would not lose my daughter."

"But if you knew, all this time..." His voice cracked. His spine spasmed, and he leaned his arms on his knees. "Why didn't you tell me?"

"Tell you?" Harrison scoffed. "Have you suddenly forgotten the hate you've harbored since that awful day? What a bitter man you've become, believing I killed her? Do you think for one minute I'd want your wrath turned upon little Frannie?"

"But to keep insisting it was suicide—"

Harrison shook his head impatiently. His color was returning, and his stature grew more commanding the more he spoke.

Devon envied him his certainty as he struggled to

comprehend the magnitude of his sister's mistake. Or his father's decisions.

"It was better for everyone if her death was labeled a suicide. Life could eventually go back to normal."

Devon inhaled a shaky breath, and a half laugh escaped. "Life was never normal after that."

"It was as normal as I could make it."

Devon gazed at his clutched hands. His lifelong perceptions of so many events had detonated in minutes. His father wasn't a murderer; he was a protector. He hadn't locked himself in his office for weeks afterward out of callousness; he'd been scrambling to stymie the investigation. His cloying overprotectiveness toward Frannie was completely understandable, given her childhood secret and her early history of depression. And Harrison's hatred toward an enraged son was to cloak fear—fear of Devon finding out the truth. It was too much. His brain was numb. "Frannie should've seen a psychiatrist," he said through stiff lips. "Look what holding it all in did to her."

"I couldn't take that chance. There's no statute of limitations on murder."

Devon looked up. "Murder? It was an accident." He spoke succinctly. "She was seven."

"Murder, accident—it makes no difference!" Harrison scowled and swept out a hand. "She's a Wickham. Imagine what the investigation and the press would have done to her at seven. I was not going to have my baby stigmatized. Think of how this one second in her life would've defined her, followed her like a frenzied whisper everywhere she went for the rest of her life."

But that one second had defined her. "Did you and Joseph tell her you knew?"

"No."

And there it was. The ultimate mistake in a father's

need to protect his child. Devon shook his head in wonder. "So you let a seven-year-old grow up with a secret she could never share or talk about, and you let her believe she was the only one carrying that burden. You let her rot away inside her head—"

"I did what I thought was best!"

Devon stood abruptly. His back quivered in protest, and he felt slightly nauseated, but the urge to get as far from his father as possible propelled him toward the door.

"Where are you going?"

He paused. "I chose my family's welfare over Hannah's half an hour ago. It's a mistake I don't plan to make again."

"The restoration girl? She'll be fine. You stick by me. I need a united family front to deal with this."

"You've never had a united family. That died with Mother as well."

"But we still have to discuss Ashby Enterprises and plan for the SEC tomorrow."

Weariness crept into Devon's limbs, and he almost sagged against the wall. "You know, Father, at this particular moment, I couldn't give a fuck about my company."

CHAPTER 32

HALFWAY TO EVANSTON Hospital and impatient to be there, Devon grudgingly pulled over on the stormy, empty street, flicked on his hazards, and grabbed the ringing cell phone. *Eric.* His throat thickened with the effort to speak. "They're onto you."

"Who?"

"Turns out my father's reason is as old as time—trying to make up for the guilt of being a shitty parent. He tendered the offer to cover up your fraud." The silence was as complete as if the call had dropped. He almost didn't care. Hannah was waiting.

"I never meant for it to go this far," Eric finally said. "The more I tried to make things right, the more it snowballed. I could've fixed everything, but Tucker began liquidating massive amounts for your wedding deposits. I even had to sell my shares to cover it."

"Did you not connect the dots that if you told him I was disinherited he'd take his bat and go home?"

"No, Devon. He's a greedy motherfucker. He'd make sure you weren't his son-in-law, but he'd stay in an insanely profitable company."

"Profitable?"

Silence.

Devon stared at the wipers swishing rapidly, never clearing the windshield for long. Eric stumbled through more reasoning. The legitimate attempt at the currency market. The Chinese yuan promptly tanking. His margin called.

A traffic light in the distance changed from red to green to yellow to red. Repeat. Life just went on.

When the rain slowed, Devon tapped the speakerphone icon, stuck the phone in the cup holder, and shifted into gear. His spirits lifted in anticipation. He'd be at the hospital in minutes.

"I never meant for it to go this far," Eric finished. "You believe that, right?"

Days ago he'd have said no, burned bridges, and never looked back. Nicole had taught him how to elevate it to a fine art. Or maybe it was his genetic makeup. He'd done it when he was eighteen. Frannie, Hannah, and Rick had all compared him to Harrison, but he wasn't, not deep inside. Harrison wasted time with his glorified mind games. Devon would be straightforward and honest, no matter how hard that was. "Yeah, I believe you. I'd love nothing better than to smash your face right now, but I believe you."

"Will you be back tomorrow? Help me face the SEC complaint?"

"No."

"Come on, Renegade."

"Don't call me that." The side of him that worshiped money, status, and power above all else had died. He had to figure out the emotional wreckage inside before he made any promises to either Eric or his father about business going forward. He had to sift through everything with his sister, and the revelation of how fucked up she really was. And even if Hannah was able to do backflips off her ER bed when he got there, he wouldn't be leaving her anytime soon. Business wasn't everything. Besides, he was starting over again, probably penniless. Why not in Chicago this time?

"Don't worry," Eric said hastily, "I'll totally fall on

my sword. I just need your support, man. Look at all the things I did for you when you came to me in trouble."

The lights of the hospital appeared ahead. "I gotta go. We can talk about it more in the morning."

The conversation had been surprisingly reasonable. His company was done, his inheritance was gone, Rogers Park would probably be auctioned to repay the fraud, and both he and Eric faced arrest and an extensive investigation. Tomorrow, he'd problem-solve what he could salvage, what he could partner with his father on, and how to live up to the bargain he'd made with O'Callaghan two days ago.

But Hannah's health and well-being took precedence, then untangling the depth of his sister's mental health issues and Joseph's unholy motivation for attempted murder. It was past time to put family first.

❧

"MISS MOORE, YOUR brother is here to see you."

Hannah spied a broad shoulder and a bit of dark, damp hair towering behind the nurse technician. Before she could refuse him, the woman parted the privacy curtain, and Devon slipped by, walking gingerly. The navy sweatshirt he'd borrowed glared neon words: *I'm Not Speeding, I'm Qualifying.* His face looked pinched and pale, and although he was smiling, exhaustion seeped from him.

When the curtain swished closed, she croaked, "Please. Don't come any closer." Each word pulled on her puffed-up lips and bruised facial muscles. He froze, his brow creasing. She had to do this before she lost her nerve. "I've loved you for so long, Devon. I probably always will. But I deserve someone who puts me first." The words she'd practiced since the ambulance ride came out stilted, slurred. But she'd said them. Confronted conflict. She'd have passed the bravery off on the morphine drip, but her emotions were intact. Her heart ached at the devastation on his face.

He spread his palms. "You do come first. I'm sorry it took twelve years to figure that out." Those long-lashed, deep-blue eyes were filled with such tenderness that tears filled hers.

God, how she wanted that to be true.

He stepped closer, a cautious look on his face. When she said nothing, he closed the distance and groped for her bandaged hand, holding it lightly. "You believe me, don't you?"

"Until you leave for New York," she whispered, and tried to shrug, but her torso muscles revolted. She flinched.

He smoothed the rat's nest of hair off her forehead. "I won't lie to you, I have to go back for a while, but not by choice. I'll have legal issues that'll take time. But the second I'm free, I plan to super-glue myself to your side. We belong together."

"I've wanted that for so many years." It came out a croak of a whisper. "I almost don't believe this. Maybe I'm daydreaming again."

"You're wide awake and in immense pain, sweetheart." He grinned and braced his palms on either side of the mattress, lowering himself on sturdy biceps instead of engaging his spine, and gave her a feather-soft kiss on the corner of her mouth. "Let it be known throughout the universe," he said lightly, "that I will always come back to you."

Her throat convulsed. "What happened with Frannie?" she whispered.

A look flashed across his face, too fast for her drugged mind to catch. Anguish? Betrayal?

"Do you remember anything about why…my sister…?"

Hannah stopped nodding when the room spun.

He pulled over a nearby chair and sat, grimacing.

At her expression, he waved a hand. "I'll let them take my temperature later. Tell me what happened after I left the library." He leaned forward, touching her arm, smoothing her hair, cupping her face. The worry on his face warmed her more than the blankets.

She tried to take a deep breath, but even her lungs seemed sore. "I was trying to feel my way…" She stopped and cleared her throat. "To the bathroom in the dark, and Frannie turned the corner." The encounter was still starkly vivid. How had she missed the clear signs of mental breakdown after living with her mother's highs and lows? Maybe if she'd figured it out sooner, she could have done something to prevent what happened.

He pulled the top blanket closer to her chin. "If this is too much—"

"It's okay." Stilted by her sluggish facial muscles, she recounted Frannie's fury over Hannah reconnecting with Devon, the shattered teacups, the pendulum mood shifts and distorted reasoning. "When Joseph walked in, I could have cried with relief," she said hoarsely. "I had a rolling pin, but his presence fooled me into letting go." *Oh, Frannie. What have you done?* "I heard you calling, and was so sure Joseph would deal with your sister that I began walking past them to the swinging doors. That's all I remember."

"She hit you with a flashlight." Devon's brows furrowed. He described Frannie's demeanor in the foyer, the blood smear on the light, and the split-second image of Hannah being dragged toward the cliff. "Here I was, immersed in my company's problems while you were out there fighting for your life. It's a moment I'll never forget." He closed his eyes, but not before she caught the guilt burning in them. "Why Joseph?" he murmured, shaking his head. "Why resort to murder?"

She'd had time to wonder that too. "He's always been there for you kids, even for your nephew with the fire. Once he realized Frannie killed Honey, and that I knew, he probably panicked when she knocked me out. How could he fix everything, and cover up her secret before I regained consciousness?"

Devon frowned. "It's not the only time he's done that." His voice breaking, he recounted Frannie's confession, the horrible secret she'd held in since she was seven. Hannah gasped, and the heart monitor beeped out a faster tempo. He glanced up at it, brow creasing, and fell silent.

"No. Tell me the rest. Talk to me." She reached for his hand, burying the need to howl in pain. He hesitated, and she gently squeezed her fingers. "I'm bruised on the outside, Dev, but I can handle this."

He told her about Harrison's control over the investigation, and the old man's warped belief that his actions all these years had been in Frannie's best interest.

"So you were right," she whispered. "Your mother never took her own life. And no one listened to you." He nodded again, the desolation on his face so acute she quickly added, "Quick. Use a feeling word now."

He looked at her like she was speaking gibberish. "That doesn't solve anything."

"It's not about solving. It's about sharing."

He scrubbed his face and sighed. "I'm fresh out of words. Can we do this later?"

She paused, not knowing how to break through this last barrier. An idea formed. "Let's try this. Every time you express an emotion, I'm going to kiss you. And I don't mean a peck on the cheek."

A ghost of a grin lit his face. "No offense, but your lips look like a cosmetic procedure gone horribly wrong. I can't imagine you'll enjoy kissing for a while."

"Try me."

His eyes crinkled.

Good, he was on board. "Now, what are you *feeling*, knowing the truth about your mother's death?"

He opened his mouth, then looked around the room as if the words were written somewhere. She could see the wheels spinning as he thought and frowned even harder. Finally he spoke haltingly. "My sister accidently killed my mother. My father lied about it, even when his suicide explanation drove such a wedge that I cut off ties with my family. Joseph and my sister tried to kill you. And my cousin committed fraud and bankrupted my company."

She stiffened, the last news coming out of nowhere. It was on the tip of her tongue to ask more about that, but now wasn't the time. He needed to get in touch with the inner damage.

Devon huffed out a harsh exhale as his gaze landed back on her. "I can't do it. How do you label an emotion for all that?"

"Well," she said gently, "it's okay to have more than one emotion for the same set of events. Maybe you feel confused? Betrayed? Enraged?"

"Yes," he whispered. Devastation crept over his features again. "All that. Keep going." The hurt in his tone tugged at her.

"I think that's enough of a start. Kiss me."

His expression cleared, and he cautiously stood. "You're sure you can handle this?"

"I could ask you the same thing." She tried to arrange her battered face into a wicked grin. He leaned down, his lips soft, the pressure light. Sure, it was uncomfortable, but so worth it. And there was nothing wrong with her tongue. When she darted it out, he eased away, kissing her earlobe, about the only part of her that didn't feel swollen and achy.

He groaned in a low, sexy way. "I don't want the nurse investigating why a visit from your brother keeps making that damn machine beep so fast," he murmured, and she tuned in to the rapid, high-pitched alarm.

She emitted a half giggle, half groan and patted his hand. "*Now* tell me how you'll problem-solve all of this."

He shook his head, pinning her with that all-encompassing stare. "I almost lost you, Hannah." He smoothed away a few strands tickling her cheek, and they bounced back. "For God's sake, I'm still getting over the image of you disappearing off the cliff. Everything else takes a back seat. The only problem I'm prepared to solve is how to help you and Aunt Milly move to a better place with the minimum amount of stress."

Maybe it was the painkillers, but all of a sudden, her muscles felt like jelly.

He braced his arms on the mattress again and drew closer. "And under no circumstances are you selling your partnership." His voice was intimate and authoritative.

"You've got an uphill battle. I've researched places all week."

"Yeah, but did you look for places that had room for me?"

Her breath caught. "I think Aunt Milly—"

"Is going to love the opportunity to unload some of her snark on me." He grinned crookedly, like a naughty schoolboy, but quickly sobered. "I'm not just in love with you, Hannah Moore. I'm crazy, sick, obsessed in love. Remember when you'd drive me nuts asking 'why me'?"

She nodded faintly.

"Well, listen up. I admire your grace, I crave your sweetness, and boy, does that angry, bossy side turn me on. We're going to have lots of conflict ahead, you can bet on that."

She placed her hand on top of his and squeezed gently. "Brace yourself, Dev. You just used a whole bunch of feeling words."

His lopsided grin was back, along with a seductive gleam in his eyes. "I know." He leaned in, his breath streaming warmly across her lips. "This is gonna be fun."

ALSO BY SARAH ANDRE

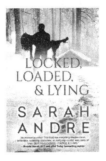

LOCKED, LOADED and LYING

"Cheese and monkeys this book is intense! A piece of advice: when you read this make sure you have no other plans for the day because you won't want to put it down." —*romance4thebeach*

"There was nothing formulaic about it all, meaning the story and characters weren't what you'd find in your typical romance novel, so kudos to Sarah Andre for her inspiring creativity and more than laudable writing skills...a debut novel so worth reading! This gets five stars." —*bookaholism*

"I was completely drawn into this story very quickly. I couldn't put it down and spent every opportunity I could get dipping into it- before work, at the breakfast table etc." —*justbooktalk*

"Wow – what a fast paced thriller full of unexpected events, mysteries and enthralling action. I really enjoyed this superbly written page turner and didn't want to put it down till I found out the truth about what happened to Tiffany – and when I did, what a shock!" —*splashesintobooks*

FROM *LOCKED, LOADED AND LYING*

Locklen Roane turned from the onslaught of stinging flakes and hurricane-force wind, flicked his jacket sleeve and squinted at his watch. Almost midnight. Three hours ago when he'd slipped into Sam's Bait and Tackle Shop, lit only by purring beverage refrigerators, the flakes had been sparse. Now that the hellish clandestine meeting with Parker had wrapped up, snow pummeled down. This would probably turn into a blizzard before he reached the top of the hill.

Out of the corner of his eye, headlights barreled around the bend of Highway 145 far below. *Has to be a tourist—who else would drive like a lunatic in this mess?*

As if on cue, the car skidded sideways on the highway. He stiffened, squinting through the swirling snow and dense mist of his breath.

The car swerved the other way, then in an ominous pirouette, sliding across the second lane. Either the wheels had just locked up or the driver stupidly fought the slide instead of turning into it.

Another 360. *Christ!* Lock stared helplessly at the unstoppable disaster hundreds of yards away. Time stretched out. The car now faced backward but skated forward, gathering momentum as it slid straight for the guardrail and the San Miguel River beyond. *Oh shit! It's gonna—*

A grinding screech echoed uphill as the rear fender smashed through the guardrail. The car sailed in the air and disappeared into the dark abyss below.

"Shit! Hold on, just—I'm coming!" His voice sounded tight in the eerie silence, and his knees shook as he stumbled downward, the horrific grinding sound still echoing sickly in his head. Damn it to hell for not having a cell phone! This was gonna be bad.

The thick forest would have made this descent treacherous on any given night, but combined with the stinging snow and thin, bobbing beam of his flashlight, his journey became one of survival. Flakes blinded him and clogged his breathing. Slashes of frigid wind whipped him until he staggered. He pushed on, slipping and sliding, and twice collided with cottonwood branches, the second one clocking him so hard it sheared off his knit cap.

Uttering an oath, he continued on, his breath now ragged. He reached the highway and half-ran, half-skated across. He halted at the guardrail's serrated hole and swept the flashlight in an arc. A Honda Civic lay upside down on the embankment. The headlights shone with morbid stillness into the swirling river three feet away.

"Hang on," he hollered, sidestepping carefully down the embankment. A blanket of innocent-looking snow hid jagged rock and loose stones. One misstep and he'd pitch right into the howling river.

When he reached the upside-down driver's side door, he shone the light through the shattered glass.

ABOUT THE AUTHOR

Romantic Suspense That Keeps You Up All Night.

 If daydreaming were an Olympic sport, Sarah Andre would be buried under gold medals. She lives with her husband in Southwest, FL, and is a 2014 and 2011 RWA Golden Heart® Finalist in Romantic Suspense. She is an active member of SWFRW, WHRWA, NWHRWA, KOD, TGN and WRW romance chapters. When she's not writing she's either volunteering for these chapters, playing with her (very naughty) Pomeranian puppies or exercising like a demented fool. Sarah is a member of a successful romantic suspense blog: www.KissandThrill.com. For more information please visit her at www.SarahAndre.com, her Author Facebook: Sarah Andre Author Page, or Twitter: @SarahRSWriter

Winnetka
Public Libra   stri
Northfield Branch
1785 Orchard Lane
Northfield, IL
847-446-5990

Date charged: 2/9/2017,12:40
Author: Andre, Sarah,
Title: Tall dark & damaged
Item ID: 3124000553625
Date due: 2/23/2017,23:59

59044931R00188

Made in the USA
Lexington, KY
22 December 2016